Disraeli in Love

A glance across the opera-boxes at the King's Theatre in 1833 might have changed Britain's history. For with that glance, the fashionable young novelist and would-be Member of Parliament, Benjamin Disraeli, fell in love with Henrietta, wife of Sir Francis Sykes, and embarked on a romance that nearly destroyed him.

His situation was ready-made for one of his own novels. A brilliant though debt-ridden hero (himself) meets a beautiful and aristocratic woman (Henrietta Sykes), friend of a great statesman (Lord Lyndhurst), who becomes Disraeli's patron and protects them in their affair. But what was the truth about this curious trio? What part did Lyndhurst really play in Henrietta's life?

Against the turbulent background of England in the 1830s, with its duels and gambling halls and sponging houses and Grub Street bullies, Maurice Edelman with a novelist's empathy recreates a Disraeli far different from the stereotype of the grave courtier and statesman presenting the Queen with India and the Suez Canal shares. This is Disraeli, armed with his genius and fighting in the service of his ambition not only against his political and social enemies, but also against the lulling temptations of a sensuous and beautiful woman.

At the heart of the scene is the House of Commons which Maurice Edelman knows so well. With his first Parliamentary novel, *Who Goes Home*, he established a distinctive post-war genre. But with *Disraeli in Love* he has married it to a period of history which he brings to dazzling life through the person of Disraeli, novelist and politician, whose adventures and achievements are as fascinating today as they were when they first startled and excited the nation over a hundred years ago.

Maurice Edelman
Disraeli in Love

COLLINS

ST JAMES'S PLACE, LONDON

1972

William Collins Sons & Co Ltd
London · Glasgow · Sydney · Auckland
Toronto · Johannesburg

Endpaper and title page drawing
by Charles Mozley

First published 1972
© 1972 Maurice Edelman
ISBN 0 00 221180 7
Set in Monotype Garamond
Made and Printed in Great Britain by
William Collins Sons & Co Ltd Glasgow

To Jean Ennis

Chapter One

'The lady, sir!'

' "Gallomania",' said Disraeli, reaching for the papers on the writing table near his couch. 'Close the window, Baum. I dislike the morning air.'

On the mantelpiece, the Boulle clock with the entwined nymphs struck ten hurriedly, as if anxious to dispose of the matter. Disraeli glanced at the inscription 'Love Triumphing over the Flight of Time' at the base of the globe encasing the movement.

'A melancholy hope, Baum, that experience disappoints . . . Never mind! *England and France: Or a Cure for Ministerial Gallomania.* Gallomania – how d'you like the title? Doesn't it sum up Lord Palmerston's unnatural passion?'

Baum opened his mouth, but Disraeli waved his hand to anticipate his reply.

'It's no matter,' he said. 'I want you to take these sheets to Baron de Haber with my compliments.'

'Yes, sir,' said Baum, standing at the side of the couch with his long arms pressed against his nankeen breeches. Disraeli wrapped the black silk dressing-gown with the embroidered panels around his hips, and said,

'Gallomania – it sounds like a female demon, an Afrite.'

'Yes, sir,' said his servant. 'The lady, sir!'

'Yes,' said Disraeli absently. He looked at himself in the gilt glass opposite his couch, and brushed aside the small dark curls that fell over his forehead. 'It's growing, you know. After Dr Bolton bled and shaved me, I thought I'd stay bald for ever. Frightened me more than death itself. Do you think, Baum, I look older than twenty-eight?'

'It depends, sir,' said Baum with his light Swiss accent, 'whether you've spent the evening at Mr Bulwer's or Lady Cork's.'

Disraeli raised himself on his elbow.

7

'That is very percipient of you, Baum,' he said. 'Which of my hosts is the more rejuvenating?'

'Oh, Lady Cork, sir,' said Baum. 'She being ninety or more makes you feel you have a long life of pleasure before you.'

'And Mr Bulwer?'

'He's young, but he isn't what you'd call youthful. He's married.'

'Draw the curtains a little wider,' Disraeli said stiffly, and he watched as Baum limped across the room towards the window of his chamber overlooking Duke Street.

Edward Bulwer's turbulent marriage was the only aspect of his life that he had no wish to adopt. Bulwer, almost his own age, had already published *Pelham*, a novel of high society, described by a hostile critic as belonging to the 'silver fork school', but which everyone read. He was a Member of Parliament, a Radical in politics yet an elegant in his own person, the editor of a literary journal, a connoisseur, his house in Hertford Street a brilliant focus of society and intellect. Bulwer had succeeded in everything except in his relations with his wife Rosina.

'The lady, sir,' said Baum for the third time, anxious that his master shouldn't neglect his chief theme. 'Mrs Austen, sir,' he added, forced from his delicacy by the other's indifference.

'Tell her I'm dead,' said Disraeli.

'Dead?'

'Yes – tell her that I expired following a syncope last night.'

Baum drew the curtains and began to move towards the door.

'No,' said Disraeli, rising. 'I'll write her a letter from my death-bed. Is she in her carriage?'

'Yes, sir.'

'It's better she should be. She'll be able to set off more quickly.'

He stretched himself, and Baum looked up at his six-foot master as he stroked his chin before seating himself at the writing desk.

My dear Madame, he wrote
    A severe influenza has kept me indoors since I returned

8

from Bradenham. Sa told me that you yourself had equally been a victim of a malady which creates between us a kinship of misery, though you are happily recovered. I have been wholly involved in political thought for the last two months, and have been accused of writing a pamphlet. But more of that when we meet, which now can only be on my next return from Bradenham. And how is Mr Austen? *Toujours le même?* The phrase is yours, and is for me a perpetual reminder of his enduring and exceptional qualities. Pray remember me to him with much affection.

Believe me to be,

Yours ever –

His quill hesitated, then he signed the letter with a flourished 'D'.

'Take it,' he said, 'and come back quickly.'

He looked out of the window towards St James's, glittering in the sunshine, and he recalled happily Bulwer's party the previous evening at Hertford Street – his talk with Lord Stanford about Constantinople and the dolphins in the Bosphorus and Bayukada, and his introduction to Count D'Orsay, the Parisian who had married Lady Blessington's daughter, and all the *blues* – Mrs Norton, Miss Laetitia Landon, the poetess, in her satin dress and white satin shoes and her red cheeks and snub nose; and then in the press of the crowd he had seen Lady Sykes and met her husband, Sir Francis, who had insisted on talking to him in Italian; and the affable Lord Mulgrave had praised his novel *Vivian Grey*, and said, 'Disraeli, you must be found a seat in Parliament' – yes, it had been a flawless evening except for the hissing animosities of Rosina and Bulwer, the icy allusions of a quarrelling couple, though in their love-match in defiance of his mother Bulwer had willingly forgone an annuity and the prospect of a legacy. 'Love Triumphs over the Flight of Time.' Disraeli touched the nymphs with his finger-tips and said, 'But transiently!'

He picked up *The Times* and began to read the leading article.

'We have never described Lord Grey,' it said, 'as wanting in all the qualities necessary to the Prime Minister of a country like this.' ('Not all, but most!' he said to himself.) 'Let his advocates who have raised the phantom lay it at leisure . . . Our great object is to impress upon his lordship the dreadful calamities which must result from the failure of the Reform Bill, of which calamities the first, though assuredly not the last, would be Lord Grey's downfall.' Absurd! That the Whigs should fall scarcely seemed a calamity.

He turned the page to the column headed 'Cholera Morbus, London. Central Board of Health, Council Office, Whitehall. March 5th, 1832,' and he traversed the statistics from the boroughs – *Poplar, Ratcliff, Limehouse, Bermondsey. Cases* 258. *Deaths* 112. *Afloat in river* 21. That was a melancholy thought. Neither dead nor alive. Afloat on the River Styx. A letter signed by John Luff and Thomas Smart, District Surgeons on Bethnal Green, protested that the disease notified in their parish was enteritis and not cholera. That might be. Yet it didn't mean that the epidemic had been contained. Other doctors had established that the disease was spreading. Cholera was bad for trade, and the merchants didn't hesitate to dispute for their self-interest even the evidence of impartial doctors. He had seen cholera on his travels in Gibraltar, Aleppo and Jaffa, and the wasted dead, blackened with flies, rotting in the streets of the *medinas* . . . Ah well, it wasn't a subject to contemplate before breakfast. Inshallah! If it was God's will – ! That was what the Moslems said, and as for himself, he was well persuaded that he had the *baraka*, the divine protection that gave him immunity amid public disasters. At any rate, he thought, looking at the invitation cards over the fireplace, the cholera wouldn't interfere with his social life in London.

From below came a distracting clash of voices, remote at first, with the words gradually becoming more precise.

'But, madam,' Baum was saying in a duet with Mrs Austen's overlaying emphasis that finally reached the landing.

'I must ask you to stand aside at once,' Disraeli heard her insist, and he quickly applied some scented cream to his hands and opened the door.

'My dear Mrs Austen,' he said with a smile and a bow, 'I rather hoped you'd defy my prudence. But the influenza – '

'I believe it requires an interval before it returns.'

She entered the room suspiciously, and glanced at the azaleas which his sister had sent him from the conservatories at Bradenham, and then at the miniatures on the side table.

'I see,' she said, 'you have disposed of Mr Maclise's drawings of Mr Austen and myself.'

'Oh, no,' said Disraeli hurriedly, 'I've moved them to Bradenham for safe custody. Besides, the Guv'nor said they were his as much as mine. Please be seated and excuse my morning disarray. Will you take tea – or a glass of hock?'

'Neither,' said Mrs Austen. 'I haven't come for refreshment.'

'And Mr Austen – ?'

'He is busy as always, and sends you his regards.'

Baum, who had been waiting for his orders, glanced at Mrs Austen's pert face with her steady eyes, tilted nose, small mouth, and her wide brow surrounded with ringlets; she looked back at him, and he withdrew, apologizing and closing the door.

Disraeli went up to her quickly and took her hand.

'Sara,' he said, 'you shouldn't come here.'

'Why shouldn't I? It's two months since you came to Guilford Street. That's a long neglect – even though Bloomsbury may seem a far distance from Duke Street and Mayfair.'

'Believe me – ' Disraeli began.

'I've little reason to believe you,' she said sharply. 'When you wrote *Vivian Grey* – when I treasured and copied each page to give to Colburn – you had no difficulty in making whatever journey was necessary. I looked after your manuscripts as if they were children.'

Her voice faltered and she looked up at him.

'Please, Ben, tell me – what happened to change everything? We were all so happy – Austen and you and myself – when we travelled to Italy – it was so beautiful – And when you were ill, I helped you to get better . . . It was so beautiful – the Grand Canal, and the palaces – Foscani, Grimani and Barberigo, and all the marble and jasper, the lapis lazuli and the agates in St Mark's Church. And the tomb of Petrarch at Arqua and Tasso's cell at Ferrara, and Byron's name scratched on the door of the dungeons, and the lovely Val d'Arno – '

'Yes, yes,' said Disraeli. He listened absently to her relentless voice. She spoke English almost as rapidly as she did French. What he remembered most of their journey was Austen spoiling their visit to Florence by eating poisonous mushrooms and how, though nearly dying, he still managed to draw up, like the good lawyer that he was, a bill of claim against the hotel-keeper. Austen at thirty-seven had seemed to him a middle-aged man, and when they had taken a trip on Lake Maggiore, his most gratifying memory was that Austen had fallen asleep after drinking a bottle of Burgundy, thus leaving him with Byron's old boatman to enjoy the glory of the lake. The best thing about his companion was that he had been good at changing money and keeping accounts, and Disraeli respected him without deference and liked him without warmth. He also owed Austen three hundred pounds, the balance of a loan that had enabled him to make his tour of the Orient.

Disraeli observed Mrs Austen warily as her reminiscences accumulated. He was due to take breakfast with Lord Mulgrave at White's, and he didn't want to be delayed. Besides, he disliked the way her nose had begun to redden as her excitement rose, and how slowly the redness receded when her excitement was over. She was too eager, too earnest, too garrulous, and the flattery that he had felt at the age of twenty-two in the enthusiasm, the gravity and the communications of a woman eight years older than himself had long been superseded by wider and more exciting attentions.

She was beginning to cry, and he glanced at the clock. Twenty past ten.

'It's unkind of you to neglect me, Ben,' she said, and he noticed that her face was mottled all over as if with the onset of small-pox. She was sitting in an armchair, and he knelt at her side.

'You mustn't neglect me, Ben,' she repeated, and he took her hand and kissed it without speaking. Her head was drooping, and he raised her chin and looked at her.

'It's not my wish to neglect you,' he said. 'You'll see. I have two surprises for you – no, three – two novels and a political tract, anonymous, of course.'

She half-smiled as he held her chin.

'After all,' he went on. 'It was you who gave *V.G.* the first puff of anonymity that made everyone wonder till, alas, they found the author was B. Disraeli.'

'Not "alas",' she said. '*No*, not "alas".' She folded her arms around his head and pressed it against her breast, where Disraeli remained, listening to her thudding heart and waiting for the clock to chime so that he might rise decorously.

'Please, Ben,' she said, kissing his head again and again, 'come and see us soon. I won't bother you, I promise. I know what wonderful work you have yet to do – I won't bother you. But just to be in your company – to be where you are – it was always so.'

Disraeli raised his head, and said,

'I promise, madam. I promise. I want you to know how – how very close I feel to you – and Mr Austen too. I – '

Outside the door, Baum's voice raised itself angrily.

'No, no,' he was saying. 'Mr Disraeli can't receive anyone.'

Disraeli rose quickly to his feet, and Mrs Austen looked up anxiously.

'You can go out through the other room,' he said. He helped her to rise, pressed her in his arms with her warm, wet face against his, smiled to her as she smiled back, half in contentment and half in apprehension, and led her through the outer door as Baum came in, followed by a small, ill-shaven man who kept his hat on as he waved a document.

'My respects, sir,' said the visitor, approaching closely and edging his chest almost up to the lower part of Disraeli's diaphragm. He gave off a smell of regurgitated gin and stale snuff, and Disraeli retreated a step. 'You are Mr Benjamin Disraeli of Bradenham in the county of Buckinghamshire?'

Disraeli took out his handkerchief and nodded, his eyes on the paper in his visitor's hand.

'Well, sir,' said the sheriff's officer, 'my respects, sir. This is a warrant. I have come to take you into custody.'

'Shall I throw him through the window?' Baum asked, pulling up the sash.

'Oh, no,' said Disraeli quickly. The sounds of rolling carriages and the morning cries of street sellers rose from outside like taunts from another world, free from bailiffs and the extortions of creditors. He hurriedly reviewed his debts, which at his last reckoning he believed to be three thousand four hundred pounds, excluding the accumulated interest that he had lost track of and a few bills he had underwritten. Recently he had borrowed from Lawson, the merchant in Golden Square, to meet his commitments on quarter day. He was satisfied with his economy, and he put out his hand silently for the warrant.

'I will save you the trouble, Mr Disraeli,' said the bailiff, smiling with his well-shaped yellow teeth. 'You underwrit when you was in Malta a bill of Captain Waters of the Third Regiment. For six hundred pounds. The Captain has defaulted, and Mr Rossi – well, he doesn't waste his time. You are my prisoner, sir, taken in execution – '

'This is an unusual experience. Can you wait here while I seek some legal advice?'

'No, sir. You are taken in execution, and my orders are to take you to the spunging-house – pardon the term – till you or your friends can pay the sum. If you'll accompany me, sir – '

'How?'

'In my hackney coach. My follower – the constable – he's waiting downstairs.'

Six hundred pounds – six thousand – six million. He could scarcely remember what Captain Waters looked like, except that he had been his host at the Malta mess where he had been quarantined for weeks on his way back from Egypt. Six hundred pounds. No – not the Guv'nor. He had made it a matter of self-esteem when he had taken chambers in London that he would live on his own fame and his earnings and his father's quarterly allowance to him. His younger brothers? They, like Sa, had nothing. And Austen? That wouldn't do either. Each time he drew on him, he became more obliged to Mrs Austen, the self-appointed Egeria who had turned into a succubus. There was, of course, Bulwer. But Bulwer himself was hard-pressed. Only the previous evening when he was admiring a marble Apollo by Canova that Bulwer said he had lately bought at an auction, Rosina had added malevolently, 'Not bought, hired.'

Hired. Borrowed. They were harassing words that covered

almost everything there was in Duke Street – the writing-table, the lamps, the bibelots, the wardrobe. Only the silver daggers, the Turkish carpets on the wall, and the pistols were his. He was a nominal possessor but, in fact, a debtor tied to his debts in an infernal marriage without divorce.

'Sir?' asked the bailiff.

'Yes,' said Disraeli. 'This is an early hour. As you see, I've scarcely begun my toilet.'

'I am to ask you to dress quickly – sheriff's rules.'

'But you haven't breakfasted, I'm sure,' Disraeli said desperately.

'No,' said the bailiff, inhaling a fragrance of cooking pies that seeped through the window.

'Perhaps,' said Disraeli, 'you'll permit me to be your host while I write a few letters, and so perhaps relieve you of your rather disagreeable duties.'

'For breakfast,' said the bailiff, taking an armchair, 'I eats steak and drinks porter.'

'That you shall have,' said Disraeli. 'Baum, send out for Mr – Mr – '

'Mr Mayley, sir,' said the bailiff, wiping his nose with the back of his hand.

'Mr Mayley's breakfast,' said Disraeli, his voice fading as the bailiff stretched out his hand for a book that lay on the table. It was an advance copy of his new novel delivered that day from his publisher, John Murray.

'*Contarini Fleming: A Psychological Autobiography*,' the bailiff spelt out slowly.

'Big words,' he said thoughtfully. 'Big words. You literary gentlemen uses very big words.'

'And then,' Disraeli said to Baum, ignoring the bailiff, 'lay out my red velvet coat – my green trousers with the gold braid – yes, and, I think, my brocade waistcoat. You would agree, Mayley, that on these occasions a man should dress with a certain appropriateness.'

'That is right, sir,' said Mayley. 'A gentleman in debt is taken at the value he puts on himself.'

An hour later, after Disraeli had written a note to Lord Mulgrave excusing himself from breakfast and to his sister Sarah explaining that she might not hear from him for a little while as he had some private and important business to deal with, he set off with Mayley and the sullen constable for Lawson's mansion in Golden Square. The bailiff had wanted to take him forthwith to the spunging-house in Oxford Street, but soothed by his rump steak and four pints of porter, he had agreed that Disraeli might visit his chief creditor 'on the grounds that you don't move out of my sight'. Now, Mayley was relaxed, interspersing his anecdotes of the warrants he had served at cockcrow outside various gambling hells, including Crockford's, with liquid belches as the cab lurched, the driver swore and Disraeli, his knees jammed against the constable's, leaned towards the open window to avoid the bailiff's increasing familiarity.

'Perhaps,' he said, when they reached Lawson's house, 'you will wait around the corner.'

Mayley, who had a wen over his forehead that depressed his left eyelid in a look of complicity, winked with his other eye.

'It's against sheriff's rules.'

'I'll give you my gentleman's word – '

'Gentleman's word? Ho! Ho! If every gentleman kept his gentleman's word, there'd be no work left for Mr Mayley . . . But I'll tell you what. I'll wait around the corner for fifteen minutes.' He fingered a remnant of steak from inside a back tooth. 'Then, I'll come in and see how you're getting on. Right?'

Disraeli got out of the cab hurriedly, put on his hat, and walked with determination but a faint tremor in his legs through the open door into the counting-house, where three clerks were sitting on high stools.

He announced himself to the youngest of the three, and stood examining an engraving of the Duke of Wellington on the wall while the messenger went slowly up the broad mahogany stairs leading to the merchant's private apartments. He took out his fob-watch, and saw that the time was five minutes to twelve. After waiting for ten minutes while the clerks scrutinized his clothes and he exhausted his interest in the Duke's posture, Disraeli asked the oldest of the three clerks to present his compliments to Mr Lawson and to assure him that if he wasn't concerned to do business with Mr Disraeli, Mr Disraeli would transfer his custom elsewhere.

'Oh, yes, sir,' said the clerk. 'Mr Lawson said we was to keep you waiting for ten minutes for you to get cooler, and then to bring you up.'

At the top of the staircase, Lawson, a middle-aged, portly, gravely dressed man in a black coat and a cambric ruffled shirt hung with a gold chain which Disraeli at once envied, was waiting for him with an outstretched, bejewelled hand.

'Mr Disraeli, sir – I am sorry to have kept you. The accumulation of business – come this way – you can scarcely imagine – in our mercantile age – money, Mr Disraeli – it's never been more difficult – tighter – tighter – there, pray – take a seat.'

His jowls were loose, and he panted between each phrase. Disraeli looked around the room giving on the Square, and at its furnishings which were sad tales of other people's distresses.

'Ah, yes,' said Lawson, following Disraeli's glance. 'That drop-front secretaire – *secrétaire à abbatant* they call it – that's a beauty – by Riesener – belonged, they say, to Marie Antoinette – came from the Château de Saint-Cloud – from Lord – well, let's not go into that – poor chap – he borrowed at fifteen per cent and charged his tenants a five per cent rent. It's not arithmetic, Mr Disraeli. Believe me, it's not arithmetic.'

'No,' said Disraeli, glancing around at the armchair upholstered in Beauvais tapestry that Lawson had at some time acquired in a foreclosure. 'There's little sentiment in arithmetic.'

'None, sir, none,' said Lawson, slowly shaking his head. 'It's a disease like the cholera – it strikes without discrimination.'

'I doubt that,' said Disraeli. 'The poor are much more susceptible. But let that pass. If I can put this to you – '

'Unnecessary!' said Lawson, with a wave of his left hand in which the sunlight from the Square touched his sapphire ring. 'It is well known among my friends. Mr Disraeli has backed too many bills. He is too obliging.'

'I don't recall having failed to repay my debts to you, Mr Lawson.'

'No,' said Lawson. 'You have borrowed to repay me – and that I know. But your credit, sir – it doesn't stem from that – when you go from me to Mendoza and from Mendoza to Cardozo, and then on to Nahum and Laredo – oh, we know about it very fast . . . No, your credit, Mr Disraeli, is your father's reputation – he was – '

Disraeli stood abruptly.

'I shouldn't think of leaving yet,' said Lawson, still sitting. 'You're not in a position to take offence . . . I was saying . . . yes, your father left our community long ago – but he remains an ornament – an ornament – he is well remembered at Bevis Marks synagogue.'

'Rossi has carried out an execution on me,' said Disraeli, his voice lowered as in a confessional. 'The sheriff's officer – '

'Yes,' said Lawson, rising and looking out of the window. 'I saw you arrive – I knew the hackney cab.'

'I have no wish to pain my father by landing in a spunging-house – perhaps in gaol.'

Lawson shuddered.

'Gaol! That's a terrible thought. Even with privileges – the food – the restraint! God forbid, Mr Disraeli! That would be terrible.'

'Can you help me?'

'No.'

'No?'

'I thought that was explicit, sir.' Lawson returned to the table, and sat down again. 'No! . . . You are deeply in debt. You've already pledged your payment from John Murray for your next book. You foolishly allowed yourself to get involved with Baron de Haber, a financial pusher – got into trouble, you have.'

'That – '

'No, please don't say it – it's true. And now, you come to me and ask me to lend you still more money.'

'Don't you understand, Lawson?' Disraeli said, rising. 'You think I don't pay my debts because of wilfulness – even witless-ness. It isn't that at all. It's just that I haven't got the money to pay.'

Lawson frowned.

'That's ingenious reasoning . . . The question is whether you are entitled to borrow when you have no prospect of repayment . . . Tell me, Mr Disraeli – have you ever thought that you might engage in some commercial transaction?'

Disraeli looked back at him cautiously, and didn't answer.

'If I'm not mistaken,' said Lawson, 'you once went into business – as they say – on the Stock Exchange with a Mr Evans – Spanish American shares. Did you not?'

'I did,' said Disraeli.

'Yes,' said Lawson. 'I recall your pamphlet on the American mining companies – very persuasive, Mr Disraeli – very persuasive, though I confess I wasn't wholly persuaded. And how much did you lose?'

'I lost my share of a seven thousand pounds' investment. I was a "bull" at the wrong moment. It was an indiscretion at the age of twenty-one that I'm still shackled to.'

'Never mind,' said Lawson cheerfully. 'Never mind. It's a pity, though, that Lord Eldon was right – American mines are our modern South Sea Bubble – but never mind. It shows, sir, that you do not spurn the operations of industry.'

'What are you recommending?'

'Well,' said Lawson, 'finance and trade are very close. As you know I trade – I trade in coal as well as finance. Coal, Mr Disraeli, mined from the earth, is gold.'

'And how does that concern me?' Disraeli asked. 'I have no means to invest.'

Lawson shrugged his shoulders.

'You have many fine friends in London now. They must use – say, one town house – say – yes, it must be – ten thousand cauldrons a year – the clubs – yes. Say you draw on me for five hundred – discounted at ten per cent. Take on top of that five hundred pounds' worth of coal.'

Disraeli picked up his hat.

'I'm not a coal merchant,' he said. 'Good God – I'm not.' His hopes that had mounted collapsed again.

'No,' Lawson said. 'No – you're not. Too proud to trade but not too proud to borrow. That leaves you only two courses.'

'And what are they?'

'There's Parliament,' said Lawson. 'Take Mr Rothesay. He owed Crocky five thousand – got Lord Chandos to give him a seat – and there he sits at Westminster – debts and all – immune from arrest or seizure – like an honest man.'

Disraeli looked thoughtful.

'And the other course?'

'Is marriage – or, at any rate, the prospect of marriage to a lady with, say, ten thousand a year. What do you say, Mr Disraeli?'

Disraeli said, 'You're jesting, Mr Lawson.' He looked around the room at the assorted pledges, now Lawson's own property.

'And what have you to offer by way of collateral?'

'Collateral?'

'Yes – security, backing, guarantees, reversions – anything you like, Mr Disraeli, since you are too proud to be a coal-merchant.'

Disraeli fumbled with his fob-watch.

'I have no collateral.'

'Sad,' Lawson said. 'Very sad for a young man – a talented young man if I may say so – a good-looking young man. Perhaps your father would underwrite – ?'

'No,' said Disraeli emphatically. 'I wouldn't ask him.'

'He won't like it,' said Lawson as if to himself. 'He's a proud man too . . . a pity he refused to serve the synagogue. But never mind!'

'Look here, Lawson,' said Disraeli desperately. 'I must have the money at once.'

'Must? Must?'

'Yes – must . . . You can take a lien on my next two books after Murray's. Colburn is urging me to write a new novel.'

'Authors are bad risks,' said Lawson.

'I promise you – '

'No – don't promise. I want guarantees, not promises, copper-bottomed guarantees . . . Tell you what, Disraeli – ' Lawson's manner had now become off-hand, and he slouched in his armchair – 'I'm prepared in view of the risk to discount a short-term bill – say, six months – '

'Thank you.'

' – at fifteen per cent.'

'Fifteen per cent!'

'You can take it or leave it.'

'Fifteen per cent! Good God!'

'That's it – for a thousand pounds – and you will assign to me the first charge on any receipts from your next three books after this one.'

'Fifteen per cent!' Disraeli muttered a third time.

'For six months. It's generous,' said Lawson.

'Generous,' Disraeli said weakly.

Lawson sent one of his clerks for the bailiff, and after he arranged the formalities of a release, Disraeli handed Mayley a sovereign and thanked him for having concluded his attentions. Mayley spat on the money, rubbed it in his palm, and said,

'My pleasure to serve you, milord!'

Disraeli left the counting-house with the feeling of a condemned man on the gallows when the trap-door jams; the noose was still around his neck, but he had been given a short reprieve. Once again as he walked into Golden Square, alert to every passing carriage in case some acquaintance might have seen him coming from Lawson's, he went through the sums of his debts, considered where he might find a new source of cash, and ended with the despairing judgment that only some Biblical miracle, a seat in Parliament, or, as Lawson recommended, a well-endowed marriage could save him from bankruptcy and a debtor's prison.

Perhaps a widow – perhaps a young heiress enjoying an annuity. He imagined a woman, say, of thirty – no, thirty-five or so – not necessarily beautiful, but certainly not plain, amiable, self-effacing, highly-bred, admiring, sufficiently rejected by life to value his hand, yet not humble, well-connected, with a large country house and a few hundred acres, and above all, several thousand pounds' worth of liquid or convertible capital. He went through the list of possibles whom his father had been urging on him. Miss Cardozo with the red-bridged nose? No – he'd rather have Newgate. Lady Flint – the hectoring, stupid Lady Flint? Better the *bastinado*. There was, of course, Miss Hill, alternating between melancholy and mania, who had a large estate in her own right and sang; but that would be the equivalent of a stay in Bedlam. There must be others. Lady Wendover, Miss Charlesworth, Miss Warren – exquisite Miss Warren – and Lady Charlotte, the daughter of Lady Lindsey. Yes – Lady Charlotte, pretty, eager, young, untouched as yet by the aspirants who would always crowd around a nubile girl with a fortune. He would have preferred a more mature object for his fantasy. But Lady Charlotte would do. He had seen her a few times at the opera, and admired her fresh and eager face, and he had been pointed out to her by the novelist Plumer Ward.

Marriage, after all, was a social contract. To that extent, he would agree with the French philosophers. Within that social contract there was, inevitably, a contract of mutual economic support. Love should not be a preliminary to marriage; it should be its consequence, the warmth from the hearth set up by two people. Yes – he must apply himself to marriage. Time was passing too quickly, and if he wasn't careful, the bachelor sought out by the hostesses to complete their dinner table might lose his bloom.

Without giving the matter thought, he had turned away from Mayfair as if to disclaim its temptations and pleasures, and was walking in the direction of Bedford Row, his childhood home, intending to eat at a chop-house. Behind him he heard hurrying, thumping footsteps, and his hand tightened on his cane. At any moment he expected the disgusting bailiff to reappear with some new writ.

'Begging your pardon, sir,' panted Baum, who had run most of the way from Duke Street, and had seen him leave Lawson's. 'This letter, sir, Mr Bulwer – he asked me to give it to you urgently.'

He waited while Disraeli took the letter, unsealed it and read it with accumulating delight.

Under the blazon of the House of Commons, it said,

My dear Ben,
 The crisis is certainly approaching, and unless we are all smitten by doom as Mr Perceval prophesied in the Chamber

last night if we leave God out of the preamble to the Reform Bill, a dissolution must come very soon, whether their Lordships accept or reject.

Whatever may happen, there is much talk at Westminster that old Sir Thomas Baring will flee from High Wycombe to Hampshire. There will certainly be a vacancy, and the Treasury will contest it.

Already Mr Huffam and Mr Nash have said that the man for the borough is none other than Benjamin Disraeli, and this letter is to urge you to prepare your canvass, for I feel that the Duke will be more fearful of the buckshot of Lord Grey's new creation of peers than he ever was of the cannon of the French. The Bill, I prophesy, will be carried on the deserted plain of the Lords with the Duke's men in full strategic retreat.

Meanwhile, Mr Joseph Hume has quoted to me your sentence, 'I am neither Whig nor Tory – my politics are described by one word, and that word is England.' That is excellent. And Mr O'Connell has also written wishing for your return in the Borough.

More when we next meet.

Edward Bulwer.

'Is there a message, sir?' Baum asked, observing the expression on Disraeli's face.

'Yes,' said Disraeli. 'This is a message. There are signs that tell us our direction. For the moment, it's the direction of Bloomsbury.'

Mrs Austen appeared timidly at the door, and Disraeli, who had been reading the cards over the fireplace, turned slowly, unsmiling.

'Why – ' she began.

He took her hands, and looked at the knot of violets in the centre of her corsage.

'Primavera!' he said.

It was the name he had given her when they had visited the flower-covered Isola Bella on Lago Maggiore, and she looked up at him hesitantly.

'You – you – '

'I – what?'

'You make me forget to be angry.'

He laughed, and she laughed back, and he led her to the chintz sofa and said,

'I have news for you, Sara – most wonderful and exciting news.'

Her fingers closed around his, and for a few seconds their hands explored each other in a parallel conversation with their voices.

'Tell me,' she said.

'Only if you assure me that it will be a close secret.'

'I am the most secret of women.'

No, not the most secret, he thought. She had already said too much about his private affairs to his grudging cousin, the architect George Basevi, who regarded novel-writing as a frivolous activity. But never mind.

'You promise.'

'I promise.'

Disraeli stood, releasing her hands, and said in a portentous tone that gave a still greater resonance to his normally deep voice,

'I have been asked by a number of gentlemen – not Whiglings nor Tories – but gentlemen of independence in the borough of High Wycombe, to stand as a candidate for Parliament.'

'My dear Ben,' she said, practical again. 'But is there to be an election?'

'The election is certain. Only the date is in doubt. What is more, next week I go to see my supporters and make a preliminary canvass. I am assured by those who've studied the registration that my victory is certain.'

'But, Ben,' she began, her expression alternating between joy and anxiety, 'the Ministry – the Treasury – surely they will – '

'I have no doubt,' said Disraeli, 'they will send down a troop of ruffians and some stammering retainer to claim the seat. It won't help them. I estimate – that's not important.'

Disraeli put his hands on her shoulders, and studied her pink-and-white dress at arm's length.

'Yes,' he said. 'Pink and white! Those will be my colours, and during my campaign, you'll wear them!'

'You mustn't tire yourself,' she said. 'You know how when you tire – '

'Tire myself?' he said exultantly. 'They'll sooner all fall dead than I will tire . . . Sara!'

'He'll be home in an hour. The maidservant – '

'Send her on an errand.'

'Where?'

'To Peru . . . Tell her not to return without the Great Auk's egg.'

She turned at the door, hesitated, and went out to instruct the servant.

Disraeli let the curtains fall. Once, he had known the room well, the sofa, the umbered portraits, the gesso ceiling that he had often contemplated – and Sara Austen, attentive, childless, eager, ambitious, the self-appointed handmaiden to genius, bending over him. It was strange that she bore his sister's name and he her husband's. The women were not unlike. But Austen – Austen with his thin hair and pale eyes, dear, good Benjamin Austen! Ah well – Disraeli removed the heavy fob-watch from the hip pocket of his trousers as Sara Austen returned. She had taken off her kerchief, and he felt her quiver as she turned her back to him, and he placed his hand over her small, firm breasts.

The gesso ceiling again, half seen through watery colours, cascades of hair, drift and lassitude, lassitude, lassitude, the small kisses over his face, the fingers entwining his curls, and the voice asking and asking for assurance.

Her weight was above him, and her nose had reddened again. He propped himself on his elbow and reached for the fob-watch that he had placed on the table.

'Was it wonderful?' she asked. 'Was it wonderful?'

'The word,' he said, 'falls short.'

His face became solemn.

'What is it?' she asked anxiously. 'Have I said something wrong?'

He stood, and put on his coat.

'No,' he said. 'Everything you say is perfect.'

'Well, why do you look like that?'

'I – '

'Tell me, Ben. I must know.'

He walked about the room while she watched him anxiously. At last he said,

'Sara – you know my feeling for you. My deep, deep feeling. You gave me belief in my genius. You made me feel an Alexander who could conquer the world.'

She stood up, buttoning her dress.

'For God's sake, Ben,' she said. 'What's changed?'

'Nothing,' he said, turning to her earnestly. 'Nothing – except that I am a conqueror without an army.'

'What do you mean?'

'I mean that for my campaign I must have money – I must have the means to pay my election expenses. I lack them.'

'Oh, Ben,' she said, and went up to him and put her head on his chest. 'I can't bear you to be worried about money.'

'I came to you elated – indifferent to the material hazards of destiny . . . But in the last few moments – '

'No, Ben,' she said with determination. 'Austen shall lend you the money. Yes, he shall!'

'No,' Disraeli replied. 'No – that's impossible. Our connection – no. It would be too indelicate. Besides, I owe him too much already.'

The sun had gone down, and the room was in shadow, lit only by the failing firelight.

'I will have to write to Wycombe,' Disraeli said, stirring an ember with his foot. 'I must decline.'

'No, you shall not,' said Mrs Austen emphatically. In the street they heard a door slam, and Mrs Austen pulled the bell for the manservant to light the candles.

'How much do you need?'

'A thousand pounds.'

'You shall have it – if not from Mr Austen, at least through me.'

'Sara – '

The manservant with his tapers entered at the same time as Benjamin Austen.

'Ben!' Austen said to Disraeli with delight. 'You've been neglecting us. Mrs Austen has been complaining.'

Disraeli shook his hand warmly, and said,

'I called at this late hour to await you – to see you before I left for Bradenham.'

'Very kind – oh, most kind – and how is your father, your dear mother, and Sarah?'

'All well, and send you greetings.'

'Well, pray be seated . . . a glass of port, perhaps – when can we expect you for dinner?'

'When Mr Disraeli is next in London. I have been conspiring with him.'

'Good! Good! And what are you working on now, Ben? Some new work of fiction?'

'No,' said Disraeli. 'The time has come for me to translate fiction into action.'

Bulwer had asked him to attend the Service of Intercession against the cholera which was being held at St Margaret's, Westminster, under the auspices of the Archbishop of Canterbury and the Speaker to mark the Fast Day. Tomorrow he would learn from the Parliamentarians about the chances of a Dissolution. But, come what may, he thought as he assessed the prospects of Mr Austen's bounty, his fight had begun.

Chapter Two

Outside the church, a few hundred yards from the House of Commons, MPs and their guests stood discussing the correspondence in *The Times*, agreeing and disagreeing with the doctors, some of whom claimed that cholera was a contagion while others declared its origin to be spontaneous. They spoke quietly, almost in whispers, as if they didn't want to conjure up the disease which so far had left the centre of London untouched. But no one could deny the startling rise in the number of cases in the riverside boroughs and the City, nor could the merchants ignore the silent quarantined ships in the Port and the unrelenting spread of the epidemic to Bristol and Plymouth.

As the bell began to toll, the congregation filed into St Margaret's with a funereal air, but Bulwer, who had walked with Disraeli from Mayfair through St James's Park, already daffodiled by an early spring, was in good spirits and declined to put on what he called 'a Sunday expression'. Disraeli too was elated. When he had returned to Duke Street he had found a letter from Mr Nash, Lord Chandos's political agent, confirming Bulwer's forecast by inviting him to stand as a candidate for Wycombe 'in certain eventualities', and he had sent an immediate reply, agreeing. He realized that the Tories wanted to split the Whigs' vote by detaching some of their liberal wing in favour of a third candidate. No matter! Whatever Nash's purpose, Disraeli intended to serve his own.

'Behold,' Bulwer said sardonically, reading from a plaque as they entered the church, ' "An Israelite indeed in whom there is no guile." '

'You refer to me?' Disraeli asked.

'I refer,' said Bulwer, 'to the whole of this assembled hypocrisy.'

They took their seats in the fifth row behind Mr Speaker, Sir Robert Peel, Lord John Russell and Lord Durham, and Bulwer looked around him unsympathetically.

'We've come on our knees to God,' he said, 'to beg Him for his intercession when we ought ourselves to have taken action long ago.'

'In what respect?' asked Disraeli.

'In providing a better water supply for the poor. You won't cure disease till you've cured poverty and the squalor that goes with it. I wonder how many of those here have been to Rotherhithe – how many even to Woolwich . . . You've been to Arabia, Ben, but I bet you've never visited Limehouse.'

'No,' said Disraeli. 'I haven't. Have you?'

'Yes,' said Bulwer, straightening his elegant green surtout. 'Everyone should visit Limehouse. The trouble is we don't know what is happening in England. Our labourers are aliens in their own country. Look at the evidence on the Factory Bill. There are children who start work at one o'clock in the morning and slave without rest till midnight the following

day. Children, imagine it! Take Sadler over there.' He pointed
to a quietly dressed, grey-haired man sitting by a pillar. 'What
chance has his Short-Time Bill got? I'll tell you – none – not
so long as the manufacturers can help it.'

The clergy were entering in procession from the West Door.

Against the church's sepia stone, the crimson copes, the
Bishops' golden crooks, the rochets, the decorated mitres and
the silver pectoral crosses flashing silver and ruby scintillae
where they met the twin bands of light from the perpendicular
windows behind the altar, seemed to Disraeli, as Bulwer
continued his discourse on the conditions of the working class,
a Byzantine pageant, but none the worse for that. Every nation
needed its ark, every priesthood its ephods. Without a hier-
archy, there could only be anarchy, and the duty of a priest was
to identify himself with insignia to separate him from the laity.

Yet he had to admit to himself that ritual was one thing,
faith another. He recognized that the abstractions of theology
must take form and flesh in order to be comprehended by
the multitude, and that only through collective worship could
a church be sustained; yet, like his father who had resigned
from the synagogue rather than accept the duty of an office-
bearer after having renounced the *corvée* of communal prayer,
Disraeli himself, though reared in the Christian faith since
boyhood, regarded ecclesiastical rites as more accidental than
essential, more useful for others than for himself, and their
celebration more necessary for public decorum than personal
salvation. For his own part, he preferred religion to be a
mystery rather than a display, the invisible Shekhina and the
arcane Holy of Holies to its priests and Levites and censers,
and the Name too sacred to be spoken to the explicit rituals of
the genuflecting masses, whether in temple or cathedral. At
Bevis Marks as a child, he had wondered at the solemn, top-
hatted gentlemen, dressed in the English mode except for their
prayer-shawls, reciting in Hebrew the incantations of their
desert ancestors. And at St Margaret's his wonder returned at
the brilliance of the princely celebrants with their English
faces and Graeco-Roman robes that remembered the splendour
of a still earlier priesthood.

Disraeli bowed his head. Awe was a state of grace that could

29

be achieved in many ways. And ceremony was one way of achieving it, even if he had no compelling need for it himself. Order was the consequence of awe, and the Church was the metaphor of an ordered society.

But today there were other considerations than reverence in his mind.

'Isn't that Lady Charlotte near the east transept?' he asked, interrupting Bulwer's mumbled diatribe against the mill owners.

'It is,' said Bulwer, displeased at being moved from his theme. 'And look at old Wilberforce, the humbug. He'll have an apoplexy over slavery in Jamaica. But what is he doing to end it in Lancashire?'

'Did you know her father, Lord Lindsey?' Disraeli went on.

'No,' said Bulwer, bowing as the procession passed. Disraeli kept talking through the murmur of the organ music.

'Perhaps,' he said, 'you'll be good enough to present me to her.'

The Bishop of Durham, representing the Archbishop of Canterbury, stood stony-faced with the congregation as the choir sang, 'I am the resurrection and the life, saith the Lord; he that believeth in me, though he were dead yet shall he live; and whosoever liveth and believeth in me shall not die.'

'Lady Charlotte,' said Bulwer, anxious to discourage his companion, 'has a weakness for clergymen of mature years. You don't appear to satisfy that inclination.'

'She's young enough to modify her views.'

'I'm afraid,' said Bulwer, 'her decisions are made by the lady at her side – her mother. She's the Argus of Lady Charlotte's twenty-five thousand.'

'We are gathered here,' the Dean intoned, 'on this Day of Fast, to remember before God those who have died in the great pestilence known as *cholera morbus*, to make penance for our sins that have brought us this visitation, and to pray for those who are its victims, seeking in our prayer with contrite and humble hearts a deliverance from further ills.'

'Amen!' the congregation mumbled.

'Twenty-five thousand?' Disraeli asked Bulwer. 'Twenty-five thousand?'

'First Corinthians, chapter fifteen, verse fifty,' intoned the Dean. 'I tell you this, brethren; flesh and blood cannot inherit the kingdom of God, nor doth corruption inherit incorruption. Lo! I shew you a mystery . . .'

The Dean's voice went on and on, and Disraeli idled again with the recollection of the sumptuous dinner-party at Bulwer's, where the champagne glasses were objets d'art, and Rosina presided like a Juno at the dinner-table – except that her peacock was a snarling miniature lapdog called Fairy. Fairy! Pity she disliked him so much. But then again, it wasn't surprising. The glittering Irish beauty, sprung from a bog in Ballywire and brought up as a poor dependant in Guernsey, resented him as a competing parvenu. Then Lawson's face, menacing and vindictive, superimposed itself over the Dean's, and Disraeli fixed his attention on Lady Charlotte, who glanced over her shoulder at him.

'Humble yourselves, therefore, under the mighty hand of God,' declaimed the preacher, the Very Rev. Dr Webber, 'that he may exalt you in good time.'

With his face orange-red against his white surplice, he represented all the healthy beatitude that virtue might bring.

'I sense,' said Disraeli, 'that our preacher has had a good breakfast.'

He wished he could pray away Lawson's bills, but his debts were more tenacious than the cholera.

'On this Fast Day,' said Dr Webber, 'let us remember that the Lord will never be tardy in delivering the penitent from the evil that flies by night and day.' He paused and blew his nose. 'A great pestilence hath fallen on the city, and the people are in great distress. They cry to the Lord for salvation that they have not yet merited. Therefore has this day been set aside for a repentance to make an end of calamity through the grace of God and the mercy of Jesus Christ our Lord. Who is there shall seek His mercy and not be answered? Who shall come to the seat of the Almighty and not be spared?'

The voice, plangent and interrogative, waited for an answer. Three, four, five seconds passed. The congregation shifted uncomfortably, but Mr Speaker and the Parliamentarians around him sat unmoved. They had listened to too many rhetorical questions. At last the preacher, satisfied that his pause had gone on long enough, said slowly and emphatically,

'For him who doth not offer a true penitence – for him who doth not appear before the throne of the Lord on the knees of his heart, for him there shall be a retribution. For the sin of arrogance, for the sin of vainglory, for the sin of concupiscence, and luxury, for the sin of immodesty – '

The church was getting hotter, and some of the ladies in the pews were beginning to fan themselves.

' – for the sin that was punished in Gilboa by excision – '

'I wonder what that was,' said Bulwer.

Near the north door where the poor were standing crushed together, a woman collapsed like a tumbling sack of potatoes and was carried out amid angry looks from the front rows of the congregation, already displeased that the ill-smelling lower classes had been admitted to the church.

'Our aristocracy think,' said Bulwer, 'that Christianity is too good for the poor.'

' – for all those sins, may the Lord have mercy on us in that we declare our true repentance.'

The Dean paused to examine the effect of his sermon on the assembly. They looked chastened, and he was satisfied.

'And so,' he went on, his expression changing from a frowning admonition into ecstasy as his gaze moved upwards to the apex of the Gothic traceries, 'our nation shall be delivered from the pestilence, the sick shall become whole, and those who have known the dark shall live in light again through Jesus Christ our Lord. Amen.'

In a great exhalation the congregants answered, 'Amen.'

The choir sang the anthem, and twenty minutes later the procession, headed by Mr Speaker and the clergy, reformed and filed out of the church, followed by the shuffling congregants, deferring to rank and putting their shillings into the collecting-boxes. Sir Robert Inglis, Hardinge, Paget, Duncannon, Duncombe – the Tories, the Whigs, the Radicals – passed in front of Disraeli stiffly without looking to right or left, and he felt it a mortification that others had a precedence over him. Nobody in this parade of M.P.s and their attendants could exceed him in ability or improve on him in appearance.

All that he lacked was Ministerial influence, some patron, the assurance of ten thousand a year, a respite from Lawson and the other duns, and a seat in Parliament which would give him immunity from the fear of a debtor's prison that poisoned every pleasure and denied him an appropriate ambiance. After all, what were his acquaintances – let alone his friends? A handful of literary men, his father's admirers, a few women enthusiasts of *Vivian Grey*, that youthful climber of his first anonymous novel, whose author the Blackwood sophisticates, on discovering his name, had tried to sneer out of society.

And yet, *Vivian Grey* had survived the critics. The great Goethe in Weimar had praised the novel, and the author's reputation continued to grow. Standing in the sunshine of the parvis, Disraeli felt that he drew at least as much attention as Bulwer. Besides, although Bulwer, with his aquiline nose, his handsome angular features and his ginger whiskers, was the son of a General and could trace his family to the Conquest, he, Disraeli, with his ancient race and Venetian descent – well, he didn't have to argue that with himself.

The fashionable gathering was relieved that the service was over and the duty in church done. Here, as the carriages assembled and the greetings and farewells overlaid the creaking of coachwork and the impatient clopping of horses on the macadam, the cholera seemed exorcized, as remote as the distant parishes in which it raged. In a small group where Disraeli recognized Sir Francis Sykes and the beautiful, detached Lady Sykes, Lady Charlotte was chattering happily. But when Bulwer approached, the Sykeses turned to greet Lady Cork, and Bulwer drew Disraeli towards Lady Charlotte as she made to follow her mother into a crested coach.

'May I present – ' he began, removing his tall hat.

She smiled a dimpling smile, and said,

'I am well acquainted with Mr Disraeli through his novels.'

Disraeli bowed.

'But that character Mrs Felix Lorraine,' she went on. 'What a monster you created – a vampire! Have you really such a low regard for our sex, Mr Disraeli?'

Disraeli flushed.

'I'd be unhappy for you to think that. Perhaps you'll allow me at some time to correct your misapprehension.'

She paused with her foot on the carriage step.

'She's such a fiend. Is she drawn from life? . . . Don't tell me. I've guessed. I think I know her. I'd be very much afraid to know you better, Mr Disraeli, in case you put me in a book.'

'We are prepared to leave, Charlotte,' her mother called from inside the carriage.

Disraeli handed Lady Charlotte in, and she turned to smile.

'We are leaving,' her mother said sharply to the coachman, prodding him in the back with her parasol. He flicked his whip and, with the horses slipping, the carriage slowly drew away.

'How beautiful,' Disraeli said wistfully. 'A fairy princess with twenty-five thousand a year imprisoned by a hirsute witch!'

Lawson the usurer and Lady Lindsey the old witch – what a match they would make!

'There's something infinitely nauseating,' said Bulwer, 'when the rich pray for the poor, and pay farm labourers nine shillings a week.'

Disraeli wasn't listening. He had decided to call on Charlotte's mother.

Since early morning tens of thousands of men and women had converged on Finsbury Square in answer to the Metropolitan Political Union's slogan, 'Make the Fast Day a Feast Day', which Henry Heatherington, editor of the *Poor Man's Guardian*, had supported with the words, 'Deprivation not indulgence is the cause of the working people's present distress.' Some marched in procession with banners, others in family groups, some dressed in their best clothes, others in fustian rags, a vast shuffle of feet, a happy murmur, accompanied at intervals by music and drum-beats as if the funeral of some dead tyrant had been turned into a festival.

After leaving the church, Disraeli and Bulwer had attached themselves to the crowd that became steadily thicker as they moved eastward.

'I'm always nauseated when I see the Party leaders side by side on ceremonial occasions at St Margaret's,' said Bulwer. 'They're as indistinguishable as Chinese. Where does a Whig begin and a Tory end? The Parties are a sham confrontation.'

'All oligarchs resemble each other,' said Disraeli. 'Look at the portraits of the doges.'

'It isn't so much the men as the system. It always turns a Party into a conspiracy united by the prospect of plunder.'

'That's true. You can't have faction without patronage. That's precisely why I doubt your idea of a Party of Independents. A Party is an organization of opinion held together by mutual obligations. Once you have a Party, you must feed its members with opportunities of advancement – offices, decorations, purses of gold, bishoprics. Or at least dinners. They're very important.'

'You don't believe that men of independence and integrity – men of liberal and rational mind – could ever serve the nation more disinterestedly than the present Parties?'

'For a time,' said Disraeli. 'But in the end, you have to acquiesce in the system. The Thing, as your friend William Cobbett calls it.'

'No friend of mine,' Bulwer protested at the mention of the editor of the *Radical Political Register*.

'Let it be so. But the Thing exists. The question is whether we can transform it from a confrontation of chiefs with their *sbirri* into a confrontation of opinion.'

'But you yourself – at Wycombe – '

'I will fight as an Independent . . . a Radical in favour of strong government. But the day must come when we have to use the structure of power as it exists. Everything else is fantasy.'

'And if those in power reject us?'

'Ah, then,' said Disraeli unsmilingly, 'it all becomes easier. We will replace them.'

'And how will you deal with Reform?' asked Bulwer. 'There's an irresistible demand among ordinary people for an extension of the franchise. However often the Lords may throw the Reform Bill out after we pass it in the Commons, the demands will grow. There must be an end of Old Sarum, an end of the Rotten Boroughs, constituencies with Members but no voters, while cities like Manchester and Birmingham are unrepresented. You can't hold two opinions on Reform.'

'Reform?' said Disraeli thoughtfully. 'I support it.' Then he added, 'In moderation.'

'Moderation!' said Bulwer dismissively. 'It's the eternal excuse for inaction. Reform is a means, not a programme. It's a means to effect change. There's a far greater issue than Reform that we've left so far to the busybodies – to the Society for the Correction of This and the Association for the Protection of That. The problem of our time is poverty – the poverty of the exploited artisan, the unemployed labourer. We call ourselves a Christian nation . . . Are the children of the poor so different from the children of the rich that their mortality rate must be ten times as great? Is that some Heavenly Law?'

'There must always be a relative poverty,' said Disraeli. 'Some will always rise and others sink. The task of government and philanthropy can only be to improve the condition of the poor – not to abolish their relative status. The English Jacobins made the mistake of assuming that they could alter a natural law by burning something down – Bristol or Nottingham or the Home Office.'

'And yet,' said Bulwer, 'it's the labourer and the craftsman who create the wealth of our nation.'

'With guidance,' said Disraeli, 'with our guidance. Let's take a cab.'

'St Giles,' said Bulwer to the cabman. 'I'll show you a London you don't know, Ben.'

'Do I have to be educated today?' Disraeli protested.

Bulwer didn't answer, and for a few minutes as the cab moved at a trot down Oxford Street, Disraeli lay back, inspecting pleasurably the mansions, the shops, and the well-dressed strollers, themselves observing with curiosity the demonstrators on their way to the Square.

'Come, Ben,' said Bulwer when they reached St Giles. He paid the cabman, and within a hundred yards of the cheerful scene in the fashionable streets, he led Disraeli into the rookeries of St Giles. Across the gloomy alleys, the sunlight touched the tops of the four-storied tenements hung with festoons of grey rags, the counterpart of the grey faces of the inhabitants slouched against the shadowed walls, the children scrofulous, with weeping sores under their noses or on their lips. From the garbage outside the houses came a stench of ordures and decaying fish, and Disraeli put his handkerchief to his nose.

'Good God, Bulwer,' he said, 'this is a high price to pay for education.'

A curious tail had now attached itself to them – women beggars, toothless, grinning and bleating, a few dozen silent children who had summoned each other without words, and who, after following Disraeli and Bulwer at a respectful distance, began gradually to press around them. A girl of six or seven ran in front of them, splashing in her bare feet in the sewage that crawled through the alleyway.

'Perhaps,' said Disraeli, 'we might return.'

'In a moment,' said Bulwer, whose interest had risen in proportion to Disraeli's nausea. 'I want to show you how these immigrants are obliged to live when they get here with a fourpenny deck ticket from Belfast.'

He led the way carefully over the refuse to the ground floor of a tenement house whose window panes and doors had long been broken in, so that it was open to the street as if it were a stable. He crouched in order to see into the barn-like room, and beckoned to Disraeli.

'Come and look!'

Reluctantly, Disraeli peered. On piles of rags and straw, like that of a *lazaretto* he'd seen in Turkey, about sixty men, women and children lay heaped together in a stinking mass, and he drew back.

'No, look,' said Bulwer relentlessly.

Disraeli peered again. Lying close to an enormous, bloated and completely naked woman were two men and a group of huddled children.

'No,' said Disraeli. 'It's too much.'

Then he looked again. What he had thought in the semi-darkness a naked woman was a sow.

The rumour that the Feast Day meant a free distribution of food had brought a crowd of hungry dockers, unemployed because of the quarantining of ships, into Finsbury Square, where they joined the thousands of weavers, carpenters, metalworkers, butchers, sewermen, bird-catchers, water-carriers, chaunters, costers, herring-sellers, old-clothes men, pedlars, patterers, vagrants, half-pay officers and out-of-work farm labourers gathered around the speakers' platform on the carts. The manes and tails of the percherons were plaited with ribbons as if on a May Day, while the tapestried banners with slogans of liberty, unity and Reform added to the general carnival air. Fresh columns of demonstrators, led by bands and drummers and union marshals on horseback, were arriving from City Road, Chiswell Street and Sun Street, with children tugging at their mothers' skirts as Heatherington spoke of a larger suffrage and the need for the 'middle and artisan classes to form a union', protested against the hardships of the farm labourers, and bitterly attacked the Bishops who had voted against Reform.

On the main platform sat the ponderous, twenty-stone Dr Wade, dressed in the full canonicals of a Doctor of Divinity. Around and behind them in the light breeze that blew across the square, flapped the banners of the silk weavers, the cord-wainers, the caulkers, the journeymen paper-stainers, the coach-painters, the trimmers, the wheelers, and the shipwrights, the scarlet and green sails of a huge armada of landlocked galleons, rising and falling in a swell with the movement of the crowd, which applauded each time that Heatherington paused for breath and greeted the end of his speech with a great roar.

Disraeli looked at the scene glumly as Dr Wade introduced the following speaker, a farm labourer called Joseph Hardy of Aylesbury.

'You see,' he said, 'they're spreading disaffection. I've seen that fellow in Wycombe. He's an agitator for the trade unions.'

Hardy began deferentially, speaking in a broad country accent with his head bowed. He said that to provide mutual succour in time of need was a Christian duty which he and his friends in the Agricultural Friendly Society had tried to fulfil. He recognized that illegal oaths were a form of sedition, reprobated by respectable men. But since 1824, trade unions had been legal. The laws against combination had been repealed.

'And now,' Hardy said, raising his lined face, and seeming to Disraeli to look straight at him with his large, hollow eyes, 'our masters treat us as felons because we don't want our wives and children to starve. Tea and potatoes – that's our diet. The cattle is better housed than us. Cattle, yes, we rear cattle – but meat we never see.'

A rumble of anger went through the crowd, and Disraeli and Bulwer edged their way from the fringe towards the dray. In his fashionable coat with dazzling neck-cloth and high collar, Bulwer was treated with a mixture of deference, curiosity and derision as he advanced through the crowd.

'You look like Moses parting the waters of the Red Sea,' said Disraeli, close behind him.

'There's always a rational explanation of miracles,' said Bulwer. 'In this company no one would want to touch us.'

'Boiled puddin's,' said an Irish girl, pushing her tray towards him. 'Ha'penny each!'

'I'll have one,' said Bulwer, 'and one for this gentleman.'

'I think not,' said Disraeli, concealing his distaste. 'Boiled puddings always make me feel faint.'

'In that case,' said Bulwer to the smiling girl, 'here is a shilling, and you will eat them for us. I never eat alone.'

The crowd had thickened, and Disraeli, Bulwer and the pie-girl were now wedged between the cart and a noisy body of demonstrators who had arrived from the east end of the square. Some wore greasy, half-fashioned surtouts; others were in rags with the collars of their paletots rubbed through the canvas; others were dressed in rusty black with their waist-coats buttoned to the throat; most were unshaven, coated with dust.

'And who are these?' Bulwer asked the girl.

'The lumpers, sir – they're from Blackwall and Limehouse ... they work on the timber ships, sir, in the ballast and loading or on the tide-work. Are you sure you wouldn't like a boiled puddin', sir?'

In between the speeches, the crowd sang a hymn beginning in a minor key with a slow and solemn verse, the anthem of the unions.

> *God is our guide! From field, from wave,*
> *From plough, from anvil and from loom,*
> *We come, our country's rights to save,*
> *And speak the tyrant faction's doom.*

Dr Wade stood, and in a magnificent *basso profundo* led the triumphant chorus in a major key that was taken up with even greater fervour by those who hadn't known the words of the verse.

> *We raise the watchword 'Liberty',*
> *We will, we will, we will be free.*

'Look at their faces,' said Bulwer. 'Look how a word can transfigure a multitude.'

Disraeli said,

'I see that Dr Wade is getting more and more purple.'

There was a silence over the gigantic assembly, only broken by the slapping and creaking of banners. Then Dr Wade sang the second verse, with the whole concourse joining in the chorus like a great army drawn in line and singing its battle-hymn.

> *We raise the watchword 'Liberty',*
> *We will, we will, we will be free.*

'I think,' said Disraeli, as the crowd surged and swayed, 'I think we might retire.'

'Good God, Ben,' said Bulwer with excitement, 'this is just the overture. Look over there.'

Disraeli followed his glance to the exit from the square, where rank upon rank of the police, backed by two troops of the 2nd Dragoons, had been deployed with their newly-issued sabres at their side. Only occasionally could the words of the speakers be heard beyond the first few rows of their audience, but the demonstration had fused into the anger of a single personality. When the speakers asked, the huge crowd answered. Reform? A monstrous bay came back as if from one throat. Lord Grey? A sigh. The Duke? A groan. The wind blew a few words from Wade's platform.

'. . . There's a moment in a nation's history when facts take precedence over dogma . . . The assault of events is more powerful than rhetoric . . .'

Disraeli, his arms pressed to his side by the weight of the crowd, looked towards a lighterman smoking a clay pipe between his blackened teeth, and said contemptuously,

'Would you give him a vote too?'

'Why not? The ugly aren't disfranchised even now. Dress him up in a violet coat, a white satin waistcoat, a pair of kersey-mere pantaloons – and he'll be making you a Ministry at White's in next to no time. Besides, what's the difference between him and the country gentlemen who come into the Chamber with mud on their boots?'

'Responsibility,' said Disraeli, forcing himself at last to the edge of the crowd, where he stood uncomfortably near a foul-smelling, gurgling sewer.

'Responsibility,' said Bulwer, 'isn't an innate condition. It's a gift – today an inheritance, tomorrow – look what happened in Paris – responsibility is something to be seized.'

'They've no wish for it. They'd rather have a bottle of gin.'

'No,' said Bulwer. 'You undervalue them. An aristocrat can beggar his family in one night at Crockford's, and they call him a gentleman. He can spend his leisure in the Hells of St James's and the brothels of Montagu Square and still be treated as a man of sensibility and refinement. Whereas if I visit the rookeries and talk to the poor, I'm charged – '

He stopped in mid-sentence as a volley of stones and bottles exploded like buckshot at the feet of Mr Commissioner Mayne, the superintendent of K Division, who was standing with the police blocking the exit to Chiswell Street.

'I think, sir,' said the superintendent to Bulwer, kicking aside some of the jagged glass, 'this is no place for you. Have you any business here?'

They were joined by a solemn-faced, middle-aged man in black, Mr Walters, a magistrate. He raised his low-crowned top hat and said,

'Good afternoon, Mr Bulwer. I'm afraid there's trouble already at Gosford Street. They've set fire to two oil-shops.'

Bulwer greeted the magistrate, and introduced him to Disraeli as the police advanced ten paces and the group of shouting demonstrators and taunting children moved back.

'You see, sir,' said Mr Walters, 'they were promised a dole of food. All they've got is speeches . . . What's the situation, Mr Mayne?'

'Well, sir,' said the Commissioner, 'we've got fifteen hundred police at the exits, and two detachments of the 12th and 17th Lancers are backing us. We want to channel the demonstrators out through Sun Street. I've spoken to the organizers from the Union. They're no bother. The trouble is the thieves . . . They've come out like lice on the coat-tails of the processions. The police surgeon reports ten of our men already injured, two seriously.'

His last words were overlaid with shouts and the obscenities of a squad of drunken women, gaudily dressed but capless, who had pushed themselves to the front of the mob.

'I see,' said Disraeli, 'they've brought up the *vivandières*.'

'The reserves,' said Bulwer. 'There are twenty thousand prostitutes in London today . . . My dear woman,' he began.

'My dear woman,' the drunken woman answered, mimicking his voice, and making a mock curtsey.

'They're very articulate,' said Disraeli. 'The Finsbury Volunteers, no doubt.'

'No,' said Bulwer, shaking his head. 'I pity them. They've been starved into surrender.'

A new salvo of rotting vegetables, garbage and stones soared over the heads of the front row of demonstrators as Disraeli stood immobile, leaning slightly on his cane, studying the mob and repressing a cough from the smoke that drifted across the Square.

'You know,' he said to Bulwer, 'I've never been in a situation like this before – though when I was in the East at the time of the Albanian uprising I seriously thought of joining the Turks.'

'What stopped you?' asked Bulwer irritably.

'The Grand Vizier. He was less tolerant of sedition than we are. In three months he hanged and shot four thousand rebels and it was all over the day I arrived . . . Since I was too late, I simply sent the Palace my congratulations.'

'You're exaggerating.'

'Ah, well – in the East everything is exaggeration. It's catching.'

'You'd better withdraw, sir,' said Mayne. 'The magistrate is about to read the Act. I will then give warning, and my men will clear the Square. Withdraw, gentlemen – the situation is dangerous – and you're in the way of my officers.'

Two policemen, struck in the face by stones, stumbled to the ground bleeding, one on his knees, the other half-conscious, and the sight of the wounded made the demonstrators bold. Disraeli pointed his cane at the now dishevelled women.

'I doubt if they'd satisfy even the bashibazouks . . . Mind you, Mr Commissioner – ' with a wave of his hand – 'all this is an ancient custom. Tacitus, you'll remember, in *Agricola* – or was it *Germania*? – you remember how the tribes would go into battle egged on by their camp-followers.'

Bulwer put his arm over his eyes as another volley of cobbles bracketed the group in front of the police.

'Withdraw, sir,' said the Commissioner. 'I order you to do so.'

At that moment a heavy tar-block struck Disraeli in the chest. He staggered, and looked indignantly at the missile on the ground, and then at the delighted mob. Bulwer was already retreating behind the police who were standing with their batons drawn as Mr Walters, amid the jeers and chanting that had now become an unbroken roar, stumblingly read the Riot Act. The blow had hurt Disraeli, and he put his hand to his chest. Then he bent down, picked up the missile, and offered it to a policeman who was standing stiffly at attention.

'Pray, officer,' he said, 'return this to that gentleman over there.' He waved his stick towards one of the lumpers. 'I'd do so myself, but frankly, I dislike ball-games.'

The Commissioner gave the order for the police to charge, and shortly afterwards the demonstrators, screaming abuse as they fell back, were driven through the smoke to the Garford Street exit from the Square.

After that tumultuous afternoon, Disraeli looked down from the Gallery of the House of Commons at the scatter of self-satisfied, intent, flushed, exhausted, indifferent faces in the

43

candled Chamber below. His chest hurt where the rioter had struck him, but he scarcely thought of it as he followed the debate.

The constitutional problem remained. How could an institution endure – even an aristocratic institution – if it had no connection with its popular roots? He had never believed in the mythology of Rousseau. That afternoon he had seen the French philosopher's idealized savages, the mechanics and the paupers and vagrants and labourers, uniting in a form of Jacobinism which he prayed would never be naturalized in England. Yet what could be said of an established, hieratic order that blinded itself to the movement of history and ignored the mass of the people? The House was debating Lord Mahon's Motion for the rejection of the Reform of Parliament (England) Bill – 'that the Bill be read a third time this day six months'. But if there were valid arguments for a wider franchise, the young and aristocratic Tory now on his feet was certainly not presenting them. He spoke in short sentences like an angry, barking dog. Nothing was a reason; everything was an affirmation or a rhetorical question. This was a Bill, he said, to create anarchy. Its inspiration was alien.

'Good God, sir!' he went on. 'Abolish the Boroughs? Accept the Schedule A? You'll deny the elder sons of peers a time-honoured right. The right of studying in the Commons. The right to study the processes of law-making which they may bring to fulfilment in the Lords.'

Leaning over the rail of the Gallery, Disraeli observed the Members as if they were the cast of a drama, some lounging half-asleep in the hot, vinous-smelling Chamber, others joining in a chorus of 'Hear, hears!', cockcrows from below the gangway, and groans of 'Anarchy!' whenever the word 'reform' pierced their consciousness. Mr Slaney mumbled in favour, then Mr Pemberton mumbled against, while bored Members drifted in and out between the Chamber and Bellamy's, the tavern connected by a corridor with the lobby. Below the gangway Bulwer was sitting, lost among the dandies, the Irish and the 'rads', surrounded by a litter of the oranges with which they refreshed themselves as the night wore on. Yes – Bulwer was too sensitive to criticism, too eager for praise, too idealistic for reality, too petulant in argument – hag-ridden by a mother at once obsessive and vindictive, a wife romantic and susceptible and, as she put it, bored by authors, and a mother-in-law whose preoccupation with women's rights overrode the personal rights of her family. Bulwer, Disraeli felt, would never be able to dominate more than the paper he wrote on.

Disraeli felt a tightening in the pit of his stomach, the tension that he always felt when he thought of power. Beneath him in the Chamber were the squires, the philanthropists, the aristocrats, the wealthy radicals, men who had been born into politics while he himself had been born, he often said, in a library. But he had an eloquence they would one day listen to. And just as at the opera he sometimes had a fantasy of rising in his box and singing the tenor's aria, so tonight he wanted to join in the debate, instead of being a stranger ignored with a blank indifference by the Parliamentarians.

After Mr Pemberton had sat down, the Speaker called Mr Macaulay, the young, dark-haired member for Lord Lansdowne's pocket borough of Calne. Immediately, as the attendant in the corridor leading to Bellamy's shouted, 'Mr Macaulay on his legs!', the Chamber began to fill with Members hurrying in from a supper of steak and table-beer, till at last every place was taken and the Bar at the farther end was crowded with standing M.P.s. Disraeli strained forward to see better the speaker, only four years older than himself, who had attracted such a large audience.

Early established in the *Edinburgh Review* as one of the most brilliant critics of the day, a protégé of Lord Lyndhurst who had given him a Commissionership in Bankruptcy, Macaulay had quickly gained the ear of the House with his maiden speech. Now he began with the flattering assumption that everyone present was as well informed and had the same reasonableness as himself.

'Yes, there is a simple alternative,' Macaulay said, 'the Bill or anarchy. But it is the status quo not reform that can lead to anarchy. On March 1st, 1831, we took no slight step in voting for Reform, one that can't easily be retracted . . . Before us lies glory; behind, disgrace.'

Though the House listened coolly at first, the 'Hear, hears!'

gradually accumulated till they blanketed dissent. Then, after speaking for an hour, Macaulay sat down to a crash of cheering and smiles and nods over their shoulders from the Ministers in favour of reform.

But the cheers faded when Mr Croker, the Secretary to the Admiralty, followed. Disraeli observed him with curiosity and unwilling admiration. The two M.P.s had been enemies since the previous year, when Macaulay had written a lacerating review of Croker's edition of Boswell's Life of Johnson. 'I hate Croker,' Macaulay had said, 'as I hate cold boiled veal.' Disraeli was glad that the arrogant Croker had met his match. Only recently Murray, his publisher, had got Croker to read the proofs of *Gallomania*, and Croker had tried to push Murray into restoring some anti-Reform passages which Disraeli on second thoughts had crossed out. Disraeli had angrily forbidden the proposal. Whatever he might think of the Whigs, he certainly wouldn't ally himself with the Tory anti-Reformers. Besides, Croker, he'd been told, had blackballed his application to join the Athenæum, the club which his own father, Isaac D'Israeli, had helped to found. That was a good enough reason to detest him, and looking down on the tall, self-confident, bald-headed, middle-aged form, he discovered to his satisfaction that his reluctant esteem of a few seconds earlier had rapidly changed into positive aversion.

'If the Bill is passed as the honourable Gentleman proposes,' said Croker, his finger menacing Macaulay, 'we shall arrive at a Directoire. There'll be a dissolution of public credit, and finally a confiscation of public property.'

His 'r's turned to 'w's, and as he spoke he moved his head from side to side, now addressing the Speaker, now the Members near the Bar.

'He's like a bun on a hot griddle,' said Disraeli's Irish neighbour, but Disraeli didn't answer because Croker had paused before launching his main attack on Macaulay's claims that a constitutional change would benefit the people.

'What the honourable Gentleman wishes to do is to give power not to the people but to the mob.' (Loud cheers from the squires.) 'Let them have it, and they'll pull down in savage sport the Houses of Lords and Commons and the *Church* . . .

The populace, like a wild beast, will only be satiated when there's no longer an object to prey on . . . Will things stop there? No – the next step will be anarchy.' (More cheers, now spreading over the benches.)

Anarchy! Disraeli savoured the word and thought that there is no scarecrow like a scarecrow word.

'Yet even that couldn't last for ever. As in 1660 and 1688,' said Croker, 'society will revive again in its full majesty.'

At his peroration, Croker turned and faced Macaulay, who sat with his hat tilted over his eyes.

> '*Fond impious man!*' he quoted. '*Think'st thou yon sanguine cloud*
> *Rais'd by thy breath, has quench'd the orb of day?*
> *Tomorrow it regains its golden flood,*
> *And warms the nations with redoubled ray.*'

There was no question, Disraeli thought, listening to the prolonged cheers, that Croker, who had sworn that he wouldn't sit in a reformed Commons, had the regard of the House. Well, so much the better if he carried out his threat to resign if the Bill went through. For his own part, Disraeli himself would be well content if Croker, who had already stood in his political path, ended his own political career with a poetic fancy.

Watching the Serjeant at Arms remove the mace after the Speaker adjourned the House at 1.15 a.m., and hearing the loud conversation of Members as they shuffled from their places towards Westminster Hall, Disraeli had no doubt that it was here that his antagonisms and alliances would always lie, that the sound of cheers and counter-cheers would be the natural music of his future, and as for Mahon, Slaney, Pemberton, Croker, even Macaulay – all indifferent to him as he looked down from the Gallery – yes, one day they would take note of him, and he would outdo them all.

Power! That was the goal. Trade, industry, social change, the poor, that great and hungry animal with its baying mouth – all that could wait. His need was power. And the first means to power was a seat in Parliament.

Yes, he would call on Lady Lindsey.

Chapter Three

'And what, Mr Nash, is the view of his Lordship?' asked the Reverend Holgate. Fifteen years before, he had come to stay with Squire Lowther's family in the manor house at Radnage as tutor to his two sons, and had stayed on with the family, practising a careful diplomacy of flattering his host and mediating between him and his wife in the course of their marital rages.

'Indeed, sir,' General Sir Arthur Cropley Gurden answered, crossing his trousered legs. Their elegant buttoned straps beneath the instep contrasted with the Squire's breeches and Hessians which he hadn't removed since his morning ride over his thousand acres. 'His Lordship's views are all important, given that the *Bucks Gazette* has already described this gentleman as a popinjay and a galloper in every direction.'

For greater comfort, the Squire hoisted his belly with his left hand, and helped himself to more port before passing the bottle to Nash. Then he said in his flat, loud voice, dropping his aitches as if to emphasize his bluntness,

'Disraeli! It's not a name I've ever 'eard of. Disraeli! It's a 'igh-macaroni name. Where d'ye find such a man?'

Nash took a sip of port, and said,

'You will realize, gentlemen, that Lord Chandos is ill-disposed towards the Whig predominance in High Wycombe.'

'God's firkins, yes,' said the Squire in an access of fury. 'They want to enlarge the franchise by telling the tenants not to pay rent. Look what happened in Nottingham and Bristol. Rick-burners – only a week ago, one of my farmers lost two ricks – burnt down like that!'

He swept his hand over the table and knocked over his glass.

'Gosling!' he shouted at the top of his voice, and a servant came running with a napkin, anxiously dabbing at the table and his master's waistcoat. Lowther pushed him away.

'Your candidate,' Mr Holgate said meekly to the agent, 'Mr

Disraeli – if I'm not mistaken – has expressed himself in favour of Reform – '

'Reform,' the Squire rumbled. 'They want to take the franchise from the burgesses.'

'I think not, sir,' said Nash calmly, speaking with the assurance that the views of Lord Chandos, the greatest land-owner in the county, would carry even more weight than the Squire's. While the others had each drunk a bottle of port after a lunch which had included a whole Aylesbury duckling a head and a joint of roast beef, he had merely picked at a chicken bone and sipped at his wine. In an electorate of less than a hundred, he badly needed the three votes represented by his drowsy table companions. Through the windows and beyond the terraced drive he could see Mr Lowther's fields, interspersed with copses of beech trees, descending in glittering folds slashed by the June sun towards the valley; but there was no sign of Disraeli, who had promised to arrive by four o'clock. Nash wondered how he could hold the attention of Lowther and his friends before they fell into a stupor.

'Now in his Lordship's view, the corn – '

'God's firkins,' the Squire exclaimed, leaping from his chair at the word, 'the corn – there's your cry. The corn – if your man – what's-'is-name Macaroni? – if Macaroni says he'll hold up the price for the farmers, he'll be home and dry. What d'you say his name is?'

'Mr Disraeli,' said Nash coolly.

'Doesn't sound a countryman's name to me,' Lowther grumbled. 'Sounds a foreigner.'

'He has already given a remarkable address at the Red Lion setting out his views,' said Nash.

'Yes,' said the General. 'A very strange performance. Mind you, Colonel Grey's performance was even stranger. I happened to be riding through High Wycombe last Thursday. Heard a band. Never could resist a band. What do you say, Holgate?'

'No, indeed not,' said Holgate deferentially. 'I'm not a martial man, but I never could resist a band.'

The General stroked his whiskers that met under his chin, and said,

'In the Peninsula – the band, sir – well, there's nothing like a band to hearten the troops . . . what was I saying, Holgate?'

'You were in High Wycombe last Thursday.'

Nash eyed him carefully. He wanted the General to be drunk enough to pledge his word to Disraeli, but not so drunk that he would forget his pledge.

'Yes, I was saying, along came this band into the High Street with Colonel Grey's open carriage and horses unharnessed – all the townspeople pushing it along. There he gave us his election address.'

'If he promised no better than his father, he's a rascal,' said Lowther.

'The Prime Minister – Lord Grey – ' said Nash, ' – has promised too much and delivered too little . . . And what did the Colonel have to say?'

'Well, he began by saying he'd never spoken in public before. Then he stammered and stuttered for a quarter of an hour, and two gentlemen from the Treasury Bench – I imagine they were Lords Commissioners – they called for cheers, and the Colonel disappeared for dinner.'

'That's as it should be,' said Lowther. 'I fear, sir,' he said to Nash, 'your man isn't coming. Pray give my respects to his Lordship, and assure him of – '

The door burst open, and Mrs Lowther stood clasping her hands in excitement.

'He's arriving,' she said. 'He's here.'

Lowther heaved himself, scowling, to his feet, angered by the intrusion and the flush that had spread over his wife's arms and throat.

'Who the devil's arriving?' he roared.

Nash rose quickly, and bowing over Mrs Lowther's hand, said,

'Delighted, ma'am, to see you earlier than I had hoped. I imagine Mr Disraeli is here?'

'Oh, yes,' she said, seeing the expression on her husband's face. 'Oh, yes,' she said, retreating and her voice fading. 'Yes – Mr Disraeli is here.'

Disraeli got down slowly from his phaeton, handed the reins

to a groom, and drew in his stomach where the stays pressed comfortably under his black morning coat lined with white satin. His damasked waistcoat was unruffled by his drive from Wycombe, his white silk shirt was open, and his gold chains clinked pleasantly as he left the driving seat. He took up his white gloves and his ivory cane, adjusted its black tassel, and prepared to advance through the porch where Gosling was waiting to conduct him.

It hadn't been a bad morning's canvass. Accompanied by his chief aide, Mr Huffam, an old friend of his father, he had called on Benthamites, Latitudinarians, Wesleyans, radicals, liberals, dissenters of every kind, and rallied them to the cause of independence. He had been delighted with the reception they gave him. At Mr Wright's chair factory, the mechanics had looked at him in stupefaction and followed him into the street with cheers. At any rate, he hoped they were cheers. Pity that in the register of the unreformed constituency almost none of them had votes. But it didn't matter. Before long, the Reform Bill would certainly be passed, and this by-election – well, it was a means of gaining experience, and preparing himself for the time when he could appeal to a wider constituency than the burgesses of Wycombe.

Until then, he would have to show he could make his mark in a fight which, however hopeless, he would never admit to be lost. Above all, he must save himself from humiliation, and Squire Lowther, who carried at least three and perhaps even five votes, was the man he had to win. Damn the Whigs and damn the Tories! Why did they have to have labels? He could beat them all in argument. But would that get their vote? The answer was, he must try.

He took the bunch of roses presented to him earlier in the day by Mrs Bolton at Wycombe from the arm-rest of the driver's seat, and followed Gosling into the saloon. Mr Nash advanced towards him, and said,

'Well, Disraeli. You were detained, I see . . . Mrs Lowther, may I present Mr Disraeli?'

Disraeli bowed, and handed her the bouquet of roses.

'My sister, ma'am – Miss Disraeli – asked me most particularly to present you with these few flowers. I'm honoured to be her Mercury.'

'Mercury – mercury,' said the Squire in a loud aside to Holgate. 'The fellow looks he could do with some.'

Mrs Lowther primped her day-cap, and curtsied slightly so that her breasts welled up under her low-draped bodice.

'Please give Miss Disraeli my compliments – '

The Squire glanced at her, and she withdrew, only turning at the door to offer Disraeli a smile.

'Let's make a beginning, gentlemen,' said Lowther, whom the transition from the table to the door had awakened. 'Your purpose, sir, is to canvass our votes.'

Disraeli crossed his legs and said,

'Perhaps, better, to offer myself for your opinion.'

'We know ours,' said the Squire hostilely. 'What we want to know is yours. We want to know who seeks to represent us.'

Disraeli looked around them, and addressed himself to Holgate, the only one of the three voters who regarded him if not sympathetically at least without visible unfriendliness.

'My qualifications I derive from the gift of my father, Mr Isaac D'Israeli of Bradenham; my encouragement from Lord Chandos, whom Mr Nash represents today; and my hopes from my energies which have been proved elsewhere.'

'Elsewhere?' said the General. 'You have served, sir?'

'Not with the sword, General, though I have faced brigands in Andalusia and pirates in the Levant.'

'Mr Disraeli,' Nash quickly interposed, 'is, of course, one of our outstanding novelists.'

'You're a reading man,' Lowther said to Holgate. 'What do you know of Mr Disraeli's work?'

Holgate shifted his black-stockinged legs, and said,

'I'm afraid, Mr Lowther, I never read novels. Were you to question me on historical biography – '

'Well,' said Lowther, walking over to the carved oak fire-place, 'perhaps you'll tell us something, sir, about your family. . . . Mr Isaac D'Israeli. Does your father hunt?'

'In Arcady,' Disraeli said. Nash smiled, and Holgate laughed, smothering his laugh into a cough as he saw the Squire's look of displeasure.

'My father,' Disraeli said, 'is a literary man – Isaac D'Israeli – author among other books of *An Essay on the Literary Character*, much praised by the most famous Englishman of our times.'

'The Duke?' said the General.

'No – I refer to Lord Byron. But the Duke has praised him too.'

The General looked respectful, and Disraeli rose and walked to the middle of the carpet, standing head and shoulders above the Squire.

'You may, of course, ask how the descendants of the ancient family of Disraeli have their seat today in Buckinghamshire – how Isaac D'Israeli, descendant as he was of those who shared in the governance of Spain when her fortunes were at their zenith, became an illumination of English literature? Permit me to tell you.'

The Squire prepared to interrupt, but Disraeli went on.

'For centuries after the conquest of the Romans by the Goths, the Saracens who overcame the Goths in turn lived in amity with the Hebrews. Then, at the end of the fourteenth century came the triumph of the Dominicans over the Albigenses.'

He turned to the Reverend Holgate, who was impressed not so much by Disraeli's historical prelude as by his dismissal of the Squire.

'Imagine, gentlemen – a gifted people, owners and cultivators of the soil – there lies your true aristocracy – suddenly exposed to an Inquisition which had already taught the Mexicans and Peruvians the atrocities that can be committed in the name of our Lord.'

He paused, and waited for the Squire to speak.

'Them Romans,' said the Squire, pulling at the bell for the servant to bring claret, 'damme – I'd disembowel 'em!'

'You will understand then how at the end of the fifteenth century my ancestors left Spain for the hospitable Republic of Venice, abandoning their Gothic surname and affixing instead the proud and unique name of D'Israeli in a tribute to the Lord of Jacob who had succoured them through many perils.'

'The Battle of Lepanto,' said the General irrelevantly, 'was one of the great battles of the world.'

'You see, Mr Lowther,' said Disraeli, 'how mysterious forces can move men to a point in history where their interests converge. My grandfather came to England nearly a hundred years ago with the Villa Reals, the Medinas, the Laras, the Laredos, the da Costas. They brought wealth to England.'

Mr Nash nodded.

'At a time of mercantile expansion, they helped England to be great . . . As for my father, a contemplative man, he chose to settle in Buckinghamshire where he has many friends – first at Chesham and now at Bradenham . . . Sir,' he lowered his head modestly, 'that is the summary of a journey through history which brings me to your house in search of your support.'

'I'm obliged, Mr Disraeli – very much obliged,' said the Squire uncomfortably. 'But let us imagine you have our votes. How can you be sworn in Parliament on the true faith of a Christian?'

Disraeli picked up his cane which he had placed across a Jacobean chair, and flicked his toe-cap with it.

'My oath as a Christian,' he said, 'will be as true and valid as I hope your own would be. I was received into the Church – baptized – at St Andrew's, Holborn, at the age of thirteen. Mr Thimbleby performed the ceremony. Do you think I could forget such a name?'

'God's firkins – no!' said the Squire, suddenly aware that he might have offended Disraeli by his question. Gosling had brought in two decanters of claret, and the Squire poured Disraeli a glass.

'You are very welcome, sir. At Radnage, you see, our politics is very simple – not too much reform, a good price for corn, and the established church.'

Disraeli raised his glass to the others, and they all drank.

'You have summed up my policies,' said Disraeli. 'I trust I may meet at the hustings with your support, gentlemen.'

Mr Lowther spread his legs and cracked his knee joints, and said,

'You can rely on our consideration. What about them rick-burners?'

'We shall make it unprofitable for them,' said the candidate.

'Transportation – it ain't enough.'

'We will think of other forms of penalty.'

'Hanging – pulling out their guts!'

Disraeli put down his half-finished glass of wine, and said,

'A procedural point. I'll bid you good-day, gentlemen . . . Tomorrow, sir,' he said, shaking hands with Nash.

Outside in the porch, Mrs Lowther was waiting to give him a sachet of herbs. 'So that you'll have happy dreams!' He took her hand and kissed it lightly. In her corsage, he noticed, she was wearing his ribbons.

He climbed into the phaeton, handed a shilling to the groom, and flicked his whip over the horse's head. He was satisfied with his canvass and he felt happy. As the carriage moved away, he could hear the General's voice coming loudly through the window.

'I wouldn't refuse anything to Lord Chandos . . . but why that bumptious Jew-boy?'

Returning to Wycombe, Disraeli left the phaeton and ordered a horse at the Red Lion Hotel. In the livery yard, he was greeted by a number of supporters, among them Mrs Clara Bolton, the wife of his doctor, who had come by the 'post' from London. He had first known her at Hyde Heath near Chesham, the house rented by his father during Disraeli's adolescence after he and Sarah and his younger brothers Ralph and James had been the constant victims of bronchitis in the chilly Bloomsbury air. Dr Buckley Bolton had a simple panacea for bodily ailments – to bleed the arm, to shave the head, and to leave the patient in solitude, except for his nurses, in a darkened room.

Since Disraeli's mother had a horror of disease and rarely appeared in Disraeli's sick-room, his adolescent illnesses were a memorial of the tenderness of strangers, chief among them Mrs Bolton during his illness at Bradenham before he left for the East. Long after he was grown up he remembered the scent of her rounded arms, where in the privacy of the sick-room she would envelop his head, and her voice, normally loud and rather coarse, but in the miasma of his high fevers a secure and tranquil connection.

After he moved to London they had met a few times secretly at Brompton, where Dr Bolton had taken a house, though in the society where she liked to move, her dyed fair hair, her powder and rouge made Disraeli regret a relationship which was convenient and pleasurable for secret occasions but made him feel restless and ill at ease, like a man after a masked debauch who, unmasked, meets one of his partners in broad daylight.

'Here he comes,' said Mrs Bolton, clapping her hands and waving a pink-and-white favour. The ladies around her joined in the applause, and Disraeli said,

'Thank you, ladies. We haven't yet captured the heights, but we've taken the outer redoubt.'

Mrs Bolton turned to her friends in delight. Despite Disraeli's detachment, she still had a feeling of ownership.

'Wonderful,' she said, patting the neck of Disraeli's horse as he mounted. 'Mind you,' she went on, 'you have your enemies.'

'Yes,' said Disraeli. 'You can't have friends without making enemies. I'm indifferent to them.'

He collected the reins, and frowned.

'Who are they, madam?'

'Well,' she said, 'perhaps I shouldn't have told you. I don't want to make mischief.'

The horse began to caracole, and Disraeli controlled him expertly.

'Who are they?' he said icily. 'It would be for my convenience to know.'

She chuckled, and he listened with distaste to the throaty sound that seemed to roll from beneath the flesh under her pretty chin.

'At the Red Lion yesterday,' she said confidingly, ' – I really shouldn't tell you this – there was a Mr Turtle at Lord Pennington's breakfast. And he didn't know my sympathy with your candidature.'

Disraeli smiled encouragingly to her.

'Well, he was saying to Lord Nugent – Mr Disraeli was a man without social standing – '

'Ah!' said Disraeli, his face becoming white as if he'd been punched in the solar plexus.

' – without family – '

'Continue!'

' – without principles – '

'I see.'

' – and without any hope of winning High Wycombe.'

Disraeli raised his hat to her.

'I'm obliged, Mrs Bolton.'

'Not angry with me, I trust – I did tell him I knew your father – that he was an excellent – '

'Not another word, Mrs Bolton.'

Disraeli tugged at the reins, and the horse reared its head.

'A knight who isn't ready for wounds shouldn't go jousting. But when I meet Mr Turtle, I'll cane his shoulders.'

He laughed, and with that laugh the sting of Mrs Bolton's report faded. Turtle! How could he feel resentful of a man called Turtle? Benjamin Disraeli – that was a name! A line of poetry! He liked it. And as he rode from Wycombe through the Vale of Hughenden, the hedgerows aflower, and skirted the dark beech trees stirring in the summer air, he felt exultant. The road was iron-hard, and he turned across the fields, where a surprised hare started up and fled zigzag in front of him. The countryside between High Wycombe and Bradenham was a series of meadows, patchworks of purple clover and yellow sainfoin abutting the cornlands and rising up to wooded hills broken only by the thatched cottages of a few hamlets. His horse knew the way, and stretched into an easy canter as Disraeli held the reins loosely. Only thirty miles or so from the wen of London, he felt himself translated already into the quiet world that his father had chosen for his secluded life. London, the hustings, and Bradenham – Disraeli needed them all, and the words matched his horse's stride – London for fame, the hustings for battle, the harmonious Jacobean manor with its huge rooms, thick walls, deep cellars and broad windows looking down from high in the beech woods to the village in the valley – Bradenham was comfort and balm.

What did the bite of his enemies matter? The more abuse he received, the more he was armoured against it.

Yes – he would endure wounds, he'd break lances, and one day he would triumph. The image of a great medieval tournament took shape in his mind, where a mysterious knight, a stranger in black armour, clashes with the champions of the court, observed by a châtelaine, a princess – no, a queen from above. The horses thunder towards each other; the lances shiver; the champion falls; and Disraeli raises his visor to the royal person as she tosses him a bouquet of jonquils.

Meanwhile, he could see ahead the Saxon church and beyond it the huge iron gates of Bradenham, the glade-like terraces of yew trees heightening the whiteness of the old hall with its gable ends and lattice windows, and he dismissed the fantasy. He was wondering if the Guv'nor could advance him a few hundred.

Sarah put down the flowers she had gathered and turned towards him with her arms outstretched. He had intended to greet her with an elaborate salute that he had been practising in imitation of Count D'Orsay; but leaving the horse to Tita, the servant he had inherited from Byron, he ran to meet his sister and held her affectionately in his arms while he kissed her on both cheeks. She disengaged herself from him, and held his hands.

'Ben!' she said. 'You look wonderful – but so thin! Why are you so thin?'

'In this country of fat men,' he said, 'the thin man is king. Besides, I have to fit my last year's wardrobe. I can't afford a new one.'

She took him by the arm and led him to the door of the manor opening on to the lawns.

'Let's walk a little,' Disraeli said. 'I've a lot to tell you.'

She put her shawl around her shoulders, and they walked slowly together through the apple-orchard to the rustic house on the fringe of the beech wood. Beside her, he felt robust as he looked at her vulnerable face with its shadowed, luminous eyes, her nose slightly too large for a woman though excellent perhaps in a duke, her warm, full lips and her sallow complexion. He spoke to her about the progress of the election, told her anecdotes about his supporters and opponents and about Mrs Bolton's intervention on his behalf, about his successes in London and his hopes for his two new novels, *Contarini Fleming*, which had just appeared, and *Alroy*, the poetic romance of a Hebrew Messiah whose head even in death sneered at his executioners. Sarah listened happily to his monologue. She laughed as he told her of his triumphs, of his repartee which, even if edited after the event, still bore his authentic stamp; she frowned when he described his critics, and smiled when he spoke of their undoing.

'When the election's over,' she asked, 'will you go back to town?'

'Yes,' he said.

Her face became sombre.

'But only for a short time,' he added. Her face lightened.

'I will confess to you, Sarah,' he said, leading her to a log seat which he brushed with his handkerchief so that she could sit. 'I want to get married. I am obliged to.'

She smiled, and asked indulgently,

'Why "obliged to"?'

'Because,' said Disraeli, 'everything – yes, everything, depends on my contracting a successful marriage – all my hopes of success – in Parliament – in society – even as a novelist – everything depends on my having a secure domestic base.'

She wagged a finger.

'Ah, Ben, still after Lady Charlotte and her twenty-five thousand. I tell you – beware of her improvident blood. She'll get you more quickly into debt than you can yourself. You must marry for love. Love – that seems to me to be the radiance that gives light and value to life.'

Disraeli looked at his sister's face tenderly. It was a face that was an exaggeration of his own, and he felt for it a deeper compassion because of the memory of his sister's fiancé James Meredith, who had died of smallpox when they were travelling in Egypt.

'That may be,' he said. 'Love in marriage is a bonus paid in deferred instalments. But those who get it in advance – ' he laughed – 'they normally use most of it before they reach the altar . . . No, dearest. I have observed that people like Bulwer who marry for love doom themselves to a permanent infelicity.'

'What do you know of love, Ben?' she asked.

Disraeli took her hand.

'Nothing, Sarah – except what you have taught me.'

She touched his face again with the tips of her fingers, and said, 'You must be careful with speeches like that. You'll win all the women and lose all the men.'

'Don't worry,' said Disraeli. 'I have other speeches for the men.'

He walked away from her and breathed deeply.

'I love the air of Buckinghamshire,' he said. 'I only feel well when I'm breathing this air or when I'm smoking.'

'Smoking?' she said.

'Yes,' he replied. 'I have taken to the *narguilah* – the one given me by the Bey in Alexandria that filters the noxious fumes.'

He came back to her, and looked into her eyes that had filled with tears at his mention of Egypt.

'Sarah – ' he said.

'It's all right, Ben. I think of him every day of my life. I didn't need you to speak of James to remember him.'

'I've tried not to remind you.'

'It doesn't matter – really it doesn't. You spoke of love before. I loved James. That's all I know, and that's what I will remember all my life.'

'But Sarah – you're still very young.'

'Young?'

'Young – you're only thirty-one. You'll get married.'

She looked at him ironically.

'No,' she said. 'I will never get married. I have decided – ' her face became firm – 'I have decided. I'll stay in Bradenham with Mama and Father, and then when they are very old I will care for them.'

She stood, smiling, and said,

'And I will live my life joyfully. We'll have neighbours and friends, and I will listen – rather like listening to distant church bells – I'll listen for news of all the triumphs of your genius, Ben.'

60

'If I succeed – '

'You will succeed – and I will applaud you, and love all those who love you, and hate all those who hate you.'

'In that case,' said Disraeli, 'I can conquer the world.'

He gave her his hand, and they walked back contentedly to the house, now piled in silhouette against the dusk, as the rooks swooped low over the tree-tops.

In the library, Isaac D'Israeli was standing reading at the tall lectern, his pen on the mahogany table by his side, ready for writing notes.

A single lamp above his head lit his embroidered skull cap and his hair that fell to the collar of his brown velvet banyan. For a few seconds his son stood contemplating the absorbed expression in his father's large brown eyes as he bent closely over the book, his private glee, his translation as if by a djinn from Bradenham to the exotic places of antiquity and legend where his researches led him. Almost since Disraeli had been aware of his father's existence, he had known him as a scholar, whose joy was in bookshops, the company of a few literary men like Mr Douce and Mr Southey, but above all in his own library, where each morning he would betake himself, with his velvet jacket reaching to the top of his old-fashioned stockings, and where he would stay, uninterrupted except by meals.

And it was here in this library that Disraeli himself had obtained his education and his knowledge of the world before he left for London. Not at the preparatory school of the Reverend Eli Cogan. There he had learnt to fight, to assert his authority against the crowd. That had been, perhaps, as important a lesson as any he had learnt from books when, as a small boy, with his back against the school wall, surrounded by a taunting mob – what was an Ikey, he had wondered? – he had dashed at the biggest of the bullies, dragged him to the ground, and bloodied his nose.

But his knowledge of literature he had gained from a private tutor, his father, and from the countless books that he had read in this library where Isaac had always seemed to be standing with a gentle smile on his lips, though now his back was a little more bowed, his eyes more myopic, his figure more portly, and his hair whiter than he remembered.

'Father!' he said quietly.

His father peered into the shadows, and then said,

'Ah, Ben! Yes – yes. Ben – how are you, Ben? Where have you been?'

Disraeli approached the lectern, and his father awkwardly gave him his hand.

'Canvassing the votes of my prospective constituents, sir.'

'Of course – of course, I forgot. Well done, Ben – well done. Take a seat. Sit here!'

He pointed to his favourite armchair with its worn silk brocade by the escritoire.

'Oh no, sir,' said Disraeli, smiling affectionately to his father. 'I can scarcely sit in your chair while you stand.'

'My dear boy,' said Isaac, 'we're not in a royal palace. The purpose of etiquette is to keep order in court. Now take your Standing Orders in Parliament. The object of rules and etiquette is to prevent great concourses from becoming a rabble. It's etiquette which determines the order of coming or going.'

'Exactly, sir,' said Disraeli. 'I defer to you. Therefore I will stand.'

He knew how to debate; he had learned how to do so in a thousand syllogistic dialogues with his father, who despite his agnosticism and his estrangement from the Sephardic community was an accomplished Talmudist, and who in argument still followed the Rabbinical method of dialectic alternatives reinforced by parable and example.

'But by standing,' said Isaac, 'you defeat the object of etiquette which is the regulation of conduct for mutual advantage. Let me tell you about the case of Philip the Third at the Spanish court.'

Disraeli bowed his head. This was one of his father's favourite anecdotes.

'Philip the Third was one day sitting by the fireside.'

'Father – there's a matter I want to discuss with you.'

'Yes – yes . . . Let me just tell you about Philip the Third. Where was I? Yes . . . Well, the court fire-maker had kindled so much wood that the monarch was nearly suffocating . . .'

Disraeli composed himself patiently.

'From the heat, you see. Now the monarch – and this is the point – the monarch couldn't stir because of etiquette, and the servants couldn't enter without being called.'

'Why not?'

'Because of etiquette . . . After a time, the Marquis de Polat appeared. "Damp the fire," said the king. "Sir," said the Marquis de Polat, "I cannot. Etiquette forbids it. It is the task of the Duke d'Usseda." Well, Ben, the Duke had left the Palace. The king got hotter and hotter rather than derogate from the Marquis's dignity.'

'I trust, sir, he eventually got cooler.'

'Alas, yes,' said his father. 'He developed a violent fever from his blood being overheated, and in 1621 in the twenty-fourth year of his reign it carried him off . . . One cannot refrain from smiling.'

'No,' said Disraeli, smiling politely. 'It is a monitory story. I will take your seat, sir.'

'My dear boy,' said his father, closing his book, *The Life of Sheridan*, by Thomas Moore, 'it's much too late – much too late. Let us dress for dinner.'

Disraeli gave his father his arm, and together they walked slowly to the door as Isaac began an anecdote about the harvest customs of the Thracians.

Shortly before dinner, Disraeli came face to face with his mother at the bottom of the stairs. He was happy to see her again after an absence of several months, and he went forward eagerly to kiss her cheek. She drew away a fraction, enough for him to realize that she was offering him her outstretched hand rather than her embrace. He took her hand, slightly fleshy and moist, and bowed over it.

'Good evening, Benjamin,' she said, and withdrew her fingers quickly. 'You will do someone an injury with all those rings. Wouldn't three be enough?'

She turned away, and Disraeli watched her move along the corridor, self-confident, with her Babet-shaped cap perched on top of her plaited hair. He tried to think of her as a grey, elderly woman, living in the country, on whom most of his fashionable friends would scarcely bestow a glance. And yet, always in her presence, his assurance ebbed. As a boy, he had been treated by her as sullen, rather stupid and ill-favoured; she had wanted her first-born son to be a Norman Paladin; instead, he would always look like an Arab on horseback, the true descendant of the Basevis and the Disraelis who bore in their name and their features the ancestral blessing and curse.

Others he could always look straight in the eyes. There wasn't a challenge that he wouldn't accept. For every tart word he would always have a sharper answer. But his mother had an early, irreducible advantage over him. She had seen him grow up; she knew what he meant and what he feigned. He had no mystery for her, and she had rejected the warm love that he had longed to give her. Never mind. The D'Israelis would one day descend from him, and as for the Basevis they didn't bear thinking about.

'Benjamin,' his mother said in the saloon, 'you will sit on my right hand, and you'll tell me all about the new fashions in London.'

She smiled to him, and he thought that his mother in her décolleté was very beautiful, except for her somewhat Bourbon (or was it Basevi?) nose.

Chapter Four

'The new performance of the Opera *Tancred* by Signor Gaetano Rossini, given at the King's Theatre, Haymarket, on May 18th, 1833, with the collaboration of Signora Pasta.'

Lady Lindsey read the title on the silk programme, and turning to her daughter Charlotte, said in a voice that could be heard three boxes away over the tuning of instruments and the excited conversation,

'I could bear opera if only it ended with the singing. But the applause – there really should be an ordinance to limit the applause!'

'Perhaps,' said Lady Charlotte, 'it would be better if every opera ended in silence like a sermon.'

'What an excellent idea, Charlotte!' her mother said. 'I find it grotesque that after the heavenly singing there should be such a terrible brouhaha from the audience. It's almost as if they were all determined to murder the effect. We'll leave immediately the opera ends.'

'Yes, Mama,' said Lady Charlotte. 'Mr Disraeli can escort us home.'

'It won't be necessary,' said Lady Lindsey, shaking the spray of feathers in her hair. 'I have asked the carriage to return. In any case, where *is* your Mr Disraeli, and where are the Sykeses?'

'There's still another ten minutes to go,' said Lady Charlotte, looking towards the heavy red draperies at the back of the box. 'Mr Disraeli said the other day he's often late but always timely.'

'What he meant,' said Lady Lindsey, 'is that he tries to make a great entrance. I can't say I'm sorry he failed at Wycombe.'

'Beaten but not failed at Wycombe,' said Disraeli, parting the curtains as if on a cue. 'Madam – Lady Charlotte.'

He bowed over their hands.

'My dear Disraeli,' said Lady Lindsey graciously, 'I should have been unhappy if you'd deserted literature for politics. Anyone can make a speech in Parliament. Who else could have written *Vivian Grey* or *The Young Duke* or *Contarini*? Come, Mr Disraeli – come and sit between us and let's ruin a few reputations.'

Disraeli took a chair between them and glanced quickly around the great theatre, ornamented along its tiers with Neptunes, tritons, mermaids and hippogriffs festooned with floral wreaths, supported by cupids and domed with a flame-coloured sky. Each box was like a three-sided room in which men in coloured coats plastroned and ruffled in white, and women with naked shoulders and aigrettes and tiaras displayed themselves as if they were actors and not spectators. They were all there, the friends and acquaintances whom he had accumulated by introduction and recommendation during a winter season in which he had had great social success, even though he had lost two elections at Wycombe. In the by-election he had been defeated by the Prime Minister's son, Colonel Grey; but from June to December he had engaged in a prolonged campaign till the passage of the Reform Bill and the subsequent Dissolution. Then at the General Election he had tried again, proudly declaring in his address, 'I wear the badge of no Party,' and making a virtue of the fact that none of 'the blood of the Plantagenets' flowed in his veins. Despite those boasts, perhaps because of them, the Whigs had pushed him a second time to the bottom of the poll.

It was true however. Though beaten, he hadn't failed. In fighting the election, he had gained experience, learning the lesson that in politics faction is all, independence an illusion. At some time, though not yet, he would have to enrol under the banner of a leader, a man whom he could respect and who would recognize his qualities, a patron he could serve and who in turn would promote his fortunes. But the matrimonial dowry for which, since Bulwer introduced them, he had wooed Lady Lindsey as attentively as he had her daughter was at least as important as a political patron. The trouble with both women was their fatal enthusiasm for venerable gentlemen. It was a family vice. After the Earl, Lady Lindsey's first husband, died, she had married an elderly vicar, the Reverend Peter Pegus, who, it was said, beat her systematically and died of drink.

Undiscouraged, and pursuing the hope that her daughter would correct her own misfortunes, Lady Lindsey had set her sights on Mr Ward, the distinguished novelist, a sixty-one-year-old bachelor. To counter this strategy, Disraeli had dressed himself in a frock-coat of clerical black when he first called on Lady Lindsey. Useless! She had received him with an aristocratic detachment, and maliciously repeated a story told to her by Mrs Bulwer that when Disraeli at one of her parties had risen in his velvet breeches from a wicker chair, old Samuel Rogers – that wicked monster! – had declared 'he bore the mark of *Cain*'. And Lady Charlotte had laughed. It was discouraging when a pretty woman laughed at a social jibe, though a pretty woman who was also an heiress had privileges which he could wait to cancel. But the mother was more than a hurdle. She was a fortress.

Now, at the Opera, he had decided to change his tactics and storm Lady Lindsey with magnificence; he wore a purple velvet coat lined with satin, black breeches with a gold band running down the outside seam, and a scarlet waistcoat which heightened the effect of his three chains – the watch chain, the filigree chain attached to his quiz-glass, and the Turkish chain with the heavy gold amulet from the great covered bazaar of Constantinople.

He was, he noticed, much observed. Or were the glances for Lady Charlotte? No, they were for him. He bowed to Lord Henslow and Colonel Greville Parker, who greeted him very civilly. There was no doubt that the Wycombe elections might not have made him a Member of Parliament, but they had certainly established his reputation.

He leaned forward in the box in order the better to be seen. The flutes and strings were tuning and practising cadenzas, and Lady Charlotte asked,

'Tell me – which of your heroes are you closest to? Which of them is you?'

'All of them,' said Disraeli. 'And the villains too – the good and the bad – the women as well as the men. They are all myself fragmented into a thousand roles – the cooks, the duchesses, the swordsmen as well as the swooning ladies.'

'You're making fun of me.'

'No, indeed not. A novel is a confession of feeling, delivered in fragments, and a novelist must feel like all mankind.'

'Yes, but surely, Mr Disraeli, you must have based Alroy on some reality – on your travels in Syria and Egypt.'

'Oh, certainly,' said Disraeli. 'The geography. But Alroy, the Prince of the Captivity, is an ideal expression.'

'Of yourself?'

'I have no doubt.'

He turned to her mother. 'Do you know the desert, Lady Lindsey?'

'No,' she said haughtily. 'It has always seemed a singularly *barren* subject.'

Disraeli gave her a bored look, and turned to her daughter. He was beginning to think that not even Lady Charlotte's fortune could compensate for her mother's conversation.

67

'You should see it in springtime,' he said. 'The desert becomes strewn overnight with flowers – cyclamen, narcissi and anenomes – like a sudden remembrance of its fertility. When you wake, with the sparrow and the partridge above you, you know how pure the earth was before it became corrupted.'

'Oh, how beautiful!' said Lady Charlotte, clasping her hands. The boxes were filling fast, and there was a rising conversation in the parterre and the boxes that joined with the orchestra in an expectant discord. 'Please go on!' Lady Charlotte said.

'What shall I tell you?' said Disraeli, encouraged. 'Only that in Galilee I understood why Our Lord chose the Holy Land for his revelation.' He began to declaim. 'The scent of the myrtle trees, the pomegranate, the orange blossom blowing its fragrance over the lake, the shrines revered by all mankind – the places stained with blood for the sake of the Holy Name – the graves of saints and crusaders – in that small compass by the ruins of dead civilizations, where the Bedus camp in their black tents, you'll find the story of – '

'Mr Guest is greeting you, Charlotte,' Lady Lindsey interrupted.

Lady Charlotte bowed to the pleasant-faced, middle-aged ironfounder who smiled to her from a few boxes away. Then she turned back to Disraeli, and said,

'It's one reason why I wanted to hear *Tancred* tonight. How magical it must be to have seen Jerusalem.'

'Yes, indeed,' said Disraeli gravely. 'It's a very worthy ambition to go to Jerusalem. The problem is, what do you do once you get there?'

'I never thought of that. But is Jerusalem really golden?'

'Golden? Yes, the dome of the Mosque of Omar built on the site of the Temple of my ancestors is golden. But in everything else, Jerusalem's glory is only a memory. The sanctuary has fallen to the goats.'

They became silent as the overture began. Then the opera opened in a palace in Sicily where the Christian knights were rallying to face the Moors, and the ladies in the chorus were giving each of them a white scarf in the presence of Argirio, the old president of the Senate, and Orbazzano, suitor of his host's daughter Amenaïde, whom the exiled Tancred loved.

68

Amenaïde sang a desolate aria, lamenting that her father had promised her hand to the detested Orbazzano when he knew she loved Tancred.

Charlotte and Disraeli joined in the applause that followed as if together they could keep alive the voice whose vibrations the uproar was already extinguishing. As Disraeli applauded, he looked across two boxes at Lady Sykes whom he had last seen talking to Charlotte outside St Margaret's. Lady Lindsey was fanning herself, and Sir Francis Sykes had his arm flung indifferently over the back of Lady Sykes's chair as if he found the clamour slightly undignified. Lady Sykes was applauding too, and Disraeli rose to his feet and shouted in a resonant voice that made people turn to look upwards from the pit of the theatre, '*Brava! Miracolo!*' From the corner of his eye he could see Lady Lindsey cringing in embarrassment, and he repeated his cry '*Brava! Miracolo!*' even more enthusiastically. Then he subsided reluctantly into his seat, a partner with Charlotte and Lady Sykes in appreciation.

The audience became quiet again as Tancred landed on the beach with a party of knights, and now La Pasta, the superb and portly contralto who took the part of Tancred, sang '*Di tanti palpiti*', the throbbing avowal of joy at the exile's return to his ungrateful country.

Lady Charlotte leant back in her chair, and her hand touched Disraeli's as the anguish of the music rose. Disraeli kept his hand still, but turned his head slowly towards Lady Sykes, who met his glance, and they looked at each other for a second till she quickly turned away towards her husband.

But now Amenaïde was telling her father she'd rather die than marry Orbazzano.

'Most unfilial!' said Lady Lindsey as the pit vigorously applauded the refusal. Unhappily the rejected suitor had forged the heroine's signature to a love-letter addressed to the Captain of the Moors, and the Act ended with Tancred shattered by his loved one's betrayal.

The audience called and whistled its approval, and Disraeli opened the door of the box at the interval to allow his companions to pass into the foyer.

'Too shrill!' said Lady Lindsey. 'Much too shrill!'

She went ahead in search of acquaintances who were now emerging from the boxes. Lady Tollemache, Lady Gordon, Miss Mary Pelham, Lord Walsingham, the Hon. Mr Wyndham, Lady Shaftesbury, Mrs Blair, Lady Buckley, Baron Eckstein with his blue sash, Sir George Warren, Miss Ellis, Colonel St Leger, Colonel Fitzpatrick and Mr Brudenell – she knew them all, and moved from one group to another, sniffing, inhaling, rejecting, ignoring – a sally here, a pause there, a note of approval, questions that didn't wait for an answer, comments that admitted no reply.

'You're so fortunate,' said Lady Charlotte, taking his arm as they stood by the sherbet stall near Sir Francis and Lady Sykes. 'You know all these Eastern places as well as Tancred. Are the costumes authentic?'

'I scarcely know how a crusader looked,' said Disraeli, 'but in Turkey – in Syria – in Egypt – you see a pageant that has changed very little since the age of miracles. In fact, everything is a miracle. The sunsets and sunrises, the light on the water, whether it be Galilee or the Bosphorus. The brilliance of the East is always in my mind . . . Tell me,' he asked, drawing her aside, 'tell me a little more about the Sykeses.'

'Sir Francis? Oh, one of Mama's London friends – they sometimes invite us to their box, though I must admit I find him a very cold person with that peculiar expression of disdain on his face.' She dropped her voice to a whisper. 'You know the old baronet seduced the wife of a brother-officer in the Dragoons – and when he complained, he tried to cut his throat.'

'His own?'

'No – his friend's. I thought everyone knew,' Lady Charlotte went on. 'He was tried in Westminster Hall, and had to pay ten thousand pounds in damages.'

'*Damnosa hereditas*,' said Disraeli.

The crush-bar was getting hotter, and Lady Charlotte was guided away by her mother towards Mr Ward. Disraeli found himself deserted, and after drawing out his cambric cuffs, he took his glass and, standing on the stairs, looked down on to the crowd as it formed and reformed into groups. He looked for Lady Sykes, and followed her with his glance as she moved, escorted by a court of smiling men attentive to her wishes, while an inner group of praetorians, including her husband, surrounded her.

Without quite knowing why, Disraeli resented the privileges of those who were claiming her interest, who addressed her and were chattering around her. He turned his back, and began to read the programme again.

Suddenly he heard a woman's voice behind him.

'I don't think it appropriate for Mr Disraeli to stand alone.'

He turned, and looked straight into the eyes of Henrietta Sykes. Over her wide forehead, her dark hair was parted in the centre and surmounted by a small chignon. Her black velvet dress, cut away from her shoulders, was clasped with two clusters of diamonds and sapphires, and on her wrist she wore a small bracelet of jade. She looked at Disraeli with her mouth slightly open as if in a hesitation that she had to overcome before asking a question, and her eyes were inquiring.

'A moment ago,' said Disraeli with a bow, 'I could have borne it easily. But now no longer.'

She smiled and fanned herself lightly, and Disraeli observed that there was a faint tremor in her hand. She presented him to Lord Horsham and Sir Henry Campbell, and went on,

'How do you find the opera, sir?'

'I'm always interested in the drama of duty and love.'

'Which side do you take?'

She spoke to him as if the others weren't present.

'I'm on the side of duty.'

'That's very sad.'

'Love is sadder.'

'Do you think so?' she asked. 'I would have thought from your novels that love is something wonderful, elevated, a mysterious fulfilment.'

'That's why it's sad. It's a dream.'

'What is sad?' asked Sir Francis Sykes, who had left her but now rejoined the group. '*Buona sera, caro Disraeli!*' He affected the belief that Disraeli was an expatriate Italian. 'What is sad?'

'Good evening,' said Disraeli coolly. 'I was saying it's sad that all the dreams of poets and composers die nightly when the last note fades away.'

'I don't take the opera very seriously,' said Sykes in his languid voice. 'Prefer the ballet any time. Can't wait tonight, though. Will you come back with Lady Lindsey, madam, or shall I send the carriage?'

'I think the carriage,' said Lady Sykes.

'We share a physician, I gather, Mr Disraeli.'

'So I understand.'

'Very good man, Bolton. Excellent man. Fine woman, Mrs Bolton . . . Good night, sir. Come along!'

Sir Francis retreated a step, bowed together with his friends, and they were submerged in the crowd, leaving Disraeli alone with Henrietta.

'I'm afraid,' she said, 'my loss is Crockford's gain.'

'No – mine,' said Disraeli. 'Will you stay for the ballet, madam?'

'Yes,' she said.

'Dear child! Dear child!' cried an imperious voice from a nearby sofa. Disraeli and Henrietta turned towards the aged Lady Cork, rouged, with the powder caked between her wrinkles, and lost in layers of organdie and muslin as she sat surrounded by a court of ladies and gentlemen, with a black page-boy in livery at her side. 'Come here at once!'

Henrietta moved across the room to greet her, closely followed by Disraeli.

'May I present Mr – '

'No, no, you may not present him. I know Mr Disraeli. I know his father too. Everyone knows Mr Disraeli. Have you read his last book?' Lady Cork didn't wait for her to answer. 'It's very beautiful. I've just laid out seventeen shillings to have it bound in crimson velvet.'

She turned to Disraeli.

'And you, sir. Why do you not take greater care of this beautiful person – there, my dear, come and sit next to me.'

Disraeli and Henrietta glanced at each other.

'She is seen too much alone in society. Are you not, my dear? I hear your husband is about to travel abroad.'

She took Henrietta's hand, and went on:

'Everyone is travellin' nowadays. When I was a girl – in Dr Johnson's day, you know – no one travelled more than they could help, and when they did, they travelled with their household.'

'I shall be joining Sir Francis soon.'

'Yes – yes,' said Lady Cork, indifferent to her comment. 'You must come to my next rout . . . Bring Mr Disraeli. I will not have bores around me. Bring anyone but that terrible Jeemes Smith . . . Never bring Jeemes Smith . . . I don't dislike his neck-cloths so much as his *bons mots*! And don't bring Jekyll either. He tires me. I can't bear deaf people. I feel for them so much. Besides, I can never repeat myself – not even for the Duke.'

She tapped with her ivory stick on the ground, and her page helped her to her feet.

'I like Mr Disraeli,' she said as if to the air, ignoring Disraeli, who hadn't said a word. 'He has a great gift of repartee.'

The bell was ringing, and she joined the general movement to the amphitheatre. Henrietta put her hand lightly inside Disraeli's arm, as Lady Lindsey invited her to join them in her box.

At the end of the second act, Lady Charlotte and Henrietta, stirred by the singing and the sorrows of Tancred, again joined eagerly in the applause that rose in a succession of storms from the audience as the singers bowed. Lady Lindsey sat glumly.

'We will leave,' she said.

'May I escort you to your carriage?' asked Disraeli.

'It won't be necessary.'

Disraeli stood, and opened the door.

'I'm sorry,' whispered Lady Charlotte, embarrassed and disappointed. 'Shall we take Lady Sykes to the Paganini concert?'

'If she consents,' said Disraeli. He was happy; nothing could have pleased him better than Lady Lindsey's departure. Lady Charlotte too, whose delicate figure contrasted so inadequately with Henrietta's tranquil beauty – a felucca to a galleon in full sail; he was delighted she was leaving. He bowed to her and her mother. Lady Lindsey kissed Henrietta and said, 'I will leave you in the care of Mr Disraeli.'

'Lord Lyndhurst,' said Lady Sykes, 'has already promised to escort me.'

'That, I fear, was an invention,' she added as Lady Lindsey left. They both smiled, and Disraeli said,

'But he is here. I've always wanted to meet him.'

'In that case,' said Henrietta, 'I will present you. But for my own part, I've always wanted to meet the author of *Contarini Fleming*.'

'You prefer Contarini to Vivian Grey?'

'I love them both. But perhaps Contarini is just a pseudonym of Vivian?'

'So they say.'

'And Alroy – another of his masks?'

'That is so.'

'I'm very glad,' said Henrietta. 'I would have been disappointed if in reality they'd proved to be three different people. You see, I know a lot about you already . . . I hear you're going to be a Member of Parliament.'

'Have you anything against that?'

'No – except that my father-in-law was a Member. He had a great talent for making politics dull. But he had a rather lively youth, you know.'

'Politics, of course, is the end of youth.'

'Yes – I imagine it has a very taming effect. I shouldn't like you to become tame, Mr Disraeli.'

'That isn't my most pressing ambition.'

'What is?'

The introductory music to the ballet had begun, and before Disraeli could answer, a rustle of hisses calling for silence ended their conversation.

When the ballet that followed was over and Disraeli had called Henrietta's carriage, he returned to find her talking to some friends, among them a handsome man of about sixty, Lord Lyndhurst, the Chief Baron and a former Lord Chancellor.

'Do you believe in platonic love, Lord Lyndhurst?' a dowager lady asked.

'After . . .' Lyndhurst answered. '*After*, madam, not before!'

There was a burst of laughter, and the lady frowned.

'I hear, my lord, you are proposing a new Matrimonial Bill.

Are you really in favour of a man marrying his deceased wife's sister?'

'If she's pretty enough – certainly,' said Lyndhurst.

The laughter rose again, and Henrietta introduced Disraeli to Lyndhurst, who gave him an amiable greeting. The party broke up, and the Chief Baron was drawn into another gossiping group of friends. Henrietta smiled.

'I wish you'd been here a few moments earlier. I was talking to Lord Lyndhurst about you. He admires your work greatly.'

'You know him well?'

'He's a very old friend of my family. My father sat for his father, Mr Copley – such a superb painter. I have a passion for painting.'

'The English School?'

'Yes – but the Venetians most of all.'

Disraeli walked happily with her through the foyer towards the entrance in the Haymarket.

'May I call on you, madam, tomorrow?' he asked in a tone that was an affirmation rather than a request, as he handed her into her coach in the rowdy street where the grooms holding the horses' heads were jostling and swearing.

'Not tomorrow,' she said. 'Sir Francis is leaving for Basildon.'

He stood downcast.

'The day after tomorrow,' she said, 'at eleven in the morning.'

He half-smiled at her, but she looked at him gravely.

Among the link-men and the coachmen, lit by the gently roaring flambeaux, Disraeli watched the coach draw away. Henrietta didn't turn her head.

He walked through the warm spring night towards Duke Street, excited and disinclined to sleep. Through the windows of St James's he could see the clubmen at ease beneath the chandeliers in a way that he usually envied, but he had no wish to join them. Henrietta – Henrietta Sykes. Her face was in front of him – her large eyes, her dark hair, her pale shoulders, her warm voice, her tranquillity. Yes – that was a rare quality. Almost all the women he met for the first time treated him as an adversary whom they had to engage in a clash of badinage and provocation. They never knew when to be quiet. But Henrietta had stood serenely, and spoken of his work with courtesy. He had answered extravagantly, seeking to draw from her the familiar bantering response. Instead, she had listened attentively – *courteously* – so that the chatter, the heat, the intrusions, the inquisitiveness, the inspections, the malice of the crowd disappeared, and he was left with an exalting pride mingled with uncertainty.

When at last he lay in bed at Duke Street, he opened his eyes in the darkness and thought of Henrietta. Pride and possession. Was that the nature of love? Perhaps in part. He had wanted her to choose him. The true possession was to *be* possessed. In a quick parade, the women he had known in his life hurried in front of him – the casual, disappointing, regretted *amourettes* of his travels – Gibraltar, Granada, Constantinople – the frivolities of Malta in the dissipated company of James Clay – the roué with a Cupid mouth, the Wykehamist school-friend of his younger brother Ralph – and Mrs Austen and Mrs Bolton, cocooning mistresses who had happened rather than been chosen, women who had enveloped him through the accident of environment. And there had been other intimations of love, flirtations at a ball that made his heart beat quicker in a fantasy that lasted a few hours. Lady Charlotte? Pretty Charlotte. She might have been beautiful if Henrietta hadn't existed. And that was now over. Goodbye to the boredom of placating her Gorgon mother! Goodbye to the fairy gold of her dowry! To be a sort of matrimonial curate would never have done. Lawson and Austen and Rossi and all the other debtors he had happily forgotten would have to wait once again.

The love he sought had to be a giving and not a taking. Only once in his life had he loved like that – and that was his love for Musaeus, his private name for the boy at school whom he had worshipped and sought to serve as he had never done before or since. No woman had ever had in his eyes the pure beauty of Musaeus, Musaeus the accomplished, the Alcibiades in whose eyes he saw the sun rise and set.

In the afternoon, when lessons were over, he would stand to watch him pass. To receive Musaeus's smile was to know why he had been born; his frown to know the suffering of an outcast soul. The walks by the river; the secret embraces; the poignant ecstasies; till the holiday when Musaeus came to stay at Bradenham, that fateful holiday when Musaeus, the paragon, the peerless oracle, spent three weeks in Buckinghamshire. Unhappily, not even Socrates could have endured the transformation of one of his beloved friends into the pimply youth that Musaeus had become.

There was, he thought, nothing like a bad complexion to free one from an infatuation. Nor was there any liberty like the escape from an obsession. And since that time, Disraeli prided himself that he had never surrendered to an illusion.

He was free, and he stretched himself in bed with exultation. Within thirty hours he'd see Henrietta again. The joy that he had on the hustings, dominating the angry faces, uplifted by the cheers of his supporters, was of the same kind, though only a fraction of what he now felt. He imagined his dress for his morning call. It would have to be splendid. The new brocaded waistcoat.

His flesh rose at the prospect of his visit. They would be alone, and he would press his mouth against her neck and bosom. But there was, of course, the door – the damned door that he would have to keep his eye on. He frowned in the darkness. Sir Francis Sykes – he wished he could have disliked him, but that was because it was always more comfortable to cuckold a man you disliked. He turned over in bed. That a woman who seeks a lover must be discontented with her husband was an axiom. And yet – perhaps he had misunderstood. Could he have misunderstood?

No, he couldn't have misunderstood. 'Not tomorrow. Sir Francis is leaving for Basildon.' Did that mean he'd return the following day? That he would have to look at the door the whole time?

The whole time? What whole time? Perhaps it was all a fantasy. It didn't matter.

'*Di tanti palpiti*'. He heard the music from Tancred in his

77

mind, the soaring voice, the chords. He could see her mouth in front of him – Henrietta! How could he pass the hours ahead? Henrietta. Again his body tautened at the name. Henrietta. Her violet eyes beneath her dark brow. The music. He drifted half-asleep with the brilliant colours of Sicily confusing themselves with the jewels on her corsage, the snake of the bracelet uncoiling and raising its tongue.

At three-thirty in the morning, Henrietta still lay awake, watching the shadows cast by the candles in her bedroom. Her husband hadn't returned from Crockford's, or wherever he might be, and the candles, twice renewed, were guttering again. After the opera, she hadn't wanted to sleep, and she had lain in bed thinking for hours of the strange, pallid Disraeli whom she had longed to meet and talk to after she had seen him at Bulwer's and then at St Margaret's. The extravagant Disraeli with the black curls, who had applauded so vigorously and ostentatiously in public and then relapsed into hesitancy when they were alone.

Yet even in his restraint there was boldness. He had announced his intention to call rather than asked permission, and so far from resenting his enterprise, she had enjoyed it.

When she had married, her family had been delighted that she would be the wife of Sir Francis Sykes of Basildon in Berkshire, descendant of the first baronet, his grandfather, who had made £300,000 in the service of the East India Company. Henry Villebois, her father, a rich man himself and a partner in the brewers Truman and Hanbury, was willing to overlook the peccadilloes of the second baronet, especially as Francis was only five when his father had died. It was strange. Francis himself often complained to Henrietta that, orphaned on both sides by scarlet fever which carried off his parents within weeks of each other, he had never known the intimacy of family life. She herself had had too much of it as a child, constantly resisting the imperiousness of her own father and sister at their home at Marham Hall in Norfolk. Yet she loved her father, who stared back at her gloomily from the painting above the fireplace.

Her marriage had begun by being a release but had faded

after four pregnancies into a weariness when she found that Sykes had inherited his father's late conversion to public respectability, but none of his early dash, and that his enthusiasm for her had evaporated in a hypochondriacal fear that domestic passion exacted an undue toll on his energies. And so they had gradually become more and more remote from each other as Sykes, depriving himself of the attentions of Henrietta, turned to the care, first of Dr Bolton and then of Clara Bolton, whom she detested. *Sapiens qui assiduus.* That was the motto of the Sykeses, and it certainly applied to the ever-present Dr Bolton and Mrs Bolton.

But Disraeli was different from them all. He was the realization in flesh and blood of a reverie that always came into her mind when she had looked at her husband's light blue eyes, his wispy hair and pursed lips, and dreamed of a consort who looked like the dark and vigorous young man who had asked to call on her.

She had known his name for several years, and had been half in love with it even before she had met him. Benjamin Disraeli. It was a bold name, a poetic name that fitted him, a name her father would disapprove of, and that too excited her. Villebois – Disraeli! The names were foreign, Norman and Venetian. Sykes. She frowned. Sykes. Villebois. Disraeli. Then she smiled to herself, and put her arms behind her head so that the sheets touched her knees as she arched her back. Benjamin Disraeli. It was a beautiful name, and suddenly everything around her seemed beautiful, the canopy, the large looking-glass with the cupids, the fresco on the ceiling, the window frames, the waxen stalactites hanging from the candle-holders. She felt a great benevolence for everything in the world, for the house, the servants, even for Francis whom she could hear opening the door.

Sykes entered the bedroom and said aggressively,

'Still awake?'

'Yes,' she said. 'I've been waiting for you.'

He went into his dressing-room, and spoke from there.

'You know,' he said, 'I don't like to disturb you

'It doesn't matter. I wouldn't have slept. Did you win?'

'Yes.'

'I'm glad.'

She could tell from the defiance of his monosyllable that he was lying.

'Where did you sup?' he asked.

'At home.'

She held her breath for a moment, and went on calmly,

'I came back alone in the carriage. And you?'

'At Crockford's.'

And that too she knew was a lie, since he was surrounded with an aura of the jasmine scent that Mrs Bolton wore.

He returned wearing a *robe de nuit* and a red night-cap which he believed to be a specific against influenza. He doused the candles, and climbed into bed beside her. He was very tired.

'Good night,' he said.

'Good night,' said Henrietta.

She smiled in the darkness, and turned her back on her husband. Then, thinking of Disraeli and the prospect of his call and feeling very happy, she curled up her knees and folded her arms over her breasts.

Chapter Five

'No,' said Bulwer, examining a scimitar that hung on the wall at Duke Street. 'I can't stay in London. People are too rancorous.'

Baum held the plum-coloured coat as Disraeli carefully fitted himself into it.

'But, my dear Bulwer,' Disraeli said, 'your *England and the English* is quite splendid. How many editions so far? Three? I'm racked with envy. And *Godolphin* – '

'You mustn't father that on me,' said Bulwer, whose publisher wanted to tease the readers of his novel by maintaining the author's anonymity. 'Much too Gothic . . . Don't you think so?' he added cautiously. '*The Age* and *Fraser's* and the *Spectator* have been very violent.'

'You accused me falsely, yet you – '

'I'm sorry.'

'I'll be content if – '

She turned her tear-stained face to him.

'I'd be content,' she said, 'if we lived together – I have great affection for you, Francis – '

He took her hand.

'I'd be content if – you see, I must have an escort – someone who'll escort me in public – Disraeli – you must know – '

'Know what?'

'Disraeli could never be more than a friend. You must believe me . . . I don't mind if you see Clara Bolton. Although I hate her. How vulgar the woman is! How could you associate with her?'

'Perhaps that's what I like and want,' said Sykes, releasing her hand and leaning back. 'Someone without pretension.'

'I'm not willing to be abandoned,' said Henrietta. 'Even though a wife is no more than a piece of property.'

'What is it you want?'

The coach was approaching Park Lane, and Sykes said,

'I will leave you at the house. What is it you want?'

'If you want to go on seeing Mrs Bolton, and we live together, you must at least let me have an escort. I can live like a nun, but not like a hermit. I *must* have an escort.'

'You mean Disraeli?'

'Or anyone else. Bulwer, Castlereagh, Pollock – anyone. I must have an escort.'

'Perhaps,' said Sykes, 'Disraeli it should be.'

Henrietta's expression didn't change.

'No,' she said, shaking her head. 'Not Disraeli. He's been too much abused – too humiliated.'

'I'm sorry,' said Sykes. 'I can see that you need an escort in society when I'm not available. Why not Pollock?'

'No – I loathe him.'

'Then Disraeli.'

She hesitated.

'I'm not sure. But if that's what you want . . .'

There was a truce of silence.

'You've made me very unhappy,' she added as the coach arrived at Upper Grosvenor Street, 'but I forgive you.'

Sykes bowed his head.

In a triumphant letter to Disraeli at Bradenham, Henrietta had described her clash with Mrs Bolton. Accompanying it was a note from Sykes inviting Disraeli to spend some time at Southend in February. 'There will be hunting with Sir Henry Smythe's hounds,' it said, 'and some Essex friends may visit us. But otherwise, we would be happy for you to find whatever solitude you may require to complete the new work in which you are presently engaged.'

· And so, Disraeli had arrived at the Grange to find himself part of a suspicious quintet.

Disraeli looked cautiously around at his table companions. Dr Bolton was describing to Sykes the virtues of the homeopathic treatment of influenza, and Sykes, hypochondriacal and always interested, as Disraeli already knew from Henrietta, in disease and its cure, was listening deferentially, their social roles reversed. Over many years Bolton had achieved a growing practice as a society physician, and although balding at the age of forty-two, he was a handsome man with a cheerful, open face, firm in his judgments without being dogmatic. In his healthy patients, his frown cultivated an anxiety adequate for dependence. In his sick patients, his smile that revealed his regular teeth produced an immediate reassurance. He had studied at Edinburgh, and acquired the basic qualifications for his profession, but the secret of his success with both women and men lay in his willingness to listen. He never hurried a consultation; his watch remained in its fob, however tedious and prolix his patient. Thus he was able to acquire not only a detailed knowledge of his patients' maladies but also of their private affairs, which rapidly gave him a wide authority over his fashionable clientèle.

An added strength was that he rarely abused that authority. Always smiling, he gave everyone the faith that his consultation was as secret as a confessional, and that his prescription was as lenient as healing would allow. After Disraeli's return from

Malta, Bolton had treated him for a few ailments, but since then, Disraeli had seen him less and less.

Yet Dr Bolton and Clara were a popular couple. Aristocrats, arrogant in good health, felt humbled in sickness by the probing of their physician, but Dr Bolton had the art of making light of most maladies. Liver? The *bon vivant*'s complaint. Gout? A gourmet's hazard. Rheumatism? The national handicap. The clap? A temporary indisposition. Because he was always well dressed as well as sympathetic, Dr Bolton was regularly invited to dinner-parties where, even if he sat at a lowly place at the table, he always paid for the invitation by his friendly, tolerant demeanour. He was a quiet counterpart to Clara Bolton, whose yellow hair and resonant and brassy laugh made the most austere assembly seem like a pump-room.

She was laughing now, interrupting her husband and diverting Sykes's attention to herself. As she addressed him, her eyes darted to Disraeli, but Disraeli had known Clara long enough to recognize that this was an old habit, not an invitation. She could never talk to a man at a party without her glance prospecting the room to see if there was some other fit for her attention. Not that she wanted an alternative to the one she was concerned with. Her exploring look meant merely that she wanted to be admired and observed in the process of being admired. It had to be known that she was desirable and, under certain circumstances, available.

She smiled to Disraeli, and he gave her a fleeting acknowledgement, enough not to antagonize her and start again the rift between what Henrietta called 'the two parties', and not enough to antagonize either Sykes or Henrietta. Despite Clara's incipient double chin and an excess of powder, she was certainly pretty. Perhaps a little plump. But that, too, was agreeable.

'And how,' asked Henrietta beneath her breath, 'is my darling love?'

'Very happy,' said Disraeli.

'Can we wave something and make them all disappear?'

'The flesh, madam, is too solid,' said Disraeli, looking at Clara.

'Are you being unkind, Mr Disraeli?' said Clara, wagging a reproving finger.

'Mr Disraeli is never unkind,' said Henrietta, springing to his defence. 'He was merely speaking well of you behind your back.'

'It's always dangerous to speak well of people behind their backs,' said Disraeli. 'If it's thought you want it to be known, it could be construed as the ultimate form of hypocrisy.'

'If I know you, Ben,' said Clara familiarly, 'I doubt that even your hypocrisy would go to such extreme lengths.'

'The beef is excellent,' said Disraeli.

'For the time of year,' said Sykes. 'Ah – yes, for the time of year.'

He didn't want the allusions of Clara and Henrietta to develop into personal acerbities.

'You will make a rubber later?' Bolton asked Disraeli.

'I have forsworn cards,' said Disraeli. 'They have cost me too many friends.'

Bolton finished his glass of claret to hide his disappointment. At an early age, he had developed a passion for gambling which had superseded every other appetite. Women, food, drink – they had all disappeared in the face of his enthusiasm for what he euphemistically called '*le jeu*'. Unable to play at Crockford's, he frequented private gaming-houses in Kensington, where, like a debauchee who disappears to a brothel for days, he would remain till he had exhausted his resources. His favourite game was *écarté*, and among the French croupiers he was known as '*le docteur flambeur*'. And so, despite the fact that he was reputed to earn £10,000 a year, he was also known to be chronically in debt, and to use Clara as a social stalking-horse to enlarge his practice and the obligations of his wealthier patients towards him. Disraeli suspected that the size of the fees Sykes paid Bolton were more relevant to the doctor's complaisance than to his professional attentions. Because there was no doubt about it – Sykes was besotted with Clara. When she smiled, he smiled. When she scowled, he scowled. When she reached for a sauce-boat, he was there before her. When she mopped her brow, he watched anxiously in case she swooned. He was besotted with her, and all that he wanted beyond that was a quiet life, with Bolton acquiescent and Henrietta entertained.

What a strange couple they were! Sykes, a *fainéant* English baronet – Clara, a brash, haberdasher's daughter. Yet that was what Sykes liked in her – her irreverence, her earthiness, her female insolence. She and Bolton were more conspirators than husband and wife, Disraeli was sure, and that Sykes knew it too. But, compulsively yet coldly, Sykes wanted Clara Bolton, and had accepted the cost. Disraeli shrugged his shoulders. She wasn't worth it. But that was Sykes's business.

In the morning, Disraeli came down early to breakfast and was helping himself to devilled kidneys from the sideboard when he heard Henrietta greet him.

'Good morning, Mr Disraeli.'

He looked around quickly, and went over to the fireplace where she was warming her hands over the crackling logs.

'Good morning, my darling,' he said, dropping his voice. 'I trust you slept well.'

'No. Did you?'

'No.'

'Was this a good idea?'

'Yes – I'm near you. It's what I wanted.'

'But it's – it's anguishing to be under the same roof and apart!'

'Yes, it is. Are the others awake?'

'No – they kept Manners Sutton playing cards till four o'clock in the morning . . . What would you like to do today?'

'To be near you.'

She smiled, and sat at the table.

'Will you ride?'

'If you like – or what else might we do?'

'Let's walk by the sea,' Henrietta said.

Disraeli looked through the window beyond the frost on the panes to the steely blue of the sky, and said,

'Yes – it will be a new experience.'

From the rear of the Grange, a path led down to the shingle and sand hardened and rippled by the cold night breeze, and as soon as they were out of sight from the house, Henrietta put her arm beneath the cape of Disraeli's fur-lined cloak. She had loosened her own redingote, and turned her face to the wintry sun. The wind had fallen, and the sound of the waves, a shimmering and distant fringe, fell on their ears like a cat's hiss.

She leaned her head on Disraeli's shoulder, and he said,

'Be careful, darling.'

And she said, looking at the sands stretching for miles on each side, deserted except for a fisherman mending his nets,

'No one will see us. No one ever walks – certainly not Francis.'

'The fisherman – '

She didn't move her head.

'He's very busy.'

Around them the gulls were swooping and screaming, and Disraeli said,

'How agitated nature is! The only really peaceful place is London!'

His side-laced boots had become sandy, and he was wondering whether they ever would be the same again after this walk, when suddenly he became conscious of the crisp air, the smell of seaweed, the scent of Henrietta's face, and the tingling of his own cheeks. Though he knew the Mediterranean Sea and the Atlantic shores of Spain, he had never, except for an embarkation at Falmouth, felt the marine air of England. It was a discovery, and he stopped and held Henrietta's hands.

'Shut your eyes!'

She did so.

'Inhale!'

She breathed deeply. Then he kissed her on the mouth, breathing with her in a single breath.

'Oh, Ben,' she said, drawing away, 'I love you – I'm happy and unhappy all at once.'

He was silent.

'I want to be with you all the time – to go away somewhere.'

'Where?' he asked.

'Anywhere.'

She waved towards the sea.

'It's too far away.'

They walked on till they came to a sheltered sand-dune sprouting with winter grass.

'Do you think,' Disraeli asked her, 'do you think he knows?'

She prodded the sand with her black-lace parasol.

'No,' said Henrietta, 'he doesn't *want* to know. It's very convenient for him.'

'It's convenient for him now,' said Disraeli. 'But in a month – two months – a year – !'

Henrietta was thoughtful.

'Yes, it could be different. Years ago – there was some young man who was attentive to me – '

'Who was he?' he asked quickly.

'I've even forgotten his name – I really have. He helped me with my shawl at a soirée – and Francis, afterwards, said that if he saw him do it again, he'd kill him.'

'Why, then, is he so benevolent towards me?'

'Because what he wants is Clara Bolton. That's what he wants, and nothing else matters. You see, he's like his father although he is terrified of being so. His father was mad – yes, really – quite mad. After his trial in Westminster Hall, he became as set on being returned to Parliament as he had been in chasing his brother-officer's wife.'

'I can see nothing mad in that,' said Disraeli, enveloping Henrietta with his cloak, and kissing her again. 'To achieve anything at all, you must be obsessed.'

'Are you obsessed?'

'Totally!'

She hesitated, and then she repeated,

'If only we could go away!'

'Would you leave Francis?' he asked.

'Yes – I'd leave everything.'

'Where would we go?'

'To Italy – to Florence. We'd take a palazzo, and we'd be together always away from all these people who grudge us our happiness.'

Away, thought Disraeli, from Lawson and the bailiffs. Away! There was nothing he wanted more.

'I would make you so happy. We'd only have a few servants,

and a very few friends from England – like Lyndhurst. What do you think, my darling one?'

With £300 from his allowance and £1,000 from Colburn, he thought, he could keep Austen, Lawson and perhaps Rossi satisfied for another quarter.

'What do you think?' she repeated.

'I think,' he said, bending to pick up a piece of seaweed in their path, 'that we must be patient, dearest. You must be careful – your children – he could deprive you – '

'Yes, he could.' Her face became sombre. 'They're so happy to play with you.'

'We mustn't misunderstand his tolerance.'

'No,' said Henrietta.

They walked back in silence; the sun had become warmer, the sky had lost its cobalt tone, and their arms touched till they reached the Grange and saw Sykes and Clara Bolton leaning over the balustrade, while Dr Bolton helped Eva to fly her box-kite.

'You look,' said Dr Bolton to Henrietta, 'as if you've drunk an elixir.'

'I have,' she said calmly. 'The morning air. I recommend it for all your patients.'

'What is its effect?' Sykes asked.

'It heightens the faculties,' said Disraeli. 'You know, they say in Jerusalem that its air makes men wise.'

'And what, sir,' said Mrs Bolton, 'does the Southend air do for men?'

She looked at Disraeli sharply before changing her expression and giving a private and indulgent glance at Sykes, whose hand she was holding beneath the balustrade.

'It makes one happy to be alive.'

'Yes,' said Sykes. 'It's a rare condition. Queen Caroline discovered the virtues of Southend – when was it, Disraeli?'

'*Non mi ricordo*,' said Disraeli, and they all laughed.

It was the catchword, still popular, dating from the evidence of Majocchi, Queen Caroline's servant, who would only reply when examined concerning the charges of adultery against her, 'I don't remember.'

'That's very good,' said Sykes. '*Non è vero* – eh, Disraeli – eh –
eh? *Non mi ricordo* – that's very good. I like these *cavalieri* with
short memories. Come along, my dear,' he said to Henrietta,
leading the way back to the house.

Clara lingered behind, and said,

'I want to talk to you, Ben.'

Disraeli paused, and watched Henrietta as she walked along
the terrace with Eva hopping at her side. Mrs Bolton was
obstructing him, and he smiled at her courteously.

'I was expecting you might. Did you win last night?'

'No – but never mind that. I want to talk about something
else.'

He waited, leaning on his cane.

'I am greatly worried about you, Ben.'

He had taken off his hat, and his hair was blowing in the
wind that had risen again.

'Ah,' he said, putting his hat on, 'you're concerned for my
health. You would like me to cover myself.'

'Pray don't be flippant. I'm telling you this for your own
sake. You realize that?'

'Of course, that's the nature of advice. What is it?'

She framed the words in her mind, and said,

'You must go away, Ben. You must stop seeing Lady Sykes.'

'Why?' said Disraeli. 'Am I in some danger?'

'Yes,' said Clara.

'From whom?'

His voice was now icy.

'From whom?' he repeated. 'From Francis? From you?'

'Not from me. Not from me. You can forget quickly. I
can't . . . No – not from me, Ben. Not even – not for the present,
at any rate – not from Sykes, though he's capable of great
violence. Not even from my poor husband. No, Ben – the
danger is from yourself . . . You see, for her you'll neglect
everything – your work, your career – your chance of arriving
at the pinnacle . . . But she won't care – no, indeed she won't
so long as she can have you for herself. That's all she's concerned about. She's greedy and destroying.'

'Shall we perhaps go in?'

'No – not yet. Not till I've finished. She'll use you, Ben –

and then, at the end, she'll do to you what she did to Colonel Sharpe.'

'Colonel Sharpe?'

'Yes, Colonel Sharpe.'

'Who is he?'

'Never mind – ask her!'

Clara's face was flushed, and she went on as if she couldn't stop.

'She'll do the same to you. Remember this, Ben – a woman who is unfaithful to her husband will be unfaithful to her lover too.'

Disraeli, feeling a dark rage rising as Clara Bolton spoke, looked away from the small veins that mottled her agitated face.

'Perhaps we might return,' he said in a half-articulate voice.

'No,' she said, 'there's something more.'

'Are you telling me all this,' Disraeli asked more firmly, 'because you feel yourself to be qualified – ' he paused, wondering how much he could say without provoking her into a hysterical flight into the drawing-room – 'are you now – '

'Yes,' she interrupted him, her voice loud. 'I am. I make no claims about myself. But I can see through others who make such claims. You're blind, Ben – blind. Didn't you know she's been Lord Lyndhurst's mistress?'

'No,' said Disraeli. 'No,' he repeated emphatically.

He felt cold, and his hand trembled.

'No,' he said again. 'It's not true.'

Mrs Bolton shrugged her shoulders and drew her hood over her hair. From Disraeli's expression, she was satisfied that at last she had touched him.

'Very well,' she said. 'It's not true. If you don't want to believe it, it's not true.'

'He could be her father!'

'Could be – but isn't . . . You mustn't let it worry you. Lyndhurst has many other women.'

She turned and went inside.

Disraeli returned to his room by a side entrance, and lay on his bed for two hours. Whatever effect Clara Bolton had had on his relations with Henrietta, he was sure of one thing – that he hated Clara with a keen, defined hatred which made him want to take her by her thick throat and squeeze it till her already exophthalmic eyes burst from her head. The thought that he had ever made love to her, the memory of her squirmings and pantings, all filled him with a violent self-disgust. Sharpe – an amorphous, unidentified figure! Lyndhurst – the handsome, powerful *bon vivant* whom he had seen command Henrietta's smiles! Was this love – the shaking and throbbing of two bodies, something that Clara and Sykes and Henrietta and Sharpe and Lyndhurst and he himself and animals mounting each other in a farmyard could do equally well? Was there nothing unique in his private and triumphant joy with Henrietta that separated them from the brutish pleasures of all those others? The sweaty gropings, the ribaldry and odours of pleasure – did they come from the common trough of experience where Clara and Sykes and he and Henrietta, together with Lyndhurst and all the others, came to gobble?

He would return to London as soon as possible. Clara had poisoned his stay at the Grange; it was her purpose, and she had achieved it.

A servant knocked at the door, and a woman's voice said, 'If that's Mr Disraeli, Lady Sykes 'ud like to see him in her 'tiring room.'

Disraeli rose painfully and opened the door. Henrietta stood there laughing.

'Would I make a good actress?' she asked.

'I hope not,' Disraeli murmured.

'They've gone driving in the barouche,' she said. Then, seeing his expression, she added, 'What is it, darling Amin?'

She called him by a name which they had discovered in the *Thousand and One Nights*.

'Nothing,' he said. Then he turned to her as she looked at him steadily, and repeated, 'Nothing. I just want you to tell me, who is Colonel Sharpe?'

'Colonel Sharpe? – I don't know anyone called Sharpe.'

'Do you swear that to me?'

'Ben – why are you talking to me like that? I've never known anyone called Sharpe.'

'You must swear to me that – that you have not had another lover since you were married.'

'Oh, dearest one,' she said, putting her hands on his shoulders, 'has that wicked Mrs Bolton been telling lies?'

'I want you to swear.'

'You don't believe me? Look at me.'

'I believe you,' he said after a pause. 'But swear!'

She frowned.

'I had such wonderful news for you. I think I must go.'

'No, don't go. What is it?'

She looked up at him, and said,

'They're all leaving tomorrow.'

'No!' said Disraeli. 'Why?'

'They've decided to go to Baden. Francis wants you to stay on and write your book.'

Disraeli pushed his fingers through his hair.

'Good God!' he said.

Henrietta kissed his cheek and before he could stop her, hurried to the door.

'Mrs Bolton,' she said, 'is an evil woman, a jealous and destructive woman.'

She closed the door behind her, and Disraeli sat on the bed, looking out towards the sea and listening to the clock. Sharpe – Lyndhurst? No, he didn't believe it. Clara Bolton was a woman whom the happiness of others poisoned, and Lyndhurst was an old man, a man of sixty, a friend of the Villebois', a cicerone in London to Henrietta. All that Mrs Bolton wanted was to alienate him from them both. But he liked Lyndhurst, and would benefit from the connection. And as for Sharpe, Henrietta had disclaimed him, and that was enough. He loved Henrietta. That was the only truth, and Henrietta loved him. In forty-eight hours the others would be on the way to Baden, and he would be left in possession.

In possession. They would be gone, and he would still be there with Henrietta. That was what mattered.

Chapter Seven

Lyndhurst lay comfortably against the cushions in his coach bringing him from the Court of the Exchequer to his house in George Street. The Whigs were out. It was now certain. Earlier in the day while still on the Bench, he had received a letter from the Duke announcing that the King, anxious to get rid of his Reform Ministers, had summoned him to Brighton to form a Government. The lawyers and officials who had seen him take the letter from the messenger had looked at him with inquisitive side-glances because of the rumours of change, but Lyndhurst had continued to preside calmly over the case of Rex. vs. Marchmont.

In his hurry the King had asked the Duke to demand the seals from the Secretaries of State immediately, without waiting for Sir Robert Peel, who was still in Italy. The Duke wanted to see Lyndhurst next day at Apsley House with a view to his becoming Chancellor again. The Great Seal! It would be a sacrifice to give up the security of the Chief Barony, that high and lucrative judicial office, for the uncertainties of the Woolsack. On the other hand, his tenure would be ensured by the fact that Melbourne was an intractable figure, unwilling to make any concession to the basic liberal principles by which one day he might still unite his party, although for the time being the Whig majority was fragmented. But for how long? The Whigs might soon be back. The Chief Barony or the Great Seal? It was a choice between two high offices, a choice that expressed the regard felt for him by King William, who had, indeed, once asked him personally to form an administration, an offer which he had refused, partly through his difficulty in getting support, partly through a lethargy which, as he felt, sometimes disqualified him from politics.

The November fog had thickened, and linkmen were guiding the coaches through the Westminster streets. Lyndhurst remembered his wife – dead in Paris a few months after the passing of the Reform Bill – and his mood of elation sank as the carriage rumbled over the stones. They had been on holiday – he, his thirty-nine-year-old wife, and his younger daughter, and they had already reached Beauvais on the way home when she fell ill and they had returned immediately to the Faubourg St Honoré. All that beauty the food of worms. She had been virtuous, and had never avenged herself on him for his foibles; when the King's brother, the Duke of Cumberland, had forced himself on her one afternoon, she had rung for a servant, and sent the Duke packing. *The Age* had printed an account. The King had learnt of it. And Lyndhurst, then Lord Chancellor, had been obliged to go to Windsor to explain that nothing but his attachment to his sovereign had prevented him from personally turning the King's brother out of the house. The King had understood, and Lady Conyngham, his *confidante*, had approved. She believed in the protection of women.

The coach lurched, and Lyndhurst sighed. Compared with the funeral wreaths, what was the pride of judicial precedence with its nosegays and trumpets? A cortège of the dead he had loved, one of his daughters among them, passed through his mind in time with the sad clopping of the horses. He was sixty-one – a time for reflection.

And yet, not for pessimism. His old mother, who shared his home with his sister, was still alive at the age of ninety. The thought cheered him, and when the footman opened the door of his carriage, he went quickly up the stairs with the youthful stride that always surprised and sometimes displeased his graver colleagues.

Dr Maginn rose as Lyndhurst entered the library, and bowed with a scrape of his leg behind him.

Lyndhurst waved him to a seat, and examined the square-faced, broken-nosed Irish scholar and his snuff-covered lapels. With his unrelenting feuds and passions, his parodies and satires of the Whigs and Radicals, Maginn was undoubtedly the most detested journalist of the day. No anti-Tory could write a novel or an essay or publish his verses without being excoriated by Maginn with cruel personal innuendoes. Yet even his fellow-Tories weren't immune from his malice, and many of them deferred to his whisky-laden eloquence rather than hazard a lampoon or a libel.

But Ministers found him useful, even though he was a man whom Lyndhurst preferred to receive before dinner at home rather than greet in public. If there was a rumour to be directed against an opponent, Maginn could be relied on to start it. A *pasquinade?* Maginn had the art. He was a ruffian, a talented bully, a bravo whom Lyndhurst had advised many years earlier when Maginn had been threatened with an action for criminal libel. If there was anything that Maginn hated it was the success of others, and he regarded it as his mission to be a censor of morals, a humbler of *hubris*, an advertiser of peccadilloes. Lyndhurst enjoyed his slanders, and diluted them in his own table-talk into indiscretions.

'I'm obliged to you for receiving me, milord,' said Maginn. 'Am I to congratulate you? There are rumours – '

'Rumours, rumours!' Lyndhurst interrupted him deprecatingly. 'Nothing definite can be said till Peel returns. Let's have a glass of madeira. Tell me what's happening in the wider world outside Westminster Hall and the Carlton Club.'

Maginn smirked.

'*Non omnia possumus omnes,*' he said.

'Well, I rely on you, Doctor. After all, you have the advantage of me in having been educated at Trinity College, Dublin, and Edinburgh, not to mention Fleet Street.'

Lyndhurst's tone was amiable, but he observed the other carefully.

Maginn took a pinch of snuff and said,

'London's always the same. Lord Melbourne's carriage still stands daily outside Mrs Norton's. You can set your watch by it. Five o'clock.'

'Well,' said Lyndhurst musingly, 'I've sometimes wondered why beautiful young women consort so desperately with old politicians. Office must be a great aphrodisiac.'

'For those who possess it – or those who perceive it, milord?'

'For both. When a girl is past the first blossom of romantic enthusiasm, she'll more readily invest in an ugly man of experience than in an Apollo. But Mrs Norton – '

'Lord Melbourne, I hear, is bewitched. Mrs Norton, as you

will know, is now the great go-between. She determines his audiences. Even Miss Eden is playing second fiddle.'

'What a beguiling picture,' said Lyndhurst. 'Melbourne surrounded by two Muses – one on his knee, the other playing the fiddle.'

'Your father would have done it justice. Marsyas the Satyr with Calliope and Melpomene.'

Lyndhurst said, 'Yes – we might add Apollo flaying Marsyas after their musical contest.'

'Apollo?' said Maginn. 'You nominate Peel as Apollo? Rather yourself, milord.'

Lyndhurst sighed.

'My poor father!'

'Would you rather have painted the *Death of Chatham* or be first Baron of the Exchequer?'

'Ah, Maginn – I would alas, prefer to be first Baron, yet what will happen to all my judgments – to my speeches in the Lords? They'll disappear one day like myself. My father's pictures will survive. But there are few financial rewards in the arts. My father toiled almost to the last day of his life. The only legacy he left me was a taste for beauty. I have some sympathy with Melbourne, you know. Why should a man exhaust himself in the service of the state without some reward of his own choosing?'

'And your reward?'

'Mine?' Lyndhurst felt at ease with Maginn as he couldn't be with his peers and fellow judges. 'The reward I seek is pleasure – and the more I must deny myself pleasure, the more I feel moved to seek it.'

'You find it in society?'

'No – society is a mournful extension of duty. It's only when I'm abroad that I feel free. Since my wife died – '

He looked gloomily at the portrait of his wife on the side-table, and said,

'The last time we all travelled together – my wife, my daughter – it's all a long time ago. The house is bereft.'

Maginn stood uneasily, and said,

'Milord, there's a matter I must discuss with you.'

'Yes – it's a great sadness, though bereavement takes men

'I've learnt indifference,' Disraeli answered, adjusting his cravat before adding another gold chain to his waistcoat. 'Who will remember Dr Maginn's reviews in a hundred years' time? Or even next week?'

'But we live this week,' said Bulwer, walking about the room. 'Posterity can take care of itself. What matters are our present satisfactions. The truth is, Ben, I can't live in a caravan. I go on, but the company irks me – the domestic entourage, the prospect of a brood of children, a household filled with din – my library invaded when I want to work – I find that rebarbative.'

Disraeli examined himself in the looking-glass, and adjusted the curls falling over his temples.

'Well,' he said, continuing his inspection of himself, content that he didn't have Bulwer's matrimonial anxieties, 'in marriage there must be a compromise between a variety of inclinations. You have a pretty little daughter. Isn't that a reward for your sacrifice of privacy?'

'Is it?' said Bulwer sombrely. 'I don't know. It's very hard to know the permitted limits of selfishness. Just think, Ben. When Rosina gave birth to Emily, I asked her not to nurse the child. What was my motive? To spare her strain? . . . No – to preserve her figure.'

'In that,' said Disraeli, 'you've amply succeeded.'

'But that isn't all,' said Bulwer. 'We have children for our pleasure, and we banish them to Siberia. Emily lives with her nurse like a stranger in some remote part of the house. I see her for a few seconds in between a meal and a new chapter . . . Yesterday I walked up the stairs, and there was Emily, pale and thin and embarrassed. I greeted her, and she said, "Good morning, Mr Bulwer." *Mr* Bulwer! She had heard the servants address me thus.'

'That's sad,' said Disraeli. 'But Rosina – '

'I must take her away,' Bulwer said. 'I've finished my work on the *New English Monthly*. I want to travel and see Rome, Naples, Florence. But I don't mind admitting, I wish I could go alone. You see, when a man wants to write and a woman wants to be entertained, tell me, for God's sake, Ben, how you harmonize the two? Should Rosina hold soirées in my study – or should I keep a writing-table in her drawing-room?'

'I see the difficulties,' said Disraeli, with a quick glance at the clock. It stood at twenty to eleven.

'And then again,' said Bulwer, persisting, 'what hope is there of serenity in a household where two women combine to lecture me on women's rights?'

'Two?' said Disraeli.

'Yes,' said Bulwer. 'Mrs Wheeler – Rosina's mother – had the luck early on in her life to get rid of an unsatisfactory husband – the misfortune thereafter to see all men in his image. She can't forget that under the Directoire she was elected Goddess of Reason in Caen, and ever since she's regarded it as a licence to have the last word in every argument. So you'll understand why I'm less than appreciative of militant females.'

Disraeli took his cane, and said,

'I agree. Travel is the cure. A few months away in Florence, and your mother-in-law will become a memory . . . And, by the way, what about Mrs Stanhope?'

Bulwer looked uneasy at Disraeli's mention of his mistress's name.

'I hope,' he said, 'that if we go to Italy, Mrs Stanhope will accompany us – for part of the way, at least.'

'Lady Sykes will see you, sir,' said the footman. And Disraeli, leaving his hat on a card-strewn table, followed him as he moved up the staircase of the house in Upper Grosvenor Street in a stately pavane. Through the door, he could hear the happy prattle of a child, and he thought to himself how little he knew of Henrietta. He hadn't even been aware that she had children. Her father, he had learnt from Lady Charlotte, was Mr Henry Villebois, a Norfolk gentleman, and she herself had married the year after the king died – when Disraeli himself was only seventeen. Apart from his knowledge of the scandal affecting Sykes's father, that was all.

He entered the room, and saw that it was furnished in a Louis XV style with arabesques and singeries over the fire-place. the furniture made with exotic veneers framed in gilt, bronze mounts. The turquoise blue and apple green of the Sèvres porcelain blended in the sunlight with the roses clustered on the table by the chaise-longue where Henrietta was lying with a child playing on the ground at her feet. On the walls were paintings from the Schools of Canaletto, Watteau and Fragonard; Disraeli, pleased by the scene which fitted his anticipation exactly, decided that Sir Francis had lived much abroad, and that the house was probably a home for his collection rather than for himself and his family.

Henrietta offered him her hand, and he bowed over it.

'I'm so glad you were punctual,' she said. 'I was afraid you might have been a minute late ... This is Eva, my daughter ... my other children are in the nursery. And this is Mr Disraeli.'

The little girl curtsied, and pushed back her fair hair so that the visitor could see her at her most advantageous.

'One day,' said Disraeli, 'when I describe perfect beauty, I'll write about Eva.'

'Where's Tou-Tou?' Eva asked. 'Tou-Tou – where's Tou-Tou? Nana,' she called, 'where's Tou-Tou? I want to show him to the gentleman.'

Her nurse came hurrying in with a beribboned miniature dog in her arms which immediately it saw Disraeli leapt from her arms on to the armchair where he was sitting.

Disraeli looked at the dog with distaste. Like Rosina Bulwer's animal, for which he had formed an unqualified antipathy, Tou-Tou had a long silken coat now moulting, he could see, on to his trousers.

'Isn't he lovely, sir?' said Eva. 'He won't bite you.'

Tou-Tou had now settled on Disraeli's crotch and instantly fallen asleep, though troubled by dreams that made it snap intermittently at invisible enemies. Afraid to move, Disraeli sat with his knees close together, while Eva toyed with Tou-Tou's ribbon.

'Perhaps,' said Henrietta, 'Mr Disraeli will let you have Tou-Tou all to yourself.'

'Oh yes,' said Disraeli.

'All to yourself,' she added in her slow, graceful voice, 'so long as you promise to keep him in the nursery and not let him run away.'

'I promise, Mama,' said Eva.

'And Nana will stay with you both all the time till I send for her, and won't let either of you out of her sight.'

The nurse gave a quick glance at Disraeli, then looked at the ground and made a reverence.

'Come and let me kiss you,' said Henrietta. The child stood and allowed herself to be kissed on the forehead and cheeks, and then gave Disraeli her hand and curtsied before taking the growling Tou-Tou in her arms. Disraeli rose, and said,

'Do you ride?'

'Oh yes,' said Eva.

'Next time I'll tell you about the mare I rode in Spain.'

'We've got an Arab mare,' said Eva. 'At the Grange.'

'Perhaps one day,' said Henrietta, 'you'll go riding together.'

Disraeli walked to the door with Eva and the nurse, and closed it behind them. When he returned, Henrietta was standing. For a moment they looked at each other, and Disraeli took both her hands in his.

'I wanted to be twenty-four hours early,' he said. She was almost as tall as himself, and again they looked at each other, now solemnly. Then she turned away abruptly with a cool expression on her face.

'Will you take tea?' she asked.

'Yes – thank you.'

She pulled the sash, and they sat facing each other on opposite sides of the occasional table.

'I'm afraid,' she said, 'that Sir Francis has left for Basildon.'

She spoke as if their hurried complicity at the opera had never taken place, and Disraeli searched her expression to see if perhaps she was mocking him, but she had already turned to the maidservant who brought in a tray with a silver tea-pot.

'Yes – leave it here,' she said. And then she added to Disraeli, 'I enjoyed the opera the other night. Even Francis had to admit it had merit. What he really likes more than anything is German chamber music. Do you like chamber music, Mr Disraeli?'

She poured the tea, and handed him a cup.

'My opportunities of hearing chamber music,' said Disraeli, 'have been confined to the courts of the Palatinate. What I've heard makes me long to hear more. At Weimar,' he went on, but Lady Sykes's expression had become more and more absent as if she were waiting for someone else to join them. She returned to him with a start, and said,

'I'm sorry . . . You were saying – "at Weimar".'

'Yes,' said Disraeli, uneasy at the thought that he was failing to capture her attention. 'The Grand Duchess was good enough to invite us to a soirée where we heard some of the most remarkable violinists in Europe play quartets, Beethoven quartets. Though I must tell you that Jupiter nodded.'

'Jupiter?' she repeated distantly. 'Beethoven – '

'No – Goethe. He was there but he fell asleep.'

'Ah, yes,' she said indifferently. 'He must be very old.'

At that moment a footman announced, 'Miss Maria Villebois,' and Henrietta rose to greet a thin lady in her late thirties with a sallow complexion and a sharp, delicately veined nose, who came hurrying in, and kissed Henrietta on both cheeks.

Scarcely acknowledging Henrietta's presentation of her guest, she rushed into a narrative of her domestic concerns, their father's maladies and his social arrangements, the whole embellished by anecdotes about people whom Disraeli had never met and, from what he heard, hoped never to meet.

'We were talking about music,' he interrupted at last, seeking to end an otherwise endless tale which, he felt, was drawing the blood from his heart and making his nerve-ends tingle.

Miss Villebois stopped speaking, and in the pause Henrietta asked,

'Have you ever heard Paganini play, Mr Disraeli?'

'Yes,' he said. 'He plays like a conjuror.'

'And how, pray, is that?' Miss Villebois asked, condescending to address him.

'With a skill more attractive to the eye than to the soul.'

'But it enchants the ear,' said Henrietta.

'That's illusion too,' said Disraeli. 'Can you remember a theme of Paganini when he has finished playing?' He couldn't bear to hear praise for another man coming from the mouth that even after it had spoken still stayed with parted lips as if the question was incomplete.

'We are hoping to hear Paganini at the King's next week,' he went on. 'Will you still be in London, Miss Villebois?'

She looked at him as if he had committed a solecism.

'I haven't yet decided,' she said. 'It depends to some extent on my brother-in-law's arrangements.'

'Francis is very unpredictable. He says travel should be an improvisation,' Henrietta explained.

Disraeli withdrew into silence.

By the time he had finished his second cup of tea, he had counted eight references by Lady Sykes to her husband, six allusions to their joint domestic activities, and had decided that under Miss Villebois's baleful eyes, the drawing-room was not a suitable place for a siege. And in any case, though his view of her radiance and beauty was unchanged, Henrietta seemed to have developed towards him a discouraging and puzzling indifference.

He stood up, bowed briefly to Miss Villebois, and turned to Henrietta. She gave him her hand, and said,

'It was good of you to call, Mr Disraeli. I'm sorry Sir Francis is away. I expect him back very soon.'

Then she rose and walked with him to the door. He wanted to speak to her, and as he looked at her face with its expectant gaze, his mouth twitched. But seeing that Miss Villebois was staring at him, he bowed silently over Henrietta's hand and opened the door.

'Please come tomorrow morning at eleven,' she whispered.

Outside in the square he took a deep breath.

At eleven the next day he returned, this time to find Lady Sykes's cousin Matilda, the Reverend Philip Butterworth and Lady Blaw already in possession of the drawing-room. He sat in frustration and anger, observing Lady Sykes's serene social deportment as Mr Butterworth spoke of his forthcoming volume of sermons, Matilda of the pony that died, and Lady Blaw of a new treatment for sciatica. When he rose after half an hour, Lady Sykes said,

'Are you leaving so soon?'

'I am obliged to,' he said stiffly.

'Please meet me tomorrow morning at eleven at the Putney coaching station,' she said beneath her breath. He hesitated.

'The Green Man?'

'Yes,' she said. 'We'll ride together.'

The sun was already warm, and the yard was bustling with coaches arriving and departing when he arrived at the livery stables at ten o'clock the next day. During the night he had scarcely slept, wondering if he had misheard the address of their meeting-place. There was a Green Man at Twickenham, and through thinking of their whispered arrangement, he had become unsure as to whether the riverside station was Putney or Twickenham. He could have taken a later coach and still been early. But he wanted to be certain that he would be there to meet her when she arrived.

Across the Thames the candled chestnut trees were creamy against the washed-blue sky, and he felt happy, as if he were at the beginning of some great event which he had always expected and which would determine the course of his life. He flicked his boot with his riding whip as he looked down at the water and wondered what it was in Henrietta that had so suddenly transformed his life. Her beauty? He had known other beautiful women. Her sympathy for him? Her independence? Perhaps. She whom everyone courted, who had an endless choice in society, had chosen – seemed to choose – him. But had she really chosen him? Had she? He walked along the bank strewn with marigolds, and his uplifting pride was chastened by the uncertainty that had made his heart race ever since the day he had first called on her.

Behind him he heard a clop of hooves, and the snort of a horse. Henrietta, in a black habit and veil, accompanied by a groom leading a bay, had come up at a trot.

He raised his hat, and said apologetically,

'I was early.'

'So was I. I wanted to make time shorter.'

The groom handed over the reins and left as Disraeli mounted.

For a few minutes they rode in silence along the bridle path that led to the Heath, till Henrietta said,

'Let's canter.'

She removed her veil, and they cantered rhythmically together, smiling to each other from time to time as the warm breeze struck their faces and the cottages of Putney disappeared behind the trees. Then, after a mile, they walked their steaming horses, and Disraeli said,

'I thought we'd never be alone.'

'You saw how difficult it is – when Francis is in England, there are always callers.'

They had reached an oak tree, and Disraeli dismounted.

'Shall we stay here a little?' he said, looking up at her.

'Yes,' she said, and he helped her to the ground. 'Is this more discreet than meeting in London?'

'Yes,' she said, and echoed him. 'I wanted to be alone with you.'

Disraeli leant against the tree and put his hands on her face.

'There hasn't been a moment,' he said, 'that I haven't thought of you.'

She looked away, and then looked back at him.

'I – it's very difficult – I don't want you to think – '

'No – that's why I'm here.'

'But you mustn't think that if anyone – since I've been married – you must believe me – there's never been anyone – no one at all. You do believe me?'

She studied him with her grave eyes, and he said,

'I believe you.'

They turned their backs on the party of riders making for Putney, and when they had gone past, Disraeli said,

'Will we always be disturbed?'

'Not always. We'll meet tomorrow at Upper Grosvenor Street.'

They mounted again, and as they rode along, Disraeli took her hand in his.

When he arrived the following day, Henrietta was lying on the chaise-longue in her bedroom, wearing a peignoir.

'How many callers will you have today?' he asked.

'None,' she said, shaking her head. 'I've said I'm *souffrante*.'

He knelt and put his face against hers, conscious of the warmth of her cheek on his mouth as she moved closer to him. In his arms he could feel the weight of her body, her breasts against his jacket, the crisp ruffles of his shirt and his chains.

'Let me lock the door,' he said, and drew away from her.

'It's not necessary,' she said with a half-smile. 'No one will come.'

He turned the key and came back. Beyond the chaise-longue in the penumbra was her canopied bed with its tightly drawn coverlets and silk bolsters, and at its side a huge bowl of peonies.

'Isn't it strange,' said Henrietta thoughtfully, 'that two persons knowing almost nothing of each other, should seek each other out?'

'It's the finding, not the seeking, that's strange,' said Disraeli. 'The person I've found is one who's always been in my mind.'

She touched his face with her hand.

'You are very kind – very generous. I am everything that can make you be uncomfortable. I have four children.'

'That's an ideal number.'

'I – I'm older than you.'

'Since you say so, it's true – but that for me is a special delight. Your husband – '

'My husband has other occupations.'

She walked to the window, and looked towards Grosvenor Square.

'How beautiful the day is – how very beautiful!'

They stood together by the window where the curtains stirred.

'But you – you have many attachments.'

Her voice was playful, but a slight frown lay on her forehead.

'None that matters since the night at the King's.'

'But everyone says – the handsome Mr Disraeli with those fatal black curls – they say he's made more women desperate than all his heroes.'

Preening himself, Disraeli took a gold seal suspended by a filigree chain from his waistcoat pocket, and then replaced it.

'I have known many women in my life,' he said. 'Some I have known closely. A few I thought I loved.'

He drew her from the window, and took her face in his hands.

'But since the last few days, I know that I have never known love – love that takes precedence over everything, that annihilates every other feeling – love that makes the greatest ambitions trivial, the greatest achievements insignificant.'

He covered her face with kisses, and opened her lips with his fingers and pressed his mouth in hers. Her négligée parted, and his hands moved over her white shoulders till she sat on the edge of the bed, and he knelt again in front of her with his face between her breasts. She didn't speak.

He was encumbered by his jacket, too tight under his armpits, sawing painfully against his shirt. His trousers too, that had fitted him so well when he had tried them on at Lumbs', were now particularly constricting. He looked up at Henrietta, and saw her eyes behind her dark lashes, looking down at him with a grave intensity. His stays had moved, and a whalebone was sticking into his ribs, and he rose, straightening himself as his clothes resumed the tailor's original disposition.

'Draw the curtains,' said Henrietta in a whisper.

He drew the curtains, and returned to the bed, where he could see in the shadows that Henrietta had thrown off her peignoir and the silken shift that she had worn beneath it. Now she was lying naked, watching him, and his eyes travelled over the curve of her breasts, the darkness of her navel deepening towards her thighs.

'Come!' she said again in a whisper. 'Hurry!'

He had hardly taken off his coat when there was a hammering at the door, accompanied by a rending wail of 'Tou-Tou! Tou-Tou! He's run away, Mama!'

Disraeli hurriedly replaced his jacket.

'Go and find him with Nana!' Henrietta called sharply in a loud voice that contrasted with her whisper of a few moments before.

As the sound of panic-stricken sobbing receded, Henrietta raised her arms towards Disraeli, and he began again to undress, and was about to fling his coat on the carpet till he remembered that his tailor, Mr Lumbs, was still unpaid, and he hung it neatly over the back of an upright chair. With a single flick he undid his cravat, his eyes passing over Henrietta's body that stirred in front of him like a quiet sea moved by a ground-swell.

'Hurry!' she said urgently. 'Hurry, my dearest one.'

As he fumbled with the buttons of his brocaded waistcoat, he saw that the gold chain he had bought in Constantinople had become caught in the lining of a pocket. He tried to detach it, but the chain had got inextricably tangled with the chain of his eye-glass. He tugged at it, but still it wouldn't budge.

'This chain,' he said, as if to excuse its obduracy, 'was given to me by Ibrahim Pasha.'

Henrietta didn't answer. Her extended arms slowly drooped as Disraeli, still tugging, went towards the thin trickle of light through the curtains in order to release himself. At last with a tearing sound the chain came away from his waistcoat, and Disraeli slipped off his shoes, removed his fob-watch, undid his shirt and took off his four rings one by one and laid them in his shoe. His first excitement at the view of Henrietta stretched out with the cushion behind her head had ebbed, though all that remained was for him to remove the stays (which, with the other dandies, he had imitated from the officers of the Malta garrison), and to take off his trousers.

It was difficult for him to reach the knotted laces at the back, and he cursed Baum for having encouraged him to wear his stays that day. Could he – without – no, that would be ludicrous. A trouserless man in a shirt was absurd enough. In stays – ! With his face flushed and almost rending his back muscles with the effort, he pulled at the laces, one, two, three, the pain increasing with each wrench, till the undergarment dropped limply to the floor. With aching hips, he slowly straightened himself, and stood naked and white in front of Henrietta, who lay unmoving.

'My beautiful one! My beautiful one!' Henrietta murmured.

He glimpsed himself in a quartered looking-glass, and his pale body seemed to him strangely out of place in the unfamiliar and well-ordered room, inhabited by the woman who lay on the bed with one leg dangling over its side, almost a reflection of the Boucher above her head. He hesitated for a moment. The excitement that he had felt before he began to undress had dwindled. He looked at Henrietta's opulent body, his eyes moving from her hair which she had suddenly loosened over her shoulders, to her half-closed eyes examining him as he stood in front of her, and to her nipples, dark smudges in the room's shadows. But the magnificence that awaited him was daunting. He wanted to cover himself, and abandon a posture that he found ignominious, but she put out her hand and drew him to lie close against her.

'Now,' she said, and kissed his mouth, holding his left hand pressed against her breast.

A light sweat broke out over Disraeli's back, and he could feel a chilling draught blowing over his shoulder-blades.

'Henrietta!' he said, and feeling her fingers moving towards the inside of his thighs, he drew away and laid her fingers on his lips. She was holding him clutched tightly against her, and making small, inarticulate sounds. He wanted to feel the great surging power that he had felt as he lay sleepless the night before. Nothing! Henrietta! She was moving slowly against him, her eyes closed. Nothing! He tried to remember how her arm had felt at the opera – the round arm that had stirred him as she leant against him in the darkness of the box. Instead, the face of Lady Cork with her raddled cheeks came into his mind. Nothing! Failure! His body was as despondent as himself. He conjured up lecherous images, remembered pleasures. The sweat traced the valleys between his muscles in rivulets. Nothing – nothing, nothing, nothing.

'Lie still,' said Henrietta, opening her eyes at last. 'Lie still, my darling.'

She raised herself up on the bolster.

'I – ' he began.

'No, don't speak,' she said, and drew his head against her breast, till one eye could see only a white bosom panting. 'The snowy bosom' – the phrase of his novels. Her fingers felt their way through his hair, and she said,

'Just be still. I'm very happy. You are my darling, my beautiful darling. I'm very happy. Just lie still.'

And as he heard those words, sheltered in the warmth of

her armpit, with the room blotted out by the darkness of her body, he recalled Mrs Bolton holding him closely in the secrecy of his convalescence, Mrs Austen cosseting his head and playing with his hair. The strange and intimidating landscape of Henrietta's beauty became one with the remembered regions of his adolescent pleasures, and he felt a faint and promising stir.

'My darling,' she said, 'my dearest darling. You are as beautiful as a boy!'

He lay quietly, feeling for minutes the fullness and maturity of her throat and shoulders. And suddenly it was as if an army had assembled in his body with trumpets and banners, horses neighing and drums thundering. Powerful and conquering, he heaved himself above her, and she received him with a great sigh of joy.

In the afternoon, Disraeli came back to see Henrietta. Together they mounted Sir Francis's carriage and drove at a trot towards Hyde Park. Henrietta wore a dress of white muslin with a large bonnet, and Disraeli had changed into a plum velvet coat.

'I want to see you every day of my life,' said Henrietta. She pressed close to him, holding his arm beneath the coverlet.

The carriage was rolling through an avenue of trees leading towards Kensington, and the coachman snapped his whip in the air.

Goodbye, Mrs Bolton! Goodbye, Mrs Austen! Disraeli smiled to himself. This was the long-sought woman of his imaginings, the dreamed-of mistress who would be his companion and ally and embellishment in society, she who had given herself to his virile assertions. Goodbye, Sara! Clara, goodbye! And a special farewell to Lady Charlotte! He was in love with Henrietta – her graciousness, her elegance, her firmness to the outside world, her tenderness to himself. Benjamin Disraeli was driving with the beautiful Lady Sykes.

Sir Francis? No matter. She had told Disraeli that she and her husband shared a home but not a marriage bed. For his own part, he felt that he had neither guilt nor responsibility.

Their love could flourish in an aura – well, perhaps not of innocence, but at least of insouciance.

Insouciance. He liked the word. The sun glowed through the trees, and he smiled to Henrietta and she smiled back to him. They were accomplices in happiness.

Disraeli raised his hat to Lord Mansergh driving past with his wife in an open landau. Lord Mansergh acknowledged the salute, then, hesitating, raised his hat a second time to Henrietta.

Chapter Six

At one end of the table, Sir Francis Sykes sat between Dr Bolton and Mrs Bolton, while Disraeli himself was on Henrietta's right hand. He had only been two days at Porter's Grange, the Sykeses' Southend house, but already the sea air had improved his health, curing the headaches that he had suffered at the beginning of the year. In the large gabled house with its gardens leading down to the sand-flats and the grey sea beyond, he had immediately been put at ease by Sykes's friendly welcome, the chatter of Mrs Bolton, the earnest, if calculating, reassurance of Dr Buckley Bolton, his former doctor, Eva's prattle – that enchanting child! – the callers from the county, and Henrietta, serene and commanding, and adoring. Disraeli felt at home.

Yet, only recently, their whole happiness had been at risk. Some malevolent gossip had written to Sykes at his country estate in Basildon to tell him that in his absence Disraeli had been visiting Henrietta daily in Upper Grosvenor Street, that they were seen together at every ball and rout, that no river party was complete without them, that his box at the Opera was in constant use by Disraeli and his young friends in company with Henrietta, and that she was 'generally regarded as being his mistress'. Since at that time Sykes was happily entertaining Mrs Bolton at Basildon, he had decided out of a familiar inertia, combined with an unwillingness to give up his present enjoyment, to send his reprimand to Henrietta by post.

He had every faith, he said, in her discretion, but there were times when it was necessary to respect public opinion, even when it was in error. His own father's misfortune had taught him how undesirable it was to flout in public conventions which had been established for centuries by religion and society. He ordered her, therefore, to give up the company of Mr Disraeli, and to have no further communication with him.

Disraeli had already returned to Bradenham, and so Henrietta had no difficulty in protesting against the outrageous suggestion that she was at that time engaging in an intimacy with him that the most exigent husband could disapprove, and when Sykes at last came back to London for a few days, Henrietta was able to swear to him on the souls of their children that she hadn't seen Disraeli (meaning for the last three weeks) and that Sykes's charges which had reduced her to bitter tears proved his own inadequacy and lack of chivalry in believing an anonymous letter-writer rather than the woman to whom he had been married for eleven years and who had borne him four children.

Sykes had eventually apologized for his allegation, but persisted that it was undesirable for her to associate with Disraeli. She had wept and wept and Sykes had locked himself away in his room before, as he announced, returning to Basildon the following day.

But the next morning, so Henrietta had written to Disraeli later, she had walked to the Boltons' new house in Park Lane, and there, standing outside, was Sir Francis Sykes's coach. Without hesitating, Henrietta had entered through the open door, inspected the empty drawing-room and dining-room, and then strode upstairs with a thumping heart, pausing outside Mrs Bolton's boudoir from which she could hear Clara's contralto laugh and Sykes's giggles. The door was unlocked, and Henrietta went straight in. Clara, with one heavy breast exposed, was lying on the chaise-longue, while Sykes was at her side drinking hock. Looking at Henrietta with fury, he rose to his feet and said,

'Leave at once, madam!'

'Yes,' said Henrietta, drawing herself up so that she rose

above Sykes. 'Strike me! Strike me! Let everyone know that you're a brute as well as an adulterer.'

The glass in Sykes's hand shook and spilled its contents over the silk cover.

'Leave at once,' he repeated.

'No,' said Henrietta, calmly taking a seat. 'You have dared to insult me – you forbade me to see Disraeli, whose kindness –'

'Kindness?' said Mrs Bolton, who had now recovered her poise. 'That man doesn't know the meaning of the word. He's cruel – cruel – you'll find him so.'

'He isn't!'

'Yes, he is!'

'He is not!'

'He is! He used to write me letters protesting his devotion and love, and – '

Watching with astonishment the change of subject from himself to Disraeli, whose merits and demerits now flitted like shuttlecocks between his wife and his mistress, Sykes collected himself.

'That will do,' he said emphatically. 'That will do!'

'No, it won't,' said Mrs Bolton, sitting up on the sofa. 'You'll see,' she said to Henrietta, 'he'll treat you as badly, madam, as he treated me. I did everything for him in his contest at High Wycombe. I canvassed for him – I nursed him – I walked miles and miles for him – I gave up my bed at the Red Lion – '

'That's enough,' shouted Sykes.

'It's not enough,' said Mrs Bolton.

'No, it's not enough,' said Henrietta, weeping again. 'You've served me ill – with this woman – with Disraeli, who only wanted to help me.'

'I will see you home,' said Sykes, combing his hair with one of Mrs Bolton's combs. 'Pray leave us, Henrietta.'

'Yes, I'll go,' she said desperately. 'I'll go. And everyone in London must know how shamefully you both have treated me.'

They drove back without speaking, till at last Sykes said,

'I'm sorry, Henrietta.'

differently. I remember when the Duchess of Wellington died – her corpse lay at Apsley House – the mob was stoning the windows – and the Duke went about his duties as if at a parade.'

'Ah, yes,' said Lyndhurst. 'But that was a marriage that died at the altar. I would doubt if he'll easily recover from the loss of his late friend Mrs Arbuthnot. They say he's invited Mr Arbuthnot to move in with him, and both are mourning together.'

Maginn smirked. This was the sort of conversation he enjoyed.

'They say Mr Arbuthnot said to the inconsolable Duke at the graveside, "Don't worry, your Grace. I'll marry again." '

'Damned wicked tongues!' said Lyndhurst, but he smiled. Then his face became sombre. 'Poor Mrs Arbuthnot. She once told an assembly at Apsley House, "Reform is worse than the cholera." And it was of the cholera she died. It could make a man superstitious.'

Maginn shook his head slowly.

'She was a woman with a masculine cast of mind,' Lyndhurst continued. 'Did you know she wouldn't speak to her brother Cecil for a month because he was weak enough to swoon at the execution of Thistlewood?'

Maginn nodded reminiscently.

'I wish there were many more Mrs Arbuthnots. Yet I must admit that the influence of women in our political affairs is excessive.'

'D'you think so?' said Lyndhurst noncommittally.

'Yes, indeed,' said Maginn. 'Mrs Arbuthnot used to make Cabinets, it was said. I recollect, though, *The Age* – ' he began to laugh – '*The Age* – Westmacott – once wrote in all good faith, I do believe, that at a great fancy-dress ball at Covent Garden for the relief of the Spitalfields weavers, she appeared on the arm of the Duke dressed in male apparel.'

'Good God!' Lyndhurst exclaimed.

'Well,' said Maginn, puffing with his attempt to speak through his laughter, 'she actually went as Mary Queen of Scots.'

'A strange confusion!'

'What happened,' said Maginn, 'was that someone told

Westmacott – who wasn't at the ball – that as between Mrs Arbuthnot and the Duke, Mrs Arbuthnot wore the breeches. Westmacott took it literally!'

'Ah, well,' said Lyndhurst, assuming a stern expression, 'peace to her ashes!'

Maginn sat awkwardly, and said,

'Milord, there's a matter I must discuss with you.'

'By all means,' said Lyndhurst. 'But first of all, tell me about the Nortons. I hear they fought a pitched battle in their carriage all the way to Calais?'

'Not exactly,' said Maginn. 'All that happened was that Mrs Norton tore George's hookah from his mouth and threw it through the carriage window. I believe he throttled her.'

'How very impolite! Not to the point of death, of course!'

'No, she jumped out in time. But the lines are drawn. All the beautiful girls, her sisters Helen and Georgina and their admirers, versus Norton and Miss Vaughan, his old aunt.'

'I have the impression,' said Lyndhurst, 'that husbands will tolerate almost anything in their wives except an interference with their vices.'

'Yes, that is a very personal matter, though possibly he didn't like her books.'

Lyndhurst waited. He could see that Maginn was fidgeting to tell him something special.

'To revert,' said Maginn with a frown. 'I must tell you, milord, you have enemies.'

'That's nothing new. Duncannon? Brougham? Campbell?'

'No – I refer not to political enmities but to more personal ones.'

Lyndhurst looked at Dr Maginn's mottled face with its mutton-chop whiskers and it seemed to him that he was unnaturally hesitant.

'Sir Francis Sykes,' said Maginn, 'has gone to Baden.'

'Indeed?' said Lyndhurst without showing any emotion. 'He often does go there.'

'He has taken Mrs Bolton with him.'

'That doesn't surprise me,' said Lyndhurst. 'And what about the worthy doctor?'

'The worthy doctor,' said Maginn, 'remains in London. He

has received a compensation for his non-professional services.'

'That must be very satisfactory for him. But what's all this got to do with my having enemies?'

Maginn rose and walked to the window.

'Last year, milord, you were a frequent visitor to Lady Sykes. As a family friend. Her interests were your close concern.'

Lyndhurst frowned. He had decided that whatever the occasional advantage of Maginn's acquaintance, the time had come to get rid of him.

'At the Carlton, I'm told – they were saying that Sir Francis might be seeking to part from Lady Sykes. I felt you should know.'

Lyndhurst laughed contemptuously.

'To marry Mrs Bolton?'

'That could be.'

'And the basis?'

'Milord, I don't need to tell you that since a certain Royal trial thirteen years ago when you were an advocate against Queen Caroline, the charge of *criminal conversation* has become a fashionable one. They are saying that Lady Sykes had engaged in certain public indiscretions.'

'Indiscretions?' Lyndhurst echoed in surprise.

'I fear so,' said Maginn. 'It's said she's living openly with Disraeli – one of Bulwer's closest friends. I knew Disraeli briefly as Murray's emissary to Scott and Lockhart when they launched *The Representative*. You know, milord, I was to be their Paris correspondent. But Lockhart didn't trust young Disraeli. Said he was an adventurer and a scoundrel, and he was right. Because of Disraeli I lost five hundred a year when the paper collapsed.'

'But Disraeli tells me you hastened the paper's demise – that you were profligate with its funds,' Lyndhurst said maliciously.

Maginn's face reddened, and he waved his hand as if to brush the matter aside.

'That's a lie – but I won't dwell on it. I came to you, milord, because I felt that at this moment, with a new administration in prospect, it would be untimely, however ungenerous the imputation – '

'All imputations are ungenerous,' said Lyndhurst.

'Indeed,' said Maginn. 'I felt it necessary to bring this matter to your attention in view of your friendly intimacy with Lady Sykes, though I must apologize, since evil communications sometimes tend to be less than gratefully received.'

'Yes,' said Lyndhurst, resuming his easy manner, 'that is true. Now tell me, Maginn, what remedy would you advise me to seek in this situation?'

'I fear, milord,' said Maginn, 'that there is a specific remedy.'

'And what is that?' asked Lyndhurst.

Maginn fumbled uneasily with the hound's head pin in his cravat.

'It is, my lord, to deny yourself the society of Lady Sykes.'

Lyndhurst rose.

'I am taking leave of you, Dr Maginn,' he said. He pulled the bell-rope, and a footman entered.

'This, Wardle,' he said, 'is Dr Maginn. He will, in future, not be received here.'

'But, my dear Lyndhurst,' said Maginn in astonishment, 'what's taken possession of you? I spoke only for your advantage. Peel himself referred to the matter only the other day.'

Lyndhurst studied him icily.

'You have been insolent, Maginn. I desire no further communication with you.'

Maginn looked back at him, and said at last, 'I see . . .' He stood. 'I've known you for some years, milord. I've known you turn your coat about many matters – Reform – Catholic emancipation – and personal matters too . . . You will wish one day you hadn't insulted me. With courage, you might have been a leader . . . As it is – ' he spat out the words – 'you're a flunkey in silken hose!'

Involuntarily Lyndhurst looked at his breeches and embroidered silk stockings.

'You have gratuitously insulted me,' Maginn went on, raising his voice. 'Lady Sykes – anyone – I – Even Judges must be prudent. You should have been more careful.'

He turned his back on Lyndhurst and strode to the door.

Henrietta surveyed the table. It had been a successful dinner-party although, to begin with, Lyndhurst had seemed con-strained and Disraeli at the other end had scarcely turned his eyes to her from his neighbour, Lady Tavistock. But Hertford, Lady Dudley Stuart, Lord Tavistock and Lady Cork were all there, despite the mutterings of her father and her sister Maria that if she went on seeing Disraeli she would be 'excluded from decent society'. She had defied them as she had defied her own husband earlier that year.

'No one,' she had told Disraeli when he stayed with her at the Grange, 'can drive me from your company.' Marriage was an effort that spent itself and required repose in order to be renewed, was what Francis Sykes had said when she had first heard of his visits to Mrs Bolton. Well, let it be so. And yet, the symmetry of their relationship, the coincidence of their feelings – Disraeli's and Sykes's – never failed to astonish her. She wasn't jealous that both her husband and Disraeli had been Clara Bolton's lovers. For Disraeli, it was a dead experience which he had donated to his successor, just as she was an exhausted episode for her husband.

No two men could have been more different, externally and inwardly, than Sykes and Disraeli. Sykes, fair-headed, physical-ly weak, ill-disposed to public life, English in essence yet more at home abroad than in England, a dilettante of letters, dis-liking the *ton* yet much concerned with its opinion – and Dis-raeli, strong and determined to play the leading role wherever he might be. In her presence, Moore had once said of Disraeli that he was an Ephebe, D'Orsay's Ganymede, a *mignon*, and Sykes had nodded assent; she had said nothing, since it was an image convenient to accept. Yet she and her Amin had lain together a hundred times since that first morning when Disraeli called at Upper Grosvenor Street. She loved him – his ardent body, his skin that became paler, his eyes darker, when he held her with an insolent familiarity that she craved and that had turned from an indulgence into an obsession.

When he was at Bradenham, she used to write to him every day, sometimes twice a day. Now she looked at him across the table. How happy she would be when the dinner was over and she could be alone with him, listening to his talk about his new poem, the 'Revolutionary Epick', about the men and women they met together, about his family, and at last, when the sounds of the household had died and the streets were still, feeling his mouth, his hands, his close possession!

'Life must be composed as art,' he had once said. And in the happy months since their first meeting, she had indulged him and surrounded him with all the beauty at her disposal, dazzling women like Lady Tavistock, handsome men like Lyndhurst and Daniel Maclise, the tall young Irish painter, silent but watchful in the torrent of conversation. She looked at Disraeli, and he looked steadily back at her, gravely unsmiling. He nodded. Henrietta rose and led the ladies from the room. The men regrouped themselves.

Lyndhurst took a place on the red-striped ottoman next to Disraeli, apart from the others who were still drinking port, and said in a tone that was neither condescending nor ironic to one half his age,

'Tell me, Mr Disraeli – you view our affairs with some detachment. How do you think things will turn out?'

'I'm ill-qualified to comment,' said Disraeli, 'except perhaps as a prophet. What strikes me is that the Whigs can't exist as a party without Lord Durham, and the King will never agree to have *him* in. Besides, Durham's getting very violent in his demands – triennial Parliaments, the ballot! It's all very revolutionary. I'm reminded of my own youth.'

A smile spread slowly over Lyndhurst's handsome Roman face.

'The young and the old,' he said, 'are always in a hurry. I'll trust you with a secret. Tomorrow I'm going to see the Duke, who'll draw up a Cabinet while we wait for Sir Robert Peel.'

Disraeli nodded conspiratorially, flattered by Lyndhurst's confidence.

'The danger is, of course, that the Whigs will coalesce again. For the time being, we'll have to do the best with what we've got – Hardinge, I imagine, for Ireland, Lord Ashburton for the Board of Trade, Goulburn Home Secretary, Scarlett for the Chief Barony – ' He spoke the names ruminatively, and Disraeli caught his thought.

'A singularly weak list,' he said boldly. 'I can think of a dozen members of the Party more intelligent, more energetic and more able.'

'Able?' Lyndhurst said reflectively. 'Since when has ability been the general test of Ministers? In every administration, you'll learn – oh, yes, when you're part of it yourself – you'll learn that only three men need to be able. The rest, as far as ability is concerned, is *chair à canon*. They're there to carry out the Prime Minister's bidding.

'You see,' he went on, throwing his head back and looking at the painted ceiling where Flora, surrounded by *putti*, was disposing herself against a cærulean sky, 'a Ministry isn't an assembly of talents. History, I think, proves me right. Do you not agree?'

'That, my lord, is the historical enigma.'

'It shouldn't be. The object of government is to exercise power. It follows that a Ministry should reflect interests rather than talents. What use would it be to have ten of the most brilliant minds in the kingdom gathered around the Duke if the dunderheads in the House or in the country said, "What's that to us? How does it affect the corn or the wool?" '

'You mean,' Disraeli said thoughtfully, 'that there is no room in our politics for intellectual pre-eminence?' Then he added quickly, 'I would have thought, my lord, that you illustrate the opposite.'

Pleased by the flattery, despite its inevitability, Lyndhurst said,

'There are a dozen lawyers in the House who, but for a few accidents, might be in my place. I was captured young from the democrats, and grew with the Tories. Lord Liverpool needed a pleader, and found me. But let me advise you, Disraeli.'

He turned his gaze from the ceiling, and said,

'To succeed in politics, it's no use waiting to be asked. You must ask. Politics isn't a game of cricket – or even a dinner-party – where you wait till your captain or hostess picks you out and sends you an invitation. In politics, you must invite yourself.'

'And if one is snubbed?'

'A political snub is a battle-wound. It heals fast, and when the snubber is forgotten, you'll still be there.'

Lyndhurst's advice chimed with Disraeli's own experience that quietism was no path to advancement. He had often observed that many politicians of impeccable claims to gentility were amongst the most coarse, aggressive and thrusting when there was an occasion for self-interest. Those who abstained from the rush usually had some alternative resource to fall back on. There was, indeed, as much contradiction between the ideals of political life and its reality as there was between the nursery precepts of social life and the way it was actually lived. What he liked in Lyndhurst was that he didn't shrink from baldly telling the truth which others masked in hypocrisy. 'You must invite yourself.' Disraeli was glad to have the sanction for a form of conduct which he had long accepted as appropriate.

'Still,' he said, 'what matters is a majority – it's the best repartee. As long as O'Connell coquets with the Whigs without commitment, you'll have your majority. But beware, sir, the greater issues.'

'Well, what *are* the issues of our age, Mr Disraeli?'

'First the need to transform the oligarchy into a real aristocracy, an élite that can at once guide and impress its authority on the nation.'

'And then?'

'Then we must return to the policy of Lord Bolingbroke at Utrecht – and Peel after him. We must protect our commerce.'

Lyndhurst glanced quickly at Disraeli as he mentioned the name of the Tory statesman of a century before their own time.

'Bolingbroke?' he echoed. 'I see we share an enthusiasm.'

'I imagined we might,' said Disraeli brashly. 'Bolingbroke took a rag-bag of pragmatic attitudes and made it into a Tory tapestry. One day, my lord, you will see how the Tories will recover from their present disorder when they find again Bolingbroke's national pattern.'

'Yes,' said Lyndhurst. 'That's like searching for the Grail. Now the Irish situation – Mr O'Connell – how would you deal with him?'

Disraeli hesitated. He feared Lyndhurst might be mocking him.

'I'd forget Oliver Cromwell,' he said, 'and remember Charles I. Daniel O'Connell is a patriot – and that is greatness.'

'It doesn't prevent him from being a nuisance.'

'That's part of his greatness,' said Disraeli. 'It would be easy for O'Connell to compromise, to renounce his people and his heredity – to turn his back on his depressed and wasted land! Instead of that, he has put his talent as a lawyer and a statesman at its service. He has risked – no, invited, imprisonment – not for his own interest but for what he regards as a great cause. Are there many men of such fixed principles?'

'I'm happy to say there are not,' said Lyndhurst. 'Ireland can keep its agitators! I dislike idealists. Let us behave as pragmatists.'

'By all means,' said Disraeli. 'But it is the idealists who give shape to history.' He didn't want to antagonize Lyndhurst, but he was enjoying his response to the provocations which Lyndhurst's faint smile blunted.

'I can't accept, my lord, that the tribune of a people degraded by the legislation of its masters is himself degraded by sharing their cause.'

'I quite agree – I've defended many scoundrels since I defended Dr Watson and the other incendiaries of Spa Fields,' said Lyndhurst.

'What is a scoundrel?' asked Disraeli. 'Is he an Irishman condemned by poverty and ill-usage to barbarity? Is he O'Connell, evading the law with his hundred and one associations? The Irish have been reduced by their conquerors to a life of peat bogs and mouldy potatoes. In a way, they're like the Jews. The Jews have been degraded by their oppressors. Those who are forced into a ghetto of squalor must eventually produce some who are squalid. Yet the greatness of the Jews – I think of the Irish too – is their tenacity . . . Go to Bishopsgate, my lord. See the impoverished Hebrew, who when the Sabbath eve comes spreads his table with a cloth as white as ours, lights candles to welcome the holy bride, and in the gloom of the smoking City celebrates the glories revealed to his ancestors of the Arabian desert.' Disraeli's eyes glowed. 'In the East End of London you will see the Jew celebrating the Feast of Tabernacles. My lord, a race that persists in celebrating its vintage though it has no fruits to gather must certainly regain its vineyards.'

'But you are a Christian,' said Lyndhurst.

'Christianity,' said Disraeli, 'is the completion of Judaism. That was the mystery Our Lord revealed.'

Lyndhurst was silent for a few seconds. He wanted to turn the conversation.

'Well, so much for the next world,' he said. 'Let us look nearer home. How would you dispose of our domestic questions?'

Disraeli pondered.

'At home, I'd pay more attention to the condition of the people. And I'd effect change within our ancient forms and so avoid political revolutions in the Continental manner. I am happy to think that in Parliament we've been able to continue our Civil War by other means.'

'Good God,' said Lyndhurst, 'you shall be the first philosopher of the Tory Party.'

'No, Lord Lyndhurst, perhaps the first philosopher of a *reconstructed* Tory Party. At present, I'm a philosopher in search of a seat.'

'You really must be found a seat, Disraeli,' said Lyndhurst, calling a footman to serve them with port. 'Wycombe obviously won't do. We're not so rich in talent that Parliament can ignore able young men like yourself. How timid the electorate is! How they fear new men! And yet, what a strange place is Parliament! What a curious assembly of genius and madness, of braggarts and stutterers, idlers and enthusiasts, self-seekers and philanthropists! And despite that,' he said, sipping his drink, 'there's a collective wisdom in the House that blankets every individual deficiency.'

Disraeli was listening to him intently, and Lyndhurst, satisfied with his audience, went on,

'One day, when you rise to speak in Parliament, you'll be faced by a body of critics who at one time or other have practised every art of pleasing, every device of humbug and hypocrisy. They're as skilled as any whore in feigning passion.

. . . When you stand up in front of such people, you stand naked.'

'How many would welcome the chance of such an exposure!' said Disraeli.

'That's true,' said Lyndhurst. 'To enter Parliament is irreparably to lose your innocence . . . That has its pleasures too.'

He abruptly changed the subject again.

'Tell me, Disraeli – what do you know of Dr Maginn?'

'Maginn of *Fraser*'s?'

'Yes.'

Disraeli reflected for a moment. Then he said,

'I knew Dr Maginn briefly when I was involved with *The Representative* . . . Everything he touches turns to slime. He's a blackmailer with a talent for journalism. It was Maginn, together with Westmacott, in *The Age*, who first spread the libel that Lady Blessington was her own son-in-law's mistress.'

'Ah, these family relationships!' said Lyndhurst. 'The poets did society a great disservice by making Jocasta's crime fashionable.'

'Yes, but Maginn's method is to condemn sin and to gloat over it. And when he doesn't find it, he goes sniffing for it. The doctor always reminds me of a pig at the foot of an oak tree, grubbing and pawing for truffles.'

Lyndhurst smiled.

'He digs and scavenges, and eventually,' Disraeli went on, 'he comes up grunting with a mouthful of decaying acorns.'

'That must be very disappointing for Dr Maginn.'

'Oh, no, my lord,' said Disraeli. 'I doubt if he or his friends would know the difference. Why do you ask me about Maginn?'

'No special reason,' said Lyndhurst, shaking his head. 'No special reason, Disraeli, except that I have much regard for you.'

'I am obliged.'

'And great affection for Henrietta – ' he spoke her name familiarly – 'she's been a daughter to me for many years. Dr Maginn is a reptilian figure – a vicious enemy, as you know, of your friend Bulwer – but that isn't important. There are some inferior men who can't bear the happiness of others – they want to claw down everyone to their own lowly state.

Be specially careful of Dr Maginn, Disraeli. Maginn is ugly and rejected. He made some approach to Lady Sykes a long time ago. Then he wooed that poetess – what's her name?'

'Miss Laetitia Landon.'

'Ah, yes, Miss Landon. He failed even with her.'

They laughed together.

'I don't expect to have any further occasion to deal with Dr Maginn.'

'In politics and journalism there's often a malice that nothing – not even sublimity – can repel. You must be careful of Dr Maginn . . . And pray, come and see me at the Court of the Exchequer tomorrow at noon. We can talk further about politics, and I'd welcome your advice.'

He gave Disraeli a friendly smile, and as the footman opened the door into the drawing-room, Disraeli stood back to let Lyndhurst pass. Maginn? It was strange that Lyndhurst had warned him against a man he despised but scarcely knew. Maginn, like Clara Bolton, belonged to the rejected who compensated for their hurt by seeking viciously and arbitrarily to give pain to others.

It didn't matter. Lyndhurst, the Chief Baron, the former Lord Chancellor, the future Lord Chancellor, Lyndhurst, after Peel and the Duke the most eminent of the Tories, Lyndhurst had invited him to call. He lingered at the door so that he could observe the ladies before deciding whom he would sit next to.

'Mr Disraeli! Mr Disraeli!'

The quavering but imperious voice of Lady Cork summoned him, and Disraeli moved quickly towards her. She sat on the sofa, a sugar-puff fairy embellished with a white silk bonnet and a frothing dress of white crêpe. Disraeli never met her without a sense of awe that for over ninety years she had spent her life as if at a ball attended by Dr Johnson, Boswell, Charles James Fox, Canning, Byron and Alfieri, not in fancy-dress but in their own person. She had known Brighton as a fishing village and Manchester as a country town, and had seen wars and revolutions change the map of Europe. Her taste was for the talented, the beautiful and the aristocratic, and although, as she once told Disraeli, she despised wealth, she liked her favourites to be rich, or at least to live and look as if they were.

He took the seat that she patted at her side, as she summoned Henrietta to join them.

'Darling Henrietta,' she said, stroking her cheek. 'I love you best in the world – I love Miss Thingumybob over there too – ' she indicated Lady Tavistock – 'but I've forgotten her name. Henrietta! Are you kind to her, Mr Disraeli?'

'Very!' Disraeli murmured.

'Yes,' said Lady Cork. 'There's no beauty like love. Be very kind to her, Mr Disraeli. I've seen love bloom and wither many times in my life. Where is your husband?'

Henrietta hesitated.

'In Venice. He went there from Baden. He'll be returning very soon – he says.'

'You must not be made unhappy,' said Lady Cork. 'He mustn't come back too soon. Mr Maclise!'

The tall Irishman joined them, and Lady Cork waved him to a seat.

'You must paint Henrietta,' she said. 'They say there's no one like you for taking a likeness.'

'Mr Maclise,' said Disraeli, 'has drawn a superb and flattering portrait of me.'

'I like flattery,' said Lady Cork. 'It's very vulgar to be too truthful.'

'There'll be no need to flatter Lady Sykes,' said Maclise. He sat clumsily in front of them, an artist with large hands that were the instrument of a tender and delicate line that had made him the most fashionable portraitist in London.

'You must paint her,' said Lady Cork, 'in a balldress showing those superb shoulders – with Mr Disraeli behind you so that she can look just like that!'

Henrietta glanced at Disraeli, and he smiled back. Lyndhurst approached, and bowing low over Henrietta's hand, said,

'I must leave, madam. I have business tomorrow with the Duke.'

He turned to Disraeli.

'Perhaps, sir,' he said, 'I may have the pleasure of spending a night at Bradenham on my next travels.'

'We should be honoured, my lord,' said Disraeli.

'That will be wonderful,' said Henrietta, clapping her hands in delight. 'I am already invited by Mrs Disraeli for the autumn.'

'In that case,' said Lyndhurst, 'why do we not all go *en famille*, perhaps first to Bradenham then later with my daughter to Paris. Mr Disraeli – you must think of it!'

'Yes, indeed,' said Disraeli. 'Indeed – I will give your kind invitation some thought.'

'Travel,' said Lady Cork, 'is an absurdity. My macaw can never get used to it, and my manservant and maid invariably fall sick. Stay at home, Mr Disraeli. You too, Henrietta. Neither of you is as vigorous as Lyndhurst. I'd like a glass of champagne!'

My dear Disraeli, (the letter read),

Not knowing your present whereabouts, since my last letter to Duke Street was returned to me in your absence, I am writing these lines to you at Upper Grosvenor Street, where I understand that your correspondence may be delivered.

I will not conceal from you my disappointment at your failure to pay the £500 on Quarter Day as you had promised, all the more so since, I repeat, I have urgent need of the money for the new house I intend to buy. Your delays and explanations about the repayment of the £1,000 which I advanced to you for your election expenses seem to me both unsatisfactory and contradictory. Nor is my understanding in any way forwarded by your failure to arrive for dinner last week when Madame expected you to give a second reading from your Epick.

I must now ask you most specifically to discharge your debt without further delay. I would be pained to have to make application to Mr Isaac D'Israeli. There are strains to which the most devoted friendship should not be exposed.

Yours,
B. Austen.

Disraeli read the letter, then carefully tore it in small pieces.

He sighed. Through the wall he could hear Henrietta preparing for bed in the next room – the sounds of glass, of brushing, the movement of chairs, curtains being drawn. For almost six months he had been intermittently the guest, as he put it, of Sir Francis Sykes. The baronet himself, acquiescing in the idea that Henrietta required protection in his absence, and re-assured no doubt that a dandy-bachelor would be a more appropriate guardian than some earnest supplanter, had written to Disraeli from time to time about Henrietta's financial affairs, treating him as a major-domo rather than as a rival. It wasn't an inconvenient situation, except that Sir Francis in his travels had detached himself from the expenses of the household, and Henrietta herself regarded money as an irrelevance to their happiness.

It had been a stimulating year – of that there could be no doubt. There was nothing that people couldn't get used to – sickness, indiscretions, death, even the happiness of others. And so after the spiteful tongues had exhausted themselves, his relationship with Henrietta had seemed to be taken for granted. At the opera, at the delicious suppers afterwards, at Almack's, at the balls where they were invited together, it was accepted that Sir Francis Sykes was travelling abroad for his health, and that he had left Henrietta in the care of Mr Disraeli.

And Henrietta, released from her ailing and anxious husband, had grown more beautiful with the passing days as she became more contented. Soon, he knew, she would stretch her round white arms towards him. Disraeli looked at his face in the looking-glass, at the dark pouches under his eyes, and decided that he must either use more wrinkle cream or go to bed earlier. But Henrietta liked the silences of the night, the lecherous talk that banished sleep, the languid acrobatics of love, the exhaustions and the awakenings. And so did he. The sounds through the wall of her movements stirred him, and he sat down to answer Austen.

My dear Austen, (he wrote),
I never fail to rejoice when I see your handwriting, even though your last letter was a timely reminder which antici-

pated by only an hour my intention to write this letter. I have greatly missed your company in the last few months, my only justification being that I have been toiling night and day to finish the Epick, which I hope will make some contribution to the restoration of my fortunes.

It explains too why in the turmoil of my enthusiasm I neglected what would have been my greatest pleasure – namely, to see you and Madame again, to dine with you, and to read you more of my work.

I am leaving tomorrow for Bradenham, and rely on your forbearance, dearest friend, till next Quarter Day, when I propose to repay the full sum of £1,000 plus the interest you have hitherto so generously renounced.

Believe me to be,

Your very sincere,
B. Disraeli.

He re-read the letter, and decided that it would do for the time being. Meanwhile, he must arrange for Henrietta's lawyers to provide some support from Sir Francis. When he had moved into Upper Grosvenor Street, he hadn't bargained on having to make so large a contribution to the establishment. But the expenses, the unpaid bills, the creditors in the ante-rooms, had multiplied during the summer, a sinister accompaniment to their pleasures. The music of the water-parties to Twickenham had begun to be haunted by the ghostly voices of duns. When he took Henrietta in some splendid gown to the King's Theatre and every eye turned towards them, he had begun to think that his happiness would be even more complete if the robe and his coat had been paid for.

He began to undress, and thought of Lyndhurst, his open friendly face, his coolness in power, his generosity, his affection for Henrietta. Here indeed was the leader he had dreamed of when he wrote *Vivian Grey*, the man who was at a pinnacle of power in public affairs, yet who would seek the service, the imagination, the dynamism, of youthful genius. Friendship and love! Was there anything else that a man needed for happiness? Disraeli was seized with a fit of coughing, the aftermath of influenza, and he quickly shuffled himself into his slippers and drew his dressing-gown around him . . . Yes, there was something else. Health – and money.

He couldn't go with Lyndhurst to France. He couldn't be dependent on him for hospitality. Far better that Lyndhurst should be their guest at Bradenham. But if Henrietta travelled with Lyndhurst and his daughter? . . . Disraeli sat on the bed despondently. In a way it would help, since it would give him a few weeks' respite from the crushing problem of her bills. But on the other hand, to be away from her at Bradenham had been pang enough in the past. That she should travel alone with Lyndhurst – ! He liked him; he was a splendid-looking man; old enough to be Henrietta's father. And then he remembered the vicious gossip of Clara Bolton. But that was absurd. *In loco parentis.* That was the relationship, and the thought soothed him.

The house had become quiet, and Disraeli looked at the clock. Twenty to two. He hesitated deliberately, knowing that now Henrietta would be waiting for him in the wide bed, delaying the moment when she would raise her arms towards him, renewing the surge of pleasure between them that their contact never failed to stir. Her dark hair falling tent-like over his face, the dry peppery scent of her armpits, the slow sinking into delight. He was tired, and wanted to sleep. Best of all, he would have liked to smoke his *narguilah.* He waited. Ten minutes – a quarter of an hour.

At last there was a timid knock. He didn't answer. The knock became louder, and he rose and opened the door. Henrietta, in a pale blue peignoir, stood there and waited.

'Won't you ask me to come in?' she said.

He looked to the top of the stairs and then downwards to the hall, now in darkness, and beckoned her in without speaking.

She drew him to her side on the bed, and said,

'Dearest one – what is it? You're sad. You must tell me why you're sad.'

He didn't answer, and she took his hands.

'Tell me, Ben, my darling heart, what is it? I can't bear it. Weren't you happy tonight? The dinner – everything I did and said was for you. Please look at me.'

He turned his face away from her, and she laid her face on his shoulder.

'Please, my love, my darling, tell me what it is.'

'It's nothing,' he said. 'Nothing.'

'But there is something. There is. You must tell me. Please tell me. You're destroying me.'

Disraeli stood, and the candles threw fluttering shadows over the walls.

'It's just that – I can't go to Paris with you and Lyndhurst.'

'But why – why? He thinks you're the most – the most talented of all the young men he knows – he said you light up every conversation as soon as you speak.'

Disraeli's sombre expression changed.

'Did he really say that?'

'Yes, he did, my darling. So why should you say you won't come to Paris?'

Disraeli's face reverted to its original gloom.

'I'll tell you, Henrietta. It's because I have no money. There you have it! I have no money – nothing.'

She thought for a moment. Then she said happily,

'But what does it matter? Lyndhurst will be our host. He's such a dear man. He'll do anything I ask. We'll stay in all the best houses. Lyndhurst has many friends – the Rothschilds, the Goldsmiths.'

'It's an illusion,' Disraeli said mournfully, 'that it's an economy to stay with rich friends. The rich, alas, rarely carry cash when they move outside their houses.'

'Oh, but what does it matter?' she repeated. 'We'll all be so happy.'

'All?' said Disraeli, glancing at her sharply. 'How long have you known Lyndhurst?'

'Oh, Ben, Ben,' she said, drawing him down towards her and covering his face with kisses, 'you're not jealous of Lyndhurst? He could be your father – even mine. And that's how he is. I've told you so often. I've known him since I was a child. He was always like that – *galant* and inactive.'

'Inactive?'

'Yes – inactive. Not like my great strong love – my beautiful Amin – my wonderful, darling boy.'

She was lying over him, and her mouth moved restlessly over his neck and his chest.

'Ben,' she said. 'Ben.'

The *narguilah* with its pouting mouthpiece and its bulbous bowl stood tantalizingly at the bedside. He would have liked a brief solitude, a quiet contemplative hour of sucking his oriental pipe, inhaling and blowing smoke. The water in the hubble-bubble was simmering with a gentle splutter as he turned Henrietta on her back.

'Oh, Ben, Ben,' she said. 'I love you. I'd die if I had to leave you. You must never leave me. Oh, Amin!'

Still holding her, he took the mouthpiece of the *narguilah* and puffed.

'Ben,' she said, 'you are very wicked . . . You *will* come to Paris.'

'First,' he said, 'to Bradenham.'

Again he drew on the thick ivory tube, and she opened her eyes and said,

'Oh, Ben, you are *very* wicked.'

After about ten minutes, like a white dolphin that he had once seen harpooned by boys in the Bosphorus, she arched her back, struggled convulsively, and sank back exhausted. Then she lay quietly, her forehead glistening with sweat as she contemplated the pale ceiling.

'I'll tell Lyndhurst,' she murmured.

When she returned from a brief languor, she said,

'I'm looking forward to meeting your sister. Tell me, Ben – is she beautiful?'

'Less beautiful than you – more beautiful than me. You won't be jealous.'

'But is she terribly clever? She understands all about politics, and I won't know what to say.'

'We'll talk about London. It enthrals her.'

'You told me she reads André Chénier.'

'*The Times* too.'

They laughed, and he kissed her neck.

'I have an idea,' said Henrietta musingly. 'Do you think Sarah might – that she might take to Lyndhurst?'

Disraeli's left hand, which had been caressing her cheek,

paused. Lyndhurst, the dashing and sophisticated statesman, the *coureur*, somehow didn't consort with Sarah attending her parents in the country.

'She will like him – certainly. Would he like her?'

'Since she's your sister, he will have a prejudice in favour – and then, imagine it, he might even become your brother-in-law.'

It was an intimacy which she seemed to find pleasing, but Disraeli, eliding some of the processes of his thought, said,

'I shouldn't like anything to make Sarah unhappy.'

'No,' said Henrietta, and changed the subject.

Chapter Eight

All day long at Bradenham Mrs D'Israeli had been superintending the arrangements for the visit of Lady Sykes and Lord Lyndhurst. For the third time Benjamin was standing at High Wycombe against Colonel Grey, and since she knew he was anxious to use the occasion of Lyndhurst's stay to promote his candidature on the basis of an alliance between Radicals and Tories, though doubtful that his persistence would ever lead to a happy conclusion, she had asked him to draw up the dinner invitations. As far as she could see, all that he had succeeded in doing so far in politics was to accumulate a crushing burden of debt through his election expenses, and to get a reputation in London as a climber scrambling with little consistency between Lord Durham the Whig and Lord Lyndhurst the Tory in search of a foothold which would not give way, as had happened before, beneath his tread.

Literature had turned her husband into a monastic. Now, as her nephew George Basevi warned her, the pursuit of a seat threatened to make her son into a laughing-stock, and she often wished that instead of following his heady caprices, Benjamin had continued with his early apprenticeship as an articled clerk to a city solicitor.

And yet he had won some social success in Mayfair. In the

last few months, Sarah had often shown her his letters, dappled with the names of the London *ton*. If half his stories of brilliant excursions into society were true, he must have been one of the lights of the season, attending like some brilliant star the great planetary figures – D'Orsay, Lady Blessington, Lady Cork, Lord Lyndhurst, Devonshire, the Musgraves. But even if his claims were only half-true, no one could deny his social dash and tenacity.

She wondered by what accident Benjamin had developed in such contrast to her husband, herself, and his younger country-loving brothers. From what ancestor had he derived the cheek, the combination of sensitivity and bravado, the persistence, the defiance, that enabled him, a young Italianate Jew, to present himself at ease among the squires of Wycombe, the dukes of St James's, and the gentlemen of Westminster? What strange affinity had brought him, an exotic *littérateur*, and Lyndhurst, the Anglo-Saxon lawyer, into so close a friendship? Perhaps it was the same spirit that had led her own grandparents from Verona to England seventy years before.

Lyndhurst, they said, had been something of a Jacobin in his youth, and even now was a man of pleasure, enjoying the company of actors and actresses as much as of men and women of breeding. No one was more ardent than he about the much-rejected Jew Bill which would enfranchise the Hebrews. Perhaps the reason for the ill-assorted friendship was that the Tory Chief Baron, the past and prospective Chancellor, a man of simple origins, the son of an artist who had first made his name in America and of a woman with little or no family background, felt some kind of democratic and cosmopolitan intimacy with Ben. The thought disturbed her. To receive Lady Sykes in the company of Lord Lyndhurst was an idea of Sarah, who had lived for months in a romantic fantasy of her brother and the beautiful and, some said, abandoned Lady Sykes travelling in Lyndhurst's glistening cavalcade to Braden-ham. For his part, Ben had shown more enthusiasm for the visit of Lyndhurst than he had for that of Henrietta, though Mrs D'Israeli knew he had been the Sykeses' guest at Southend.

Accompanied by Mrs Fawcett, the housekeeper who had worked for the family for over thirty years, Mrs D'Israeli walked through the rooms of Bradenham House, making her last dispositions for the visit. Lyndhurst had been assigned to the main guest-room, Lady Sykes had been given Ben's bedroom which overlooked the park, Ralph was to stay in the old nursery, and Ben himself was to move to the east wing, which was an advantage since immediately after dinner he had to leave for Wycombe in order to begin his canvass early next morning, intending to return the following day.

Lord Lyndhurst, Lady Sykes, Mr Nash, Lord Chandos's agent, Squire Lowther and his wife, Mr and Mrs Huffam, the Reverend and Mrs Holgate, General Sir Arthur Cropley Gurden and Lady Cropley Gurden – that was more or less all. This was Ben's campaign committee at dinner. But what mattered was the occasion. She stood at the broad windows and looked with satisfaction over the lawns, closely scythed and trimmed, leading to the beech copse and the cypress trees. The gardens with the roses blighted by the frosts of late autumn looked sad, though every now and again the white doves, tempted by the pale sun, swept with a startled quiver from the gables on to the grass, posed there in a dignified formation, and then with a sudden impulse flew fluttering back to the roof.

'Is everything arranged, Mama?' Sarah asked.

'Yes,' said her mother. 'Here is the *placement*.' She produced a sheet of paper. 'Your father will have Lady Sykes on his right, Lady Cropley Gurden on his left . . . you'll have the General . . . No, I'll have him . . . you'll have him on your left . . . yes, and Squire Lowther . . . the Holgates at the bottom of the table. Heavens, I've left out Mr Nash!'

'Mr Nash next to Lady Sykes,' said Sarah. 'Ben was anxious that – '

'Yes, we'll certainly have Lady Sykes between Lord Lyndhurst and Mr Nash.'

'And what about Ben?'

'Ben will have to fit himself in.'

'He was anxious,' said Sarah, 'that there should be champagne.'

'I don't require any advice from Ben about my hospitality,' Mrs D'Israeli said stiffly. 'I wouldn't like Lady Sykes to leave with the impression that we have been failing either in grace or style. I'm sure she'll be as happy as she was last time.'

'But Lyndhurst – he's really quite unknown to us. Don't law lords bring their servants with them?'

'If he does,' said Mrs D'Israeli, 'there will be suitable arrangements.'

'And will he want his servants to attend him at dinner?'

'That, I think, would be excessive,' said Mrs D'Israeli. 'After all, we're not a Royal household or the court of some German princeling where every guest has his Jäger. I don't imagine that when Lord Lyndhurst entertains domestically his arrangements are any more elaborate than ours.'

'Yes, Mama,' said Sarah.

By ten o'clock, Mrs D'Israeli had proved that, despite the apprehensions of her son, who had wanted to import the famous chef M. Ude from London, she was capable with the help of Mrs Fawcett of providing a dinner as delicate and as ample as any to be found in London. Lyndhurst had complimented her on the soufflé, and Squire Lowther, a connoisseur of simpler dishes, had twice exclaimed, 'God's firkins, but I've never known such a saddle of lamb!' To her surprise, Isaac had proved himself an expert in military history, and the disdainful General Sir Arthur Cropley Gurden had rapidly been reduced to a pupil's deferential posture as Isaac, who had never seen a cannon except on the ramparts of Göttingen, described the role of artillery in the Battle of Corunna where the General had fought. The Reverend Holgate was happy to be left alone. Sarah, her sallow cheeks pinkened, had absorbed Lyndhurst's attention. Disraeli, always reserved when his mother presided over the table, had barely spoken, but felt content. He had been ill at Bradenham after a fall from his horse, and was satisfied to listen rather than to participate.

He stood by a pillar, listening to the conversation that had moved from gossip and anecdote to politics and law. Lyndhurst had told Lowther a bawdy story about a whore at a drunken orgy who had lain with a king's messenger, and pocketed his dispatch instead of her fee.

'God's firkins,' said Lowther, choking himself in a paroxysm of laughter, 'I recall – I recall . . .' But he didn't finish his recollection. Unbuttoned, he lay with his legs outstretched, the picture of a satisfied snoring guest.

'*Gravis cibo et vino*,' said Lyndhurst to Disraeli who approached him. 'What a happy evening, Disraeli,' he added with a glance at Lowther. 'Don't underrate the squires! You must always care for the agricultural interest. The Tories of Wycombe will back you as long as you have friends like Lowther.'

The squire awoke at his name.

'A splendid fellow, Disraeli,' he said, opening one eye. 'Can't tell an oat from a barley-beard . . . But he cares for the land.' He began to sing in a tuneless voice, 'The land – the land – heigh-ho, the land . . .' Then he fell asleep again.

Disraeli looked down at him benevolently.

'Whatever happens,' he said, 'I must move on from Wycombe.'

'I'd talk to the Duke, but he wants retainers not allies. You must enrol under the Tories.'

'You have the advantage, my lord,' said Nash, who had joined them, 'of being a lawyer. A lawyer can speak with equal fervour on both sides of any case.'

Lyndhurst ignored the innuendo, but turning to Disraeli he said,

'It's true that legal eloquence is very attractive to partisans. It was after I helped defend the Jacobin Dr Watson that the Tories sought me out to defend the interests of property. Mark you, sir,' he said to Nash, 'I count it a great advantage that I once helped to save a Cabinet from being blown up at dinner. Would you believe it,' he said as the other gentlemen gathered round him, 'Arthur Thistlewood, the very man I helped to save in 1817 when he was tried together with Dr Watson, was the man I helped to hang at the time of the Cato Street conspiracy.'

'That's true impartiality,' said Mr Huffam, 'but I must confess, milord, that I never fully understood its circumstances.'

'Well,' said Lyndhurst, 'it's very long ago. It's part of the history of England. Imagine, gentlemen, this fellow

Thistlewood plotted to assassinate the whole Cabinet over the dessert – Lord Westmoreland, Liverpool, Castlereagh, the Duke of Westminster, Mr Canning, Lord Harrowby. Very uncivilized!'

'Was there no protection?' asked Huffam.

'They aimed,' said Lyndhurst, 'to take advantage of the absence of the London garrison for the funeral of the King at Windsor. It was all very carefully planned. They'd even provided themselves with bags to carry off their trophies – the heads of Sidmouth and Castlereagh, and then they intended to set up a provisional government at the Mansion House.'

'Good God!' said the General.

'Well, there they were, twenty-five of them, in a loft over a stable in Cato Street, waiting to invade the dinner-party. Luckily we had an informer. They were surprised, a few shots were fired, a police officer was killed; and though most of the plotters escaped, they were captured a few days later.'

'It all ended satisfactorily,' said Nash.

'Satisfactorily?' Lyndhurst said ruminatively. 'On May 31st, 1820 – remarkable how well I remember it – five of them – Thistlewood, Ings, Brunt, Davidson and Tidd – were hanged and beheaded.'

'Beheaded?' asked Disraeli, speaking for the first time. 'Wasn't that overdoing it?'

'The charge,' said Lyndhurst, 'was high treason.'

Disraeli hesitated, and walked off towards the drawing-room as the conversation continued. For a few seconds he stood behind Mrs Lowther's chair, and she, sensing his presence, turned her head and said,

'This time, Mr Disraeli, you must succeed. We are all determined. I've completely turned twelve voters in your favour.'

'*Your* favour, madam,' said Disraeli, 'is all the success I require.'

She blushed, and applied her attention to the embroidery that Mrs D'Israeli had shown her as an example of her needle-woman's skill. Disraeli half-smiled to Henrietta, and she rose and joined him at the door.

Isaac, who had sat in silence while Lyndhurst was dominating the conversation, looked up as he saw Henrietta move towards his son, and said,

'Ah, Lady Sykes, you must let me show you some of our antiquities.'

Disraeli gave him an amused glance, but Henrietta said quickly,

'I'd like nothing better.'

Isaac heaved himself from his chair, and said,

'The great time of Bradenham was in the Lovelace-Wentworth period. Ah, yes – it was bought by Sir Edmund Pye the baronet. He was a staunch Royalist, and was fined over three thousand pounds by Cromwell's Parliament. *Vae victis.* You see here over the door his coat of arms.'

He led her into the hall, and pointed to the fireplace.

'There's the date – 1628 – and here you see the initials, C.R., of Carolus Rex. Now come along.'

And with Henrietta lightly taking his arm, he shuffled towards the main staircase, where he pointed upwards to the azure ceiling with its design of cherubim peering down over a *trompe l'œil* balustrade.

'Why did they always paint cherubs on ceilings?' asked Henrietta.

'To recall our innocence as we go to our slumbers,' said Disraeli. 'Shall we walk up and study it more closely?'

'Perhaps,' said Isaac, 'you had better show Lady Sykes the seventeenth-century Dutch tiles on the fireplace in the oak room.'

'Oh, yes, please,' said Henrietta eagerly.

'They're scenes from the Scriptures,' said Isaac, returning to the drawing-room, and talking to himself.

As soon as he had gone, Disraeli and Henrietta went into the hall and took their cloaks. She stopped in front of the portrait of a beautiful woman, with an arrogant but embittered expression.

'Who is that?'

'That,' said Disraeli negligently, 'was my grandmother. She never spoke a kind word to me, though she once gave me a guinea – when she thought she was on her death-bed.'

Henrietta smiled, and they walked out over the stone path

leading beneath a pergola to the woods, where, as soon as they were out of sight of the house, Disraeli took Henrietta's hand, and said,

'I wanted to talk to you before I left.'

'You abandoned your supporters?'

'I fled from them. They were talking about the gallows.'

She drew closer to him, and he felt her breast pressed against his arm.

'Yes,' she said, 'I couldn't bear to hear anyone talk of death. How beautiful the world is! Look at the sky.'

The night sky was cloudless, hard and star-filled.

'Two days,' said Disraeli, pausing at the end of the path. 'You won't forget me?'

She laid her face against his, and said,

'My dearest one, I think of you every moment of my life. I'll never forget you. If anything happened to you, I'd die.'

She drew away from him, and took his hands.

'Till I met you, Ben,' she said, 'I'd never been happy – never.' She dropped her glance. 'I've told you. Before you, I'd never looked at another man – let alone been unfaithful to Francis. I love you – your sweet head. When you are away from me, I – I – '

He raised her face.

'Darling Henrietta,' he said, 'why can't we always live in the country?'

She laughed.

'Because you'd get bored very quickly. You'd ask me when we're going to the next party, and who'll be there. And then, there's money – it's so difficult.'

'Money!' said Disraeli bitterly. 'The entail and the heirloom are the hereditary curse of the aristocracy.'

'It doesn't matter,' said Henrietta, taking his arm and walking on. 'I must tell you something wonderful. Francis is sending me a thousand pounds – I heard yesterday from the solicitor, Mr Pyne. I wanted to keep it a secret. And Lyndhurst has promised to help me.'

Disraeli stopped.

'Lyndhurst? Why?'

'Because he is our friend – he is fond of us both – I'm sure of it. You should hear how he speaks of you.'

'And you?'

'He makes me feel a child – and that's what I am to him. Oh, Ben, it would be very harsh to reject such kindness.'

'Have you ever – ?'

She put her fingers on his mouth.

'You must never say it again. Never! Lyndhurst has always been kind and generous. But I've told you . . . darling Ben!'

She drew him to a tree.

'Darling Ben! You know I'd give up everything in the world for you – my husband, my friends, even my children. Is that what you want?'

He didn't answer.

'You know,' she went on, 'you only have to ask me. Look at me!'

He had averted his face, and she repeated,

'Look at me! But remember, darling Amin, if I give up society and live like Lady Blessington, both our lives will be different. D'Orsay dazzles London in his barouche, while Lady Blessington receives only gentlemen. Is that how you'd want us to live?'

He took her into his arms and kissed her.

'No,' he said, 'it's just that I'm tormented by the contradictions between what I aspire to do and . . .'

'And love?' she said, finishing the sentence.

'Yes,' he said.

'In that case, you must choose.'

'I have chosen,' said Disraeli. 'While I can, I'll try and fulfil the purpose of my life – to love you and to deserve you. But if I can't be worthy of you by the situation I make for myself – well, then, I'll still love you.'

She smiled happily, and they began their walk back to the house. Mr Nash was returning to Aylesbury, and Squire Lowther and Mr and Mrs Holgate to High Wycombe. The carriages had already assembled in the drive, and Isaac D'Israeli was bidding farewell to the guests. Disraeli hurried to join them as the groom, carrying a lamp, was putting his travelling case into Lowther's carriage.

'Ah,' said Mrs Lowther, 'we feared you were lost, Mr Disraeli. Mr Lowther will travel on the box.'

'Yes,' said the Squire. 'You will travel inside and I'll have some air . . . She talks and talks and talks.'

Sarah left her bed and went to the window. The moon had risen and laid a hoar-frost, magically warm, over the grass and the trees. Everything was now silent, the house, the gardens, the dogs. Everyone, she felt, was asleep, the excitement ended of the arrivals and departures – everyone except herself. The monotonous days had been interrupted by the great event of Lyndhurst's visit, but soon that would be over too, and after Lady Sykes and Benjamin had left, she herself would return to the task of listening to time shuffling past and enjoying vicariously Benjamin's adventures. Yes – she loved her brother, so that his achievements, his pleasures, his social conquests were almost her own. Ever since James Meredith, her fiancé, had died of smallpox in Benjamin's arms in Egypt, she had often faced as in a nightmare the dilemma as to which of them, had she been able, she would have saved. She had loved Meredith; no one, it seemed to her, would ever replace him. Yet she felt – she was uneasy in face of that, even in privacy – she would have saved Benjamin.

Tonight she couldn't sleep because, suddenly, after choosing a perpetual widowhood without even the remembered joys of marriage, something strange and unexpected had touched her. A voice, a glance, a hand pressed over hers, a glimpse of all the happiness which she had thought impossible. Lyndhurst had greeted her, and smiled to her, not with the gentlemanly but casual attention of Ben's other friends who took it for granted that her destiny in life was to be a self-effacing attendant; no, he had greeted her as a woman who might yet enjoy her own life. He had made her laugh with his anecdotes which he addressed especially to her. He had taken wine with others, and looked at her over his glass, his eyes playful and benevolent. He had an easy, ageless charm that drew her to him, and made her feel, as her mother rarely allowed, that her opinions and judgments were important. And he had recited a few lines

141

of French poetry before she withdrew from the room with the other ladies.

His face, his voice, his tall elegant figure, the gestures of his slim, pointing hands, had remained in her mind. Even in her bedroom, his gentle, amiable expression persisted in front of her, banishing sleep. He was a widower and – no, it was an absurdity. And yet, not an impossibility. Ben claimed him as his friend, and he would perhaps return. Perhaps the memory of Meredith would become paler with time; somehow or other, his very features had become fused with the miniature that she kept on her table. He was a portrait, not a reality.

A few rooms away, Lyndhurst lay sleeping, and morning was at least six hours distant before they could meet. She thought of stratagems by which she could cross his path, perhaps walk with him through the walled garden, bring him the *Bucks Gazette*. The night was cold, and she lay on the bed beneath the blankets, thinking again of Lyndhurst's eyes above the glass that he raised in a toast, his greying hair with the small quiff over his forehead, and his voice, his voice! Miss Disraeli. Never had she heard her name pronounced with so much tenderness – not even by Meredith, dear good James with his honest, straightforward affections.

'My lord,' she said aloud into the darkness, 'may I offer you the *Examiner* – the *Gazette*?' It was too humble. 'My lord,' she said in a more emphatic voice, 'the newspapers have arrived.' That was better, but still not quite right. She should sound more relaxed, happier, serviceable yet not sycophantic.

'Here you are, Lord Lyndhurst,' she said with a laugh, her voice clear and amiable, 'the papers are here. Surprisingly – they're rarely on time. You have very little choice, I fear – the *Examiner* or the *Gazette*. Which will you have?'

She was lying with her eyes wide open in the darkness deciding whether at last the tone was right when the door opened and her father, carrying a candle and wearing a tasselled night-cap and a long nightgown appeared.

'Sarah!' he said mildly. 'Sarah!'

She closed her eyes and didn't answer.

'Sarah!' said Mr D'Israeli reproachfully. 'You're talking in your sleep again!'

Then he left.

The laudanum had given him a few hours' unconsciousness, disturbed by dreams of strangers moving as if at a ball through a Chamber of Requests, of his dead daughter holding his hand in a park, and of manacled prisoners with bowed heads. Lyndhurst awoke, stifling, not knowing where he was or where his servant had laid out his banyan. The moon had begun to set, but its light framed the heavy curtains and gradually disclosed the unfamiliar room, the canopy with embroidered cupids over his bed, and the ormolu handles of the wardrobe.

He found his slippers and dressing-gown, lit a candle, and walked carefully, in order not to disturb the household, down the oak staircase to the library.

He was happy at Bradenham away from the ceremonial of the courts or the Woolsack to which he would be restored in a few weeks' time when Peel had finally formed his administration. Here was silence and peace, the only sounds the stirrings from the woods. In London there was always the mutter from the antechambers, the press of business, the supplicants and pleaders and defenders. Here, by contrast, Isaac D'Israeli was a metaphor of nature, passing quietly through the seasons of his life, ironically contemplating those who struggled against fatality. How different from Ben – the young Napoleon who had been beaten in every skirmish yet refused to take 'no' as destiny's answer! Could he succeed? In politics, the ones who succeeded were those who had the will to outstay the others. Yes – Ben would succeed one day, provided that he didn't exhaust himself first. He had formed a great affection for Disraeli; when he was tired, the younger man spread a reviving energy; he was a David to his Saul. He liked, too, the quiet, sallow-faced Sarah who was the reverse side of her brother's coin, but with her mother he felt less easy. She looked at him with her sharp dark eyes as if to inquire the reason for his interest in her son, the nature of his friendship with Ben's menage.

Lyndhurst paused in the hall by the podium of a Silenus embracing two nymphs, and touched the statue's rough surface. Whatever his public office, the private man continued. For how long more? Five – six – perhaps ten years? Five days? Five minutes? His heart beat rapidly and painfully.

'Lyndhurst!'

He heard the voice and turned. It was Henrietta. She wore a green satin mantle chequered in black with its velvet collar done up at the neck, where her hair fell loosely.

'Good heavens,' said Lyndhurst, 'is nobody asleep tonight?'

She raised her face in the shadows of the candle-light, and said,

'I couldn't sleep.'

She took his arm as they went to the drawing-room, where they sat on a sofa with the candle flickering on a table.

'Please talk to me. Are you happy, Lyndhurst?'

'Happy?' he said. 'Almost!'

'Almost,' she echoed. 'Almost! Why must one be "almost" happy?'

'What would make you wholly happy?'

'To be able to live with Disraeli – to be married to him.'

'Might not the difference – ?'

'No – no. It is part of our completeness. He needs the love of someone who will give him the love he has never had from his mother. You saw how she looked at me – with her beady, hostile eyes . . .'

'But is that enough?' Lyndhurst asked. 'A love of that kind?'

'Oh, but there is so much more,' said Henrietta.

She looked at the flowers.

'That's how I feel so often,' she said. 'All closed up like those flowers on the table – so anxious to give, but imprisoned by myself. I feel so afraid all the time. My father wrote to me the other day that unless I stop seeing Disraeli, no one will receive me in society. He – he passed me in St James's without greeting me!'

She began to sob, and Lyndhurst took her head between his hands and held it against his chest.

'How long, Henrietta, have I known you?'

She didn't answer.

'I've known you,' he said, 'for over eighteen years . . . Open your eyes!'

She drew herself away and looked into his face that seemed unchanged from the time when she had first seen it.

'You were scarcely more than a schoolgirl. You were like a daughter to me then – as you still are today. No one will harm you, Henrietta. I promise you – I'll defend you against everyone.'

'I am grateful,' she said.

'Malice,' said Lyndhurst, 'is the first-born of jealousy. The prudes wish you ill not because you're wrong but because you're beautiful.'

She wiped her eyes.

'No, I'm not,' she said.

'Yes, Henrietta, you are,' said Lyndhurst. 'Perhaps we'd better go to bed.'

The candle was beginning to gutter.

'You were the first man I ever knew outside my family,' said Henrietta. 'When I was a little girl – when you came to the house to see Father, I'd wait for hours to see you pass.'

'What do you want me to forget of all that, Henrietta?' Lyndhurst asked.

'Nothing,' she answered. 'I would never want you to forget, John, that I was your apprentice.'

Lyndhurst smiled, and she laid her head against his shoulder.

'No,' he said, 'it was I who learned from you – but what I learned was that the season of happiness could only be a brief one.'

She turned her face to his, and in the darkness he kissed her, observing the frown between her eyebrows, her tightly clenched eyes.

'No,' she said in a voice that was half a sigh, half a complaint. 'No – I mustn't – Ben – '

He kissed her again.

Afterwards, as they climbed the stairs in darkness except for the starlight that came through the tall windows, Lyndhurst was the first to speak.

'After all,' he said, 'we've known each other for many years – long before you were married.'

'Yes,' she said, eager to accept his assurance. 'Yes, that's true.'

'Disraeli and you – that's something quite different.'

'Yes,' she said, 'yes – quite different. I'm so bewildered. If he ever knew – '

'There's nothing for him to know,' said Lyndhurst. A glimmer of light lay on the landing, and he kissed her hand and then her cheek.

'I don't want to let you go,' he said as they stood there.

'I must,' she said.

'You'd better go ahead of me,' Lyndhurst said.

'Yes,' she said uncertainly. 'Yes.'

With a contented smile, Lyndhurst watched her go.

Through the opening of her bedroom door after she heard the whispered and ill-comprehended voices, Sarah saw the two figures part. Then she returned to her dressing-table and brushed her hair carefully, saying with each stroke, 'I wish I were dead . . . I wish I were dead.'

Chapter Nine

'*Quid datur a divis felici optatius hora?*' asked Maginn benignly, surveying the crowded saloon, the tables slopped with drink, the misty and cheerful figures among the smoke. He was sitting in his usual place in the corner, his thick legs spread apart, his back to the wall, with his younger colleagues from *Fraser's* surrounding him and his most intimate friend, Charles Westmacott of *The Age*, at his right hand.

'Only another bottle,' said Westmacott, rapping on the table for the potman. 'But it's next month not this month that matters. How long can the Tories survive?'

'Only as long as the Rads and the Whigs allow them.'

Maginn frowned, and his mood darkened. This was the moment, after the cheerful hours between one and three at the Cock in Fleet Street, when an editorial or a lampoon would have its embryonic inspiration, slowly hatching in banter and malice. *Fraser's Magazine* specialized in acerbity: *The Age* in libel, and what Maginn was unwilling to publish under his own name, Westmacott was always ready to pick up.

But even those who most condemned *The Age* privately enjoyed reading it, except when they in turn became the objects, like Madame Vestris, the gossiping impresario of the Olympic Theatre, of Westmacott's exactions.

'*Oderint dum metuant*' was the motto, but Westmacott was always prepared to be merciful for cash. His first failure had been when Lady Blessington, recently widowed, was defended by Bulwer after *The Age* first spread its libels about her and her son-in-law D'Orsay. And on another occasion, Westmacott had been knocked down at Covent Garden by Kemble after writing that Fanny Kemble's real father was Kemble's own nephew. Since then, Westmacott had taken to carrying a loaded crop.

'Talking of the Rads,' said a young lawyer's clerk, an occasional contributor to *Fraser's*, 'I hear that Mr Bulwer and his missis are separating.'

Westmacott turned his face blearily to the young man. Ever since Bulwer in *England and the English* had described Westmacott as 'Sneak, who keeps a Sunday newspaper as a cess-pool for the week's filth', any mention of his name at the Cock was regarded as a solecism unless it was accompanied by vilification. ('Sir,' Bulwer had written in parody of a letter from Westmacott to a prospective victim, 'I have received some anecdotes about you which I would not publish for the world if you will pay me ten pounds for them.')

'You're a friend of Mr Bulwer?' asked Maginn.

'I do not claim that honour,' said the clerk.

'Yet you are privy to his intentions?'

'I heard about them from Sir J. Doyle's secretary.'

'And where, pray, did he get this information?'

'From Mrs Wyndham Lewis. It was after Mrs Bulwer found a person in his rooms . . .'

His voice trailed away.

'What person?' Maginn asked gloomily.

'A woman.'

'Ah,' said Maginn, 'the brothel-keepers have taken command of London, and set the tone. We live in an immoral era, do we not, Westmacott?'

'Most immoral. The Rads are its chief corrupters.'

'Well,' said Maginn, 'there's many a Radical masquerading as a Tory.'

'Labels, sir! Labels!' said Westmacott. 'Your Lord Lyndhurst – '

'It's six months since I last saw him,' said Maginn. 'He had the delusion he was the Duke. Lyndhurst's always acted a part. He began life as a Radical – a democratic Jacobin – defending every revolutionary who came his way.'

'Lyndhurst isn't a man of scruple. He'll take any brief that's marked high enough.'

'Lord Liverpool's first brief to him was to be a Tory. Once he'd prosecuted Brandreth for the Crown, it was goodbye to his past. Mind you, he still likes a lily-thighed whore.'

Maginn finished his whisky, and the potman refilled his glass.

'I hear,' said the clerk, 'he's sharing Lady S. with Mr Disraeli. It shows a lack of political partiality.'

'I doubt he'd share anything with anyone,' said Maginn.

'I assure you it's true, sir. Heard it around the Inns of Court.'

'How d'you mean – "share"? They take it in turns? Or fore and aft?'

There was a roar of laughter.

'Well, I don't know how they do it,' said the clerk, blushing. 'But Lyndhurst takes her off to Paris. Then when she comes back, Disraeli takes care of her in Bucks.'

'It's true,' said another voice from the smoke. 'I was in Taunton for Disraeli's canvass. *The Chronicle* reported it. The Whigs don't let it go. Lady S. haunts him as I imagine Lyndhurst's haunted by Brandreth's ghost.'

'Disraeli should have no place in politics,' said Maginn savagely. 'He's a cheat. He went to Abbotsford to try and inveigle Sir Walter Scott and Lockhart into that affair of *The Representative*. He offered jobs right and left to lure writers from their occupation, and then deserted them. And at the end of it all, he landed Murray with a twenty thousand pound debt. That's Disraeli. And Lyndhurst – ' his voice choked – 'Lyndhurst had the gall to allege – '

'They say,' said the voice from the smoke, 'he's Lyndhurst's Ganymede.'

'Ganymede,' said Westmacott, 'never looked like that Portugee.'

'He cut a dash at Taunton, you know. The women went wild. You must admit, Doctor, he's a very striking fellow. A fine speaker – a fulminator. He's got a great talent for excitement. You should have heard the country gentlemen howl. He called O'Connell "an incendiary and a traitor".'

'You heard it, sir?' asked Maginn.

'No – but it was said.'

'Was it, indeed?' said Maginn with interest. 'That's criminal libel. Very ungracious, bearing in mind that O'Connell was an old friend.'

'Disraeli has no old friends,' said the voice. 'Only new ones.'

The inn began to empty. It was half past three, and the party broke up, leaving Maginn and Westmacott alone. For a time, they sat in silence, till Maginn said,

'Perhaps a paragraph or two in *The Age* – a note that Mr O'Connell and Mr Disraeli aren't so close as they were when Mr O'Connell commended Mr Disraeli to the electors of Wycombe.'

'Yes,' said Westmacott, writing. 'Perhaps a few monitory words on the debts of friendship.'

'With an epigraph, "Thy friendship oft hath made my heart to ache: do be my enemy – for friendship's sake." From Mr O'C. to Mr D.'

'Yes, excellent.'

The potman was swilling the tables, and Westmacott prepared to rise, but Maginn stayed him.

'I think something like this: "At a time when the duty of an aristocracy, professing to uphold the Throne and our Gracious Sovereign, should be set to standards for the people – "'

Westmacott wrote as Maginn spoke.

' " – we cannot but regret the profligacy of conduct which some of its members exhibit – no, flaunt. That Lady S.'s

149

cavaliere servente or *cicerone*, as he may prefer to call himself, advertises publicly a liaison which contradicts propriety, is his affair. But it is timely for us to say that the Party which supports Sir Robert Peel, a gentleman of immaculate domestic life, should think carefully before admitting to its ranks and to the cause of Throne and Church one whose conduct morality must reprehend." '

'Good,' said Westmacott as Maginn paused. 'Then a few words about O'Connell.' He wrote, ' "Mr O'C. is not normally the beneficiary of our admiration or advice. Yet it is impossible to ignore the Christian charity – no, meekness – with which he has borne the criminal charge of being an incendiary and a traitor lately levelled against him at Taunton by his friend B. Dis." How's that?'

'Very good – very good indeed. Then you can again put in the couplet – "Thy friendship oft hath made my heart to ache: do be my enemy – for friendship's sake." '

Westmacott blew his nose with a handkerchief like a duster, and said,

'I think that will do it very well. What is there to add?'

'Nothing,' said Maginn, raising his heavy frame from his chair and balancing himself with his fingers splayed on the table. 'Nothing. But make sure that O'Connell gets a copy. Disraeli too.'

Chapter Ten

In the ante-room of the main hall of the Anne Street Chapel in Dublin, Daniel O'Connell unfolded the newspaper a second time, and read the extract which his anonymous correspondent had surrounded in a square of black ink as if it were a funeral announcement.

'Do we now go in, Mr O'Connell?' asked the chairman, Fergus Maguire.

From outside rose the sound of the audience, a clatter of feet on the wooden boards, a roar of talk.

'Not yet,' O'Connell replied in the authoritative voice with which he had commanded so many assemblies in Parliament, in the courts, and in the Dublin streets. 'I must read this again.'

He hesitated.

'You say it came from London?'

'Yes,' said Maguire.

O'Connell stood, towering with his broad, muscular body over Maguire, and then walked up and down, shaking his head.

'I can't allow it,' he said, 'I can't allow it . . . "An incendiary and a traitor." ' He threw the copy of *The Age* on the ground. 'Why should Disraeli speak of me like that? I've never done him an injury. I – ' he didn't finish the sentence. His son Morgan who was standing at his side, said,

'You're used to calumnies and lies, Father. You'd do better to ignore him. After all, he's spent the last two years looking for principles to betray when he hasn't been genuflecting to some peer or toadying to a duchess. He's a man who counts his dinner-parties as others count their game bags.'

'No,' said O'Connell emphatically. 'No. I must answer him. These are criminal libels.'

'They are provocations,' said Morgan. 'They want you to call them out. I beg of you – ignore them. They want to provoke you so that they can kill you with impunity. What they want is an assassination, not a challenge.'

'I've never flinched from a challenge,' said O'Connell sombrely. 'Despite my oath!'

D'Esterre. Twenty years before, when he was already forty, his enemies had embroiled him in a duel with D'Esterre. It was their habit. Whenever he spoke for his fellow Catholics, there was always someone to find an opportunity to challenge him to a fight, or, if he declined, to impugn his courage. So it had been when he used the word 'beggarly' to describe the Corporation of Dublin, and the Castle party had nominated D'Esterre, one of the Merchants' Guild, to provoke him.

He had refused to fight, not, as he said to himself, out of cowardice but because he could never believe that a trial by ordeal could settle a cause. But then, through Sir Edward

Stanley, D'Esterre's second, he had received a direct and unavoidable challenge which he had been forced to accept.

On Wednesday, February 1st, 1815 – the date was impressed on his memory – he had risen from the side of his sleeping wife, from whom he had concealed the affair, kissed her and his children on the forehead, and then driven twelve miles from Dublin with three of his friends. They met D'Esterre's party at Bishopcourt, near Naas, in a clearing where the wood led down to a bog, and in the cold air at first light, with the horses steaming with sweat, he had knelt on the damp grass and prayed; then he crossed himself and rose, his hands trembling, as he folded them inside his cloak.

He had been given, he didn't know how, the choice of ground. Perhaps the master of the duel, Sir Peter O'Rourke, had tossed a coin. Should he place his opponent with the light over the bog behind him, or might the sun rise and dazzle him at the moment of his pistol shot? It didn't matter. Everything was part of a dream, which would soon be over. He had chosen the background of the trees.

The handkerchief fell with O'Rourke's shout. He could see D'Esterre's face, pallid, his eyes tense as if to ask why he, a plump and contented merchant who hitherto had known only prosperity, stood in a waterlogged field, far from his wife and children. And in that second, as O'Connell fired almost simultaneously with D'Esterre, he realized that he was alive and that D'Esterre, struck in the hip, was dying, surrounded by his aghast friends and the sombre surgeon.

He had knelt again and prayed for D'Esterre, and vowed never again to engage in a duel.

'What they can't bear is that I should have allied myself with the Whigs for the sake of Ireland and the Catholic cause,' said O'Connell. 'But the balance of power is in our hands, and we'll teach the Tories a lesson. That's what these scribblers are afraid of. But Disraeli – '

'I think the meeting's getting impatient,' said Maguire as a trampling noise rose from the hall, accompanied by the clapping of hands. O'Connell drew himself up with the histrionic port of his head which had made juries quail in front of him, and advanced with a stern, unsmiling expression, through the narrow door on to the platform now lit by the bright April sun shining into the sour-smelling hall.

As soon as he entered, the whole audience on the floor and in the gallery rose to their feet clapping and shouting, 'Lib – er – ator!' in an ovation that went on and on.

'There must be over a thousand here,' said Maguire with satisfaction, and after a few moments when O'Connell had taken his seat, he stood and the audience gradually fell quiet.

'My friends,' the chairman began, 'there are times in the life of a nation when its spirit is represented by a single man. I speak of Daniel O'Connell.'

Immediately there were renewed shouts of 'Liberator!', calls, and cheers for Daniel O'Connell.

'I needn't tell you,' Maguire went on, 'of the hundred battles which he has fought in the courts and in Parliament for the right of Ireland to achieve its independence and fulfil its destiny, to worship in a manner appropriate to itself and to permit its people to enjoy the benefits of a free, an uncolonized and an unconquered country.'

He turned to O'Connell, who was sitting with his heavy face lowered, waiting restlessly for the chairman's eulogy to end.

'Gentlemen,' Maguire went on, 'if Daniel O'Connell has been called an agitator for founding the Irish Volunteers for the Repeal of the Union, if he's been arrested for conspiring to evade the proclamations from the Castle, it is because he has dared to be a patriot. Today he continues to fight for a repeal of the Legislative Union by which repeal alone the peace and well-being of Ireland can be preserved.'

When O'Connell rose, the whole audience rose again with cheers. In his dark green surtout, with his arms outstretched and raised in a gesture that was half benediction and half embrace to his compatriots with the pale grey faces, the farmers and the peasants and the ragged labourers who had come on foot from the villages and the city to hear him, O'Connell stood as if surprised at his welcome.

Waving down his audience, he spoke in a quiet, almost casual voice, so that the listeners had to strain their ears to hear what he was saying. He began with a contemptuous reference to the King's Speech, which had deplored 'attempts to excite the people of Ireland to demand a repeal of the Legislative Union'.

The audience groaned. Still in the same half-audible tones, O'Connell described how he had opposed the paragraph in the Debate on the Address. He had spoken, he recalled, for five hours, in a debate which had continued for nine days, though in the end his Motion had been defeated by 523 to 38, with only one English Member voting in the minority.

The audience groaned again.

From there he went on to talk about the Coercion Act which successive governments had prolonged. The Castle, he said, that stronghold of privilege and Toryism, had become an Augean stable. Lord Duncannon – more groans from the audience – had done nothing for Ireland. The Tories had now taken over, but happily it was the Irish Members who held the balance, and as far as he was concerned, speaking as an Irishman, that balance would be held in favour of Lord Melbourne and the Whigs.

There was a mutter of agreement from the floor.

'No one,' O'Connell went on, 'will be allowed to challenge or impugn my principles. When that bloated buffoon Lord Alvanley asked the price Lord Melbourne paid for my support, I'm proud to say, gentlemen, my son Morgan – ' he put his hand on his shoulder – 'defended me and exchanged shots with that bully on Wimbledon Common in token that an Irish patriot cannot be insulted with impunity!'

There was a roar of applause, and O'Connell stopped and drank a glass of water.

'But I must say,' he went on, 'of all the calumnies which have been directed against me in our Association, and that means everyone in this great hall, none has surprised and, may I perhaps say, disheartened me more than the attack by Mr Benjamin Disraeli at Taunton.'

He scanned the faces in the hall, prolonging their expectancy, and said,

'I observe from your silence that Mr Disraeli is unknown, at least to the majority of you. Very well then! Let me give you

a brief characterization of this man, who has had the impertinence to describe me as an "incendiary and traitor" – ' he
repeated the words – 'an incendiary and a traitor – the one a
qualification for transportation, the other for the gallows.'

A great sigh of disapproval passed through the hall.

'Now Mr Disraeli has lately been a candidate for Parliament,
a search which has led him from Wycombe to Taunton. He's a
political pedlar. More than that, he's a man who perhaps more
rightly deserves the title of a superlative blackguard, both in
his private as well as his public life, than anyone I've ever met
with before.'

O'Connell paused.

'He's an author, I believe, of a couple of novels – ' he made
it seem a base and trivial occupation – 'and that was all I knew
about him until 1831 or 1832, when, being about to stand for
High Wycombe, he wrote to me requesting a letter of recommendation to the electors . . . He claimed to be a Radical
libertarian. So naturally I gave him the testimonial he had
begged . . . Well, what happened next? Disraeli took my letter
with him, got it printed, placarded it everywhere – and failed.
Then I heard he was a candidate for Marylebone; there too he
failed. As you may imagine with a man so lacking in principle,
he got tired of being a Radical after these two defeats, and
thought he'd try his chance as a Tory. And so he stands the
other day at Taunton, and by way of currying favour with the
electors, calls me "an incendiary and a traitor".'

He paused again and clenched his fists on the lectern.

'Now, gentlemen, my answer to this piece of gratuitous
impertinence is that he is an egregious liar. He's a liar both in
action and words.' The audience shouted its approval. 'Liar!
Liar!'

'Now the question is, shall such a vile creature be tolerated?'
O'Connell's voice rose.

'Disraeli is a living lie; and England is degraded by tolerating
a miscreant of his abominable description.'

O'Connell had spoken the words at the top of his voice, but
now he said rapidly as if in an aside, 'The language is harsh, I
must confess; but it's no more than deserved, and if I should
apologize for using it, it's because I can find no harsher

epithets in the English language by which to convey the utter abhorrence which I entertain for such a reptile.'

The audience stamped its agreement as if it were stamping Disraeli into the ground. O'Connell wiped his mouth with a linen handkerchief.

'He is just fit now, after being twice discarded by the people, to become a Tory. He has all the necessary requisites of perfidy, selfishness, depravity and want of principle which qualify him for the change.'

Then he went on in a conversational tone, turning to another aspect of the matter,

'His name shows he's of Jewish origin. I don't say this as a term of reproach; there are many most respectable Jews. I honour them. I have urged their rights. But there are among them, as in every other people, some who are of the lowest and most disgusting grade of moral turpitude; and of those I look upon Mr Disraeli as the worst. He has just the qualities of the impenitent thief on the Cross. Yes, indeed, he has. And I really believe that if Mr Disraeli's family were to be examined and his genealogy traced, Mr Benjamin Disraeli would be discovered to be the heir-at-law of the – the *exalted* individual to whom I allude.'

The crash of laughter from the whole hall continued for half a minute till the chairman rose and asked for silence. O'Connell, who had been smiling, changed his expression like an actor into one of bitter contempt.

'My friends, I forgive Mr Disraeli now. Let us leave him as the lineal descendant of the blasphemous robber who ended his career beside the Founder of the Christian faith.'

Disraeli was happy.

For the first of the masked balls in aid of the Royal Academy of Music, the patrons – three of the much-feared ladies who presided over Almack's – had taken the Hanover Square Rooms and transformed them into a vast marquee of gold with tented dependencies for sitting-out. He disliked dancing, since he had only learned the steps and figures, and then through imitation, when he was already a grown man, too late to excel. Yet he liked the ambience, the music, the chatter with groups of aloof young men who had hated their dancing masters at school and now preferred, instead of dancing, to lean against the pillars and study the women.

He was happy because he had arrived in a fashionable party that included D'Orsay, Bulwer, Lord Stanley and Talbot, and had then joined the Chesterfields and the Ansons. He himself was dressed as a corsair with a white, long-sleeved silken shirt, open at the neck, a red sash, chains like stalactites, pleated pantaloons and a foulard around his head, a happy counterpart to Lady Chesterfield who, apart from her fair skin, was a sultana even to her turban. Lady Burghersh and Lady Fitzroy Somerset were dressed as Pompadours, but it was Lady Londonderry as Cleopatra, her eyes made up with kohl visible through her mask, her arms naked and be-bangled, her brow draped with diamond pendants and her dress embroidered with emeralds and brilliants, who caught everyone's attention. Quite early in the evening, the young Lord Castlereagh had limped over to Disraeli and said grumpily, 'A lady wishes to meet you.' Disraeli followed him to Lady Londonderry, and Castlereagh presented him. Taking her outstretched hand, he said,

'After today, madam, they'll say Cleopatra looked like Lady Londonderry.'

She smiled, a royal person accepting homage.

'And what did Cleopatra really look like?'

> '*For her own person,*' he answered,
> *It beggar'd all description; she did lie*
> *In her pavilion – cloth-of-gold of tissue –*
> *O'erpicturing that Venus where we see*
> *The fancy outwork nature.*'

'That's very beautiful, Mr Disraeli,' said Lady Londonderry. 'Do continue.'

'Alas,' said Disraeli, looking at Castlereagh's pock-marked face, 'what follows is less apt.

> '*– On each side her*
> *Stood pretty dimpled boys, like smiling Cupids*
> *With divers-colour'd fans . . .*'

Lady Londonderry waved her own feathered fan, and said,

'No, it's scarcely appropriate – though the company today is as agreeable as it's fanciful. I must talk to the Duke of Wellington, who looks like a sheep who's lost his fleece. Actually, he lent it to Lord Wilton.'

Disraeli turned towards the nobleman dressed as a Spanish grandee in a golden fleece set in diamonds.

'Philip IV,' said Lady Londonderry.

'I imagine he has his royal guards,' said Disraeli.

'Yes,' said Castlereagh. 'They are especially on the *qui vive* against corsairs.'

But Disraeli was happy. He had fought a by-election in Taunton at the end of April, and though the Whigs were back under Melbourne, he had defiantly declared himself a Tory, a fully-fledged Tory invited by Granville Somerset, a former member of the Government, to stand as a candidate. Yes, he had lost at Taunton, but he had been nominated for membership of the Carlton Club, in face of the threats of a black-ball by some of his ill-wishers. The contest had exhilarated him. Last year at Wycombe, he had put a good face on his third failure, leaving behind him a body of dedicated admirers, among them Squire and Mrs Lowther, who had both wiped away a tear at his farewell banquet. In Taunton, by contrast, he was a fresh and stimulating figure, untarnished by defeat. At Wycombe he had learnt how to handle the squirearchy, and the country gentlemen of Taunton, now flocking to his support, were full of praise that he knew their problems so well. What did it matter that his speeches were interrupted by a rabble gang shouting in cadence, 'Jew! Jew! Jew!'? What did it matter that there were malign whispers about Lady S., as the local Whig newspapers called her? What did it matter that the regular insult was to call him an apostate? His shoulders had become calloused to that cross he would have to bear through life.

The election had been exhausting; nine hours a day of canvassing, badinage and repartee, to a background of cheers, counter-cheers, the whole combined with an episode of dodging the bailiffs. Yes, the experience had been exhausting but not wasted.

Now that he was in command of his political principles, he felt that he could command his voters. Peel in his Tamworth Manifesto had shown that the Tories had assimilated what was best in the thinking of their critics, himself among them. There was, indeed, nothing so irresistible as an idea that had found a spokesman. Like Molière's M. Jourdain who suddenly realized that he had been speaking prose all his life, Disraeli felt that even at his most radical, he had expressed ideas which were the essence of a self-renewing Tory Party. The protection of the territorial interest, a proper regard for the manufacturing classes, an acceptance of the rights of labourers and mechanics and their place in the nation, the consolidation of the monarchy and a repairing of the fabric of the Established Church – those had always been his political objects, and he saw their fulfilment in the Tory Party.

Disraeli felt happy.

He looked up, and saw Mrs Wyndham Lewis, the wife of the Member for Maidstone, standing at his side. For a moment, he thought she was Mrs Austen, so startling was the resemblance, although on inspecting her again, he thought she was several years older than Sara. He had met her a few times before, once at a political breakfast at her house, and he had observed that although she was an insistent 'rattle', many of the leading Tories paid her a considerable respect, no doubt from deference to her husband, an iron and steel grandee who had made many substantial contributions to the Party.

'Will you dance with me, Mr Disraeli?' she asked. 'Mr Lewis isn't well, and couldn't attend.'

He greeted her, and she went on breathlessly, 'I am Calpurnia, a Roman matron, the costumiers assure me, but I believe a Vestal Virgin. Can you tell the difference?'

'The subject,' Disraeli said, 'would require examination.'

She smoothed the white dress that exposed her shoulders, and said,

'I think I must be a Vestal because of the fillets in my hair. Now, Mrs Norton – what is she?'

Disraeli followed her glance to Mrs Norton and Mrs Blackwood, standing together, masked, in white robes.

'A priestess,' said Disraeli.

'A Roman, like me?'

'No, a Greek.'

'Ah, well,' said Mrs Lewis, 'I always get them mixed. I can never remember who came first – the Romans or the Greeks.'

Disraeli saw Henrietta smiling at him, trapped by Mrs Lewis. When the Duke of Wellington passed and gave Mrs Lewis a specially ceremonious greeting, she offered him a slight curtsey, and when the Duke hesitated and passed, she asked, 'Shall we now dance, Mr Disraeli?'

'I should be honoured, madam, he replied.' He looked at her again. She was nothing like Mrs Austen. The Duke's greeting had somehow transformed her.

'And how?' asked Henrietta across the table, 'is the honourable Member for Lincoln?'

Bulwer took off his mask, and with his glass of champagne in his hand, sat himself in the place that Disraeli had left.

'A rather sad travesty of a French marquis,' he said. His powdered wig made him feel hot, and he wanted the evening to end. Henrietta, a Watteau shepherdess, was by contrast enjoying herself. 'No glum people,' was Lady Cork's fiat on some other occasion, and tonight Henrietta agreed. She had received a generous if rather poignant letter from her husband in Venice which assured her both of her allowance and his continuing attachment to her. He was ill, he said, in his dictated letter, but it had a postscript in his own hand that ended, 'I cannot use another's pen to write of my affection for you.' Well, so be it. This was a time for grace, not glumness.

'You must be happy tonight, Bulwer.'

'Why?'

'Everyone is happy. It's the fashion.'

His eyes became sombre, and she said more seriously, and half in inquiry,

'You miss Rosina?'

'I don't think so,' he said. 'No, I don't think so. Since we parted – since I've been living as a bachelor at Albany, my life has been more tranquil.'

'Is tranquillity enough?'

'For the time being,' said Bulwer.

'But I still don't understand,' said Henrietta. 'You and Rosina loved each other so much. I heard you were so happy in Italy.'

Bulwer shook his head.

'It was a disaster. When we were in Naples – '

'You were with the Stanhopes?'

'They'd left,' said Bulwer, giving her a side glance. 'I found Rosina excessively – ' he repeated the word in italics – '*excessively* in the company of a Neapolitan prince. It's strange, Henrietta. Jealousy is a most powerful aphrodisiac. I could have betrayed her a thousand times, and felt an untroubled indifference. In Naples, I felt a rage – an unspeakable rage at the affront – it was an injury to my dignity – and our return to England was a mixture of murderous and amorous frenzy in a rattling, uncomfortable coach.'

'And why didn't your reconciliation last?'

'The aphrodisiac spent itself. Back in London, I was no longer jealous – no longer menaced.'

Disraeli rejoined the table, and raised his glass to Bulwer.

'A new amalgamation of Tories and Radicals?' someone called out.

'We share two unshakable enthusiasms – Lady Sykes – '
Bulwer toasted her.

'And Lord Durham,' Disraeli said boldly.

'To Radical Jack!' said a drunken *mousquetaire* tauntingly.

'To the most honourable of men!' said Disraeli.

'And of statesmen!' said Bulwer.

'Damn his eyes!' said the *mousquetaire*.

'It's a mazurka,' said Mrs Wyndham Lewis, taking the *mousquetaire*'s hand and drawing him to the dance floor as Bulwer glared in fury. 'Every Polish count should know the mazurka.'

'But I'm a musketeer, not a mazurkist!' the receding voice protested.

The others laughed.

'How does one deal with an insulting ruffian in public?' Henrietta asked.

'For my part,' said Disraeli, 'I bow and walk away.'

'Why is it,' Disraeli asked as he danced with Henrietta, 'I can only perform the mazurka with you?'

She looked at him joyfully and said,

'Because we share the same pleasures. Oh, Ben – I'm happy. After Lyndhurst's dinner, we'll go home together?'

Disraeli had wanted to talk to Lyndhurst about the prospects of a General Election, and at first he wanted to say, 'No.' Taunton had been, in a sense, a holiday from love, and yet each night and morning his heart had beaten with a loud and emphatic memory, even though there were times now when he would have liked to disengage himself from an attachment which had become a compulsion. What shall we do tonight? Where shall we go tomorrow? What are you doing today, next week? When he protested at her curiosity and insistence, she had replied, 'Would you wish me to be indifferent?' And that was true. He needed her care and concern. He needed an audience in front of which he could rehearse his ambitions without pretence. After the abuse which was part of his destiny, the other part being acclaim, he wanted comfort.

'We'll go home together?' she repeated.

'Yes,' he said. 'Let's not stay very late.'

Henrietta looked over her shoulder, and Disraeli said,

'I have in my arms the most beautiful – the most desired woman in the room.'

'And what about Lady Londonderry?'

'She has asked me to dine at Rosebank – on the Thames.'

'She didn't mention it to me,' said Henrietta, pouting. 'Some people are more masked without their masks than when they wear them.'

Disraeli tightened his arm around her waist.

'She asked me if she might invite you too.'

Henrietta murmured, 'Thank you . . . Who is that man by the pillar who keeps staring at you?'

They were dancing towards a broken-nosed man in evening dress who stood masked and alone. As they approached, he stepped forward and said with a slight Irish accent,

'A letter for you, Mr Disraeli. It's urgent, now.'

Within a second he had withdrawn, and Disraeli stopped dancing as he studied the envelope with his name written in a literate hand under the heading, 'By express.'

'Read it, my darling,' said Henrietta. 'I'll wait.'

He drew her into an empty alcove, and took from the envelope a report from a Dublin newspaper headed, 'Mr O'Connell Teaches Manners to Mr Disraeli.' An anonymous note inside said, 'Mr O'Connell's reprobation of the apostate will be published in the London papers tomorrow.'

'What is it, Ben?' Henrietta asked anxiously. 'You've gone white as death.'

He didn't answer, but put the envelope and the letter in his pocket.

'Let us continue with our dance,' he said.

Chapter Eleven

Henrietta awoke with the sound of a Weber waltz in her mind. The whole evening had been music – the ball, the supper at Lyndhurst's house in George Street, and the night that had ended in exhaustion and a brief sleep from which the clamouring birds had roused her. She put out her hand idly, and stirred her body, searching in the warm sheets for her lover. 'Ben!' she said, her eyes closed. 'Ben – my darling!' She felt secure and contented. Her children were at Basildon, her husband was in Venice, and Ben, whom she now needed every day of her life like a nourishment, was at her side. She reached out to touch his head, but her fingers found only the crumpled pillow, and she opened her eyes to see that the bedclothes had been thrown back and Disraeli was no longer there.

It was already dawn, and she rose hurriedly, putting on the silk dressing-gown that lay at the bottom of the bed, and drew the curtains. The sky was opalescent, nacred with reflections of delicate pink and saffron, and she stood looking out at the honey-coloured stone of the houses opposite in the silent square, and the tree-tops yellow in the early light. In the distance a cock was crowing, and it was strange, she thought, that in the year 1835 London, where drovers came with their cattle and sheep grazed in the open spaces, was still like a Norfolk town. The air was fresh, and she breathed deeply, happily. Her body was at peace, saturated with love. She wanted Disraeli to be at her side again with his head on her breast, his limbs twined in hers, silent and floating. Floating. It was his word. Floating for hours like something ethereal, beyond the reach of her sister Maria with her constant doom-laden warnings, and her prim and autocratic father whose face frowned at her from his portrait on the opposite wall; sound-less, beyond the din of the world that would intrude too soon into their lives again.

Beyond the reach of Ben's enemies. Once, in Wycombe, she had heard him address a political meeting. He had begun quietly, rather affectedly, with the hesitation of an ibis, some-one said, that had wandered into a field of geese; and then, throwing away his uncertainties, he had made his audience roar with laughter, rage and enthusiasm. At the end, the applause had gone on and on. His opponents had tried to deflate him with cries of 'Old clothes!' and 'Jew boy!', but Ben hadn't quailed. As the interruptions multiplied, his voice had become stronger till, at last tired of their own monotony and worn down by the counter-cheers, his adversaries had faded away. It was a success she never wanted to observe again.

A pistol shot made the glass in the windows and the scent bottles on her dressing-table tremble and dance, while for a few seconds the room was darkened by a flutter of startled birds. Henrietta stood quivering, resting her hands on the table to control them. The breeze blew the muslin curtain in her face, but she didn't move. When it fell away, she saw that the cabinet where her husband kept his duelling pistols was open, and she said aloud, 'No – no!' and walked slowly towards it, feeling her knees dissolving with terror. One of the pistols was missing.

'Ben!' she called aloud. 'Ben – Ben!'

She rushed into his room, and found it empty. Then, with her hair falling over her shoulders, she hurried past the servants who had crept out of the attic and basement to see what was going on.

'Ben!' she called. 'Ben!'

Her voice was a wail as she went from room to room in a vain exploration.

A second pistol shot, still louder this time, from the small terrace made the chandeliers rattle. Dragging apart the curtains in the drawing-room, she saw Disraeli outside in an open-necked white shirt and black trousers calmly reloading the pistol. The door had jammed and she had to shake it open, and then she stood weeping at the top of the stone steps.

'Why are you crying?' Disraeli said coolly as he finished loading.

'I thought,' she sobbed, 'I thought – Francis had come back – and – '

Disraeli took her in his arms, and soothed her.

'I shouldn't worry about that. Now if he saw me using his pistol – that would be another matter! He'd be entitled to object. Pray go back to bed – the morning air is treacherous. No – watch! I'm learning how to use this weapon.'

He put her behind him, and with his left hand on his hip took careful aim at a wine bottle standing against a wall about twenty yards away. A manual on small arms lay on the bench at his side, and he lowered the pistol without firing.

'Listen to this. "The pressure on the trigger," ' he read aloud, ' "should be sustained rather than brutal, a caress not an assault." It makes poetry of death. Let's see.'

He raised his arm again, and pressed the trigger, and the bullet, hitting the wall several feet from the bottle, sent dusty fragments of sandstone into the air.

Disraeli shook his head.

'I'm damnably short-sighted.'

The bottle stood undaunted, almost with a sneer, on its ledge. Dropping his flippant style, Disraeli said,

'I'm going to fight Morgan O'Connell.'

'But why?' she asked, taking his arm agitatedly as he laid down the pistol. 'What about? What harm has he done you?'

'His father has insulted me – but he won't fight.'

Disraeli's valet Baum, struggling into his jacket, arrived hurriedly.

'Do you need me, sir?' he asked.

'Yes,' said Disraeli. 'Clean my pistol.'

Baum quickly took the pistol and ran into the house.

'What does it matter?' Henrietta said as they climbed the stairs together. 'You've been insulted so many times – politicians have to be insulted as women have to bear children.'

She closed the door behind them in the bedroom.

'Oh, Ben – please, Ben, don't fight. After last night – I don't know – I think we were reckless – there was so much love between us – and if because of it – '

Disraeli stroked her head absent-mindedly.

'You can't be a mariner,' he said, 'and never face a storm. We put to sea at times of our own choice. O'Connell abused me. The newspapers are full of the vile reports. Later today, I will see D'Orsay and ask him to arrange matters.'

'Come, Ben,' said Henrietta, leading him back to the bed. 'You look so tired. Rest your darling head on me. Oh, dearest one – ' she began to cry again – 'if anything happened to you, I'd die. I'd kill myself.'

He didn't answer, and within a few moments he fell into a deep sleep, watched by Henrietta, her happiness all gone and replaced by the thought of a bullet like the one that had splintered the wall, shattering the white brow above the dark lids, and turning it into a scarlet bouquet.

D'Orsay's handsome face was earnest as Disraeli discussed with him the service he required. Lady Blessington, with her deep affection for Bulwer and Disraeli, her favourites in the circle of friends who had defended her against the taunts and jeers of London society, looked even more unhappy.

'You must treat O'Connell with sublimity,' she said.

Disraeli waited for D'Orsay's judgment. He was, after all, London's *arbiter elegantiarum*.

'Every woman in London is in love with Count D'Orsay,' Lady Cork had once said. 'And half the men!'

It was certainly true that D'Orsay with his quiet elegance, his astounding good looks and his impeccable horsemanship was a model for the *ton*. Indeed, so excellent were these qualities that he might have become one of the least popular men in town, had it not been for the notoriety of his debts, his preference for cards over women, his young wife's early desertion, and the whispered belief that he and Lady Blessington dined but didn't sleep together. But added to all this was a characteristic which even those who called him a coxcomb had to admit – he was generous as well as chivalrous; courteous to the humble and indifferent to the arrogant. There was no misfortune which D'Orsay couldn't transmute by the alchemy of his character into an occasion for hope, no weakness of human nature which he couldn't forgive, since, even when he was its victim, he saw it as an extrapolation of some quality in himself.

'Come,' said D'Orsay, 'surely Lady Blessington is right. The proper attitude is indifference.'

'No,' replied Disraeli excitedly. 'The only answer to one blow is two. I've come to ask you to manage the affair, D'Orsay. You have some experience of these matters.'

He was sitting in a chair looking up at D'Orsay, who was examining himself in a new frock-coat in front of a lookingglass. It seemed to Disraeli that D'Orsay was taking the matter too calmly, and that he was more concerned with the cut of his trousers than with Disraeli's life or death problems.

'You must listen to the letter I've drafted for the newspapers,' he said.

'Of course – of course,' said D'Orsay, looking over his shoulder to examine how his clothes sat. 'But you mustn't be immoderate, Ben. In an affair of honour, victory always goes to the one least agitated. How d'you like the colour of my trousers?'

Disraeli was shuffling with his papers and didn't answer.

'No – tell me,' said D'Orsay. '*Cuisse de nymphe effrayée* – it's the colour they're wearing in Paris this season. Fawn with a blush. Do you like it?'

'It's very becoming. Do, I beg you, sit down and let me read my letter to O'Connell.'

With a final glance at himself in the mirror, D'Orsay took an armchair in front of Disraeli, and prepared to listen.

' "Mr O'Connell" ' – Disraeli began, and looked up. 'You observe, D'Orsay, that I don't dignify him with an invocation. . . . "Mr O'Connell, although you have long placed yourself out of the pale of civilization, still I will not be insulted even by a Yahoo without chastising it." '

'Yahoo?' D'Orsay asked.

'Yes,' said Disraeli self-appreciatively. 'It gives me the opportunity of using the word "it" to characterize that monster, O'Connell.'

He went on,

' "When I read this morning your virulent attack on myself and knowing that your son had paid the penalty of your similar virulence to another individual on whom you had dropped your filth – " '

'Filth? *Ça c'est très fort – peut-être trop fort,*' murmured D'Orsay.

' "I called upon your son to reassume his vicarious office of yielding satisfaction for his shrinking sire." '

'Now that's good,' commented D'Orsay. ' "Shrinking sire" I like very much. But when did you write to Morgan O'Connell?'

'This morning,' said Disraeli glumly. 'Here is a copy of the letter.' He produced a sheet of paper from his pocket, and read,

'To Mr Morgan O'Connell, MP
    Sir,
    As you have established yourself as the champion of your father, I have the honour to request your notice to a very scurrilous attack which he has made upon my conduct and character.

    Had Mr O'Connell, according to the practice observed among gentlemen, appealed to me respecting the accuracy of the reported expressions before he indulged in offensive comments upon them, he would, if he can be influenced by a sense of justice, have felt that such comments were unnecessary. He has not thought fit to do so, and he leaves me no alternative but to request that you, his son, will resume your vicarious duties of yielding satisfaction for the insults which your father has too long lavished with impunity upon his political opponents.

I have the honour to be, Sir,

Your obedient servant,
B. Disraeli.'

'Now it's getting serious,' said D'Orsay, standing again. 'Morgan won't hide behind his father. When you call his father a – what do you call it? – a Yahoo? – he will certainly fight.'

'It's what I wish,' said Disraeli. 'O'Connell believes that because he killed D'Esterre years ago, he can berate and insult his betters from the privileged sanctuary of a false principle. That can't be tolerated. You must call on Morgan, and present him with my challenge.'

'Ben – Ben – Ben,' sighed D'Orsay, putting his arm around his shoulder. 'We can't be answerable for the sins of our fathers. I should be very reluctant to do penance for my own. Let's have a glass of madeira and consider this business calmly.'

'No,' said Disraeli, disengaging himself. 'There are times when we place our destiny on the table like a wager. It's irrevocable. We can't turn back. I wouldn't want to condemn myself to a lifetime of regret if I felt I might have vindicated myself – if I'd only had the courage.'

'Do you need to prove it?'

'To the world – yes. To Lady Sykes, who is insulted with me,' said Disraeli. 'I ask you as my friend to be my second.'

A frown came over D'Orsay's face, giving it an unpleasant air.

'I can't.'

'You won't?'

'I can't. *Ne sois pas en colère avec moi, cher Disraeli.* I would willingly help you, but I can't. It is impossible for me to interfere in an affair which has a political bias. You see – ' and he brightened up – 'when I arrived at Calais some years ago there was a little man who sat in a little hut – and he was *le douanier.* And he said, "You are admitted to England, M. le Comte, but you are a foreigner, are you not?" "I am," I replied. Then he said, "Since you are a foreigner and a French-man, you mustn't engage in any political activity, and you must report to the police when you change your address." So you see, Ben, the key to the whole matter. I'm a foreigner, and it would be a highly political matter if I arranged for you to kill the liberator of Ireland or even his son.'

'Yes,' said Disraeli reluctantly. 'I understand.'

'But,' said D'Orsay, a sudden smile showing his strong white teeth, 'I have a better idea. I'll get Harry Baillie – Colonel Baillie – to be your second, and I will arrange everything – yes, I will personally arrange it.'

He embraced Disraeli warmly, and said,

'Have no fear, *cher ami*. If the result is mortal, it will at least take place in style.'

For the hundredth time, Disraeli visualized the prospective duel as if it were a scene in a drama that he was writing – the dialogue, the voices, the setting. And still his heart beat faster, his fingers clutching the side of the chair, and when he rose to walk up and down the room, a tremor in the legs persisted. He wanted to write to his father and to Sarah, but as soon as he took up the quill his hand couldn't shape the letters. Henrietta? If he died, would she weep for a day, perhaps a week? She would wear a becoming black. Would she forget the two years that had been a music of love, pleasure, excitement? How soon would she return to balls, to the opera, to parties on the river, to excursions and country houses? Disraeli shrugged his shoulders. Why not? Anyone who could survive the first week of mourning a lost love could be sure that eventually some other love would extinguish the pain. It wasn't true that the sadness was for those who stayed behind. It was far harder to have to leave a writing desk filled with unfinished manuscripts, the first chapters of a novel about Henrietta, for even as he had lived his life with her, he had seen it as a romance as well as a reality, a romance disturbed only by the twin monsters of envy and malice like *The Age* and his debts. He smiled wryly. The debts he could endure. It was the creditors he couldn't stand.

Dyspepsia made him long for a civil war, but the duns made him yearn for death itself. How melancholy it was to look at the invitation cards over the fireplace with the neat A – 'accepted' – in the corner for next week, next month that might never come! His anger and hurt hadn't diminished. He still wanted to make the O'Connells pay with a physical wound for the cruel insult, although the idea of actually killing O'Connell or his son wasn't in his mind since, even now, he still felt admiration for the Irishman. The report in the newspapers that had so incensed O'Connell was a deliberately garbled version of what he had said. He had never called O'Connell an incendiary and a traitor, and he could understand that the Irish leader had resented the insults. He believed, too, that the messenger who had given him the advance copy of *The Times* at the ball had been sent by Maginn – perhaps it was Maginn himself – hoping to embroil at one stroke two men he detested. But it was too late for reason. Until O'Connell had suffered an injury as great as his own, he would feel diminished, unable to move in public or even in society with the sublime independence which he had set as his own standard for himself.

Unlike his brothers, Disraeli himself had never wanted to kill even a pheasant, but he accepted that the O'Connells might take a different view of him. Lord Castlereagh had fought Canning, and the duel remained a famous example of courage vindicated and insults expunged without bloodshed. But O'Connell had already killed a man. Yes, the O'Connells might take a different view.

D'Esterre – Disraeli – D'Esterre – D'Israeli. The names succeeded each other in time with the clock's pendulum. It was already past midnight, and still there was no reply from Morgan. Yet it had to come. His second, Colonel Baillie, had called on Morgan O'Connell, and the reply could not be long delayed. Disraeli poured for himself a glass of cognac, and drank it in a single draught. Suddenly as his face began to glow, he felt released.

Yes, he would fight. He would fight, relying on his *baraka* to preserve him. He would fight, and if he died, he would be remembered by those who loved him and a posterity that would honour him. But if he lived – *if* he lived – he would have acquitted himself well. He lay in an armchair without undressing, sleepless and dozing till the next morning.

At nine a.m. Baum opened the door and ushered in Baillie.

'I'm sorry,' said Baillie at once. 'O'Connell won't apologize.'

'Ah!' said Disraeli sombrely. 'Then he must fight.'

'Nor will he fight,' Baillie went on. 'Morgan says that fighting his father's traducers would be a full-time occupation, and that he is only prepared to do so once a year, and that he has already exhausted this year's quota.'

'The man's a coward,' said Disraeli, striking the table with his fist and standing, 'I will write and tell him so, and force him to fight.'

Baillie shrugged his shoulders.

'A refusal to fight, sir, should end the affair.'

Disraeli pondered, and then he said triumphantly as if to himself,

'We've thrashed them. That's all that matters.'

He shook Baillie's hand in gratitude for his service and said aloud, 'We've thrashed them.'

'Thank you, sir. I doubt if the O'Connells will show their faces in public for a little time.'

Just as Disraeli was drawing a deep breath of exultation, Baum came into the room and whispered.

'There is a policeman waiting for you outside,' his accent thickening.

For a moment, Disraeli didn't grasp what Baum had said, although he realized that the valet was dealing with a subject of the utmost confidentiality.

'A what?'

'A policeman,' Baum said loudly with a glance at Colonel Baillie.

'I will take my leave,' said Baillie, affecting not to have heard. 'I have to see D'Orsay.'

When he had gone, Baum ushered in a uniformed officer with a heavy moustache.

'Mr Disraeli, sir,' he said, 'I have a warrant to take you before Mr Bennett, the Marylebone magistrate, requiring you to keep the peace in connection with Mr Morgan and Mr Daniel O'Connell.'

'I see,' said Disraeli to Baum, who was listening respectfully but resignedly, 'I see that the O'Connells who reject the law in Ireland invoke it in England. Never mind! Pray wait a short while till I perform my toilet. Then get me my outdoor coat, Baum, the one with the velvet collar. I may need it in the cells.'

Later that day, Disraeli wrote to his father a letter that Baum took to Bradenham by the express diligence.

Dear Father,

I have trounced the O'Connells, and I hear on all sides approval for the way I comported myself. Most newspapers today carry my philippic against father and son, who in a harmonious duet have refused to fight.

Some have been critical of my adjectives, a few of my substantives, and my description of O'Connell *père* as a Yahoo is now firmly attached to him.

One minor inconvenience of my challenge is that this morning I was summoned before the Marylebone magistrate and ordered to be bound over in the sum of £500 to keep the peace. Of this sum, I have so far been able to raise only £300, and my Marylebone links have thus become for the time being rather more intimate than either you or I could wish.

If you would be good enough to advance me £200 of my 'quarter', by the hand of my messenger, Baum, I should be free by the end of the week to discuss with you further the proof pages of my *Vindication of the English Constitution* which you have already praised beyond its deserts.

I trust, Father, that you are well and untroubled by any of the maladies which still affect the metropolis, though the new water supply has happily ended the cholera.

Lord Lyndhurst has asked me to send you his special greetings.

At the opera that evening, Disraeli appeared at the first interval with Henrietta on his arm. The story of his challenge to O'Connell had been widely reported, and his passage through the foyer was attended by much turning of heads and congratulatory handshakes. The Irish Radical wasn't a favourite of the opera-goers at the King's Theatre. The appropriate bearing for the occasion, Disraeli had decided, was one of modest serenity and manly dignity, and Henrietta supported this role by an air of clinging relief. This was all the easier since until an hour before the opera began, Disraeli had been waiting in the magistrate's office for Baum's return.

'The information, I gather,' said Disraeli, 'was laid by Ronayne, one of O'Connell's friends.'

'Yes,' said Henrietta, holding his arm more tightly.

'You know him?'

'Yes,' she said. 'I happened to meet him only yesterday . . . I would have been unhappy if you'd insisted on fighting and Morgan had killed you.'

'Did you – ?' began Disraeli suspiciously.

But he never finished his sentence, since the large figure of Lord Alvanley came bearing down on them, thrusting through the crowd, his bucolic face shining with approval.

When Disraeli and Henrietta returned to Upper Grosvenor Street, he found Baum waiting for him with a letter in his hand.

'It came to your chambers, sir,' his servant said sleepily.

The letter read:

Sir,
    I propose to call on you tomorrow, Friday morning at eleven o'clock.
    I am, sir,
                            Yours obediently,
                            Henry Villebois.

Chapter Twelve

Disraeli looked uncertainly at the light around the curtained windows. The clock, ticking loudly and angrily, was in shadow, and he raised himself painfully in bed. He knew that he had to confront something disagreeable during the day, but what it was he didn't know.

After Disraeli had left Henrietta only a few hours before, he had returned to his chambers and fallen into an uneasy sleep, troubled by dreams of duels and Meredith and a sad image of his father, silent and reproachful. The O'Connell affair was behind him, but the insult had burnt into him, an acid on a sore. It was true that at the Opera he and Henrietta had made a triumphal progress through the foyer with a retinue of admirers. A man who was ready to die for his honour could never be publicly insulted. But O'Connell's slander would be repeated and repeated. Of that he was sure, even though no one would dare quote it in his presence. Still, he had given notice that whatever the *canaille* at the hustings or of *The Age* might say, no one could abuse him with impunity. After all, he had vindicated both himself and Henrietta. Just as no one could insult him, so too would they hesitate, apart from the scribblers of scurrilous and anonymous *graffiti*, before they would again libel Lady S., as they chose to call her.

But no sooner had he warded off one set of enemies than another, like a pack of hounds, was at his heels. Lawson was troubling him again with his demands for payment of the exorbitant interest on his bills; Rossi kept pursuing him with the odious Mayley so that he scarcely risked going out before nightfall; and Austen was still plaintively requesting him to repay several hundred pounds outstanding on the ground that he needed the money to buy a new house in Montagu Square. Sleepily, Disraeli tugged at the bell to summon Baum. It was really too absurd, his debt to Austen; it was so old, it should have died on its feet long ago. Still, Austen was a good fellow. Anybody else would have been far less patient with him. Sara Austen. *Das Ewigweibliche zieht uns hinan.* He was fortunate that Mrs Austen was – had been – his friend and Austen his solicitor.

He had been fortunate in his solicitors, he thought, as Baum brought him his coffee in silence. In the early morning, Baum and Disraeli now spoke to each other rarely. They had agreed lately that till the rites of dressing had been completed, conversation was a mutual distraction, and Baum, limping to the wardrobe, demonstrated Disraeli's morning clothes in a dumbshow.

A good valet and a good solicitor were preconditions of an

easy mind. On Henrietta's introduction, he had recently met William Pyne, a massive, bushy-browed and amiable City solicitor, with a gentle, persuasive voice that had made him think at once of a bull cooing. Between the two men there had been an immediate and affectionate understanding. Disraeli saw at once that there was no human weakness for which Pyne, like a kindly priest, could not feel compassion. As in a confessional, Disraeli had admitted his debts and the complications of his personal life, and Pyne, nodding his head, had agreed to intercede for him with his creditors or any other adversaries who came within the ambit of the courts. Pyne's own prosperity and respectability were guaranteed by his large practice among the aristocracy, especially those who were interested in speculative building and matrimonial settlements, and he had accepted Disraeli as a client, not from any prospect of financial benefit but because he liked him. It was undoubtedly a relief to have lost Austen and acquired Pyne. Both of them were men of faultless character. But Austen, alas, was a creditor and Pyne, happily, was not – at least not yet.

Baum still waited.

Looking at the display of waistcoats, Disraeli remembered suddenly the cause of his displeasure at the prospect of the day in front of him. Subfusc – grey – clerical – Henry Villebois. Yes, that was it. Henrietta's father was due to call on him at eleven, a time when he enjoyed smoking his *narguilah*, relaxing in slippered feet and wearing his silk banyan. Baum had drawn the curtains, and Disraeli saw that the time was a quarter to nine. The middle of the night. He would have liked to turn over and to sleep again, but the possibility of Mr Villebois finding him in disorder and having yet another cause of complaint goaded him into flinging the patchwork cover aside, and standing on the cold floor in his nightshirt.

Baum stood in front of the open wardrobe with the patient and respectful expression of a worshipper before an Ark. Disraeli indicated a black morning coat that he wore for funerals. Baum raised his eyebrows; Disraeli repeated the gesture. He had no doubt that decorum meant a great deal to Mr Villebois.

On his writing-table lay the manuscript of the second book

of his half-finished novel, *Henrietta Temple*, that he had put aside during the Wycombe campaign, and he took up the pages and shuffled them till a passage caught his eye and he re-read it.

'Amid the gloom and travail of existence, suddenly to behold a beautiful being, and as instantaneously to feel an overwhelming conviction that with that fair form forever one's destiny must be entwined . . . to feel fame a juggle – ' he liked that phrase – 'and posterity a lie: and to be prepared, at once for this great object, to forfeit and fling away all former hopes and ties; to violate in her favour every duty of society – that is love!'

He re-read the passage. It was true. Before he had met Henrietta, he had often wondered by what criterion love could be measured. By surrender? By sacrifice? After he had met her, he had known that love meant both. The gloom and travail of existence, the endless battles with malevolent physical pain, the destiny that tied him to a rock where the waters of his debts constantly rose, nothing had seemed important to him when he had written those words except the fact that Henrietta had chosen him, that in the face of a disapproving world, she had laid public claim to him, that she had hazarded her position and her resources, even her children whom she loved with a poignant intensity, in order to be his mistress. And he for his part had proudly asserted that nothing mattered, neither ambition nor office, compared with his love for her.

Not that over the months the sublime elation hadn't been diminished by practical necessities or rivalled by the old obsessive appetite to make his way in politics. He had often wished that he could speak to Henrietta about politics as he wrote about them in his letters to his sister at Bradenham. But she was indifferent to the themes of the day. Although in her association with Lyndhurst Henrietta had accustomed herself to be an audience for able, powerful and ambitious men, she knew little of public affairs other than that Lyndhurst was a Tory, presiding over an entourage of Tories, with challenging and sometimes heretical views. Her father was a Tory too, but his opinions seemed to have little in common with Lyndhurst's or even Disraeli's. 'What is a Tory?' she had asked Lyndhurst naively. And Lyndhurst had answered, 'I don't know.'

Yet if, like Henrietta, Disraeli didn't know what a Tory was, he claimed to know what a Radical Tory Party could become – a Party in which tradition, in his view, would mean not paralysis but the foundation of change, in which, he felt, public conformity could be harmonized with personal liberty, and in which the whims of individuals might be subordinate, nevertheless, to a general discipline. And what it might become would be determined one day not by lawyers like Lyndhurst, the spokesman of arbitrary 'cries', but by a statesman who would transform the Party's empiricism and partial greed into an ideal philosophy. Disraeli kicked a piece of coal, fallen from the scuttle that Baum had brought in. If he had time, if he had the means to make a beginning, if he had a seat in the House! . . . that, at least, Henrietta would understand.

As he dressed, he visualized the occasion of his Maiden Speech. For some weeks after the beginning of the Session, he would sit quietly in his place behind Peel, studying the atmosphere of the Chamber, listening to the orators, and occasionally exchanging some friendly words in the library or at Bellamy's with his acquaintances. And then on some great issue, say the Irish Municipal Reform Bill which the Whigs were already contemplating, he would make his Maiden Speech. The usher in the corridor would shout, 'Mr Disraeli on his legs!' and he would begin his speech modestly in a low voice so that Members would crane forward to listen. Although he knew that he could speak almost better than anyone there, he would ask the indulgence of the House for his temerity in addressing it, and then, as the Bar became crowded with Members hurrying in, he would raise his voice so that it resounded clearly in the silent and attentive Chamber. A classical reference to O'Connell as a Hermes in a broad-brimmed hat and carrying a caduceus, the inventor of the lyre, the stealer of his brother's cattle. Yes, the image fitted O'Connell; his Quaker style hat and thick walking-stick were famous. And it fitted, too, his alliance with Melbourne. Yes, the House liked a classical reference, and here he would pause for the laughter and the 'Hear! Hears!' to subside. Then, while Members were still in a mood for laughter, he would refer to Melbourne, not with malice but with banter, and he would turn to the substance of the matter. A speech not too long – say, an hour. Applause. Peel turning his head in appreciation. An engaging bow from Melbourne. The greetings and congratulations in the Lobby. A hurried letter to Sarah, telling her of his triumph.

Well, all that would have to wait. He brushed his hair, and examined himself in the looking-glass. His black coat made his face seem whiter than ever beneath his dark hair. At the corners of his eyes was already a faint tracery of lines. To exclude some of the light and eliminate them, he changed his position. At some time or other, if he wished to have a stable position in society, he would have to marry and set up a house where he could receive instead of being a constant guest at other people's tables. He looked at the cards that had arrived in the previous few days from the Talbots, the Marquis of Worcester, Lady Londonderry, the Ossultons. Each was a compliment, but compliments tended not to be repeated.

'Pray, take a seat, sir,' said Disraeli, and Baum took Villebois's top-hat and helped him out of his Petersham greatcoat. The climb up the stairs had tired Villebois, and he stood for a few seconds, trying to regulate his laboured breathing. In Henrietta's bedroom, his portrait had often frowned down on their naked bodies, and Disraeli, observing his visitor as he sat in the armchair, a country gentleman calling on his daughter's lover, felt that they were partners in unease. Yet Villebois's face had the traits of Henrietta, and Disraeli felt a reluctant bond with him.

'May I offer you some refreshment, sir?' asked Disraeli. 'Coffee – tea – a glass of wine?'

'No, thank you,' said Villebois, sitting squarely in front of him. 'I will not stay long.' He glanced around the room at the daggers and the hanging Turkish carpets on the wall.

'Relics of my travels. Yes, let me have some more coffee,' he added to Baum.

'You have spent a long time abroad, sir?' asked Villebois.

His heavy frame, his fresh complexion and his voice, too large for the room, gave Disraeli a sense of physical inadequacy.

'In my travels,' Disraeli said, 'I have spent perhaps a year of my life abroad.'

'In Italy?'

'Partly in Italy. But mostly in the Levant.'

'Ah yes, I see. The Levant!'

He spoke the word distastefully, and Disraeli watched him without speaking.

'You were, I think, born there.'

Baum had brought in the coffee, and Disraeli waited for him to leave.

'No,' he said. 'In Bloomsbury. As was my father.'

'Ah,' said Villebois. 'I was mistaken. Yet your name, sir . . .'

'My name,' said Disraeli, 'requires no further explanation.'

'No, no, indeed not,' said Villebois, taking snuff from a silver *tabatière*. He felt that he had exceeded the limits of verbal curiosity, though, at the same time, he had put Disraeli at some disadvantage. He was silent for a few moments, and Disraeli sat silently too.

'I have heard of you, of course, Mr Disraeli, from my son-in-law, Sir Francis Sykes.'

'I am acquainted with him. I trust he spoke of me in cordial terms.'

'He said you were an Italian Jew.'

'Would you regard that as a hostile reference?'

'No,' said Villebois. 'I have no prejudices against your race. My concern today is with my daughter.'

'Yes,' said Disraeli, helping himself to coffee. 'It's a natural concern. I wouldn't wish to interfere in so personal a matter, but the fact is, sir, that your daughter has been abandoned by her husband.'

Villebois's hand clenched the carved top of his stick.

'I imagine,' said Disraeli, 'you have come to see me to confide your anxieties.' He stood and walked around the room. 'It's something which agitates and distresses her friends – Lord Lyndhurst, Lady Cork, Lady Blessington, myself. You, sir, your estates are remote from the speculations of London life. If you hear about them, they are at second-hand, inspired as often as not by malice. Believe me, we all have Lady Sykes's best interests at heart. My sister, who is her friend, is deeply distressed.

'I am under the impression, from what I hear, that the distress is of your making, sir.'

'Mine? . . . Mine? . . .'

Disraeli stopped his promenade, and said,

'Lady Sykes's difficulties exist. They are real. What does Sykes tell you?'

'What he tells me is between him and me. It's reasonable that he should travel on the Continent for the sake of his health. You know very well, Mr Disraeli, there's nothing unusual in such separations even in the happiest marriages.'

Disraeli opened his mouth to speak, but stopped.

'But in fact,' Villebois went on, 'he has absented himself because of the pain – the anguish – he's been caused by your intrusion into his marriage.'

'That is what he says?'

'It is what I say – what the world is saying.'

Disraeli hesitated, and said,

'What is it, sir, that you've come to discuss with me – not, I imagine, the price of corn?'

'No,' said Villebois. 'I doubt if you could instruct me in that. I want you to leave my daughter alone.'

Disraeli looked out of the window at the heavy rain that splashed the streets in shining puddles. Then he turned, and said,

'I have no wish to be discourteous to you, Mr Villebois, even though you've just used language and made inferences that I could reasonably resent. You've come to see me on the basis of some gossip to ask me to leave your daughter alone.'

'Yes,' said Villebois. 'I'm a countryman. I address you plainly. Leave her alone!'

To control his hands, Disraeli tidied some papers on the table.

'Henrietta,' said Villebois, 'grew up after her mother died. In the absence of that care, I took the place of two parents. You must understand, Disraeli, that I love my daughter with a double intensity. She was happily married with four beautiful children. Then you met her, and are preparing to destroy her. Everything! Her marriage, her home, her family life. That is an evil thing to do – a very evil thing.'

'Have you spoken to Henrietta?'

'Not yet – I will speak to her today. But the responsibility is yours.'

Disraeli took his seat again and said,

'Lady Sykes, sir, is an adult. She must make her own choice. If she says to me she wants no more of my company, I won't see her again. But you must understand, it is she who must decide . . . But then again, you must also consider that a woman in London – abandoned, deserted, neglected, call it what you will – is exposed and vulnerable. If I don't see her, would you rather she were assailed by those gentlemen who would like to take advantage of Sykes's absence?'

'My daughter,' said Villebois, standing, 'knows how to comport herself with English gentlemen. You, sir, do not belong to that company. You can't even imagine how you'd feel if your own sister were debauched in a similar situation by some other Disraeli like yourself.' His voice was raised, and Disraeli observed him coldly.

'Or perhaps,' shouted Villebois, striking the table with his cane, 'among your people you wouldn't care. I warn you, sir. Leave my daughter alone! I know about you. You want to make a career in politics. I warn you. If you don't leave her alone, I'll see to it that every door in London is closed to you.'

Disraeli bowed to him, and handed him his hat.

As Baum closed the front door on Villebois, Henrietta's coach drew up. Her father glanced at her angrily, and without speaking, stepped into his waiting cab.

Chapter Thirteen

Tilting the silver tea-pot, Mrs D'Israeli sat erect and poutered beneath the oak tree as she might have done at home while her guests lay on rugs striped with the shadows cast by the late afternoon sun. She looked at Sarah's face with its downcast eyes, and at the highly polished, pointed shoes of Lyndhurst who was stretched out languidly like one of the dandies whom Benjamin both cultivated and imitated. Till recently, his intimacy had seemed flattering to the family; yet gradually the strange caravan of Ben and Henrietta and Lyndhurst had begun to be remarked on in the county.

This was the second time that the trio had come to stay at Bradenham, and although Lyndhurst himself, both as Chief Baron and Lord Chancellor, had never failed to treat his hosts with a due courtesy, she suspected that Lyndhurst was using the family for some interest outside the pleasure of their company.

Whenever she had given him one of the baleful and penetrating glances which she knew made her sons as well as servants and strangers cringe with guilt, Lyndhurst returned her look with the immune composure of a judge who had stared down many an advocate and many a criminal. He wasn't afraid of Mrs D'Israeli, yet he respected in her an insight which amounted almost to a complicity, since although in her disapproval she might wish to deny him the hospitality of Bradenham, for Ben's sake she would be unlikely to do so.

In the golden day with the woods gently ochred and the meadows dry after a long drought, Mrs D'Israeli had proposed the picnic in order to observe Lyndhurst more closely, especially in his demeanour towards Sarah. Isaac, of course, had declined to come, his theory being that the emanations from the grass, even when partially stifled by rugs, were the cause of intermittent fevers. Besides, he had reached a point in the revision of his second book on Charles I when he couldn't face any interruption.

Despite her reserve about Lyndhurst, Mrs D'Israeli had nursed the idea for some time that he might form an attachment to her daughter. Too late to be launched on a London Season where she would have to compete in a painful and useless contest with ingénues of eighteen, but retaining the interesting and romantic aura of a young woman stricken by the death of a fiancé, Sarah, it seemed to Mrs D'Israeli, was still nubile, at any rate in relation to a sixty-one-year-old widower who had held some of the highest offices in the state, and still had a virile bearing and a reputation for success with women. There was also Mr Hinton, the manufacturer, another widower whom she had asked to dinner.

Mrs D'Israeli handed a tea-cup to one of the servants, and she, in turn, gave it to Sarah. Lyndhurst at that moment turned to Sarah and said that it was a beautiful day; her hand trembled, and the cup and saucer rattled as if they were castanets.

She is very plain, thought Mrs D'Israeli, very plain. Why does she have to wear her hair piled up in that unbecoming style? Why does she insist on wearing the thick pelisse that's making her face glow so obviously? And why doesn't she sometimes look up from the ground when she's speaking to him?

And Lyndhurst was thinking, She's damned homely with that sallow complexion that suits Diz so well. She's really like a bad copy where everything is either too long or too short, too curly or too straight. But with a mother like that – a father who'd rather read a book on Heaven than actually go there – and Diz on top of it all – poor girl, what chance has she got?

He took from her the saucer where the tea had spilled, and poured the overflow on to the grass.

'That's very kind of you,' she whispered.

'There's a Spanish proverb,' Lyndhurst said, smiling. 'Spilt drink – departed sorrows, but I think it rhymes in Spanish.'

He had invented the proverb, and she, suspecting that this was the case, smiled back at him, raising her dark eyelashes and looking at him with her beautiful, luminous eyes.

'Good God,' he said to himself. 'She makes herself dowdy, and yet she could be – oh well, perhaps not exactly!'

Lyndhurst was always eager to discover in any woman who pleased him by her temperament some physical merit that could enlarge his appreciation.

'I wish you could be with us tomorrow at the Aylesbury Assizes,' he said. 'I think half the county will be there. The rick-burners must be taught a lesson.'

'I don't like to see people being taught a lesson,' said Sarah. 'Teaching others a lesson is usually a roundabout way of inflicting pain.'

'But if villainy doesn't suffer,' Lyndhurst said politely, 'the innocent will suffer still more. Would you approve of that?'

'I didn't say,' Sarah said gravely, 'that the wicked shouldn't be punished. All I said was that I don't enjoy the spectacle of pain – all the more, when sometimes it is so hard to distinguish between the deserving victims and the undeserving tormentors.'

Lyndhurst sat up, and then rose to his feet gracefully in order not to disarrange the folds of his coat.

'May I ask Miss D'Israeli to walk with me to the copse?' He gave her his hand, and they walked away from the group under the attentive eyes of Mrs D'Israeli. Disraeli and Henrietta were talking urgently about a letter she had received from her father following his visit to Disraeli in London. It spoke with indignation of the scandal caused by his challenge to O'Connell after 'the degrading if well-merited attack on your *paramour*'. The world, Villebois said, would have been rid of two scoundrels if they had fought their duel, and disposed of each other with a simultaneous shot.

Lyndhurst and Sarah walked in silence to the copse at the top of the mound, from which they could overlook the Vale of Aylesbury folded in the Chiltern Hills that made a low arc over the whole horizon. The sun, still high in a cloudless sky, shed a warm, benign light over all, and standing with Lyndhurst, Sarah felt that she never wanted the day to end, although Lyndhurst's earlier conduct with Henrietta had caused her so much secret hurt and bewilderment, perhaps even more in relation to Ben than to herself.

'Sarah,' Lyndhurst began, and it was the first time that he

had addressed her by her forename. 'Sarah – the last time we stayed with you, you were so happy and gay . . . Is anything troubling you?'

She began to examine a leaf on a beech branch, and it seemed to her that nothing at that moment was quite so absorbing as the shape and design of that leaf, the perfection of its fibres, its colour and texture, and the fact that on such a day she should have realized so acutely the importance of that particular leaf.

'Sarah!' Lyndhurst repeated.

'What is it?' she asked as if she had been awakened from a dream. She pulled the leaf from its stem, and folded it and re-folded it till it cracked and crumbled.

'I want to know if anything is troubling you.'

She reflected for a second, and then she said, thinking that the filigree gold chain that held his eye-glass was simpler yet far prettier than her brother's, 'Yes – I have been greatly troubled since your last visit, Lord Lyndhurst.'

'Did I – perhaps unwittingly – it couldn't have been otherwise – did I perhaps offend you?'

She looked straight into his eyes and she said,

'Not me – at least, not directly.'

'Who then? Your mother – your father? I regard your father as an ornament of our age – he's a truly great man. And your mother – ' he laughed – 'it would be dangerous to be anything but her ally.'

There was the sound of a gunshot in the distance, and she started.

'I don't like sudden noises,' she said apologetically. 'Perhaps we'd better return.'

'No,' said Lyndhurst. 'Tell me, Sarah – I wouldn't like there to be a misunderstanding between us.'

'I will tell you then,' she said resolutely but looking at the ground. 'You have been my brother's friend. He respects you, admires – even loves you. I don't think I exaggerate. He speaks of you as – as a Greek youth might have spoken of his mentor – as a knight might speak – oh, I don't know. He is devoted to you.'

'I am very touched,' said Lyndhurst. 'I think you know what

I think of your brother. His destiny is certain – and a fine one. Why do you mention all this?'

With a feeling that what had been clear in her mind had suddenly become blurred like the outline of the valley where a mist had begun to rise, Sarah hesitated.

'Because – ' she said. 'Because – Henrietta – Lady Sykes – it is indelicate of me to say this but it is known – she and Ben have a close intimacy – '

'A very moving one,' said Lyndhurst gently. 'She was most unhappy with Sykes – he treated her abominably and then abandoned her. Ben has been kind to her – he has made her happy, and I believe she has given him a happiness – and a stability – that he needed. Why do you mention this?'

'I – I . . . Oh, Lyndhurst – the last time you were at Bradenham – I couldn't sleep – I looked into the corridor – it wasn't deliberate – I swear it – I saw you and Lady Sykes – I wouldn't tell Ben – ever – ever. But I've been tormented.'

Her eyes filled with tears, and she was about to turn away when Lyndhurst took her hand, and said:

'Sarah – Sarah – what a child you are! How people can torture themselves! So much more than Torquemada ever could! My dear, dear Sarah, do you realize what Henrietta and I were talking about? Do you know how long I've known her? She's been my ward for many years.'

He tried to raise her face, but she looked away.

'Do you imagine, Sarah, I'd accept your hospitality – and Ben's – and then betray your trust?'

She raised her tear-filled eyes to him, and he looked at her tenderly.

'But I saw you,' she said. 'I saw you embracing Lady Sykes – like a *lover*!' She forced the last word out explosively.

'Let's walk back,' he said, still examining her face as if he was a doctor forming a general view of his patient. She didn't move, but looked at the hoofmarks hardened in the turf.

'Let me tell you this, Sarah,' he said sternly. 'I was discussing with Lady Sykes how best I could serve her interests and your brother's. We had talked about the matter earlier. We were agitated. We couldn't sleep, and we met – by chance – yes, by chance . . . And if I took Henrietta by the hand – ' his eyebrows twitched – 'if I consoled her – it's because I love her as a daughter.'

'As a daughter,' Sarah echoed with a sigh.

'Yes – since she was a child. There is nothing I wouldn't do for her happiness. And you thought? . . . I'm disappointed, Sarah. When I first saw you, I said to myself, "*There* is someone who will understand when the whole world may be in error." I was wrong. I'm sorry. Let's go back.'

Now Sarah's tears began to flow steadily and silently, tears of relief and guilt, and Lyndhurst stood in front of her with the sun lighting his steady blue eyes, full of reproach and forbearance.

'I'm sorry,' Sarah said in a voice that was a supplication and a surrender. 'I'm sorry.'

Lyndhurst gave her his warm, dry hand and involuntarily she was about to raise it to her lips, but he drew it away and kissed her on the forehead, and the smell of the cigar that he had been smoking earlier in the day seemed a fragrance.

'Take my arm,' he said. 'I must consult you.'

An hour before dinner was due to be served, Disraeli went to look for his father whom he hadn't seen since the O'Connell affair. To his surprise, the old man was already dressed in his formal though unfashionable breeches, silk stockings and buckled shoes, his braided swallow-tail coat a model of out-of-date elegance, with his hair carefully arranged over his upright collar.

'Ah – yes, yes,' Isaac said as if to explain away his unusual attention to his dress, since apart from Henrietta and Lyndhurst, the only other guests were to be the Basevis and Mr Hinton, the Midland manufacturer whom Baron de Haber had asked Disraeli to introduce to Lyndhurst. 'Yes – yes,' was all Isaac said, but Disraeli knew that it meant, 'The smaller the dinner, the more punctilious I must be.'

'How are you, Ben? . . . Yes – yes. I've been reading your proofs of *The Vindication of the English Constitution*. The finest thing you've ever written. And dedicated to Lord Lyndhurst! That is excellent – excellent. Take a seat, Ben. I must talk to you.'

Disraeli could see that his father, walking uneasily up and down the library instead of standing in his usual place at the lectern and addressing him from there, had something disagreeable to tell him.

'What is it, sir?' he asked.

'Croker,' said Isaac. 'Have you seen him lately?'

'No,' said Disraeli. 'I avoid him.'

'He's a man of ability,' said Isaac fairly. 'It's a pity he's left Parliament.'

'Permit me to disagree, Father,' said Disraeli. 'Croker's a talented toady, always looking for someone to be second to. He's the bully of debate, but prick him and he'll subside with a wheeze. Even his cleverness is a kind of legerdemain, a trick. He'll provoke you with a bogus paradox that might baffle the peasantry, but once you've exposed it as a logical contradiction, he'll forget he ever put it forward.'

'You don't regard him, I take it,' said Isaac, leading his son on, 'as a man of intellectual honesty? Consider his evisceration of Macaulay.'

'No,' said Disraeli, excited by his own diatribe. 'Macaulay's interpretation of England's history is false. But what moves Croker as a critic isn't a search for truth. It's envy – malice disguised as frankness. Those who are deceived by his disloyalty call it courage. But, fundamentally, Croker's chief vigour is employed like a cockerel in ousting any challenge from his farmyard.'

'I sometimes think,' said Isaac, 'that's a law of nature. Even baboons make a circumscription they won't let their rivals cross.'

'Why, Father, do you ask me about Croker?'

'He's a man to guard against,' said Isaac, lowering himself slowly into an armchair, and Disraeli saw with a pang that his father, who had seemed an unchangeable, ageless mark on which all his life he could take his bearings, had become old. His hands shook; his eyes had lost their old brilliance; and from time to time he interrupted himself, to stare in front of him as if he were occupied with some inner matter of importance that far exceeded anything that could happen outside.

'I am aware of Croker's enmity,' said Disraeli, 'and I'm

armed against it. If a man engages in politics, he must always be armed. If he seeks love, he must be ready for hatred. And if he wins love, he must be prepared for the jealousy of his critics – the amateurs and the professionals.'

'Croker has been saying at the Athenæum, and Maginn's been spreading the story, that you attacked O'Connell because you knew he wouldn't fight, and that you challenged Morgan and then secretly informed the Justices – '

'That, sir, is a lie,' said Disraeli, leaping to his feet, his face ashen, a vein standing out on his forehead. 'I will – '

'No, no,' said Isaac mildly. 'Sit down, Ben. Of course, it's a lie. But you can't have a duel every day of the week including Sundays. You can't fight all your enemies. All you can do is compose your life in such a way that whatever the insults of your slanderers and enemies, you are invulnerable.'

'And how can I do that?' Disraeli said bitterly. 'With my name and race, if I ignore an insult, I'm a coward. If I issue a challenge, I am looking for notoriety. If I win, they'll say I'm a cheat. If I lose – that I'm a weakling.'

'You must be armed,' said Isaac, 'with a carapace that you wear like a second skin . . . But never, never complain, Ben. Of all the philosophers, I like the Stoics best. Never complain, and never try and explain your reasons. After all, when you explain a poem, you turn it into prose. And when you multiply explanations, you merely add to the matters to be explained . . . And all this you'll find especially true of politics.'

Disraeli was about to speak but his father continued.

'Then again, you'll have to make some important decisions very soon, Ben. Are you a novelist or a politician?'

'I hope,' said Disraeli, 'I can be both.'

'An illusion,' said the old man, shaking his head. 'It's one or the other. You may think you're engaged in both, but one must yield to the other. If you want to succeed in politics, you must give up other distractions.'

'Are you reproaching me, sir?'

'No,' said Isaac. 'I have no reason to reproach you. I am merely concerned to offer you an opinion. With your genius, you could conquer the world. But not if you try to cross your Alps carrying more baggage than Hannibal.'

The wall clock struck seven, but neither of the two men turned his head.

'You mean – ' said Disraeli.

'I mean,' said Isaac firmly, 'that your liaison with Lady Sykes – a most amiable lady – must injure you in the end. No life – still less a political life – can be an unlimited series of parties. There'll come a moment when you'll have to decide. Do you wish – may I ask – to marry this lady?'

'She is, sir, married, as you well know.'

'If her husband divorced her – would you then marry her?'

Disraeli floundered. 'That is a matter which I'd have to consider if that case arose.'

'And if that case arose,' asked Isaac, his eyes suddenly lighting up, 'do you feel able to support her in your habitual style?'

Disraeli flushed, and then he smiled, shaking his head. 'I have never been able to win an argument with you, Father.'

He helped Isaac to his feet and they walked arm-in-arm towards the drawing-room where, over the chatter, they could hear Lyndhurst's robust laugh.

During dinner, Hinton remained silent except for an occasional acknowledgement of some observation by Mrs D'Israeli. His high black stock, his square face and his thick fingers seemed to Disraeli to personify the latitudinarian qualities of the man who was reputed to be among the wealthiest manufacturers in England. The son of a blacksmith, Henry Hinton's father had bought a small ironworks and then engaged in the manufacture of tools; Henry Hinton himself at the age of fifty-five, together with his two sons and his nephews, was beginning, in his turn, to instruct his fellow countrymen in the advantages of domestic industry over speculation in foreign Golcondas. He rarely left his home, finding little in London's pleasures to compensate for the autocratic rule which he exercised in his foundries and engineering works, where he knew his thousand workers by name and where he was always referred to as The Guv'nor.

And yet, thought Disraeli, that eponym, The Guv'nor, which Hinton and his own father shared, couldn't have been applied to two more different men. At the other end of the table, he could hear his father telling a long, involved anecdote about the spring rituals of the Lacedæmonians, which he had preceded by an equally long description of the Armenian patriarchate in Jerusalem. Mrs Basevi, worriedly groping for a point of contact, had asked Hinton which was his favourite opera. Granite-faced, he replied that he never went to the Opera. And when she had added coyly, 'But you should!' he confronted her with an unsmiling indifference which had made Disraeli, much as he disliked both the Basevis, want to enter her defence.

He was wary of Hinton, who had been recommended both by Baron de Haber, one of the Rothschild agents, and by Mr Wyndham Lewis; thus he knew very well that Hinton's interest was to meet Lyndhurst and that his role in the matter was merely to be a go-between. Hinton, although aloof from the general conversation which he regarded as flippant, and from the constant reference to the names of people he didn't know which he felt was unworthy of his attention, occasionally raised his head when Lyndhurst spoke, and contemplated him for a few seconds from under his thick grey eyebrows until he realized that Lyndhurst, whom he addressed formally as 'my lord', was more interested to talk about Signora Grisi, the singer, than about the real purpose of his visit, which was to impress on Lyndhurst the necessity of free trade.

Anxious to draw the taciturn manufacturer into the conversation, Mrs D'Israeli said, 'I hear, Mr Hinton, that Lady Charlotte is to marry your friend Mr Guest.'

Hinton paused with his knife and fork raised above the roast duckling, and eyed her for a second before answering.

'So I understand,' he said at last, in his gloomy voice. 'So I understand.'

'He is very much older than she is,' said Mrs D'Israeli, 'but he is a very handsome man.'

Hinton, interrupted in his careful chewing, frowned, as if he couldn't understand why Mrs D'Israeli wanted to discuss Lady Charlotte. After reflecting on the matter, he wiped his mouth with his napkin and added, 'He has also had some success in his industry.'

Mrs D'Israeli turned towards her daughter, who had become agitated by this exchange and, by way of distraction, was drawing attention to the flower decorations on the table in pink and white which she herself had arranged. Then she called the butler back with a frown when he went to pass her by in his second circuit of the table with the Tropfenberg, praised by Basevi for its 'delicate *parfum*'. And when Lyndhurst complimented her on the flowers, she blushed and then went pale, as if she were going to faint.

Darling Sarah. Dearest Sa! Disraeli thought, observing her. It was a melancholy prospect for a woman still young to spend the better part of her life caring first for her old parents and, if she survived them, to live on at Bradenham in solitude, unloved except by her brother and a few servants. He looked affectionately across the table at her, and she half-smiled, and he observed that she was trying with her half-smile to conceal the gap where she had lost a tooth. He caught his mother's stern glance, and averted his eyes. Then, hearing Lyndhurst's gallant attentions to his sister, he thought, Perhaps, after all, who can tell? Sa is an excellent housewife – and Lyndhurst is no longer young.

Henrietta was amusing his cousin George Basevi, 'that ungenerous, censorious prig', Disraeli called him, who had always tried to diminish him in the eyes of his mother. At one time a pupil at the Royal Academy of the famous architect Sir John Soane, as he constantly bragged, he had received a few public commissions, designed a terrace in Belgrave Square, and spoke as if his mouth held a china egg, in the loud, pompous tones much affected by the wealthy Sephardim on the assumption that this was the voice of the English upper classes.

Henrietta was wearing a dress with a deep décolleté, and Disraeli reflected that if his goatish relative bent any further over her, his long nose would be lost in the cleft. A goat, a tapir, an ant-eater! Mr Hinton had begun to talk across the table to Lyndhurst about the need for Britain to acquire a large continental market, adequate for her productive possibilities, and the other guests fell silent as, once he had seized his theme, he declined to let it go.

'We must hear what the farmers say,' said Lyndhurst at last in a mild tone.

For the first time Hinton permitted himself to smile.

'England,' he said, 'is destined to be the factory of the world. The only question is, "How long will you allow the farmers to veto our national progress for their partial interests?"'

Regretting that Hinton was more inclined to discuss the nation's affairs than to interest himself in the ladies, Mrs D'Israeli rose and Sarah followed her. Disraeli found himself next to Hinton.

'And how is Baron de Haber?' he asked. 'I haven't seen much of him lately.'

'Baron de Haber?' said Hinton with a faint frown. 'I should ask you that. He claims your confidence, sir.'

'He acts for the Rothschilds,' said Disraeli, as if in explanation.

Hinton studied Disraeli as if he were assessing his weight.

'I have no doubt,' he said, and turned to Lyndhurst to pursue the subject of free trade.

In the drawing-room after dinner, Sarah darted rapid glances from Henrietta, who was describing a water-party to Twickenham, towards the double doors, waiting for them to open and restore Lyndhurst without whom she felt deprived. Love? That was impossible, since after the death of Meredith she had vowed that she would never love again, and none of her brothers' friends, or even the intended suitors brought by her mother, had ever been able to move her. But Lyndhurst with his wisdom, his nonchalance, his combination of maturity and elegance, his deep, searching look even his mouth, well-shaped and self-indulgent, pleased her. He had repeated at dinner that he wanted to consult her, and her heart quickened each time the door creaked and feet shuffled behind it.

At last a manservant opened the doors, and the men entered, singly and in twos with the preoccupied yet liberated air of those who, having disposed of graver matters, could now be more frivolous. For their part, the ladies went on talking, though looking up to calculate their hostess's disposition of the gentlemen.

'Mr Hinton,' Mrs D'Israeli said firmly, 'Lady Sykes has an inextinguishable thirst for knowledge.'

'Yes,' said Henrietta, looking up invitingly. 'Do come and tell me about machinery. I fear I'll never understand it. I'm told that there are machines that make machines, yes indeed. Mr D'Israeli assures me it's the case. Is that true, sir?'

Hinton listened attentively. He had never yet had such a serious question put to him by so beautiful and aristocratic a woman.

'It is true, madam,' he said, and went on to describe at some length the nature of the new machinery.

'Come and join us,' said Mrs D'Israeli to Sarah's dismay, guiding her towards where her brother was talking to Mrs Basevi. But halfway, she steered her past the grand piano to the farther end of the room where Isaac was engaged with Lyndhurst.

'You are neglecting Mr Hinton,' she said to her husband. 'He's most anxious to talk to you about Mr Malthus.'

'Oh, really,' said the old man absent-mindedly. 'Really – whatever happened to Mr Malthus? Nothing untoward, I hope.'

Holding Sarah's elbow, Mrs D'Israeli surveyed the drawing-room where the servants were renewing some of the candles, and said in a firm voice,

'Sarah's going to sing two Lieder she learnt on our Rhine journey.'

Overcome by surprise, Sarah drew her arm away sharply, and said in an angry whisper,

'No, Mama – no. I really don't want to . . . I won't. I won't.'

But her mother, determined to display Sarah's talents to the company, pressed her firmly in the direction of the piano stool to murmurs of approval from Lyndhurst and Isaac.

'You do like music, don't you, Mr Hinton?' said Mrs D'Israeli as Sarah, flustered and angry, settled herself in front of her music.

'I do, madam,' said Hinton. 'The organ music of Bach – at Eastertime.'

'Then you will certainly enjoy these Lieder,' she answered, seating herself in an armchair and arranging her face in an expression of determined soulfulness.

Stretching and clenching her fingers in the air as a preliminary exercise, Sarah drew the stool closer to the piano while her brother rose lazily and stood protectively by her side.

Everyone was silent as she played the introductory bars of the *Lied 'Mondbeglänzte Zaubernacht . . .'* Then she sang in a pleasant contralto voice, without affectation and without distinction except where she exchanged a B flat for a B natural, riding nonchalantly over a mistake that made her brother's nose twitch, with a *crescendo* that in turn made the glasses on a nearby salver tremble like Chinese bells.

'Bravo!' said Lyndhurst enthusiastically, and Isaac who had dozed off awoke and joined in the applause.

'*Röslein auf der Heide* . . .' he proposed.

Sarah shook her head, and was led by Lyndhurst to the grey silk sofa where he sat beside her.

'Delicious,' he said. 'That was delicious. "Moonlit night that holds the senses in thrall – wond'rous fairy-tale splendours . . ."
How very beautiful!' He crossed his legs, and Sarah looked away from his muscular thighs and calves thickened by his posture. He sat casually but his back was straight, his stomach flat, and Sarah was conscious that she was sitting in such proximity to him that she could feel the warmth of his body through the muslin of her dress and she shivered slightly. Lyndhurst said attentively,

'May I bring you your shawl?'

But Sarah, afraid that if he left her his seat might be taken by someone else, said,

'No – no. Thank you. I am all right.'

He began to talk to her about Hinton, saying that he was the archetype of the new men who one day would have great power in Government because they had great power in creating the country's wealth.

'You mightn't think it, but they are really an Estate of the Realm.'

Sarah murmured politely, but what she was impatient to hear

was the private matter that Lyndhurst had already referred to twice. The sofa was small and as Lyndhurst uncrossed and then crossed his legs again, his left thigh rested against Sarah's. She would have moved away, but there was no room, and besides, Lyndhurst was looking reflectively into space as if totally unconscious of their intimacy.

'There is a matter I want to consult you on, Sarah,' he said, repeating the words he had already used. At the sound of her own name that seemed to be not just a verbal address but a communication of his whole person to hers, Sarah felt an exquisite sensation that began inside her knees in a nervous contraction, moving rapidly through her thigh now pressed against his to the base of her spine.

'I want to ask you, Sarah, whether you believe that happiness can ever be found in marriage between two people of different religious origins?'

She folded her hands over the small reticule in her lap where the poignant feeling seemed to be accumulating in power.

'It depends,' she said, panting a little from her effort not to be distracted by the frightening pleasure that was rising inside her. She wanted to draw away from her contact with Lyndhurst but now she felt as if she was attached to him by some magnetic connection. 'It depends on who the people are.'

'One of those people,' Lyndhurst said, 'is myself.'

She turned her face to his for a second, and looked away quickly. She had never before seen him so stern and preoccupied. Neither spoke for a few moments, and Lyndhurst waved away the butler who was offering them champagne from a silver salver.

'The other,' Lyndhurst went on, and Sarah's heart now beat in solemn thuds, accompanying the ascending feeling inside her, rising chromatically and incessantly to new octaves, 'The other is of the Hebrew race – one of the race of Our Lord . . . She isn't in her first youth.' He looked closely at Sarah's dark hair where three grey hairs were picked out by the light from the chandelier above her head. 'But she is gentle, kind and loving. She has a noble heart – ' Lyndhurst smiled as if to himself – 'she cares for the poor. She is the very model of what the psalmist called "a woman of worth" – a woman whose price is far above rubies.'

And now a sudden panic overcame Sarah. She wanted him to say what he wanted to say clearly so that she would know her destiny. She thought wildly of other women of the Hebrew race no longer in their early youth whom Lyndhurst might know, but could think of none. Could he mean her? Could he? She wanted him to speak, to declare himself before she died of the invading sensation that gulped inside her, ever more violently each time he changed his position.

'I wish to remarry,' said Lyndhurst simply, looking her full in the face. 'I have pledged myself informally to Miss Georgina Goldsmith, the daughter of Mr Louis Goldsmith.'

'Miss Goldsmith,' she repeated faintly.

At that moment the surge of ectasy broke inside her, overlaying her despair, and with her eyes closed she turned her face away. Then after a few seconds she stood up and put her hand on the back of the sofa to support herself.

'My dear Sarah – I'm sorry. Are you unwell?'

She didn't answer, but ran from the room.

Chapter Fourteen

Outside the Aylesbury Assize Court during the adjournment, a group of fashionably dressed men and women were standing under the classical portico discussing the trial of the three farm labourers accused of rick-burning. After the fetid atmosphere of the court-room, counsels' portentous voice and the jury's fixed stare at the prisoners in the dock, it was pleasant to lounge in the bland September sunshine, to gossip, and to weigh up the odds as if at a race-course.

Squire Lowther was offering three to one that Hardy, the principal accused, would get no less than ten years' transportation, especially as the indictment charged him with administering an illegal oath as well as with burning Mr Palmer's ricks.

'Give me five to one, sir,' said a young farmer from Wendover, 'and I'll take you. After all, Baron Williams has never judged leniently.'

Lowther looked at him angrily.

'Not judged leniently? . . . What did he do with them labourers from Dorchester? Seven years. Ain't that lenient? . . . Would you take a wager, Mr Disraeli?'

Disraeli, leaning against a Doric column with his cane tucked under his arm, said,

'No, thank you, Mr Lowther. I'm too superstitious to gamble on men's lives. Imagine you won, only to bring down on yourself the wrath of the gods. If I were you, I'd be very careful.'

'Well,' said Lowther, 'what they've done is a sin against God and man, so I don't see that a bet can harm. Any other time, I'd have laid a hundred guineas that Hardy'd get the gallows. But we're living in soft times. Four to one,' he said to the young farmer, and they shook hands.

Disraeli looked away to Henrietta, who was talking to Daniel Maclise and to Mrs Nash, the wife of his former agent at Wycombe. Disraeli raised his hat solemnly, and Mrs Nash curtsied.

'It's very exciting,' said Henrietta. 'The first and last time I ever went to a trial was when Lord Lyndhurst took me to the Old Bailey. I was a girl of fifteen, and I felt so sorry for the prisoners. They looked so inhuman with their shaven heads. It's degrading for people to be manacled.'

'They'd burn us in our beds,' said Mrs Nash. 'They've got to be chained, madam, or they'd do us an immense harm. The whole of Buckinghamshire would be in flames. What do you say, Mr Maclise?'

The tall young Irishman, holding his portfolio of drawings under his left arm, smiled and said,

'I'm only an artist and I don't understand these agitations. Good Lord – when I used to see the ricks burning in Connemara and the sky all red with the shadows leaping and all those shapes up above like the Apocalypse – I'd just want to paint the scene as I saw it.'

'You made no judgments?' Disraeli asked. 'Nothing between the burners and the burned?'

'Oh yes,' said Maclise good-humouredly. 'But a barn ablaze at night is a beautiful sight.'

'Not for the farmers,' said Mrs Nash.

'Please show us your sketches,' said Henrietta, turning the subject.

Maclise propped his leg on a plinth, and spread out his portfolio.

'There,' he said, 'is Judge Baron Williams who commissioned me to take his likeness. I've foreshortened his nose a little – you'll notice it's rather telescopic – when he speaks he thrusts it out, and when he broods he retracts it.'

Henrietta laughed as she looked over his shoulder.

'You've made him without blemish,' she said.

'Yes,' said Maclise. 'I like everyone to be beautiful. So do they. Here, for example, is Mr Barstow, the junior for the prosecution, with his high collar and fancy cravat.'

'And what are these?' Henrietta said quickly, pointing to some smaller sheets which Maclise was trying to shuffle under the larger sketches.

'A few notes, madam – a few notes.'

'No, show us – please.'

From his portfolio, Maclise took out a sheet of drawings, and her bantering expression became solemn.

'Look, Ben,' she said, and together for a few seconds they pored over the drawings. Maclise looked at them guiltily.

'I thought I'd do them, uncommissioned,' he said.

'But they look like saints, not prisoners,' said Henrietta.

'Most of the Blessed Saints were prisoners,' said Maclise, 'held in chains, reviled by the mob. Domenichino, they told me in Rome, would frequent the prisons to look for models for his martyrs.'

Henrietta inspected again the drawings of Hardy and his fellow prisoners.

'The eyes,' she said, 'those terrible eyes! You shouldn't do portraits like this, Mr Maclise. They make me want to cry.'

'They'll be holy tears,' said Maclise. 'I'll transfer these drawings to a great canvas, and call it – '

'The Combinators of Aylesbury?' suggested Mrs Nash spitefully.

'No,' said Disraeli. 'You must transmogrify. I've observed there's no censorship that can't be avoided by transmogrification. Call your picture "The Combinators" and you'll be held up to ridicule and shame. Worse, they'll say you're seditious. But call it "The Martyrs of Cnossos" or "The Christians Before Their Judges" and I promise you, Maclise, there'll be an admiring crowd ten deep at the Royal Academy.'

'You show them in too favourable a light,' said Mrs Nash.

'Ah, madam,' said Maclise, closing his portfolio, 'suffering is a universal kinship, unaffected by right or wrong.'

'Lord Lyndhurst says it's the unions that are at fault in this,' said Henrietta. 'And these poor men are going to get exemplary sentences to put down once and for all the spirit of sedition. Do you agree, Ben?'

She turned to Disraeli, and added before he could reply,

'By the way, we're invited to dinner with Lyndhurst at the Judge's lodgings . . . I think I see Mr Bulwer.'

Standing alone on the steps was Bulwer, who had come directly from London to be present at the trial, which had begun to attract almost as much national attention as that of the Tolpuddle farm labourers earlier on. Leaving Henrietta with Maclise and Mrs Nash, Disraeli approached his friend with delight, and Bulwer gave him a cheerful greeting.

'Nowadays, Bulwer,' Disraeli said, 'we meet only by chance – or at Lady Blessington's. We mustn't rely too much on fate.'

Bulwer shook his head slowly.

'I've been preoccupied – writing – domestic affairs. You know Rosina's now living in Bath?'

'Indeed,' said Disraeli noncommittally.

'Our separation is complete. There's a moment when the façade of public deceit about one's private affairs is too heavy to buttress. Hysteria isn't, I fear, one of the Muses.'

Disraeli smiled, and said,

'I've a certain advantage. I can always flee to my cave in Bradenham.'

'And of course,' said Henrietta, joining them, 'he takes me with him.'

'A happy provision,' said Bulwer.

'Why don't you come and stay with us?' asked Disraeli.

'Lyndhurst wouldn't find that very welcome,' said Bulwer.
Henrietta stiffened.

'Pray – why not?'

'Because, madam, I am active in presenting a petition to
Parliament humbly begging His Majesty to grant a free pardon
to the Dorchester labourers who have been the victims of a
monstrous travesty of justice. My purpose in coming here
today isn't to take part in a peep-show – ' he waved his hand
disparagingly at the visitors to the court who were now drifting
back – 'it's to provide myself with material for the defence of
the prisoners. Your friend Lord Lyndhurst takes a different
view. He – '

'You will excuse me, sir,' said Henrietta haughtily. 'It isn't
my practice to discuss my friends in their absence. Ben!' She
summoned him imperiously to join her in returning to the
court-room, but instead of following, he looked moodily at
the ferrule of his cane. Henrietta raised the hem of her skirt,
and left without turning her head.

'I've displeased Lady Sykes,' said Bulwer.

'She tends,' said Disraeli, 'to elevate personal loyalties to
political principles.'

'It makes no difference,' said Bulwer. 'Lyndhurst has never
had a political principle himself or a personal loyalty.'

'That,' said Disraeli, 'is really too much.'

They were alone on the steps of the court-house, and from
inside they could hear a confused shout from a tipstaff and the
rumble of feet as the visitors, lawyers and court officials rose
to receive the judge.

'Is it too much to criticize Lyndhurst – or to defend the
victims of injustice? Since you've applied to join the Carlton
Club, Ben – '

'I'm afraid, Bulwer,' said Disraeli, 'it's time to return.'

Bulwer watched him wryly as he entered the court-room
with his cane under his arm. Then he himself went in by a
different door.

During the day, a copy in pamphlet form of a letter from the
King to the Prime Minister, Lord Melbourne, had been widely
distributed, some thought by a group of Birmingham trade

unionists in touch with the London Radicals, indicating the Royal pressure on the Ministry for Hardy, Woolcott and Lovering to be condemned and held up as examples.

Under the heading *Windsor Castle*, it read,

> The King has received Lord Melbourne's letter of yesterday, and has given his serious attention to the communications made by Lord Lyttleton upon the state of the trade unions . . . He laments the increase of an evil which may possibly terminate with the decay and natural death of the existing causes, but which, in the meantime, may expose the country to much contest, inconvenience, loss, and possibly to actual commotion.

After describing at length the danger of the trade unions, the King urged Melbourne to act.

> Upon the whole, the letter ended, the King cannot lose sight of the importance of endeavouring to impose some check to the progress of this evil, and to impose some preventive measures . . .

But what measures? Disraeli had shown his copy of the unstamped sheet to Lyndhurst, who thought it was authentic and that its deprecatory but cautious style was characteristic of William. Between the Whigs and the Tories there was little dispute about the threat of the trade unions in seeking to subvert the relations between the classes. The growl of the farm labourers and the operatives was the counterpart of the revolutionary movement in Europe, and enough was known of that to create apprehension and a demand in both great parties for repressive measures.

'The decay and natural death of existing causes . . .' That, thought Disraeli, as he looked at the men in the dock, was an optimistic euphemism. The chief 'existing cause' of discontent was that farm labourers in Buckinghamshire living in dismal conditions, deprived of light and room, toiling from dawn to nightfall, were getting eight shillings a week. It was a fact that wouldn't disappear through decay or natural death. On the contrary, the grievance would fester and grow unless it were remedied by some political action. Yet where was this action to come from?

The invited guests, the grandees of the county, Lyndhurst's entourage, the court officials, the whispering counsel, all seemed to belong to another world from that of the grey-faced prisoners in the dock. The most notorious of the agitators, as Mr Barstow, the junior for the prosecution, had said, was Hardy, whom Disraeli, on the bench in front of the judge, remembered speaking on the Fast Day demonstration from the same platform as Heatherington. With his half-shaven head where the hairs were beginning to sprout next to a mole at the line of his forehead, Hardy in the dock looked different from the orator of a year before addressing a mass open-air demonstration. But suddenly he lifted his eyes and fixed them on Disraeli as if he recognized him. His eyes were brown and solemn, set in cavernous sockets, and dominated his long, drawn face. Disraeli looked back at the prisoner, at his shapeless tunic and at his hands, powerful, calloused and manacled as they gripped the edge of the dock. In Göttingen he had once seen a shackled bear dancing in the street to the taunts of a crowd that was prodding it with sticks. The caged men – Hardy above all – recalled the tormented bear with its solemn brown eyes and its muzzled snout. The rick-burners were doomed.

Usually somnolent in the afternoon, Squire Lowther was staring at the prisoners, mumbling as the prosecutors made a point and scowling at the defence counsel. As the witnesses entered the box or the prisoners' counsel rose to interrupt, he stirred on his wooden bench like a rider goading his horse to a series of jumps. In the jury-box were twelve yeomen farmers, some of them known to Disraeli, all Lowther's friends, three of whom had had their own ricks burnt down on other occasions. Judge Williams himself, newly appointed to the Bench and anxious to make a favourable impression in the presence of Lyndhurst, wide-awake and eager not to forfeit a moment of a trial which had attracted the interest of the whole country, kept darting his keen, bird-like eyes from counsel to the prisoners, always ready to intervene when he felt that the prosecutors had missed some argument.

The morning session had concentrated on the charge of rick-burning, and the prosecution had done badly by any standards, though almost everyone was convinced of the guilt of the prisoners. The ricks had been burnt. That was sure. Since the constables had failed to find any other culprits and Hardy and his friends were the best-known agitators in the Vale of Aylesbury, the assumption followed that they were guilty. Even when for the defence Mr Bull and Mr Derbyshire called witnesses to prove that the accused were in bed at the time when the ricks were blazing, Judge Williams felt obliged to interrupt with the caution that those who gave such evidence were interested parties, related to the accused, and that it was well known in such cases for those bound by wifely or filial duty to forswear themselves.

But later on, Mr Gambier, an impressive figure in his wig and black mutton-chop whiskers that left his well-formed chin exposed, concentrated on the charge against Hardy of 'administering an unlawful oath to a person of the name of Garroway for the purpose of binding the party to whom it was administered not to disclose any illegal combination which had been formed . . .', an indictment based on an Act of 37 Geo. III, Cap. 123, and the Act of 39 Geo. III, 79, Sec. 2, all dealing with sedition or unlawful combinations.

'May it please you, my lord, gentlemen of the jury,' said Mr Gambier for the prosecution, '. . . I turn now to the matter in the indictments concerning the administering of an illegal oath . . .'

Now Edward Garroway began his evidence, speaking in a scarcely audible voice that made Disraeli strain his ears to hear.

'I am twenty-eight,' he said. 'I work at Mr Frampton's.'

'Do you recognize the prisoners in the dock?'

'Yes, sir,' said Garroway without looking up.

'Raise your head and look at them,' said Gambier in a thunderous tone.

Garroway slowly raised his head, glanced at Hardy's eyes, and looked quickly away.

'Are you acquainted with the accused?'

'Yes, sir.'

'How long have you known him?'

'A year, sir – since I removed from Mr Bush of Great Heath and got a job with Mr Frampton.'

'The nature of your acquaintance?'

Garroway moistened his lips.

'He enjoined me in the summer to attend a Methodist service where he preached.'

Gambier put his hands on his rump beneath his gown, and turning his back on the witness, addressed himself to the air.

'So you are a Methodist?'

'Oh, no, sir – I'm Church of England like Mr Frampton.'

The court laughed, and the judge's eyes smiled.

'And then,' asked Gambier mildly, 'did your intimacy flourish?'

The witness looked back at him blankly, and didn't answer.

The judge interposed.

'You learnt to know Hardy better?'

'Yes, sir.'

'You discussed with him what he called the unhappy condition of the labouring classes?' asked Gambier.

'He – well, we talked about wages, sir.'

'Yes, you talked about wages . . . Were you aware that Hardy had incited a riot two years before on that very subject?'

'With great respect, m'lord,' Mr Bull interposed, 'there is no record of a conviction against Hardy, and I submit that my learned friend's question is inadmissible.'

'That is so,' said Judge Williams.

Gambier bowed, and said,

'Perhaps I can put it differently. Were you aware that Hardy was the secretary of the Agricultural Union at a time when there were riots at Chartridge and the Lea, and windows were broken at the County Hall?'

'It was before my day, sir.'

Gambier frowned. He wasn't making adequate progress.

'After you met with Hardy on the – er – ecclesiastical occasion, when did you next meet him?'

'Well, sir,' said Garroway, 'it was in July, and I remember it well because we passed by Mr Palmer's burnt-out rick, and Hardy said, "God's curse light on him that he'd rather burn his own ricks than pay a proper wage." '

'Pray continue,' said Gambier.

'And we walked from Chartridge to Chesham till nightfall, him talking all the time about the price of corn. Shame, he says, that men and their kin go hungry when England is so rich. What lacks, he says, is wisdom and humanity to help the poor, since the substance is abundant.'

'And what,' said Gambier in a soothing voice, 'what did you do when you reached Chesham?'

'We came to John Tulk's cottage – the leader of the Union. And Hardy – him there – he asks me do I want to be sworn.'

'And you agreed?'

'Oh, no, sir. I says no, seeing I took the Church oath.'

'And then?'

'He says to me, "It's too late. If you don't swear now, they'll find you with your neck broken in the River Chess." '

Gambier looked across the court to Hardy, who looked back at him without moving.

'So I goes, sir, and as soon as I'm in the door, someone blinds me with a handkerchief – there are several there – and I hears Hardy talking. Then when I'm blinded, they give me a book to kiss, a Bible I think it is from its weight. And then I repeats word for word after someone who says if I ever betray – '

He stopped.

'Go on.'

' – that if I ever gives away the secrets of the society I'd be damned to everlasting perdition – then, all sang a hymn – and the President says I'm now admitted to the honourable degree of brother "through the merits of Jesus Christ our Lord. Amen." '

He rattled off the conclusion.

'You had to pay for this privilege?'

'Yes, sir. A shilling for the entrance fee, and twopence a week, and the rules are that if there's anyone strikes, then all strikes.'

'I see,' said Gambier. 'Now, will you tell the court, Garroway, what happened next.'

'I takes off the blindfold, and there in front of me is Hardy and others, and behind them a painting of a skeleton and a death's head, and Hardy says that's the lot of anyone who turns traitor.'

'When did you next meet the prisoner Hardy?'

'In the court, sir – in this court.'

Garroway bowed his head, and left the witness-box as a rustle of discussion swept the court. If it had been difficult to establish Hardy's connection with the burnt-down ricks at the height of the dry summer, the evidence of his conspiracy to administer an illegal oath was clear. A second witness, Hopkins, employed by Mr Palmer, reinforced Garroway's evidence, asserting that he too on the same night had been inducted into the society with the same ritual, which ended,

> *Brethren, ere we depart,*
> *Let us join hand and heart*
> *In this our cause;*
> *May our next meeting be*
> *Blest with sweet harmony,*
> *Honour and secrecy*
> *In the labourer's cause.*

Below the judge, Lyndhurst made a ribald remark which was taken up by counsel and passed from mouth to cupped ear with spreading smiles. Somehow or other, the verse amused the visitors, who found it entertaining that so pernicious a purpose had been accompanied by such innocent lines.

Rapidly Mr Gambier called in evidence a sign-painter who had painted the backcloth, the constable who had arrested Hardy and discovered the Union's book of rules in a locked box, and the turnkey at Aylesbury Gaol who had found on Hardy's person an unstamped pamphlet.

Then Mr Bull, who had delayed his cross-examination, asked for Garroway to be recalled.

Bull was a small man of fifty with a gentle manner that contrasted with the aggressiveness of Gambier.

'You say,' he said, 'that you removed yourself from Salisbury to take up employment with Mr Frampton.'

'Yes, sir,' said Garroway.

'Would you describe yourself as an enemy of the unions?'
Garroway began to answer, and stopped.

'Are you not an enemy of the unions?' asked the judge, leading him to his answer in a way that made both defence and prosecution look uneasy.

'Yes, sir.'

'You are – or are you not?' asked Bull.

'I'm no friend of the unions,' said Garroway.

'Yet you associated with Hardy, knowing his activities?'

'We was both labourers. I don't know no other company.'

'No – really not?' Bull looked surprised. 'I have the impression that you enjoy Mr Frampton's intimacy. Is that so?'

'No, sir.'

'You worked, indeed, on Mr Frampton's estate in Dorset before coming to Buckinghamshire.'

'Yes, sir.'

'You gave evidence, I think, in the Dorchester trial.'

'I worked on the farms with them that was convicted.'

'I think you worked with the magistrates as well.'

'Is that an improper activity for a law-abiding subject of the king?' asked the judge. 'Surely not!'

'Indeed no, sir,' said Bull, 'except that most of us do not require subventions to carry out our civic duties. I put it to you, Garroway, that you are a professional tale-bearer and paid informer – that you received payments both from Mr Frampton and the magistracy to join the union, to report on its activities, and finally, to incite the commission of the alleged conduct – for which Hardy stands arraigned.'

Garroway shook his head.

'You are a man who took an oath, on your own admission, in the name of Our Lord – whether or not that oath was legally administered. Did you have no scruples about breaking it?'

'I do not accept, Mr Bull,' said the Judge severely, 'that an oath taken in breach of the law or under duress can be laid on the conscience of the witness with a construction in favour of the accused. It might conceivably be thought a burden on the witness in compounding a felony. But I cannot admit that you are following a proper line of argument.'

Mr Gambier lay back on his bench. He was satisfied that he had the sympathy of the judge.

'Hardy has three prosecutors,' said Disraeli to Lyndhurst. 'One of them is Mr Baron Williams.'

'You had better be careful,' said Lyndhurst lightly, 'or you'll find yourself in dock with Hardy for contempt of court.'

'But this isn't justice,' Disraeli muttered as the judge yet again led a witness to an answer hostile to the defendant.

'You mustn't say so,' said Lyndhurst as if the matter had now become too serious to be treated with indulgence.

'But it isn't,' said Disraeli with a shrug. It was the first time that he had attended a criminal assize, and he wanted to know why the prisoners couldn't examine others in their own defence. Perhaps, one day, he would seek to amend the law of evidence. Until then, justice would have to sleep.

Before passing sentence, the judge ordered candles to be brought as the court-room had fallen into shadow, and he had some difficulty in reading his notes. After a retirement of only twenty minutes, the jury had returned with a verdict of Not Guilty to the charge of rick-burning, but Guilty in respect of administering and taking an illegal oath. At the first announcement there had been a mutter of indignation from the benches where Mr Lowther sat with some of the other gentlemen from the Vale, and a gasp of relief from the shawled women and the handful of farm labourers in their Sunday clothes who had been admitted to the galleries. Then the foreman of the jury gave the second verdict, and this was followed by a scraping of feet and a brief clamour in the galleries, immediately quelled by the judge.

'Prisoners at the bar, have you anything to say before sentence is passed?'

'Yes, my lord,' said Hardy, raising his head. 'I have written a statement,' and a court official handed a piece of paper to the judge. Judge Williams took it with a look of distaste, studied it for a few seconds, then mumbled his way through it so that, after the first few words, even those in front of him could only grasp an occasional phrase.

'If we have violated any law, it was not done intentionally . . .

our wives and children . . . degradation and starvation . . .'

Hardy strained over the dock to listen to the perfunctory reading, and when it was finished he turned his gaze helplessly towards his wife, sitting clay-faced in the gallery.

'Prisoners at the bar,' Judge Williams said sternly, 'of the intentions of men it is impossible for a man to judge. The prisoner Hardy has declared that your intention was altogether without offence. Nevertheless – ' he paused reflectively – 'there are cases in which, whatever may be the intention of the parties, the inevitable effect of the act done upon public security is of such a kind that the safety of the public requires a penal example to be made . . . The use of punishment is not with a view to taking revenge on particular offenders; it is for the sake of example.'

In front of him, Squire Lowther was nodding vigorously. The judge, looking firmly at the prisoners, said,

'I am bound to pronounce a sentence of the law which the Act of Parliament has provided, and accordingly the sentence is that you and each of you be transported for seven years.'

There was a moment of silence, and then from the gallery a scream, a long wail from Hardy's wife, as the prisoners were hustled to the cells.

The court rose, and after the judge and the dignitaries had withdrawn, the remaining visitors filed out, chattering, into the early evening air of the High Street.

'Good God,' said Squire Lowther in a loud voice. 'It's a damnable shame. It was plain as a pikestaff – they'd burnt the ricks – hanging, I say! Hanging – !'

He'd lost his hat and was looking, Disraeli thought, as if he needed bleeding.

'Will you take a glass of wine with us at the George?' Disraeli asked.

'No, sir,' said Lowther. 'I'm already overheated – and I have my carriage.'

At the head of the long queue of coaches outside the court-house was Lyndhurst's, and Disraeli led Henrietta towards it.

'Thank heavens it's over,' she said. 'I swear I'll never go to another trial. That scream – ! What will happen to them?'

'They'll go first to the prison hulks at Portsmouth – and then the convict ships to Botany Bay.'

'Are there so many prisoners in England that they have to be kept in hulks?'

'The prisons ashore are full to overflowing.'

'But Botany Bay – '

'It's a poetic fancy. They travel in chains. One out of three dies of fever. They're flogged and brutalized. And when they reach Australia, they work for masters who are their warders with convict overseers.'

The High Sheriff's pikemen stood to attention as the coach drove off.

'Well,' said Henrietta, taking Disraeli's hand in hers. 'They are criminals after all. Pathetic, yes – but felons.'

'Their crime is poverty,' said Disraeli. 'There's surely a flaw in a society that sentences men to death for being poor.'

'They burnt the corn.'

'How many of our barons have burnt the crops of others?'

'You sound like Bulwer.'

Disraeli smiled sadly.

'Bulwer's displeased with me. But you see, Henrietta, the Radicals tell only half the story. They protest, and want to subvert. Where is the other half that deals with creation?'

'What manner of creation?'

Feeling the evening breeze, Disraeli closed the window.

'I don't want to arrive at Baron Williams's dinner with a catarrh,' he said.

'You didn't answer me,' said Henrietta. 'What sort of creation do you mean?'

'I mean a just society that conserves what is best in the authority of the past and replaces what is worst.'

'Then what would you do with the political unions and the trade unions and men like Hardy?'

'I'd give them a proper place in our society.'

'But Lyndhurst says that democracy is a form of Jacobinism.'

'He has to live down his democratic past. I begin with a belief in aristocracy. I can afford to consider a democratic amendment. Will you wear your ivory white robe for dinner and the Mantua necklace?'

It was a Sykes heirloom which he liked especially for its Italian associations.

The calendar was now complete, and Baron Williams, the High Sheriff and Lord Lyndhurst had the familiar sense of ease that accompanied the end of the assizes. Everyone at the excellent dinner was agreed that villainy had been punished with fitting sentences that included two of death, one for wounding Mr Palmer's bailiff, the other for burglary at Hyde Heath.

Without his full wig, Disraeli observed, Baron Williams had lost most of the majesty which his commanding seat beneath the Royal Arms had given him at Aylesbury. He seemed now a somewhat anxious man, worried about the roast partridge and the soufflé and afraid that in the presence of Lyndhurst he might fall below the level of the occasion. Disraeli, close to the High Sheriff's wife, who was eager for royal gossip, sat moody and withdrawn, while at the other end of the table Henrietta, as usual, had secured the attention of both her dinner neighbours, leaving the other ladies looking into the middle distance in hope of some ultimate salvation. Disraeli was evolving a phrase for an article he was planning to write in *The Times*.

'The closer you get to great men,' he said to the High Sheriff's wife, 'the smaller they seem.'

She looked at him in bewilderment.

'You mean at Court?' she asked.

He poured her some hock.

'That,' he said, 'I have yet to explore.'

But at night, listening to Henrietta's contented breathing at his side in their rooms at the George Hotel, he thought again of Hardy, the trial, the scrap of paper that the judge had taken with two fingers, the scream from the gallery. He wondered if after the self-indulgent dinner Baron Williams had slept well. He wondered; and thought that he had to find £300 in two weeks to meet one of Rossi's bills; and he wondered about Hardy in his cell. He lay awake for several hours; and he thought that he really ought to call at Guilford Street to greet

Sara Austen; and he touched Henrietta's face with his finger-tips; and she turned and nestled in his arms, and he thought that he loved her but that she was twined around him like an octopus.

Chapter Fifteen

During the night, Henrietta began to stir a little with moaning noises like a dreaming puppy, and Disraeli, half-awake, put out his hand to calm her. She was afraid of the dark, and always insisted that the curtains should be open so that the starlight could make her aware that she wasn't encoffined and entombed. Disraeli whispered her name, but in her sleep she pulled his arm suddenly, arching her back, and screamed with the distorted, strangled sound of someone who meets a faceless horror in a cul-de-sac. Disraeli kissed her face and spoke in her ear where he could feel her outspread hair, dank with sweat.

'Wake up, dearest,' he said urgently. 'Wake up!'

In the room above he could hear creaking movements and footsteps, and he soothed her as she lay awake but still shuddering, gasping for breath in his arms.

'You'll wake the whole inn. What is it, Henrietta?'

'I dreamt – it was so horrible – it was like that picture we saw at the Exhibition.'

'The Fuseli?'

She whimpered.

'That terrible monster – that goblin – lying across the breasts of that woman – The Nightmare.'

'It was nothing – a romantic fantasy.'

'I'm so frightened. I wish I hadn't gone to the trial. He had the face – '

'Whose face?'

She put her head against his chest, and said,

'I don't know. I've forgotten.'

'Try and remember. Tell me.'

'No – I've forgotten.'

'Shall I light the candle?'

She was sitting up now, and the miasma of her dream was evaporating. She took a deep breath.

'No, dearest. I'm better. I'm foolish. I went to sleep thinking of the woman in the court-room – that heart-rending scream. Such mixed-up dreams. I dreamt I was that woman, and the judge came to take away Eva. Oh, Ben, I never want to go to another trial – never again in my life. To watch another human being condemned, and then to go off and dine!'

'Now you sound like Bulwer.'

She ignored his remark.

'Even Maclise – calmly making sketches – '

'An artist has to note – to record, to interpret. I don't imagine Maclise wanted to entertain himself with another's miseries any more than I would.'

'No,' she said quickly.

'I'm going to talk to Hardy myself later today.'

'Why?'

Disraeli kissed her frowning forehead that had now become cool.

'Because there is something I want to know. You must sleep, my love. You don't want to go to the Eldritchs' ball with great puffy eyes.'

'No,' she said.

'Would you like a glass of wine?'

'Perhaps – yes.'

He went to the window with the decanter, poured each of them a glass of port, and when they had drunk it, she said,

'I think I'll sleep now,' and curled herself in his arms. But Disraeli lay awake, thinking of the judge and Squire Lowther's bet, and the court-room, and listening to his own heart-beat that thudded in his ear in the nocturnal silence.

It was market day in Aylesbury, and the clutter of drovers and their sullen, bugling herds threatening at any moment to over-turn the stalls at the roadside, and farmers making their way to the square made it difficult for Disraeli to reach the court, although it was only a short distance from the inn. The early mists had lifted from the Vale, the cockerels, as if at a second dawn, were echoing each other from the cottage plots, and the woods on the hills overlooking the town had a russet flush. For those who had come from the countryside to market, a new day had begun with new hopes for gain and flirtation and drunkenness, while the anxieties that burrow in the heart at night were abated. The morning bustle always restored Disraeli to an optimistic mood. A post-horn was a summons to a journey. A lavender girl's cry was an evocation of sweet-smelling cupboards at home. Even the scrape of the crossing-sweeper's spade gathering up the dung on the cobbles of the yard was a reminder that kings might fall and cabinets tremble, but that today and tomorrow were joined to yesterday by commonplaces that safeguarded the continuity of living. He was alive, and the pile of apples, red and firm, on a cart that pressed him against a wall, was a fragrant message of orchards and fields and walks and rides in happy liberty.

Approaching the court where Hardy had been put in the cells before being transported to the Portsmouth hulks and from there to the convict ship for Tasmania, Disraeli wanted to turn back and merge with the indifferent men and women who, if they had paid any attention to the rick-burners' trial, had now forgotten it and were absorbed in their private business, buying, selling, inspecting, weighing, assessing, rejecting, accepting, bargaining, all with the single intention of caring for their self-interest. And that, thought Disraeli, was how it should be. Why should he take the pains on this glowing autumn day to visit a seditious convict in his cell? He hesitated on the Guild-hall steps. To satisfy a shameful curiosity like those who visited Bedlam to watch the lunatics? To find material in another human being's anguish for a chapter in a novel? A beadle approached him.

'Sir?'

'I have come to visit the prisoner Hardy.'

The beadle, a small, humble man, led the way into the building, and Disraeli followed him through the court-room, now empty, silent and impersonal, yet still menacing, where only the previous week men had been condemned to the gallows.

'Yes,' said the beadle, reading his thoughts, 'looks quiet enough, sir. I looks at 'em when the judge says, "Guilty," and

I says to myself, "That'n won't live it out," but "That'n – he'll come back." '

'Indeed?' said Disraeli. 'How do you come to your conclusions?'

'Ah!' said the beadle. 'It's experience, sir. There's nothing like experience to tell you about men. It's will what counts. You don't need a lot of muscles to have will. It's will what counts. Here's 'Arry.'

Harry, the warder in charge of the six cells, had been awakened by Disraeli's visit, and he was in a surly mood.

'You've got your letter, sir, from His Honour?'

'I have nothing in writing,' Disraeli said stiffly.

'Can't let you in,' said the turnkey, moving his heavy bulk towards his small room from which he had been disturbed.

'Baron Williams, my man – '

'Sorry, sir,' said the turnkey in a portentous voice, 'court's orders. No one can visit the prisoners without a signed letter with the proper seal.'

The beadle had shuffled away apologetically, feeling that perhaps he had been too obliging to the visitor in the eyes of the massive turnkey, of whom he had a certain fear.

Disraeli eyed Harry for a second, then putting two fingers in his fob he took out a sovereign and said,

'Is this the seal you require?'

'It's against orders,' the turnkey said, but this time more feebly as he put out his hand. 'I could stretch a point, sir, for a gentleman – Baron Williams – '

Disraeli waved him on, and the warder, swinging his iron ring with the keys clinking gently, said, 'It's dark, sir. Mind them steps!'

For a few moments Disraeli could see nothing in the underground cell where the warder had brought him a stool to sit on. Then gradually he became accustomed to the light filtering through a grille high in the narrow dungeon at the level of the courtyard, and saw Hardy's shape on the palliasse spread over the stone floor.

'A gentleman,' said the warder, and Hardy slowly raised his head and lowered his shackled feet to the ground. His hands were in manacles, but as an act of grace the chain linking them with his fetters had been unlocked. Even in the penumbra Disraeli saw that he looked different, and then he realized that Hardy's head had now been wholly shaven, except for a hideous, disfiguring tuft of hair, emphasizing his separation and debasement. Thinking that he was about to start on the first stage of his final journey, Hardy tried to rise, but the warder said,

'No 'urry. There's no 'urry, lad. Ye ain't movin' yet awhile. Sit easy, 'Ardy.'

The warder gave Hardy a push in the chest that sent him against the wall.

'That'll do,' said Disraeli sternly. 'Please leave us, and come back in – in a quarter of an hour.'

Now that his eyes were accustomed to the gloom, he could see not only Hardy but also, behind him, a green ooze trickling through the grille from the courtyard, leaving a series of slippery, greenish trails like the spoor of loathsome snails. He wanted to put his handkerchief to his nose against the repellent stench, a human, debasing stench that was the residual compost of all those who had vomited and defecated and urinated in that enclosed space in transit to other gaols. Disraeli had already taken his cambric handkerchief from his pocket, but he put it back, unwilling to deepen Hardy's indignity. He noticed a spider crawling slowly and, it seemed to him, musingly over Hardy's forehead, resting from time to time near his eyebrows, then meandering along his cheek towards the collar of his canvas jacket before returning and warily pausing near his nose as if wondering where to go next, till at last it decided and raced quickly along Hardy's sleeve into the darkness. Disraeli pulled his stool back a foot.

Hardy spoke first.

'You're Mr Disraeli. I know you, sir. What brings you here?'

He spoke in a whisper, without hostility, composed like a man who, accepting the knowledge that he has an incurable illness, and putting aside all temporal ambitions and desires, waits acquiescently but with a sombre curiosity for what the remainder of life may still offer him.

'I was present at your trial,' Disraeli said. Hardy waited for him to continue. A dog, snuffling in the courtyard, began to bark through the grille.

'I have some interest in your case,' he added.

'A political interest?' Hardy muttered.

'Perhaps more a human one. I felt you lacked the opportunity of putting your case.'

Hardy raised his head and looked at him. Disraeli remembered the demonstration in Finsbury Square years before. It was the same look of recognition, of understanding, as if Hardy saw in Disraeli one who might have been an ally but had chosen to be an enemy.

'Why should it be otherwise?' Hardy asked in his slow countryman's voice. 'The purpose wasn't to serve justice but to set an example. I wasn't tried. I was put on show.'

He began to cough, and Disraeli waited for the hoarse, aching sound to end.

'Baron Williams and his satraps – and you, sir, and your friends with the wages of a hundred labourers working fourteen years on your backs – you wanted a scarecrow and scapegoats.'

He had raised his voice, but he spoke in level, controlled tones, his Dorset accent underlining his carefully chosen words.

'You are a farm labourer,' said Disraeli, patiently ignoring Hardy's charge, 'but you don't speak like one.'

Hardy's mouth twitched in the darkness.

'I speak, sir, like a farm labourer who was awakened at his mother's knee – my mother was the youngest daughter of a Dissenting clergyman – to know that the meek shall one day, however long it be deferred – to know that they shall inherit the earth. She taught me to read and write. She helped me to instruct myself, and to respect my fellow men.'

'Yes,' said Disraeli. 'But since then – '

'Since then,' said Hardy, 'in the fields and the byres – and for two years in the manufactures of Leicester – I've pondered an oppressive question.'

'And what is that?'

He recognized now in Hardy's manner the legacy of the Dissenting preacher, questioning and at the same time dogmatic.

'The question,' said Hardy in a suddenly angry voice, 'is why in England today so many millions of Englishmen are aliens in their own land?'

It was a phrase of the Radicals that Disraeli had often heard from Bulwer.

'Aliens?'

'Yes, aliens,' said Hardy. 'Why is it that the vast majority of men and women – we, the labourers and the craftsmen, their wives and children, are treated like helots – people without rights whose destiny is to slave themselves to death, alienated from the product of our hands, barely kept alive with a pittance from our toil, while the surplus is enjoyed by the owners of land and capital?'

'Do you ask me that as a question?'

'If you like. But it's a question addressed, sir, to your social order . . . Is it a divine dispensation that the mass of our countrymen should forever be condemned to a brutish life of ignorance and poverty so that an aristocracy – so described – and the exploiters of capital shall have the benefit of social grace and indulgence?'

Hardy paused, and in the narrow cell the two men could hear each other breathing.

Disraeli had kept his hat on as a precaution against the damp; but he felt that it was like a taunt to the shaven-headed prisoner, and he removed it. In a way, he was sorry that he had come because his very freedom to leave accentuated the gap between his condition and Hardy's shackles. Yet at the same time, he felt a compulsion to understand what went on in the mind of the dissident labourers, so often spoken of in the drawing-rooms and the clubs of London as a dark and undifferentiated mass of ignorance. He had sometimes heard of the eloquence of their spokesmen, cultivated in working-men's institutes and non-conformist chapels. It was an eloquence far removed from the brawling obscenities of St Giles and the groans of the mob at the hustings of High Wycombe and Taunton. It was part of the whispered alliance that had begun to form between the liberal Radicals and the newly articulate representatives of the labouring classes who, with the help of philanthropists and the clergy, had discovered the power of literacy.

'Wouldn't your question be better put,' said Disraeli, 'if you were to ask whether in an ordered society – ' he hesitated – 'there couldn't be a better distribution of its benefits so that an aristocracy that leads, a middle-class that regulates, and a labouring class that produces may all have a just share?'

'Who'll order your society?' the prisoner said in a harsh voice. 'Those who chain naked women to the coal-buckets in the mines because they're cheaper than ponies? Your Manchester philanthropists who make children of ten cough out their lives in their mills? A just share of the workhouse? Is that what you mean, sir?'

'No,' said Disraeli. 'I'm familiar with the Commissioners' reports to Parliament.'

'You must see with your own eyes, Mr Disraeli,' said Hardy. He leaned forward as if he were sitting in his own cottage. 'You're a man of intelligence. Go to the factories and see how the weavers live – the diseased children – men and women who won't live beyond the age of fifty. They're condemned to death as surely as if they were placed in front of Judge Williams and told they were to hang.'

'What you say is right,' Disraeli acknowledged with a frown. 'Our world is changing. We're in the midst of a transformation – '

'A revolution.'

'No – a transformation that will avoid the horrors of revolution. Don't you see, Hardy, we must appeal to our own tradition – to the tradition of an older England – the England of a few hundred years ago – when the people were a charge on the virtue of an aristocracy which acknowledged its duties. The structure of our society is changing with the new techniques. Can't we adapt what is best in our feudal traditions – its order and its bounty – adapt it to a new and re-invigorated England?'

'That,' said Hardy, his head beginning to droop and his voice fading from weariness, 'is a heresy. In your new Established Order, sir, merit is equated not with the fulfilment of duty but with a talent to acquire.'

Disraeli fumbled with his hat as if to leave.

'It was good of you to come,' said Hardy, as if to himself.

'Very good. You came to hear a defence that went unheard, not my defence alone – the defence of all who toil. You see, sir, at intervals society needs to purge itself of its guilt. And so, when wages fall to starvation level, our landowners and bishops and ministers – they don't say that the system must be changed so that the labourer can receive his hire. No, they say that if a rick is burnt by men driven to despair, if workers who are too much put upon combine in a refusal, if men take an oath not to submit to intolerable persecution – that is a sin in the deprived, a blemish which is the cause of their own ruin. Then we see the spectacle of your landowners and your judges and your chaplains and your militia all agreeing that the way to extirpate protest is to hang a few labourers, transport many more, starve their wives and children – There is the real revolution – the revolution of the possessors against the dispossessed.'

'Your wife,' broke in Disraeli. 'Is she cared for?'

Hardy looked down at his iron fetters, and didn't answer.

'I hope,' said Disraeli, 'you may permit – '

On an impulse, he had decided to send fifty guineas to Hardy's wife.

'She will be cared for, I trust, by the Union and by God's will,' said Hardy gravely.

'The Union?'

'There is more loving-kindness among men who toil,' said Hardy, 'than there ever was in the Poor Law or the bounty of the castle. I've no wish for charity.' He looked up at Disraeli, now standing. 'One day, Mr Disraeli, you will recognize that the power of England lies in its people. Not in an exclusive aristocracy – not even in the possessors of factories and machines – it lies in the united will of the masses.'

'Reform – '

'Reform means nothing. It's not through the suffrage but through union and unity that the working-class will establish its rights.'

Hardy raised himself heavily, and Disraeli restrained an impulse to help him.

'I may not live to see it,' he said. 'You will.'

The cell door opened, and the turnkey stood waiting.

'Time's up,' he said. 'Transport's leaving in half an hour.'

'Your friends – ' Disraeli began. Hardy cut him short.

'I am obliged to you for your visit, Mr Disraeli.'

As if leaving a drawing-room, Disraeli bowed to him, and as he mounted the stone steps, he could hear the warder through the iron door snarling at Hardy,

'Well, yer ladyship – and is yer ladyship ready for a nice sea voyage?'

Outside the Guildhall a crowd, mostly women, had gathered to watch the departure of the convicts. A few old men sat smoking their pipes on the wall facing the courtyard, and the four constables at the gate stood self-consciously opposite them, their sabres at the ready, as if they expected them at any moment to become the focus of an insurrection. A tumbril cart, tugged by two straining horses, had earlier pulled into the cobbled entrance, and the onlookers, always delighted with the prospect of a free entertainment, had drawn close, patiently waiting for the spectacle to begin. As newcomers arrived, those already established offered a commentary on the situation.

'It should be a lesson to them,' said the grey-haired wife of a tradesman. 'We'll be able to sleep more soundly tonight.'

'Rick-burners, hey?' said a farmer's son. 'I'd not transport 'em. I'd burn 'em alive. What do you say, Parson?'

'Where there's no vision,' said the parson, unwilling to be involved in argument, 'the people perish.'

It was his omnibus comment on all questions about secular problems.

But Disraeli, who stood near the edge of the crowd, noticed that at Wendover Corner where the cart would turn towards the road to the south, a group of white-faced women in shawls and forlorn children, relatives, he had no doubt, of the condemned men, were waiting with a fatalistic air of defeat and misery such as he had seen only among the humblest and most poverty-stricken peasants in Spain.

Hardy had irritated him, though his mournful lecture had a certain logic that Disraeli was reluctant to acknowledge. No Parliamentary Report, it was true, could take the place of observation. Nor could he himself share the feeling of a labourer who had worked in factories as well as the fields. On the other hand, was it necessary to have visited the Ganges or the moon to have an idea of them?

Hinton had spoken much of Manchester. He himself would like to see Manchester's mills and factories, to meet the New Men, to study the condition of the working-classes and then to write from experience about the new England, an England that had to renew itself in order to preserve its ancient glories. Yes, he would have to visit Manchester.

The crowd surged forward as the gate half opened, but it was only to admit a magistrate responsible for the prisoners' transfer.

But Hardy! The man was irritating, and yet his trial, Disraeli was convinced, had been a travesty, the ritual of justice without its substance, an exercise by its promoters in bogus piety. He stood tapping his cane, then walked towards the drably clothed women at the corner. He had made up his mind.

He would talk to Bulwer.

The thought was an act of redemption for the shame that he had felt since the day before in participating in a raree-show. He would talk to Bulwer, and urge him to set in train a petition for a pardon. Melbourne would have to listen. The Irish, even O'Connell who disliked the Unions, would support it. Peel would have the insight to recognize that reconciliation not division made a nation great, and that the civil war in England, no less bitter because for the time being the lower orders had been made impotent, must be brought to an end. A pardon! The word made his heart lighter. He would like to say to the mourning women, 'See! There's no need for despair. Mr Bulwer and I will bring your men a pardon.'

But then he saw before him the rigid, unrelenting faces of those, including Lyndhurst, who had approved of the verdict. Melbourne would never give way as long as the manufacturers, led by Ashworth, were locked in struggle with the Unions who had revived the poisoned weapon of the strike. His hope lay in Peel and the men of goodwill in Parliament, the men of chivalry, generosity and compassion like John Cam Hobhouse,

Graham and Fielden, for whom political reform without social reform had no meaning.

The gates were flung open, a constable shouted, 'Clear the way!' and the crowd exhaled an 'Ah!' as the cart with the convicts, escorted by two red-coated mounted troopers, shambled into view. The six prisoners were securely fettered with the median chain between the manacles and the foot-irons fastened again, so that they couldn't rise to their full height but stood with their heads bowed, jostled against each other with the bumping of the cart. Stray dogs ran yelping at the fetlocks of the horses, and the prison coachman in his peaked cap slashed at them with his whip. The troopers thrust their horses' flanks against the sightseers, and the cart began to get under way to a chorus of groans. As if to show that they were on the side of authority, a group of out-of-work navvies in ragged fustian who had been employed on the canal shouted their own abuse, happy to find that there were others more deprived than themselves, and a hydrocephalic boy, caught up in the carnival air, joined in with an angry, unintelligible bray.

As the cart approached Wendover Corner, the women surrounded and held it up, but the troopers urged their horses forward, then backed them into the crowd. At that moment, Hardy began to sing, in a voice at first tuneless but then firm as the others sang too, the hymn of the Unions:

> *'God is our guide! From field, from wave,*
> *From plough, from anvil and from loom,*
> *We come, our country's rights to save,*
> *And speak the tyrant faction's doom.'*

The cart swayed, and they sang still louder.

> *'We raise the watchword "Liberty",*
> *We will, we will, we will be free!'*

For a second, Disraeli caught Hardy's eye, and was about to raise his hat in farewell, but the driver lashed his horses and swore, and the cart lurched forward in an accumulating rumble as the wail of the women overlaid the convicts' fading voices.

Chapter Sixteen

From Isaac D'Israeli at Bradenham House to Benjamin Disraeli at Long's Hotel, New Bond Street, London.

October 15th, 1835

Dear Ben,

Yesterday before noon we had an unexpected visitor in the person of Mr Henry Villebois who, having announced that he had made a detour on his way to see a nephew at Oxford, hummed and hawed about a matter which, he said, delicacy made him unwilling to broach. Recognizing that this reluctance was the obverse of a certain eagerness, I invited him to my study, where after a few moments he explained himself eloquently.

He began by identifying himself as the father of Lady Sykes – a fact which I should have recognized earlier had his irruption been less sudden. After I had expressed my respect for this lady and my regard for her personal qualities, he went on to lament the circumstance that, being alone in London, since her husband was obliged to travel abroad for the sake of his health, she was exposed to the calumnies and impertinences of a heartless world, always ready to abuse an unprotected woman.

When I assured him that Lady Sykes, accompanied by Lord Lyndhurst, had been our honoured guest, and that I had never heard speak of her except in terms of esteem and admiration, he appeared to become irate, warmed, as I imagine, both by the subject and by the madeira wine I had offered him. He told me that his daughter had been placed in an ambiguous position by a certain member of the D'Israeli family, and that this was causing him considerable distress. He was a descendant of the Villebois of Normandy, and no one would be allowed to taint his honour with impunity. He confessed, so he said, that he had hitherto been denied the opportunity of meeting any of the Hebrew race, and it was possible that their customs were different from those of the Villebois.

Being anxious to end an interview which had interfered with my reading of Lord Chesterfield's Letters, I urged him at this stage to his point. 'My point, sir,' he said, emphasizing it by a blow of his fist on the study table which brought Tita into the room, 'is that I desire your son to give up my daughter's company.'

Since I was now reinforced by our major domo who stood looking gloomily at Mr Villebois as if that gentleman were a Bulgar, I explained that my influence over you was neither more nor less than his over Lady Sykes, and that you both had reached your majority, and were able to determine your own alliances and company. At that, Mr Villebois, who had become plethoric, was obliged to sit, and I sent Tita for a cordial. Now that Mr Villebois's anger had been replaced by an air of suffering, I found it easier to recognize how much paternal distress Mr Villebois felt at his daughter's situation.

My sympathy was all the greater when he urged me as a father to defend the prospects of my own son. As an old friend of his family, Sir Robert Peel, he said, viewed with displeasure the alliance of Lady Sykes with Mr Disraeli, and as leader of the Tory Party he regarded with disapprobation the involvement of a recent recruit to his Party with a lady whose name had always been free from scandal. His solicitude was scarcely disinterested, but I found it impossible to ignore its justification.

I remarked to you earlier, Ben, that I had been reading Lord Chesterfield's Letters. There is, indeed, one with which you will be familiar, but to which I will refer you again, since you have in the past answered my objections to certain of your behaviour by saying that you were a rational being and knew exactly what you were doing.

Lord Chesterfield wrote,

'. . . We need not suppose that because a man is a rational animal, he will, therefore, always act rationally, or because he has such or such a predominant passion, that he will act invariably and consequentially in pursuit of it.'

You, Ben, have often said to me that ambition is the force

that drives you, heedless of blows, towards the fulfilment of a great destiny. Now, hear once more what Lord Chesterfield has said.

'I will suppose ambition to be (as it commonly is) the predominant passion of a Minister of State, and I will suppose that Minister to be an able one. Will he, therefore, invariably pursue the object of that predominant passion? Sickness or low spirits may damp this predominant passion; inferior passions may at times surprise it and prevail. Is this ambitious statesman amorous? Indiscreet and unregarded confidences made in tender moments to his wife or mistress may defeat all his schemes.'

Shall it be said of you – shall you say of yourself in frustrated middle age – that you were diverted in your springtime from your high purpose by an amour, impossible of conclusion in marriage, and which by then must in any case have spent its force? Far be it from me to offer you instruction in the manner recommended by Mr Villebois. In my retreat at Bradenham, I have more contact with old civilizations than with our contemporary society. Yet there are cycles of feeling, action and achievement which seem to remain constant through the ages. The appetite of sensuous love is an episode in those cycles. At the height of his philosophic powers, Socrates welcomed the fact that he had been 'released from the beast'. (He meant sensual love.) The prospect of action and achievement still lies before you. But the visit of Mr Villebois has made me feel that you should assess carefully the forfeit you may have to pay in power and political success if you persist in a relationship which is censured not merely by the envious but also by your friends and well-wishers.

I cannot say that Mr Villebois, who came in anger, left rejoicing. I only hope that my handshake as he left reassured him of my benevolence towards all concerned in this imbroglio.

Your devoted father,
Isaac D'Israeli.

Post Scriptum

You must not take amiss either the above lines or my

failure to advance you a further £200 against your 'quarter'. I had a wealthy father who left me a shrinking fortune. What remains is the seed-corn. I.D.

From Benjamin Disraeli to Benjamin Austen at Guilford Street.

Long's Hotel,
New Bond Street,
London.
October 17th, 1835

My dear Austen,

As you see from my address, I am back in London, briefly ensconced near Saunders and Otley of Conduit Street to whom I have entrusted my forthcoming work, *A Vindication of the English Constitution in a Letter to a Noble and Learned Lord*. You will have guessed that the subject of my dedication is Lord Lyndhurst, and my theme the advantage of a Tory democracy over a Whig oligarchy. I propose to send Madame an inscribed copy within the next few days, and will await with anxiety the judgment of two friends who, while they have ever been generous with praise, have never been niggardly with reproof when that has been needed.

Several months have now passed since I last attended Mrs Austen's dinner-party for Dr Warren whose excellent Diary inspired me to use the Homeo-Pathic system when I was lately stricken by the Influenza. What a brilliant evening! And how I miss my excellent Austens! But swept into a maelstrom of political obligations, I have had to deny myself any personal pleasures including, dear friend, your own society.

Father has asked me to send you his especial greetings, and Mother hopes that before long we may have the pleasure of entertaining you at Bradenham.

And now to a lesser but more tedious matter. I have paid the interest on the outstanding loan, and will, of course, arrange for the same on Quarter Day. Unfortunately, the capital repayment may have to wait till I obtain the first advance from my publishers. In the light of the *Vindication*'s

certain success, I venture to hope that you will accommodate
me with a further £200 on the same terms as, with your
steadfast friendship, you have done in the past.

Believe me to be, dearest Austen,

B. Disraeli.

Mrs Sara Austen to Benjamin Disraeli at Long's Hotel.

Guilford Street,
Bloomsbury.

Private   October 19th, 1835

Dear Ben,

Your neglect since last April has caused me much pain,
especially since the O'Connell affair made me tremble for
your person, though your absence was itself a form of death.
You must not imagine that people can be plucked and discarded as if they were insensible fruit on trees. I don't want
to feed your arrogance by telling you that I think of you
every day and night of my life, but since it is the truth, I
must tell it to you. Your letter, in its reference to me, was a
refreshment, yet one which gives no security of sustenance.

I read of you and what you write, and recognize that your
preoccupations have separated you from me in the way a
great ship draws away from a small harbour. Yet I want you
to know that, however distant your journey, whatever the
tempests, you can always return to this shelter.

Pray call on Monday at eleven or four. I will give you
Mr Austen's reply to the conclusion of your letter.

Sara Austen.

D'Orsay to Benjamin Disraeli.

As from Gore House,
Kensington.
October 20th, 1835

Cher ami,

*Deux cent livres? Pour le moment pas même deux cent shillings.
Je viens de passer une soirée désastreuse à Crockford's. Après avoir
gagné mille deux cent livres, j'ai perdu deux milles. Mais ne vous
en faîtes pas. Le pouvoir est aux débiteurs, pas aux créanciers!*

By the end of the week, I propose to raise three thousand pounds, a thousand by loans and two thousands at cards. From the latter, I will arrange for you to have two hundred and fifty.

Let us meet at dinner on Friday. Lady Blessington has read the *Vindication*, and is at this moment writing to you with an expression of rapture. She wants you to contribute to the next edition of her *Book of Beauty*, a poem about a maiden at her first ball. I trust it won't turn to a political philippic.

Votre dévoué,
Alfred D'Orsay.

Benjamin Disraeli to Sir Francis Sykes, Bart, in Nice.

Long's Hotel.
October 21st, 1835

Dear Sir Francis Sykes,

I was happy to receive your letter and to learn that your health has so much improved that you have been able to travel from Venice to Nice. You have been good enough in your absence to entrust the honour of acting as guardians of Lady Henrietta to Lord Lyndhurst and myself. I hope I can say that by our attentions to her in society we have safeguarded your reputation and her name.

Yet with the greatest respect I am obliged to say that the financial provision you have made for her and your children scarcely suffices to uphold the status appropriate to you both.

I cannot but feel that either you should return and resume your care of Lady Sykes, or alternatively make an adequate and unconditional provision for her. No less than a further £3,000 will suffice to meet her pressing obligations.

I remain,
Yours sincerely,
B. Disraeli.

Sir Francis Sykes to B. Disraeli at Long's Hotel.

November 10th, 1835

Dear D'Israeli,

I recognize that it is a labour for the best of friends to

assume another's responsibilities. Still more must it be a burden for one who is but an acquaintance. I recognize that you have been generous, together with Lord Lyndhurst, in caring for my wife at a time when England has become utterly irksome to me.

I pay no attention to what the *mauvaises langues*, as Lady Sykes once called them, have to say about our ménages. No stranger is qualified to judge about the nature of a relationship in which they have no part. Nor indeed do I care a fig for the insufferable Villebois, Maria especially, who turn sour in the presence of another's happiness.

Each one of us has to make his own decision about the regulation of his life. My own decision is made. I will not return to England, and exchange the benevolent Latin skies for London's rain and mist, nor the gentle Mediterranean temperament for the malice of Mayfair's drawing-rooms.

I have instructed Coutts to allow Lady Sykes to draw on me for up to £3,000 in quarterly instalments.

Yours truly,
Francis Sykes.

Lord Lyndhurst to Benjamin Disraeli.

Palais Fouché,
rue Lafitte.
October 30th, 1835

My dear Ben,

Arrived in Paris after a laborious journey!

. . . o fortes, pejora que passi
Nunc vino pellite curas.

Not since April when our Ministry fell to the coalition of Whigs, Radicals and Repealers have I felt so liberated. But then, it is the nature of Paris to let even a peer be private and embellish himself with a red cockade. Let me first, however, say how much we enjoyed our September stay at Bradenham, and regret that you have not found it possible to accompany us. Miss Copley, one of your fervent admirers, has asked me to tell you of her chagrin at your absence.

Here the summer still seems to linger, though the chestnut

trees in the Tuileries are turning russet. The Municipal Reform Bill now seems far away. Baron Rothschild has received us very graciously at the Palais Fouché, where he lives in a splendour – Bourbon *meubles* and Renaissance *bibelots* – which will only be surpassed when he has completed the mansion he is now building in the Faubourg St Honoré. What an extraordinary family these Rothschilds are! They have what Midas lacked – the talent of prescience allied to the gift of transubstantiation. At the present time, there is much talk of railways, and a vast cabal led by Baron de Haber is seeking to obtain a private licence for a Paris–St Germain–Versailles railway now that the Ministry has thrown out the plan for a state-owned steam-coach line. Thiers, the King's first Minister, 'bloody, bold and resolute' in sabreing the mob at Lyons, has pronounced his verdict. 'Railways will never succeed.' But Rothschild with an irresistible argument, before which anti-railway Ministers, deputies and journalists fall in swathes – the argument of seven million francs' worth of free issues of shares in the proposed company – thinks differently. There is naturally some anxiety among the gentry and the peasants who will see their crops blackened by the engines, their forests in flames from the engine sparks, their cattle dropping their calves and their birds poisoned by soot.

I myself believe James's (or Jacob's) promise that there is no better investment, provided that there is no war or insurrection, than a speculation in railway shares. This is a case where self-interest can legitimately wed historic change, and the prosperity of the few will one day enrich the many.

But in case you think I am preoccupied with finance, let me say at once that Paris is the gayest and most brilliant city that I have ever known, a metropolis of light and art where the poet, whether in a *mansarde* or in the salon of King Louis-Philippe, is emperor.

Egalité, as you can imagine, is the order of the day, befitting a state whose head is the son of Philippe-Egalité and a true son of the Revolution. But revolution, he freely acknowledges, can go too far, and in the event, though nothing can stop anyone from calling on the king at the

Palais Royal where the caller may even receive a handshake, the monarchy is, in fact, an institution of the high bourgeoisie and the Funds, with men of letters and a few painters to ice the cake, so to speak.

A Jacobin past has never prohibited a conservative present. It is the genius of the French king to have lived at Twickenham, sent his sons to an English public school, placated the French middle-classes, reassured the sovereigns of Europe, and protected the *vie de Bohême* while behaving himself as a modest *père de famille*.

Rothschild, ever adaptable, has followed his example, and happily receives the most talked of artists of the day. I have lately met at the Palais Fouché Victor Hugo, an exquisite family poet with a beautiful mistress, the actress Juliette Drouet, Balzac, a sublime writer of a remarkable ugliness, and the German Heinrich Heine, author of the *Buch der Lieder*, an exile who has written that Göttingen, his old university, looks best when you face it with your back!

To steal one of his *mots*, I can tell you, dear Ben, that were you to ask a fish in water how he feels, he would answer, 'Like Lyndhurst in Paris.'

You would be happy here. Miss Copley and Lady Sykes find many distractions, and both ask to be remembered to you affectionately, and Lady Sykes, at least, will write to you in the very near future.

Ever yours,
L.

Lady Sykes to Benjamin Disraeli in Bradenham.

Fontainebleau,
November 1st, 1835

My dearest one,

Another month – the time is endless. Miss Copley is constantly unwell from the water, the food or the air, but Lyndhurst remains as cheerful as his daughter is *maussade*. Paris life is a party that doesn't stop, and Lyndhurst's connections with the Rothschilds are a passport even more effective than his being a former Lord Chancellor. The French turn everything topsy-turvy. They are relaxed in public and *very* stiff at home. They like wit, and applaud it with the tips of their lips, but laughter seems the preserve of the people in the street.

Today Lyndhurst took me to a boar-hunt in the forest at Fontainebleau where a large number of Frenchmen in scarlet with a chorus of horns and trumpets charged through a regular Stonehenge of what they call megaliths. A lot of time was spent in drinking fine wines and picnicking, and no one was wounded though many were frightened. I believe that eventually a boar was killed, and in the evening the Duc de Noailles gave a ball for all the *chasseurs* and their ladies. It was very tedious, and Lyndhurst flirted with the Duchesse.

Dearest love – I can't wait to see you again. Tomorrow we go to Rambouillet, where we will stay some days if Miss Copley's health and mood permit.

My dearest one – I miss you. Every throb of my pulse is for you, and you are my breath, my *innermost* being. Love me for ever, even as I love you.

Your faithful
H.

Benjamin Disraeli to Lady Sykes in the care of the British Embassy.

85 St James's Street,
London.
November 18th, 1835

My dearest,

Here in London everything is smoke and fog, and so it will be until you return. But my chagrin is mingled with excitement as I await the publication of *A Vindication of the English Constitution*. I confess that in my Tory hero Lord Bolingbroke I see a certain person with whom others will draw parallels – one who maintains 'that vigilant and meditative independence which is the privilege of an original and determined spirit'. But like Bolingbroke, *That Person* has had to choose between oligarchy and democracy. And I have written, 'From the moment that Lord Bolingbroke in becoming a

Tory embraced the national cause, he devoted himself absolutely to his party.'

Yes, dearest one, the decision is made, and perhaps one day with the great spirit of Bolingbroke, *another* – one you have given your love – will 'guide the groaning helm through the world of troubled waters'.

So much for the future, yet for the present there remains the irksome problem of a Parliamentary seat. Lyndhurst has made a few tentative movements but scarcely enough. I trust that in your travels that have taken you so far from me, you will at least use the opportunity to impress on him the great and pressing need to find me a place more sure than Wycombe or Taunton.

Come back soon. I am bereft by your absence, and London is empty. I can't bear to walk past your house and see the drawn curtains, so I have taken to detours and you are responsible for my taking a great deal of unwonted exercise.

Come back soon, my beloved. The world and distance are too much between us.

I send you my love – my deepest love.

B.

I also send you copies of my correspondence with Sir F.S.

Lady Sykes to Benjamin Disraeli in London.

The Grange,
Southend.
December 2nd, 1835

My dearest and only beloved,

I am in exile, but everything is exile when I am away from you. I returned from France on Monday, and I must see you soon. What genius you showed in your letter to F! What dear and sensitive delicacy! But your letter made me sad, for while it relieved me of the necessity for the time being of worrying about cash and my milliner, not to mention the household expenses which I had always thought were paid by God, it reminded me how far away you were, how others could look on your darling head, and how bereft I am without you.

236

Last night I fondled the pipes you left behind, and went into your room and it was cold and the fire unlit. I can hear the waves breaking against the shore, and I remember how many times we lay warmly together while the sea raged outside. O Amin, I am longing to return to London and take you once again in my arms. Last night I held your pillow and pressed it against me in bed, and kissed it and kissed it and kissed it. Is that foolish, and do you forgive me?

It seems so long ago that I met you at the King's Theatre. What happiness, my dearest, my best-beloved! Night and day has been a radiance. My children, who are here with me, look at me as if I am possessed by some spirit. And that is truly so. There is nothing of me that doesn't belong to you, nothing of me that you couldn't dispose of as you will. You are my fate, my love, my darling, perhaps my undoing – but even that would be a happiness.

I will return, my beautiful Amin, in the second week in January. Don't worry or doubt about Lyndhurst's assistance to me. He loves the children, especially Eva, and is very kind. Besides, you know I can do as I will with him, and what I seek is his powerful interest on your behalf which I will prove.

I embrace you a million and a million times.

H.

Benjamin Disraeli to Sarah Disraeli at Bradenham.

Park Lane,
London.
December 29th, 1835

Dearest Sa,

The Whig hounds have been hunting a quarry which to their surprise has turned on them, and now they are in full flight. *The Globe* abused me for the *Vindication*, but I have found an irresistible ally in Barnes, the editor of *The Times*. He has authorized me to write a series of letters under the pseudonym of Runnymede – pray regard this with your usual discretion, since my anonymity enlarges my freedom to write on a variety of subjects from the Lords to the populace. I intend to send the whole Whig pack over the precipice.

The turn of the year, dearest Sa, is always a time for retrospect and resolution. I can't complain that it has been a year without pleasures and excitements. Sometimes when I think of it, it seems a calendar of suppers and water-parties and music and gossip, as evanescent as the dates that have marked the occasions. And of defeats, yes, of defeats. But despite my defeats, I have advanced politically. I have gained an attention through my writings that hundreds of Members of Parliament might envy. I have now a solid political base in prospect at the Carlton and in my association with Lord L, who has returned from France and sends you his warmest regards. Offers of candidature are imminent. The time must *surely* come soon when I will have a seat in Parliament and be able to command what I can now only recommend.

I think of you always and wish that I could spend more time at Bradenham instead of attending social occasions like the New Year's Ball at Londonderry House. To dance is for me a servitude, and a ball-room a place where the deafened converse with the inarticulate. Besides, physical exercise, when one is obliged to submit to it, should have space, not intimacy.

Poor old Mrs Watson! To think that she has died. She seemed immortal. Yet there is a stage of decrepitude as on this late day of the year when only the hope of resurrection can compensate for its misery.

But enough of melancholy. I send my most loving thoughts for the New Year to the best and dearest of sisters.

Ben.

Chapter Seventeen

When Henrietta's carriage reached George Street, Disraeli saw that the snow-covered approaches to Lyndhurst's house had been overlaid with straw, muffling the wheels so that the horses, already shrouded by the drifting flakes, seemed a cortège of vaporous mutes. As the groom let down the steps, the door opened to admit them into the hall, where a number of greatcoats and fur-trimmed pelisses were hanging, giving off a wet smell which even the log fire couldn't dissipate.

From the drawing-room, as Disraeli and Henrietta were being helped out of their coats by a footman, came a murmur of voices, restrained and moderated to the occasion, a laugh quickly repressed and followed by a small cough.

Miss Copley came to greet them with her familiar expression that assured them of a courteous welcome as long as they were loyal friends of her brother.

'I trust there is some improvement?' said Henrietta.

'None, I fear,' said Miss Copley, her eyes steady and re-signed. She had known many sadnesses in her life, and she was prepared for yet another. 'Mother is dying.'

She led them into the drawing-room, where Lord and Lady Haughton, Miss Ainsley, Mrs Carpenter, Miss Anthea Copley, a niece, four cousins and two barons of the Exchequer were drinking tea and eating cakes and reminiscing about Mrs Copley as if she were already dead.

'She was so beautiful,' said Mrs Carpenter. 'That perfect complexion – those clear eyes! You would never have guessed that she was ninety-one.'

'Ninety-two,' said Miss Copley.

'Ninety-two!' the company echoed in awe. The figure related them to another century, another era.

'And so intelligent,' Mrs Carpenter went on, taking another cake. 'She never lost any of her faculties.'

'Only her hearing,' said Miss Copley.

'She never could stand old people,' said Lord Haughton, his frog-like mouth expanding into the beginning of a guffaw which a frown from his wife interrupted.

'So proud of Lord Lyndhurst she was,' said Mrs Carpenter, looking at the clock. The time was half past eleven, and every-one in the room was wondering how long politeness required them to stay when conversation was hindered by the twin dangers of being too grave or too flippant.

'He was so close to his mother,' said Miss Ainsley, drawing her shawl around her as the windows darkened with snow.

239

'He is with her now,' said Miss Copley.

In contradiction, the door opened and Lyndhurst entered. His eyes, Disraeli noticed at once, were red-rimmed as if from sleeplessness and weeping.

'Ah, my dear Lyndhurst,' said Lord Haughton, 'three score years and ten! How fortunate you are to have enjoyed your mother for so many more years than that!'

Lyndhurst gave him a displeased look, and turned to Disraeli. His voice was husky, and he avoided Disraeli's glance as they shook hands.

'I'm sorry,' said Disraeli. 'The doctor – '

'He offers no hope,' said Lyndhurst. 'No hope – ah, Henrietta – I didn't see you. I am grateful to you for coming. Please come to my room, Ben. There's something I want to discuss with you.'

Disraeli followed him to the library, where Lyndhurst, beckoning him to an armchair, fell exhausted on to the leather-buttoned sofa.

'I wish to God they'd all go away,' he said. 'Dammit, they regard it as a compliment to me that they sit there like vultures waiting for her to die . . . Do you know, she wants to live. I listen to her struggling for breath, and I know that she wants to live as much as anyone of forty or sixty . . . It's a great grief – a terrible parting – so many years – so much devotion.'

He put his face in his hands, and began to sob with a strange sound that Disraeli hadn't heard since he saw Sarah for the first time after James Meredith's death. How can one feel another's grief, he wondered. Mrs Copley was more than old. She had been cared for by Lyndhurst and Miss Copley like some antique clock miraculously preserved under a glass case, functioning in all parts. And it had seemed to all who knew her that it would always be so; her gentle face would always be there to tell her visitors of Lyndhurst's triumphs. Yet now, it was ending as everything must end. And Lyndhurst, the prosecutor with the stern eyes who had so often sought the death penalty, must now himself see time's execution of the person he had most loved.

Disraeli felt that death-bed scenes were best reserved for the theatre. In real life, he found them over-dramatic and embarrassing, and now from below he could hear constant additions to the cast, including Lady Cork, whose sharp, sibilant voice was already subduing the general talk. Crumpled and shrunken with grief, his back bowed, Lyndhurst had lost the serenity, the gravity, the philosophical poise which Disraeli had always admired in him. A lock of hair, half-grey, half-dyed, had fallen over his forehead, and for the first time he seemed accessible to mortal accidents. Lyndhurst would never be first in Government, Disraeli felt. Able in law, possessed of an incomparable memory that gave him an apparently effortless command of his brief, he would always need someone to initiate the theme, to divert him from the self-indulgences which normally he preferred to the arena, and to make the public interest rather than pleasure his chief concern.

The Irish Municipal Corporations Bill was to be brought forward in the Lords, and Disraeli tried to talk about it, but Lyndhurst was reluctant. Two days earlier, he had given a dinner for the Tories – Lord Roden, Rosslyn, Sugden, Hardinge, Alderson and a few others – where Disraeli had already heard him speak at length on the subject, referring to the Irish as 'aliens in blood and language and religion'. It had been a casual observation which had been reported first to the Whigs and then to O'Connell and Sheil, and taken up by *The Globe*. Lyndhurst had tried to deny the offensive imputation, but now the charge was firmly established that in relation to Ireland he was committed to an extreme prejudice.

'It's always very difficult,' he said, 'when you assume that you are dining with gentlemen, to find out afterwards that you were dining with village gossips.'

'It seems to me,' said Disraeli, 'that just as only a new love can extinguish an old, so it needs one's own new grievance to efface the grievances of others. You must create one!'

Lyndhurst sighed.

'Not today.'

They returned to the drawing-room, where Lady Cork was holding forth on the sofa with her negro page at her feet, her blue organza dress spread out in layer on layer, while the others listened deferentially.

'Ah, Lyndhurst,' she said, interrupting herself, 'I couldn't be kept away.'

'The weather – the snow – ' he began.

'No, no,' she said. 'The snow is very healthy. But this poor child – ' she waved towards her turbaned page – 'he does nothing but shiver. Go near the fire, boy, and warm your hands. You see, his palms have become quite white . . . I spoke to Mrs Copley's doctor. Terrible men, doctors. Do you still practise the Homeo-Pathic treatment for your maladies, Mr Disraeli? . . . I forget what they are. I've never had a doctor in my life . . . You know – ' turning to Lady Sykes – 'my dressmaker made me this robe with the neckline beneath my chin . . . I said to her, "Miss Rodgers, I dislike this dress." "Why, m'lady?" she asks. "It makes me look a hundred," I told her.'

There was a murmur of smiling appreciation as Lady Cork, demanding attention and returning nothing except her anecdotes, forged on. It was presumed in society that because she was old, articulate, aristocratic and rich, everything she said was interesting or amusing or remarkable, and that her great age was a sanction for every rudeness. Henrietta, Disraeli knew, never tired of her flow of stories and commands, but he himself had lately begun to feel that a lot of Lady Cork went but a little way. He rose, and spoke briefly to Lyndhurst, saying that he would call again. He wondered if the second January dinner which Lyndhurst was due to give would still be held if Mrs Copley died, and what part he ought to play in the funeral ceremony. It was a dismal thought, and he was preparing to leave when he heard the chatterbox voice of Mrs Wyndham Lewis, who had come to offer her sympathy.

She had been driving, she explained, with a window in her coach jammed, and her face was glowing from the wind and the snow.

'You must overlook my disarray,' she said to Disraeli who greeted her.

'It's desperately pleasing,' he replied. 'You will start a fashion, ma'am – a fashion in travel if these are the results.'

He looked into her friendly eyes, and he liked what seemed to him the genuineness of her disposition. She wasn't beautiful, nor indeed was there anything in her person that drew him

towards her. But he felt at ease in her company. She had something in common with Mrs Austen, though happily she lacked
her intellectual aspirations. Yes – that was it. An unintellectual
woman. Yet that couldn't be the only quality in her that made
him feel at ease. Henrietta herself, now surrounded by a
murmuring court, was also an unintellectual woman, though
he never felt at ease with her. From the first their association
had been excited by anxiety. Perhaps that was the condition of
their love.

'And how is Mr Lewis?' he asked.

'He isn't as well as I'd like him to be,' Mrs Wyndham Lewis
said with a trace of a Welsh accent in her cadenced voice. 'He
has had a fever, but he's been distracted by the Letters of
Runnymede in *The Times*. Tell me, Mr Disraeli – ' in a loud
voice that made a number of heads turn – 'is it true that you
are their author? Come on, do tell us!'

Disraeli, half-pleased, half-irritated, said,

'I – well, I know they've been attributed to me by one or two
hostile papers – there's certainly some imitation of my style –
I've often thought the writer is familiar with my works. But
the authorship – '

'Oh, never mind, sir,' said Mrs Lewis, smiling. 'Whoever
wrote them, everyone agrees that they are remarkably brilliant.
Everyone in London is talking about them. You must come
and dine with us next Tuesday. Yes – don't fail to come. I'll
send you a card.'

Disraeli glanced quickly at Henrietta, who was preparing to
leave.

'I shall be delighted,' he said firmly.

Maclise had agreed to paint Henrietta for the reduced sum of
£300, two hundred pounds below his normal price, and while
Disraeli didn't have that amount immediately available, he
calculated that the proceeds of the *Vindication* and his new
novel, *Henrietta Temple*, the love story that he was hoping to
finish before the end of the year, would enable him to maintain
his style of life, to pay for the picture and perhaps even to
fight another Parliamentary contest, especially if he got into
the Carlton and was aided by a subscription. He hadn't worked

out exactly what his expenses would be, and his occasional studies of his outstanding bills and notes of hand left him with impressions rather than definite conclusions about his finances. Still, he felt that he could face 1836 with some confidence.

Henrietta, wrapped in furs, sat at his side without speaking as the carriage jolted and slid through the sleet towards Maclise's studio in Fitzroy Square.

'I must say,' said Disraeli, 'visiting the sick is one of the Christian duties I'd willingly forgo.'

She didn't answer, and he went on,

'I was surprised to see Lyndhurst so stricken.'

She looked at him with her large eyes, violet in the winter light, and said,

'You mustn't underestimate his ability to feel deeply.'

Disraeli shrugged his shoulders.

'I don't imagine he will allow his grief to interfere with his pleasures.'

'She was very old.'

The horses were slipping, and the coachman reduced their trot to a walking pace.

'Lyndhurst asked me if I'd again accompany him and his daughter to Paris after – '

Her voice dwindled.

'Oh,' said Disraeli. He looked stonily ahead.

'I said I would talk to you,' she went on. 'I'm very sorry for Lyndhurst. He will be very lonely.'

'What about Miss Goldsmith?'

'I see no urgency. Her chief attraction, I suspect, is her father's bullion.'

Disraeli leaned against the other side of the carriage.

'Mrs Lewis invited me to dinner,' he said.

'I know. You accepted?'

'Yes.'

'Without me?'

'I trust you have no objection?'

'None.'

Her voice was curt.

'Her husband's a close friend of the Duke.'

'She's a very common woman. I heard her gossiping the

other day about Rosina. How can you endure her?'

'Her husband's a close friend of the Duke,' he repeated.

They didn't speak for a few minutes. Then Disraeli extended his hand to brush away a strand of hair from beneath her bonnet.

'What is it?' she asked, putting her hand to her face.

'Nothing,' said Disraeli. 'Just a few flakes of snow . . .'

Maclise's studio was on the top floor of his house at 63 Upper Charlotte Street, Fitzroy Square, and Disraeli and Henrietta climbed the narrow stairs carefully till they reached the large room with a top light and two easels, one occupied by a completed painting, the other by an empty canvas. Henrietta glanced at the picture, and Maclise said, 'That, madam, is *Puck Disenchanting Bottom* – I showed it at the Society of Arts in Cork – and you, Mr Disraeli, will you be pleased to take a seat while I consider Lady Sykes.'

He gave her his hand to the podium, and said,

'It is very good of you to visit me in this studio. The light, you understand, is all-important. How long is it since I first drew you, Mr Disraeli – three years?' He had taken a note-book and was already making sketches of Henrietta. 'Yes – that was an interesting period. I was Alfred Croquis, you know, in *Fraser's Magazine*.'

'You are the chief portraitist of our age,' said Disraeli.

'Ah,' said Maclise, his handsome Irish face beaming, 'not everyone liked my portraits. Goethe said my drawing of old Samuel Rogers frightened him . . . And then there was M. Talleyrand asleep in his chair. It was thought to be anti-French.'

'But your portraits are always kind to ladies,' said Henrietta, who till then had kept a sullen silence. 'I especially liked your painting of Miss Landon.'

'Your sex, ma'am, is by definition beautiful,' said Maclise, still sketching. 'I turned from ink to oils because the danger – always – for an artist is self-imitation. I drew a hundred like-nesses, but I was never satisfied.'

'Why?' Henrietta asked.

'It's unanswerable,' said Maclise. 'Consider my friend

William Etty. Since Rubens, there's been no painter of the human body like him. But he is never content. You will be surprised to know that Etty, old and suffering from bronchitis, goes coughing and gasping every night of the week, through fog and rain and snow, to the academy in Trafalgar Square, and there he wheezes his way to the life class at the top of the building, and at last finds his heaven there with his millboard among the students.'

'But surely,' said Disraeli, watching the absorbed expression of Maclise who didn't stop working as he spoke, 'that was – how can I put it? – a private pleasure rather than a necessity?'

'Most certainly a pleasure,' said Maclise. 'But a necessity too. A painter, like a pianist, must practise control. As you well know, sir, nothing in art should be an accident. Etty's palette – a little Naples yellow, light red, Indian red, a little vermilion, lake, terre verte or raw umber – some burnt umber and black – and out of it all comes that glorious, miraculous flesh . . . !'

After Maclise had sketched for a few minutes, Disraeli said, 'I'll return within an hour. I imagine, Maclise, that a spectator is an encumbrance to an artist.'

'Ah, no,' said Maclise, pushing back his long chestnut hair. 'Not when he makes the sitter smile with such an effulgence.'

After Disraeli had gone, Maclise, working with a silent absorption, began to prepare the surface of the canvas with a mixture of linseed oil, sugar of lead and turpentine. The studio was warm from the open fire, and Henrietta took off her cape. Apart from a couch, a table and chairs, a suit of armour, a stack of draperies and some swords and spears and a shield, glittering in the sunlight that came brilliantly through the roof light now that the snow had stopped, the room, pervaded with a pleasant smell of paint, was bare.

'Tell me, Mr Maclise,' said Henrietta, 'how did you first become an artist? Was your father an artist?'

'No, madam,' said Maclise. 'He was a shoemaker from Cork.'

'Perhaps your mother – '

'She was a pew-opener.'

'Then I must congratulate you.'

'On what?'

'On not following those admirable occupations – in order to put your talents at a wider disposal.'

Maclise looked up and saw that Henrietta was smiling, but he didn't smile back.

'An artist, like a shoemaker, is a craftsman,' he said. 'My father was a Highlander by origin, then he served in the Elgin fencibles before settling in Ireland. But all his life, he encouraged his children to acquire skills . . . When I was a schoolboy, I used to do drawings of soldiers, artillery, horses – anything I saw. Then I studied the antique plaster casts that Pope Pius VII gave to King George and King George gave to the City of Cork. And then one blessed day, when I was nineteen years old, I saw Sir Walter Scott in Mr Bolster's bookshop, and without him seeing what I was doing, I drew him in pen and ink, and afterwards he signed it and I had it lithographed, and sold five hundred copies . . . There!' He had finished priming the canvas.

'And that,' said Henrietta, 'is how you became an artist.'

'Oh, no,' said Maclise, 'that is how I first knew that there was money to be made in art. For then I opened a studio in Princes Street, and everyone flocked there to be painted by the artist who had drawn Sir Walter Scott, and Mr Sainthill, a man truly named, let me read in his library, and I illustrated Mr Crofton Croker's second edition of *Irish Fairy Legends*. And then I came to London – and here we are in Fitzroy Square, madam, with me preparing to paint the most beautiful woman in London.'

Henrietta didn't answer. While Maclise had been talking, she was thinking of Disraeli's forthcoming dinner at Mrs Wyndham Lewis's. Lately he had accepted more and more invitations without her, always explaining that his political obligations made it impossible to refuse them. Though he was reluctant to admit it, she knew there were those, including Peel and his friends, who weren't prepared to receive a man and his mistress. She had no wish to be a Lady Blessington, isolated like a demi-mondaine, with a retinue of male attendants, each one of them hoping at some time to supersede the current lover. Imperceptibly, Henrietta felt, her position had been changing. As Disraeli involved himself more and more in politics, so she had been more and more removed from the excitements of society. Nor was she interested in the stale compliments of Lyndhurst's elderly colleagues or even Disraeli's dandy acquaintances who tried to woo her behind his back. 'The most beautiful woman in London.' Did Maclise think that would enhance his fee? She was feeling tired and stiff from her pose on the backless twin-handled stool, and she said,

'I think I'll rest.'

Maclise went over to the podium and led her down, and she was pleased that he had acquiesced without discussion.

'How lovely the day's become,' she said.

She looked up at the glass roof where the last traces of melting snow were diamonded by the dazzling rays of the sun.

'May I see what you've done?'

Maclise hesitated.

'There's very little – a few shadows and lights.'

He stood behind her, his large athletic body towering, and she said,

'No, there isn't much to see – except the posture. I seem to be leaning forward. And will those be my eyes?'

'Yes – I will paint you wondering and seeking – not discontented, but seeking.'

'What should I seek that I haven't got?'

'We will explore that.'

Henrietta frowned, and looked at the clock.

'I trust Mr Disraeli won't keep me waiting.'

She felt uneasy in Maclise's presence now that he had stopped working.

'How many sittings will you require?'

'Perhaps three – or four – or five. I don't know. I will be expeditious. Perhaps, madam, you will appear one day in a ball-dress of your choice, and lend it to me for a short time so that I can drape it over a lay figure . . . A woman's shoulders are the key to a woman's person.'

'Indeed – how do you explain that?'

'Her posture – her character – her remaining proportions – all are present in a woman's shoulders. A woman's bare shoulders expose a woman totally.'

'Perhaps,' said Henrietta, 'you will bring me my furs.'

Maclise looked at her in amusement.

'If Mr Disraeli is delayed,' he said, 'you will melt away in this overheated room.'

She smiled to him, and said,

'In that case, Mr Maclise, you must divert me. Show me some of your sketches.'

Maclise set up a little table, and opened a heavy folio of drawings.

'Well,' he said, 'here are some sketches of Wicklow – ' he turned the drawings, and she looked at them perfunctorily – 'and here is Charles Kean as Norval in *Douglas*, and here are some sketches for my picture *Snap-Apple Night, or All-Hallows Eve in Southern Ireland.*'

He replaced the folio with another, and turned a page before saying,

'No – I don't think this will interest you. They are some studies – classical studies – I made at the Louvre. Student studies – I have never had great success in painting the nude.'

'Oh, I differ from you,' said Henrietta. 'These have – have remarkable strength.'

'Here you see *Mars and Venus* – Mars the helmeted figure in a barque and Venus – '

'Yes, she is Venus as I imagine her to be.'

'And here is *Hylas and his Nymphs.*'

The four nymphs crowded around a bewildered Hylas, their naked bodies repeated in the pool.

'And this,' said Maclise, 'I call *The Lovers.*'

It was executed in sepia ink and water-colour, and Henrietta felt her cheeks become warm as she looked at the naked, entangled lovers. She drew away, and Maclise closed the folio.

'Will you one day translate these sketches into oils?'

'Into oils?' he repeated. 'A sketch is for reminiscence.'

She glanced quickly at the preliminary drawings of her that he had laid on the wooden floor while he dipped his brushes in turpentine. At that moment Disraeli entered. He had been calling on Bulwer at Albany, and was filled with the virtuousness of one who has performed a good office.

'You've made progress, I see.'

'Great progress,' said Maclise. 'Pray glance at the sketches.'

'Admirable,' said Disraeli. 'Admirable.'

The drawings showed Henrietta in a contented pose, her expression aloof but not arrogant, her eyes large and interested without being unduly eager, her lips firmly closed, giving her a quality of inaccessibility which Disraeli always liked.

The three of them smiled happily, Maclise because he had made a good start with the portrait, Disraeli because the *tracasseries*, as he called them, of the morning ceremonials were over, and Henrietta because Disraeli was restored to a good mood.

'Tell me about Bulwer,' she said to Disraeli as their carriage took them at a trot towards Grosvenor Square.

'Poor Bulwer,' said Disraeli, his face sombre. 'I'm afraid it's all over between him and Rosina. They're about to part officially. He looked as calcified as his centurion in *The Last Days of Pompeii*. Public success and private failure! Albany really is the last redoubt. A man can't flee to his club without the danger of getting sympathy.'

'I shouldn't think he'll be long without sympathy at Albany.'

'Yes – but of a more intimate kind. At any rate, he'll soon be out of reach of that terrible virago.'

'But you told me yourself, Ben – she burst in on him when he was receiving another lady.'

'Ah yes, that's why he seeks the protection of the law.'

'It's disagreeable all the same.'

'What is?'

'The fact that two people who meet in love – who have children together – should in the end have to separate amid the musty smell of legal documents – constables at the door – arguments in Chambers. Is that the way for love to die?'

She moved closely towards him in the carriage, and he laid his face against hers.

'No,' he said, 'no. But you're not Rosina.'

'And you're not Bulwer,' she said, gratified. 'Let's drive through Hyde Park.'

Disraeli instructed Henrietta's coachman, and with the snow crunching under the wheels they drove in the January sunshine over the roads between the stark black trees.

'Dearest one,' said Henrietta, fumbling in her reticule, 'a letter came for you this morning – brought by a groom . . . I forgot to give it to you. Are you angry?'

'No,' he said, and held her more closely, with his arm behind her back.

The writing was unfamiliar, and Disraeli opened the letter slowly. It contained a printed page from *John Bull*, with some lines marked in red. The heading was,

'Vindication of the English Constitution in an Ode to a Scribbler known as Runnymede.'

Disraeli felt his hands tremble with rage, and his face set. He read on,

> *He who writes as Runnymede,*
> *Doth nothing wot of Saxon rede.*
> *A hybrid he of Hebrew breed,*
> *To Lyndhurst still a Ganymede.*
> *He gracious shares his Henrietta,*
> *Who being good could still be better!*

He tore the sheets carefully into small pieces, and as the carriage bounced along he let them drift through the window like confetti from his hand.

'What is it, Ben?' Henrietta asked anxiously. 'Has someone upset you?'

'No, my beloved,' he said, stroking her neck. 'No one.'

'But I can see you've become so pale. What is it?'

'Nothing – nothing. I am very happy. And that's what consumes them.'

'Has someone written something offensive about you?'

'Yes,' said Disraeli sombrely. 'And I know who it is. It's Maginn. Once, I would have tried to kill him.'

'No,' she said, clinging to his arm. 'No.'

'Have no fear,' said Disraeli. 'I propose to write his name down and put it into a drawer. I have no doubt that in three months' time it will have completely disappeared.'

The snow started to fall again, and the watery sun was overlaid with sluggish, livid clouds that reflected a blue light over the road, now ribbed with drifts where the coach skidded behind the horses. Henrietta glanced timidly at Disraeli as he looked through the window at the whitened tops of the carriages in Knightsbridge.

'Let's go back, dearest,' she said. 'You look chilled. Let's go back. We'll be all alone, and we'll have something to eat, and we'll – '

'I must call at Bond's,' said Disraeli stiffly.

'But you said you'd come home with me. What's happened to change your mind? I'm not a – a thing that you can say "Come here," "Go there." What is it, Ben?'

'Nothing,' he said, still looking away. 'I've got to go to Bond's to deal with some affairs.'

'You know that's not true. It's that note I gave you. What is it, Ben? Please, Ben.'

She took his hand, and said,

'Turn to me. Look at me. Tell me what it is.'

He slowly turned his face to hers, and said,

'I want to know – I want you to tell me the truth, Henrietta. When I've asked you before, you've always evaded the question, and laughed it away . . . I accepted what you said because I wanted to – because I was afraid not to believe you – but now I want to know.'

'What do you want to know?' she asked in a quiet voice.

'I want to know about you and Lyndhurst – whether you have been lovers.'

She withdrew her hand and said,

'If you're so jealous, so unbelieving, we can never be happy together. I will tell you for the last time. I knew Lyndhurst first when my father used to take me to see John Copley at his studio in George Street. I told you. Copley painted my father's portrait, and I was just fifteen.'

'But Lyndhurst – '

'He was a mature man already – a famous lawyer, even though his mother ordered him about as if he was a schoolboy. And he treated me like a little girl . . . He would walk with me across the Park holding my hand.'

'I see,' said Disraeli.

'Yes, and he took me a few times to the Courts.'

'Indeed.'

'Yes, with Father.'

Disraeli didn't answer.

'And sometimes he took me without him.'

'And what else?'

'What else? Nothing! Lyndhurst was a sweet, kind man.'

'What went on between you? Did he fondle you? Did he kiss you?'

'Oh yes, he always kissed me – when he arrived and when he left. And he always gave me presents at Christmas and on my birthdays. And I went with him and his wife and daughter on holiday three or four times. Is there any more you want to know?'

'Yes,' said Disraeli, his hand tightening over the window-ledge. '*Were* you his mistress?'

'His mistress?' Henrietta echoed thoughtfully. 'Why do you think that?'

'Because,' said Disraeli, 'because I know Lyndhurst well. The first words I ever heard him say were at the King's Theatre. "Do you believe in platonic love?" some female asked him. "*After*, madam," he answered. "*After* . . ." I have no wish to share you with Lyndhurst.'

She took his hand again, and said,

'Oh, Ben. You mustn't be unhappy about Lyndhurst. How could I have ever dreamt when I was a girl that one day I'd meet you and love you?'

Disraeli was silent.

'Whatever people say now – whatever they've been saying in Aylesbury – Lyndhurst isn't my lover. Indeed, he's not.'

'But he was. I must know, Henrietta. I must know. Or I must leave you, and never see you again. If you tell me, I will stay with you. If you refuse – '

The coach thumped over some hardened snow, and threw them together, but they disengaged themselves and Henrietta huddled herself in the corner.

'You must do what you have to,' she said at last. Then, making a decision, she turned to him and said,

'It was so long ago, Ben – everything – so many years ago. As a child I worshipped Lyndhurst with all the fantasy of a child who translates a fairy-tale into day-dream. But when he

253

first touched me – when I saw his face close to mine – used by time – by experience – it was in his father's studio one evening when they had all left – it all became confused.'

'Why?'

'Because – yes – what he did gave me pleasure – it seemed to me that never again could there be anyone to give me such pleasure – but at the same time, the pleasure destroyed all the radiance of love. And I wanted it, and yet I thought, What has all this, this ugliness – to do with love?'

Disraeli went to interrupt her, but she continued.

'Let me finish, Ben. Perhaps after this you won't ever want to see me again.' She flicked away a tear with her handkerchief. 'I hated what he had done, and I hated Lyndhurst. But then, after a time, like an appetite, I wanted to see him again. And I felt like an apprentice. I wanted to learn everything that pleasure could give.'

'And he taught you.'

'Yes,' she said, 'he taught me.' She wept. 'For a year. And then it was over, and later I married, but it was different. Francis – it's strange that men and women can engage in all the same motions, yet without – without a spell, it's meaningless.'

'And since then?'

'Since then – there's been nothing. You must believe me, Ben. Nothing at all. I didn't want to tell you in the past, because I didn't want to estrange you from Lyndhurst. He likes you so much – loves you. He wants to forward your career. It's all past – long ago.'

She was covering his face with kisses, and her face was tear-stained against his.

'When you were fifteen – '

'No, sixteen.'

She continued to kiss him, and when they arrived at Upper Grosvenor Street, she clung tightly to his arm as they climbed the staircase of the empty house.

Chapter Eighteen

'I never could understand,' said Lady Cork, 'why nowadays it's all the rage to wear imbecile sleeves, those great, stuffed-out legs of lamb. I like a woman's arm to be an arm. You have a woman's arm, Henrietta. Why make it a *gigot*? And not just a leg of lamb. A leg of lamb enclosed in a muff. It's enough to revolt one against one's dinner.'

Henrietta, lying on the sofa, didn't answer. She had been ill, and Lady Cork in her bouffant pink organdie, attended by her cherry-eyed page, was like an emanation from her fevered dreams of the past few days. Lady Cork dropped her handkerchief and stamped with her ivory stick till the boy picked it up.

'I'm tired of dinners,' Lady Cork rattled on. 'I don't like Bulwer. Do you like Bulwer? He speaks too faintly. I like a man to speak up. Now Francis Egerton – he's different. He is a literary man – Lord Francis Egerton – he translated Goethe – *Wer reitet so spät durch Nacht und Wind* – your Francis first told me about him – wait, dearest Henrietta – give me a sachet, boy!'

The page handed her an enamel box, and Lady Cork ate a dragée.

'Yes – then there's Buckingham – the traveller, my dear, not His Grace. Have you read his *Oriental Herald*? – a most remarkable book – you must read it. They say he wrote most of it himself. Are you unwell, darling Henrietta?'

Henrietta raised herself on the cushions and glanced around the boudoir of the Park Lane house which she had lately taken. With the help of an excellent architect and the guidance of William Pyne, she had arranged the decoration of the house in a manner which had delighted her lover. *Rococo de nos jours*. She had chosen heavy brocaded curtains in a pale biscuit colour to offset the gilt, and his praise had made her happy. The only shadow on her pleasure was that in the last few weeks Disraeli had so often absented himself from her company.

Lady Cork was examining her through her eye-glass.

'No, don't tell me,' she said. 'I see that you have become thin. You mustn't become thin, beautiful child. Men like slender women for company, but opulent women for rollicking.'

Henrietta smiled faintly.

'I'm not really thin,' she said. 'It's simply that I haven't driven out for a few days, and I suppose I look pale.'

'Yes, pale,' said Lady Cork decisively. 'It's time you were better cared for. I see Disraeli everywhere. Why don't he attend you better?'

'Oh, he does,' said Henrietta quickly. 'He couldn't be more attentive, Lady Cork. You can imagine he has much to do now that he has returned to politics.'

'Politics?' Lady Cork said harshly, tapping her stick. 'He'd do better to stay with his novels. There's no room for Jews in politics. Besides, Disraeli has no prospects – the places are all filled for the next twenty years. And on top of it all – ' she lowered her voice – 'he lacks the goodwill of Sir Robert Peel.'

'Sir Robert, I understand,' said Henrietta meekly, 'has always been friendly to Disraeli.'

'Peel,' said Lady Cork with a wave of her hand, 'is a politician who makes a show of being friendly to everyone. You must look at him, dearest child, when you next meet him. His smile is lively; he shows all his teeth. But his eyes – they're dead – quite dead, and they've been so for years, though he's scarcely fifty. Besides, he has red hair.'

'Red hair?' Henrietta repeated.

'Yes,' said Lady Cork. 'Red hair and black hair never mix . . . Tell me, what news have you of Francis?'

'I hear from him at intervals,' said Henrietta thoughtfully. 'He has a restless spirit that drives him from place to place in Europe, though I doubt that he will return to England this year.'

'Does he write about Disraeli?'

'It's strange,' she said. 'He writes about him in the most benevolent spirit. It makes me afraid.'

She looked at the old woman, seeking from her age and experience an illumination of her problems. Lady Cork sat as if she hadn't heard what Henrietta had said. Then she said,

'You must be very careful, dearest child. Sykes is unpredictable, a violent man as capable of change as a Mediterranean sea. For the time being, with Clara Bolton – '

'They've separated.'

'How d'you know?'

'I know it. She's gone to Holland. Sarah – Ben's sister – had a letter from an English clergyman inquiring about her . . .' She hesitated. 'I have the feeling that Francis simply abandoned her.'

'Good!' said Lady Cork. 'And her husband?'

'He's our neighbour in Park Lane.'

'You have no communication with him?'

'None.'

'That's as it should be,' said Lady Cork, her eyes glazing over. 'I was telling you about my macaw – '

'Your macaw?'

'Wasn't I? . . . No, not the macaw – Disraeli – yes, Disraeli.' She had stopped fidgeting, and had become grave, her embalmed old face set in a solemn expression.

'You must be careful, Henrietta, that Sykes don't return and compromise you and Disraeli in a "crim-con" situation.'

'And how could that be?' said Henrietta, sitting up. 'He acquiesced.'

'That was last year. The fact that he and Mrs Bolton have parted makes his position easier.'

'Oh no,' said Henrietta. 'No. It's impossible. "Criminal conversation?" You mean he could deprive me of my children?'

'He might say that you had deprived yourself of them.'

Henrietta rose, and went over to the coloured miniatures of her children on the table.

'No,' she said. 'It's impossible.'

'Not impossible,' said Lady Cork, 'not impossible. You must be seen more in public, dearest child. Why have you lately retired?'

Henrietta did not answer.

'Has Disraeli been occupied with other matters?' Lady Cork went on. 'You're not an old glove, dearest child, to be put on and off. I admired Disraeli – I love his father – ah, yes – did I ever tell you how well Byron thought of Isaac? *The Literary*

Character – yes, Byron once told me he'd choose that book out of all as the one that gave him most "elevation" he called it. And then – that other writer – what's his name – yes, Scott – Scott – I'll forget my own name soon – Scott said he thought Isaac his peer, but he hated young Disraeli – yes, hated him. He once went to Abbotsford – was it Abbotsford? Yes – to launch a journal. Walter Scott gave him dinner, and sent him home.'

'That isn't what I heard,' said Henrietta staunchly.

'No,' said Lady Cork. 'That's because you heard it from Disraeli. Where is he today?'

'I don't know. He has many duties.'

'Duties? Duties? He's neglectin' you – he has compromised you, and he's neglectin' you. You must be more resolute, dearest child. Come and sit next to me. You know I love you.'

Henrietta came and sat next to Lady Cork on the sofa, and Lady Cork's maculated hand closed over hers.

'He has neglected you, has he not?'

Henrietta burst into tears, and Lady Cork observed her lowered head till her sobbing ended in a hiccup.

'Yes,' she said, 'he has neglected you. I hear he's all the time at the Londonderrys' without you.'

Henrietta shook her head slowly.

'It isn't just that,' she said. 'I have many friends. The Lynd-hursts are kind to me. John – Lord Lyndhurst – has always been a sort of guardian. He understands so much that Disraeli overlooks. Lyndhurst doesn't need to be as *frantic* as Ben. That's the real trouble. Ben's so frantic – as if he's afraid that the coach will leave without him, and he has to fight for a place . . . And sometimes, he's heartless.'

She began to cry again, and Lady Cork stroked her hand.

'I sometimes have bad dreams. What will become of me? Francis will leave me, and I couldn't blame him. Then Lynd-hurst is to be married. It may be that his wife won't tolerate old friendships . . . And Disraeli! He's younger than I am. I have four children. Why should he want to burden himself at the beginning of his political career with a married woman, possessed of a family – when he could have all London at his feet?'

'And you love him?'

'Love him? Love him? Yes – I love him. I love him because I have a great willingness to love. Francis stifled it. He despised my enthusiasm. I wanted to love even more than to be loved. And then I met Disraeli. And he was a man who wanted to *be* loved.'

Lady Cork signalled to her page, and kissed Henrietta on both cheeks.

'Dearest Henrietta – I will send you six bottles of port. You must drink some each day to make yourself strong.'

Henrietta smiled wanly.

'And then again,' said Lady Cork, primping her organdie till she looked like an aged china shepherdess, 'I will give you some advice. You must not despair about any man.'

'I despair often,' said Henrietta. 'I have such evil dreams that I'm afraid to go to sleep. I dream of trying to find Disraeli who can never again be found. I dream of that all the time – and the last time I went to George Street, I took a bottle of laudanum from Lyndhurst's cupboard, and when I got home, I took a draught that made me sleep without dreams for nearly two days and nights.'

'No,' said Lady Cork sharply, 'you must promise me, Henrietta, you'll never again do that. Promise me!'

Henrietta didn't answer.

'Have you any of the laudanum left?'

Henrietta went silently to a drawer and produced a half-empty bottle.

'Give it to me,' said Lady Cork imperiously. She took the bottle, sniffed, made a face, and handed it to the page.

'You must never do it again . . . Hear me, Henrietta. You must be seen more. You must come to dinner on Tuesday – alone, if Disraeli can't come. I'll ask Egerton or Buckingham since you like authors. But come you must. You must distribute your attentions more so that the wicked tongues will stop talking about Lady Sykes and her swain, Disraeli.'

Henrietta didn't answer.

'If you move more in society, you will dilute the attention. The less exclusive you are in public, the more exclusive you can be in private.'

'Yes,' said Henrietta humbly.

'And by the way,' said Lady Cork, making for the door, 'how is your portrait getting on?'

Henrietta laughed for the first time, and rang the bell for the footman.

'It's making slow progress.'

'He's a very good artist, Maclise.'

'Yes.'

'A fine, dashing, handsome man as well.'

'Yes,' said Henrietta.

'Sixty years ago, I could have wished for a Maclise to paint me. Come, boy!'

The doors opened, and Henrietta looked after her thoughtfully.

Chapter Nineteen

Disraeli chose an armchair by the window overlooking Pall Mall, and took up a newspaper. It was the first time he had visited the Carlton Club as a member, and he tried to dispose himself nonchalantly without showing the diffidence that he felt at his unchaperoned début. It was nearly five o'clock. The club was almost empty apart from Lord Ellenborough asleep with a newspaper trailing from his hand. Two other members who came into the room, stared at him, muttered something or other, and then left laughing.

Whenever in the past Disraeli had walked down Pall Mall, the spectacle, dimly seen, of clubmen at their windows had always seemed to him to emphasize the contrast between the possessors and the excluded. To have been elected at last to the Club on the nomination of Lyndhurst with Lady Blessington as his chief canvasser had been a triumph, especially taking into account the usual cabal which had tried to keep him out as they had done successfully at the Athenæum. It meant that instead of having to rely for his Parliamentary prospects on accidental meetings in society, he was now at the centre of the market where the Tory Whips weighed ability and transacted business, where the first rumours reached of seats to be vacated, and the health of MPs was anxiously discussed, not indeed out of care for their well-being but with an eye to their succession by younger and more robust candidates; where the organization of a revitalized Conservative Party was taking form, and the mysteries and secrets whispered between Members in the Commons were submitted in the reading-room or the coffee-room to a second, even closer probing. At Westminster the interest was in policies; here in arrangements.

This was the atmosphere that Disraeli craved, and he sank back into the old leather armchair, listening with satisfaction to its bellows-like wheeze, and thinking that there couldn't be many things able to give a man a greater sense of the *douceur de vivre* than to have lunched with the Duke, not at Apsley House it was true, but in Hyde Park Gate all the same, and to take up a position as of right at the window of a famous club, reading his own contribution to the most significant newspaper in England.

Pity that Henrietta had lately been irked by the competition of his political affairs! Much as he loved her, he sometimes felt asphyxiated by her demands for attention, which had increased rather than diminished as their relationship had become known and accepted. In the last few months, Sir Francis Sykes had been writing a series of contradictory letters, one day announcing his imminent return to England, another day saying that his health made it necessary for him to move from Nice to Leghorn or Venice or Naples. He addressed Disraeli as a confidant, assuring him that he profoundly appreciated his friendship towards his wife in a hostile world that was always ready to put a disagreeable interpretation on whatever lay beyond its comprehension. Occasionally, these sympathetic letters made Disraeli feel uneasy, since if they expressed Sykes's ignorance, his awakening would be all the more brutal – and if they were written in irony, Disraeli would have to be more than watchful of their deferred confrontation.

Was it easier to live with a closed or an open secret? The advantage of indiscretion was that those who practised it could scarcely be charged with a mean reticence. But there were disadvantages too. His father had told him that Peel had made some unfavourable reference at a dinner-party to his connection with Henrietta, and he had feared it might hinder him in his election at the Carlton. Yet the fact that it hadn't was proof that his leader recognized his talent and, despite the gossip and what Swift had called 'the virulence of the dunces', wanted him in the Party. Lord Melbourne, on the other hand, always willing to injure an opponent, had said at the Reform that Disraeli was 'an intellectual investor beyond his means, a young tradesman in other men's abilities, a chaser after the wives of *fainéant* husbands'. Well, so much the worse for the Prime Minister. Disraeli took up *The Times* and read his 'Letter Addressed to the Lords' in the long, thin column on the left-hand page, signed *Runnymede*.

'In a few hours,' he had written, 'in obedience to the mandate of the Papal priesthood, that shallow voluptuary who is still Prime Minister of England' – 'shallow voluptuary!' He relished the words with their evocation of sybaritic self-indulgence combined with transparency of intellect – 'that shallow voluptuary who is still Prime Minister of England will call upon Your Lordships with cuckoo note to do "justice to Ireland" . . . But the Irish cannot be conciliated.'

Indeed, they could not. He had discussed his article with Lyndhurst, who had described the Irish Municipal Corporations Bill as a Whig project to create centres of sedition.

'Irish history,' Disraeli's Letter continued, 'is an unbroken circle of bigotry and blood.'

That, he had to admit, was a bit strong, but not so strong as O'Connell's diatribes, and if he saw the Irish collectively in the person of O'Connell, who was to blame? He didn't mind admitting to himself that he had liked and admired O'Connell. It was a pity they had quarrelled – but he had powerful political arguments as well as resentments against O'Connell and his followers. There was no doubt that this Letter would be well received at the Carlton, and he wasn't surprised that from time to time various gentlemen he recognized – Sir Henry Hardinge, Baring Wall, old Viscount Stormont, Sir Richard Vyvyan and Lord Eliot – came into the room to cast a glance at him, while he modestly occupied himself with his news-papers.

He looked up for a moment, and saw that Sir Robert Peel had walked into the room, hesitated as if to address him, and then before Disraeli could greet him, withdrew.

It didn't matter. There'd be other times when they could meet, times when Disraeli would have made a mark which even his Party leader would recognize. Peel's forehead was noble and frank, he had to admit, but his eye wasn't good. He had an awkward habit of looking askance. And then again, his mouth was compressed and his long upper lip gave him a priggish air. Disraeli had often heard him speak in the House of Commons, and admired his clarity and skill as a debater. What he lacked was the ability to move his audience. He had, as Lyndhurst once said, 'an incapacity for pathos', and when he tried to conjure up sentiment, his face became distorted like that of a woman who wanted to cry but couldn't.

Disraeli had first met Peel four years before at a dinner which he especially remembered from the way that Peel ate his turbot with his knife. He had offered one or two remarks, but Peel hadn't taken to him, and after a few seconds tucked his napkin under his chin and ignored Disraeli till the meal was over. Disraeli, undeterred, had recently sent him the *Vindi-cation*, a gift which Peel acknowledged with an ambiguous compliment about the refreshing way Disraeli had handled a worn-out subject.

A waiter, standing in front of him with a note on a salver, interrupted his thoughts. Disraeli opened the envelope and read,

'Mr James Jephson presents his compliments to Mr Disraeli, and informs him for his convenience that he is sitting in the armchair reserved by custom for Sir Robert Peel.'

Hurriedly putting the note from the Club's secretary in the inside pocket of his coat, he rose and walked to the window. Now he knew the reason for the whispering and inspections, and he had to make a decision as to whether he would retreat from the Club before his gaffe became a dinner-table anecdote, or whether he should stay and inhibit the gossip till the story became stale. He decided to stay, and sauntered warily through the reading-room to see if he knew anyone there. In the billiard-room he came face to face with an old acquaintance, Lord Glentworth.

'My dear fellow,' said Glentworth, shaking his head. 'Most exciting news!'

It was his favourite opening in conversation, and usually concerned some wager he had made, the purchase of a horse, or a change of repertoire by La Grisi.

'What is it?' Disraeli asked. 'Has the Government fallen?'

'Much more serious,' said Glentworth, drawing him conspiratorially to the sofa and lowering his voice below the clicking of billiard balls that was the only other sound in the room. 'I'm going to get married.'

'My congratulations!'

Disraeli wondered who was the beneficiary of Glentworth's rakish enthusiasm, which had already so alienated his grandfather Lord Limerick that he had disinherited him, leaving him with only his title as a marriageable attraction.

'Miss Maria Villebois!' said Glentworth gravely.

Disraeli started from the sofa and then subsided. Maria Villebois – the censorious spinster who had so often adjured her sister to reform, was going to marry Glentworth – Pery – the squire of Covent Garden and lord-in-waiting at the King's stage-door. Did that make him a sort of morganatic brother-in-law? Perhaps that was the reason why old Villebois and Maria had been so troubled by his relationship with Henrietta. Not disapproval of himself; merely the apprehension that an irregularity in Henrietta's social conduct might estrange from Maria a man who was better known among the gamblers of Crockford's, the Cyprians of Vauxhall Gardens, and the prize-fighters of Bow than anyone else in London.

'Yes,' Disraeli said. 'I've met the lady. I was much impressed by the – piety of her disposition.'

Glentworth shuffled his feet.

'Pious – yes,' he said. 'Pious! Dammit, Disraeli – d'you think I'll be able to stand it?'

'At fifteen thousand a year,' said Disraeli, 'you'd be in error not to.'

He left Glentworth looking thoughtful, and returned to the

coffee-room, where he saw that Peel and Lyndhurst were engaged in a relaxed discussion. Lyndhurst beckoned him over, and Peel waved him to a seat.

'Delighted to welcome you, sir,' he said. 'Pray join us. I have spent the morning receiving deputations, and I'm exhausted. You know, I never care how hard I work in the closet or the House. I always feel that something's being done. But a deputation is like a military exercise. So much stamping! So much dust! And everyone at the end is as they were. After all, you know the views of a deputation before their spokesman even opens his mouth. And then you have to put on a countenance of respectful candour while they're producing their impracticable systems.'

'The great art of receiving deputations,' said Lyndhurst, 'is to stifle your yawns for a period and then to allow an expression of conviction to come into your eyes – the sort of look that means that despite all your prejudices and preconceptions, you have at last allowed their arguments to break through.'

Disraeli made to speak, but Lyndhurst went on.

'One of the problems of our age is the demand for too close and early a definition. There was a time when men could be fluid in their views, and then make up their mind the moment when decisions have to be taken.'

'Would you not say, my lord,' asked Disraeli, 'that our Party will have to discard its pragmatism before long and turn to principle?'

Peel looked at him coldly, and asked,

'What principle have you in mind, Mr Disraeli?'

'The principle of having principles,' said Disraeli.

Peel said abruptly, 'Very interesting, sir. It is an excellent thing that in our Party there should be young men who aren't preoccupied with programmes.'

'I see that "Runnymede" is very severe today with Lord Melbourne,' Lyndhurst interposed. ' "Sensual libertine." '

' "Shallow voluptuary," ' said Disraeli.

'*Very* severe!'

'Swift would have called it mild,' Disraeli answered.

'I'm not sure,' said Peel, 'whether in politics an argument

ad hominem is ever more effective in the long run than an argument *in rem.*'

'But surely, sir,' said Lyndhurst, 'the character of a statesman can't be divorced from the policies he recommends? Doesn't a virtuous nation require virtuous statesmen? How can an atheist recommend religious observance? Or a libertine the merits of family life?'

'The answer,' said Peel, recognizing the cynicism in Lyndhurst's question, 'is that they do.'

'Can a man who is incapable of managing his personal financial affairs be a good Chancellor of the Exchequer?'

'Most certainly,' said Peel. 'Dr Johnson, I think, illustrated the nature of a fallacy with the false proposition: "He who drives fat oxen must himself be fat." '

'Oh, I agree,' said Lyndhurst. 'The true logic should be: "He who drives fat oxen must himself have authority." The operative part of the proposition is the quality of being able to drive the oxen.'

'Well, what do you conclude from that?' asked Peel.

'That the personal qualities of a statesman are relevant to his position.'

'You draw no distinction between his private and public life?'

'Not in their externals,' said Lyndhurst. 'Every statesman should seem a Cato, even if he can't be one.'

'And what allowance would you make for human imperfection?'

'The duty of a statesman is to conceal himself.'

'You mean,' said Peel with a half-smile, 'it's possible for a bad man to be a good statesman, provided that he shrouds his personality.'

'Bad,' Lyndhurst echoed thoughtfully. 'No – I don't say that. We live in an age when badness is regarded as congruent with adultery. That seems to me to cover only a small area of life. Are there no others where even a statesman like Melbourne, admittedly an adulterer, can practise virtue?'

'What d'you think, Disraeli?' asked Peel.

'It isn't a subject that I've thought about very deeply,' said Disraeli, disclaiming any expertise. 'I imagine that at a certain

moment in a statesman's life – when his private person becomes, in a sense, public property – he has a duty to ensure
that his public and private comportment fuse. He ceases to
enjoy the privilege of a double personality. He can no longer
say there are the rules for himself and those for the governed.
He becomes a kind of Vestal Virgin, dedicated as a symbol to
tend the altars of public good – '

Lyndhurst interrupted him with a loud laugh.

'Stop, Ben – stop. I don't recognize myself.'

'I think,' said Peel gravely, 'Mr Disraeli was visualizing his
own future.'

'Indeed, yes, sir,' said Disraeli in an equally grave tone.
'I'm comforted, though, by the feeling that that future is not
imminent.'

'Are you still interested in Taunton?'

'No,' said Disraeli. 'I am now seeking another seat.'

He hoped that Peel might use the occasion to propose a
possible vacancy. But instead, Peel rose and said,

'You must keep trying. Yes, you must keep trying. With a
lively mind like yours, you must succeed.'

Disraeli rose too, and said,

'There is one matter, sir, on which I should like to enlist
your support.'

Peel eyed him coolly, and said, 'Indeed, and what is that?'

Disraeli, having committed himself, now advanced firmly
into the subject.

'I have been asked,' he said, 'by a number of my friends,
including Members of the House of Commons, though not
all of them Tories – ' he drew a deep breath – 'I have been
asked if I could engage your sympathy for a man called Hardy,
who has been transported to Australia on a charge of rick-
burning and conspiracy.'

He observed that Peel's features had tightened, and he
faltered, but went on.

'There is, sir, a considerable feeling that this man's guilt
was not adequately proved – and having attended the trial at
Aylesbury I am obliged to say that I share this view – that he
is the victim of local malice, and that even if his guilt were
proved, the sentence of seven years' transportation is un-

consciobably hard. I hope for your support with the Home Secretary in recommending him for the Royal mercy.'

He stopped, and waited for a reply. Lyndhurst, he noticed, had picked up *The Times* and was reading it as if the subject under discussion was of no interest to him.

'You must know, Mr Disraeli,' said Peel, 'that I have always felt it my duty and responsibility to uphold the law, while none the less engaging in measures of law reform. I never hesitated when I was Home Secretary to defend civil rights even when to do so involved unpopularity. I needn't remind you that it was I who introduced the Bill for Catholic Emancipation, and I was overwhelmed for my pains with abuse as a traitor and an apostate.'

'Indeed, sir,' said Disraeli, 'those were the credentials which made me feel that I could approach you in the case of this unhappy man.'

'No,' said Peel, standing and preparing to leave. 'The law can't be set aside by partial prejudices – not even in Opposition. There have been many things within my gift. But it is not within my gift, nor would it be my wish, to interfere with the judiciary. Good morning, Mr Disraeli.'

After Peel had closed the door behind him, Lyndhurst put down his *Times*, and said,

'That was unwise, Ben. Peel often confuses self-righteousness with rectitude.'

'I imagined him a humanitarian.'

'Yes, but he couldn't offend the farmers by pardoning a trade union conspirator, a rick-burner.'

'Hardy was acquitted of that charge.'

'No matter. That is how they see him. For Peel, the cohesion of the Party is more important than the coherence of his principles.'

Disraeli shrugged his shoulders.

'I can't help that. I promised,' he said.

He was due to call for Henrietta later in the day at Maclise's studio, but he had four hours ahead of him and he decided on a sudden inclination to walk in the sunshine to visit Mrs Austen in Guilford Street, where he would be near Fitzroy

Square. He couldn't say that his first appearance at the Carlton had been an unqualified success. Peel's ironic manner always made him want to over-assert himself. There was nothing he would have liked more from Peel than a complimentary reference to the Letters of Runnymede, or perhaps some comment on the *Vindication of the English Constitution*. But nothing! It was almost as if Peel had deliberately tried to undervalue his contribution to political thought – and that, he felt, even more than writing novels was his most important achievement so far.

In the first months of his love for Henrietta, after he had begun to write *Henrietta Temple*, he had added the sub-title, A Love Story. He had completed one volume in a fierce activity when he had been separated from her at Bradenham in the autumn of that year. But then there had followed eighteen months of pleasure, of social engagements interspersed with political forays, of balls and parties, and elections and speeches and articles and leader-writing.

From time to time he had returned to the manuscript with the thought of completing it, but always there was some distraction and, he had to admit it, a decline in his original enthusiasm. He remembered again his description of first love, his first meeting with Henrietta at the King's Theatre.

'There is no love but love at first sight. This is the transcendent and surpassing offering of sheer and unpolluted sympathy. All other is the illegitimate result of observation, of reflection, of compromise, of comparison, of expediency. The passions that endure flash like lightning; they scorch the soul, but it is warmed for ever.'

Yes, that was how it had been, and that was how it remained. 'The passions that endure flash like lightning; they scorch the soul.' Yet there had been inconveniences. There were times when he wished that their names weren't so inextricably mingled. There were times when he felt more a guardian than a lover, and a guardian himself in need of protection from the pack of creditors constantly reappearing in the person of Mayley, the odious sheriff's officer. Colburn the publisher had asked him whether he had another novel on the stocks, and had offered him a substantial advance. *Henrietta Temple*? He needed the money urgently, and he calculated that if he could finish the novel at Bradenham in September, he would be ready for the task that he had set himself – to capture a Parliamentary seat and begin in earnest a political career for which his writings and his Carlton connections were merely a preparation.

Sometimes he longed for a miraculous intervention that would release him from the galley-oar of his debts. Recently he had heard from Baron de Haber, eager to promote a loan to some City investors from his financial house in The Hague. Although his experience of de Haber was that his proposals failed to benefit anyone but the Baron himself, Disraeli had decided to visit The Hague and study the suggestion. £1,000 to act as drummer for a financier! It wasn't a part that he relished, but he had little alternative. Perhaps marriage, after all, was the answer. And yet heiresses couldn't be plucked from the air. He had no wish to tie himself for life to some gaunt and elderly widow, nor, for that matter, to some chatterbox débutante like Lady Charlotte, even if he could have overcome her family's resistance.

He was thirty-two, still young but not very young, and he would have to hurry. The only fame he thought worth while was a fame that he could enjoy before he was enveloped by dismal middle age. Despite the brightness of the afternoon, Disraeli felt melancholy. In the balance-sheet of his life, he felt that he had more debits than credits, that the assets of last year's pleasures had already evaporated, and that he carried burdens of responsibility that made him feel a hundred years old.

Nor could he discuss these matters with Henrietta. When she wasn't talking about love, she was discussing her children or new furnishings, a dress or a ball. Her greatest quality was that she could move in society with a total indifference to malice or praise, and when he escorted her in public he always felt a certain sublimity, as if her style raised them both above the gossip or even the admiration of onlookers. What she required most of all was the reassurance she found in their physical union. There was no setback in her personal life – external menaces, her husband's displeasure, her children's illnesses, domestic problems – which didn't disappear for her when they were in bed together.

Sara Austen looked up in surprise when Disraeli was announced by the servant. He went to kiss her cheek, but she offered him her hand instead.

'You're not pleased to see me?' he asked.

'Very,' she said, 'but it's been such a long time since you came to Guilford Street – not since you read us your Revolutionary Epick.'

He frowned at the memory; he had once hoped that with this poem he might have been recognized as the equal of Byron, Shelley, Southey, but somehow or other when he re-read his work, it had proved to be merely a pastiche.

> *Divine Equality, thou art a God,*
> *Omnipotent indeed! Thy sacred fire*
> *Burns now in later temples, not to fall*
> *Like thine old shrines; yet who can e'er forget,*
> *Whose soul indeed thy noble faith inflames,*
> *Thy broken altar on Athena's hill!*

How splendidly the words and phrases had rolled when, with his back to the fireplace after dinner at the Austens, he had read the Epick to the polite company of his fellow-guests! But the poem had had no success when it was finally published, and he wasn't surprised.

'I fear, madam,' he said, 'the age of versification is past. In ancient times, I suppose, the poet was also the orator. That might have suited me very well. But poetry has become too metaphysical, more a matter for study rather than for passion. I feel I must restrict myself to prose.'

'And what are you writing, Ben? You know I was always your sternest critic.'

'The sternest and best,' said Disraeli, and he had a sudden feeling of tenderness for Sara, who, since he had ended her intolerable demands on his time and emotions, now looked at him with an air of modest reproach which touched him. 'I'm writing a novel, a love story,' he said.

'I wish I could have helped,' said Mrs Austen. 'Can I offer you tea?'

'Not yet,' said Disraeli, drawing his chair close to hers. 'I want to talk to you first.'

'What about? Your family – how are they? I never hear from Sarah.'

'They're well. They live a very quiet and isolated life at Bradenham. Sarah cares for the villagers – she helps to administer the household – and the days disappear.'

'Yes – the days disappear,' said Mrs Austen. 'And yet – ' she added brightly – 'it's strange how when one episode of one's life ends and it seems that everything is ended, something else begins.'

'Oh,' said Disraeli jealously, 'you mean you – '

Her face flushed, and she said,

'I don't mean anything. We have many new friends – '

'Are you saying you see G.?'

'Indeed, he is a very charming and gifted man.'

'Yes,' said Disraeli.

She tugged at the bell and ordered tea.

'Tell me, Ben,' she said, 'why have you called on me today?'

Disraeli stood and walked around the room.

'I wanted,' he began, 'I wanted – '

'What?'

'Comfort.'

'I would have thought you have a sufficiency of that.'

'No – no, that isn't so.'

He returned to his seat, took her hands in his.

'I'm very confused, Sara – very. The moment I achieve something I've longed and struggled for, I want something different – something outside my reach.'

'But Lady Sykes isn't outside your reach. Everyone in London is talking about your liaison with her. Are you so naive, Ben, that you don't realize it?'

He hesitated, and said,

'I realize it. In a way, I *wanted* everyone to talk about it.'

'In that case, you have no reason for complaint.'

'Not for complaint – perhaps – '

'Perhaps what?'

'Perhaps for regret.'

Mrs Austen released his hands, and said,

'You know I have never wished you anything but good. Eighteen months ago when I first heard about you and Henrietta Sykes, I thought I'd die – yes, quite literally. I ceased to want to live. Mr Austen – well, I needn't speak of him. My husband is a good, kind and loving man – and that is something apart. But you were like a sun that gave me warmth and light, and when you disappeared, it was like an endless night. And so, I wanted to die.'

'I'm sorry,' Disraeli muttered.

'And yet I had to know everything about you. I collected every piece of gossip like a scavenger. I read every newspaper to see if there was a reference to you. I waited – yes, I'm ashamed though it's true – I waited at Duke Street and Park Lane – I waited for hours just to see you pass by with Henrietta.'

'I'm sorry,' Disraeli said again.

'No – you mustn't be sorry,' said Mrs Austen, 'I was glad. I was proud of your ascent – happy for you. You see, Ben, I loved you.'

The servant brought a tea-tray in, and Mrs Austen's manner became formal in her presence.

'I hope you haven't been overworking with your novel, Mr Disraeli. You are looking rather thin.'

Disraeli smiled.

'I always look thin in spring,' he said. 'It's the after-effect of hibernation.'

'You mustn't become too thin,' she said. 'There's still a great deal of influenza in London.'

After the servant had gone, Disraeli said,

'I sometimes wish I could abandon everything and return to the East. It's only there that I've ever felt totally at peace.'

'Is that really so? Aren't you just saying that at this moment in London you have problems you find it hard to deal with?'

'Yes,' said Disraeli.

His visit to Mrs Austen, he felt, was a mistake, but a different kind of mistake from the one he had prepared himself to face. He had come to her for comfort, though ready to condescend.

Instead, she had offered him nostalgia without comfort, and it was she, with her hint of a successor for her favours, who was condescending to him.

He didn't want to leave defeated. She was observing him with a smiling familiarity, as if she were well-disposed towards him and bore him no ill-will for the past but had acquiesced in a new and benevolent relationship.

'Sara!' he said, rising. 'Ask the servant – '

'She won't come back till I summon her,' said Sara, still smiling.

'May I come and sit next to you?'

'Of course.'

He sat on the sofa beside her chair, and said,

'Darling Sara – forgive me if I hurt you.'

She didn't answer but continued to smile.

He stood by her chair, and drew her up and put his hands on her shoulders, looking into her pert face, her small mouth and her amused eyes.

'Sara!' he said, and tried to draw her face to his. She resisted, and he said, 'Come, Sara!'

'No, Ben,' she said. 'Lovers have a duty to be faithful.'

She pulled at the tassel to summon the maid.

On the way to Maclise's studio, Disraeli's mood, chastened by a rejection at the hands of someone whom he hadn't really wanted, began to revive. A flower-girl near Euston pressed on him a bouquet of irises and daffodils, and when he gave her two shillings her loud gratitude followed him down the street. He didn't wholly regret his call on Sara Austen. Her smiling detachment relieved him once and for all of the sense of guilt and obligation he had felt towards her. Thanks to the excellent arrangements of his solicitor, William Pyne, and the generosity of Henrietta, now that Francis Sykes had made some more substantial provision for her, he had been able to discharge his debt to the tedious and insistent Benjamin Austen though his other debts remained. He swung his cane as he walked, liberated at last from an episode which had been instructive rather than pleasurable and, on the whole, more irksome than entertaining.

At Fitzroy Square Henrietta's coach was already waiting, and the coachman raised his hat to him.

'Have you been here long?' Disraeli asked him.

'Two hours, sir,' said the coachman.

'Two hours,' Disraeli muttered. 'The tedium! The tedium!' He liked the idea of being painted, but he never found it easy to compose himself for more than half an hour at a time. Poor Henrietta! A manservant opened the door, and he hurried upstairs to the half-open door of the studio, and going straight in greeted Henrietta, who was sitting on the sofa with the light flowing in through the top windows on to her bare shoulders. She was wearing an evening dress of rose-coloured velvet with bouffant sleeves and a pointed corsage with a deep décolleté. Her skirt, embroidered with blonde lace, billowed out like a sail.

'I'm late, I'm afraid,' he said. 'I stopped for these flowers.'

'They're beautiful,' she said, and he saw that there were two spots, as if of rouge, on her cheek-bones. 'They're beautiful.'

She stood up, and in a gesture unfamiliar in the presence of a third person, kissed Disraeli affectionately on his cheek near his mouth. He studied her at arm's length, and said,

'You are beautiful – exceptionally beautiful today. What have you done to her, Maclise?'

'I have painted her,' said Maclise sombrely, soaking a brush in turpentine.

'Yes, he has. And it's wonderful,' said Henrietta. 'Come and look.'

The picture had already been shrouded in a canvas cover, and Maclise, drying his hands, said,

'I wouldn't advise you to see it finished before it is, sir. There is some way to go.'

'Ah,' said Disraeli cheerfully, 'but you have already substituted the real person for the lay-figure.'

'I so hate wearing evening dress at this hour,' said Henrietta with a glance at Maclise, and Disraeli observed that her gaiety and excitement about the picture had transformed her manner. No longer aloof and commanding, she alternated between shyness and talkativeness, and Disraeli, charmed by the change

275

in her, felt protective and intimate, as if they had begun to play a new family game together.

'Come, Maclise,' he said, 'let's all study the painting. I promise we won't embarrass you with criticism or praise.'

Maclise stood in front of the easel, and said, in his soft Irish voice,

'No – I'd rather not, Mr Disraeli. There's nothing so fatal as to show a picture before it has come to life.'

'Oh yes, please, Mr Maclise!' said Henrietta, her violet eyes looking steadily at him. 'You would do us a kindness.'

Maclise hesitated. Then he said, 'Very well,' and drew away the drapes hanging over the picture.

Disraeli raised his quiz-glass and stood back in order to focus, and Henrietta watched his expression. At first, Disraeli saw only the general design of the painting. Henrietta was in full face, sitting on the divan which had been idealized into a classical bench. The folds of her dress were still to be completed, but the background, a balustrade with an Ionic column beyond which lay a receding parkland and a blue sky, had been finished in detail. Henrietta was leaning forward, and the upper part of her breasts was visible with the faint hint of a vein giving life to the delicate surface. The formal, haughty expression of the first sketches was gone. In its place there was now an urgent, eager glance; her lips were parted, as if what she was asking was not yet answered; and the fingers of her right hand were clenched in the fold of her dress.

Disraeli stood without speaking, till at last Henrietta said, 'Well – what do you think of it?'

Maclise let the drapes fall over the picture, and waited for Disraeli's comment.

Disraeli cleared his throat.

'As you said, it's not yet finished . . . It's very interesting . . . We'll have to see how it turns out.'

Chapter Twenty

Despite his limp, Baum was agile, and as Disraeli came forward he retreated around the room, swaying out of range while avoiding the chairs that had been pushed back; then, when he was almost cornered against the bookcase, he slipped beneath the punches to take an upright stance at the centre of the carpet.

Disraeli in his shirt-sleeves squared up to his valet again, and led with a straight left to the chin that made him stagger.

'Again!' said Baum.

Disraeli again pushed out his arm, but this time Baum cross-countered with his right, and followed it up with a short left jab to the solar plexus that left Disraeli sitting on the floor, gasping.

Baum helped him to his feet, and untying Disraeli's boxing gloves, said,

'It's no good your hitting my head if you leave your middle empty.'

'No,' said Disraeli, taking deep breaths. 'You're quite right, Baum. The head is more spectacular; but we must look to the torso. Tomorrow we'll practise that double punch.'

Baum handed him a towel, and Disraeli said as he wiped his face,

'How am I getting on, Baum?'

'Well,' Baum said appraisingly, 'quite good! Quite good! But not yet Mendoza! You fight like a schoolboy, sir, with both arms swinging – like this.'

He imitated Disraeli's flailing style, and Disraeli looked at him meekly.

'You must remember,' said Baum, 'the art of boxing is to be quick. So you must move the shortest distance – not like a big circle but like this – psst – psst!' He moved his left and right fists like pistons.

'Yes,' said Disraeli dutifully.

'And then,' said Baum, 'you must look – look at the other man all the time – at his hands to see where they go. Now you will take your tub.'

For several weeks, Baum had been giving Disraeli lessons in boxing, a popular sport among the dandies, and despite Henrietta's protests at their brutality, Disraeli, who had never played organized games, looked forward to his morning battles. Baum's stocky body was as tireless as when ten years before he had worked as a strong-man in German and Swiss fairs, and he never had to exert himself unduly; but for Disraeli each of their confrontations was a metaphor of all his struggles, and though he could never hope to defeat Baum, each bruise he received and sometimes gave was a certificate of experience and education.

Around the large blue porcelain tub in the bedroom at their new chambers in Park Lane not far from the Sykeses' new house, Baum had drawn a Chinese screen, and Disraeli sank happily into its warmth that made the red patches tingle where he'd been pummelled.

'How's the jaw, Baum?' he called out.

'Impossible to move,' said Baum flatteringly. 'Lucky for me you was wearing mufflers.'

He brought in a pitcher of warm water, and poured it over Disraeli's soap-covered shoulders.

'You've got to eat a bit more, sir,' said Baum. 'You're too thin. You stay up too late – and you're too tired in the day to eat – you write and write. You'll be ill if you go on like this.'

'Ah, my dear Baum,' said Disraeli, 'I must go on like this.'

He stood, and Baum wrapped him in a huge towel.

'What a year this has been!' said Disraeli, drying himself. 'September's a sad time, Baum – when the leaves drift across the Park. I'm very conscious of mortality. Have you packed?'

'Not finished yet, sir. Shall you take the gloves?'

'Yes, Baum. We'll box every morning, and then we won't fight in the afternoons.'

'But will you be bored, sir, at Bradenham?'

'Yes – very. But it'll be a loving boredom. And I'll write too.'

'What about, sir?' said Baum, laying out his linen.

'I have only one theme,' said Disraeli, examining himself in the glass. 'At what time do I see Mr de Rothschild?'

Even during his bout with Baum, the prospect of his

appointment with Lionel de Rothschild had occupied him, but he wanted to hear his valet remind him in words so that he could savour again the thought that he was going to meet a man long admired, a member of a prestigious family with whom, he sensed, his fortunes would one day be involved.

'Twelve o'clock, sir,' said Baum.

'If Lady Sykes calls,' said Disraeli, 'tell her I've already left for Bradenham, and that I'll write to her by the next post.'

'Yes, sir.'

'And take this letter to Pyne – it's urgent.'

'Yes, sir.'

Baum hesitated.

'Is there anything else?' asked Disraeli.

'Yes, sir. My wages, sir.'

'Ah,' said Disraeli, taking two guineas from his purse. 'You are a first charge on my estate, Baum. And here's another guinea in the understanding that you teach me that cross-counter.'

'Thank you, sir,' said Baum. 'I have put out for you the green brocade waistcoat. Mr Rothschild will appreciate it.'

'Yes,' said Disraeli. 'Something a little baroque.'

Lyndhurst had arranged their meeting, and Disraeli had hoped that it might take place in grander circumstances, say at a dinner where, in the presence of politicians of his acquaintance to whom the Rothschilds for all their wealth might defer, he wouldn't be at a disadvantage. Lionel de Rothschild was due to leave within a few weeks for the Continent, and had sent a courteous note by a liveried messenger that since he was 'eager to meet Mr Disraeli, he would be indebted to him if he would call on him at New Court, St Swithin's Lane, at a time to suit his convenience, say twelve p.m. on Monday'. Disraeli had hoped to be invited to the Piccadilly mansion of the Rothschilds and to see the Grinling Gibbons *boiseries*, lovingly described by Lyndhurst, but New Court, the old family house now exclusively a counting-house where Baron Nathan still presided, was a good beginning.

He had calculated his time of arrival carefully, not too early and not too late, but he was, in fact, twenty minutes too early, and he walked up and down the narrow street, avoiding the jostling clerks and the costermongers and the bearded old-clothes-men in dirty gabardines pushing their barrows with a bleating chant of 'Clo'! Clo'!' The Jews who'd built temples when the Saxons wore woad now found a common forum with them in the Pantheon of Money. The time was five to twelve, and he entered the dark building. He had expected the din of the Stock Exchange. Instead, everything was quiet, felted. The doorkeeper who received him passed him on to an usher who presented him at the end of a corridor to a respectful clerk who introduced him to a young secretary who addressed him by name, offered him a leather armchair, and asked him to wait. As he sat there, he studied the painting of Nathan Rothschild, the founder of the London branch, bald-headed, the image of an English man of property except for his heavy-lidded eyes and voluptuous mouth. Next to it was a portrait of Betty de Rothschild, the wife of James, the head of the French family; still the dark, heavy-lidded eyes looking stead-fastly beneath the white aigrette, the black hair parted in the centre – and the bare shoulders, the elegance of a French society beauty.

Disraeli stood, and examined the picture more closely, study-ing the fan in her right hand, the jewelled bracelets, the opulent folds of her ball dress. Lyndhurst had been present at the first ball in March after the building of the Rothschild mansion in the Faubourg St Honoré, and had described the neo-Renais-sance house as everything that the sixteenth century could imagine and the nineteenth century could pay for. But Betty de Rothschild outshone her surroundings.

Disraeli heard the door open and turned to greet Lionel de Rothschild, a tall man rather younger than himself. 'Sorry to keep you waiting. Yes – that portrait is after the original by Ingres. Very good of you to come. Hope you'll have a chop with us.'

He led Disraeli into a dining-room lined with portraits of members of the family, and he introduced Disraeli rapidly. 'Mr Evans, Mr Clitheroe, Mr Norris-Browne, Lord St Albans, Mr Hinton, Sir Peter Hillyard and Mr Barker . . . A glass of madeira!'

Apart from Lord St Albans, the guests were members of the bank or City merchants, and since, Disraeli quickly recognized, it was the custom of the house not to discuss business affairs during the meal, the conversation was restricted to generalities in which he deliberately took no part. He had expected to be private with his host, and to find something brilliant behind the glum exterior of New Court. Instead, he was confronted by a dull, reserved and deferential group of businessmen in dark dress for whom the mutton was clearly an even more serious subject than finance. Rothschild led the conversation to the weather, the theatre, the Aylesbury hunt, and Ireland.

'Ireland!' he said. 'I see no outcome of its troubles till its wealth can be regenerated through industry.'

The merchants mumbled assent, and Lord St Albans whose contribution to the table talk had been limited hitherto to a languid 'Ah, yes,' now expanded his comment to 'Ah – yes, indeed.'

'The political problem of Ireland,' said Rothschild, 'is insoluble as long as there's a population that grows faster than its resources.'

'Do you believe, sir, that Mr Malthus's principles could solve the problem?' asked Mr Hinton, who had given Disraeli as a fellow guest of the Rothschilds a somewhat warmer greeting at New Court than he had as a guest at Bradenham.

'I doubt it,' said Rothschild, passing the wine to his neighbour, Mr Evans. 'I always feel that the Malthusian remedy is rather like prescribing a regime of abstinence from food to a man suffering from consumption.'

'I have, I must admit,' said Hinton, 'some sympathy with the Irish peasantry who find themselves obliged to sustain a Protestant Church which, in turn, is the instrument of their oppressors.'

'Not oppressors, sir,' said Disraeli. 'Surely not. The Irish Protestants, I grant you, take the view that because they own most of the property in the country their church has a right to support from the mass of the population. I can understand the Papists' dislike of such a situation. But what O'Connell is seeking by his alliance with Russell and Melbourne is nothing less than Repeal.'

After his gloomy silence, Lord St Albans now became eloquent.

'You will often find, sir, in politics, that some respectable, if practical, reason is used to mask a sinister and more general motive. I accept that the Irish suffer great disabilities that make them the natural victims of men like O'Connell. I accept that a people whose staple diet is the potato – '

'And whose only exercise is drinking and procreation,' interrupted Sir Peter Hillyard.

' – is at the mercy of an Act of God and the theories of Mr Malthus. But is there not an innate vice in men whose reaction to every measure of good government is violence and rebellion?'

'Rebellion,' said Rothschild, 'isn't always against its apparent object. It isn't, surely, part of the natural order that the Irish, a vigorous and pleasing and talented people, should have to subsist on steadily diminishing parcels of land. Or that if their potato crop were ever to fail – which God forbid! – it would be a vengeance of Heaven for their sins.'

'Are you acquainted with Ireland, sir?' asked Hinton.

'No,' said Rothschild.

'It is a country brutalized and paralysed by a domestic superstitition,' said Hinton.

Disraeli, choosing to take an opposing view to Hinton's, said,

'The Irish have been brutalized like any other subject people. I detest their spirit of sedition, but I respect their will.'

'What "will"?' Hinton asked sharply.

'To love and to worship, to fight and to multiply. There's your law of nature, Mr Hinton. Without that will, great peoples like the Babylonians have vanished. And with that will others – like those of the race of Our Lord – have survived.'

He drank his port and saw that the other guests, somewhat uneasy at the turn of the conversation, were beginning to shuffle their chairs and lay their napkins on the table.

'I don't doubt,' said Disraeli, 'that the Irish will survive.'

'The only question,' said Rothschild calmly, 'is "how".'

He stood, and the others rose respectfully. For a few moments, Disraeli felt a sense of chagrin that he had been invited to an omnibus luncheon as mediocre for its food and wine as it had been for its conversation. There wasn't a day of the week when he couldn't have enjoyed a better meal in better company with more agreeable talk than the eclectic ruminations of Rothschild and his guests' respectful amendments. He had hoped to shine, but he hadn't shone. He would like to have discussed grave subjects with the handsome young man who had the serenity that comes from possessions reinforced by knowledge and a family that had organized itself like the units of an army deployed for reciprocal support. With such a family behind him, he, Disraeli, could be an Alexander. But for the time being, he thought, as the guests left one by one with grave bows to Rothschild, he would have to fight alone, comforted by the fact that although his father wasn't a financial magnate, he at least provided him with the haven at Bradenham where he could dream of his campaigns.

'Pray, don't leave yet, Mr Disraeli,' said Rothschild. 'I would be delighted if you'd stay and talk to me.'

He led Disraeli into a private room, heavily furnished in a Germanic style that Disraeli recalled from his own Rhine journey with his father some years earlier. At once Disraeli felt at ease, as if the attitudes he had assumed in the presence of the others were irrelevant, as if with Lionel de Rothschild he shared a historic secret – 'the Great Asian Mystery', he had once called it – which required no verbal description to be brought to their consciousness.

'I was delighted,' said Rothschild, 'that Lyndhurst arranged our meeting. I hear he's going to marry Miss Goldsmith.'

'Yes,' said Disraeli. 'Lyndhurst's a man who needs the ballast of feminine company.'

'Melbourne, I'm sorry to say, has been rather savage with her father.'

'Melbourne,' said Disraeli, 'can be a singular ruffian. Ask Wellesley or Brougham. What was Mr Goldsmith's offence?'

'Lord Holland asked for some honour for him. Melbourne said, "No, I hate refined Solomons. God knows I hate doing anything for these Stock Exchange people!" '

'I imagine,' said Disraeli, 'that doesn't surprise you, sir.'

'No,' said Rothschild. 'My regret is that Mr Goldsmith

should put himself in a posture where he can be insulted at second hand. A Jew who is insulted face to face can be sublime – like your Alroy. That novel above all made me wish to meet you.'

'I wrote Alroy,' said Disraeli, 'when my mind was still fresh with the impressions of my journey through Syria. I'd seen Jerusalem and Bethlehem and Nazareth and the broken columns of great civilizations blown over by the desert. And I was struck by the miracle which for centuries has preserved the Jews, despite the squalor of the ghetto and the scaffold of the auto-da-fé, degraded, abused and injured, yet still clinging to an ancestral faith and a messianic belief in an ultimate redemption. And it seemed to me that despite the livery of shame that their oppressors have laid on them, the time might come when some deliverer might rise up, a saviour, who would restore this indestructible people to Zion.'

'But you based Alroy, I believe, on Sabbatai Zvi – a false Messiah who ended up a Moslem.'

'Ah,' said Disraeli, 'any Messiah who fails is a false Messiah. But the greatness of a Messiah lies in his ability to make men dream. Without the dream, there's no fulfilment.'

'Would you put O'Connell in your category of Messiahs?' Disraeli hesitated.

'Yes,' he said. 'He's a man who summarizes a nation's dreams, and articulates them. How many such men are there?'

'But dreams won't feed the peasantry,' said Rothschild. 'Is not the problem that so many Irishmen are fed on poetry and legends? I would have thought that public works are more important than dram-shop fantasies.'

'I agree,' said Disraeli, 'that it isn't enough to provide public works or charity for paupers. Today in England, there must be a million persons on the parish rates – perhaps eighty thousand literally confined within workhouses. There must be over a quarter of a million receiving outdoor relief. In Ireland, the situation is proportionately worse. The problem isn't to relieve distress but to create productive work.'

'But how?' said Rothschild again.

'By means of railways,' said Disraeli dogmatically. He was enjoying his lecture to Rothschild. 'There's a Royal Commission sitting now to consider the expansion of railways in England. Consider, sir, what might be done if instead of your surplus capital being directed to foreign loans and foreign mines, you anticipated the future – above all in Ireland – by laying the basis of a new character for the country, a change in its social relations – new combinations of industry – an improvement in its agriculture.'

'What is the basis of your calculation?' said Rothschild.

Disraeli uncrossed his legs, and crossed them again easily.

'I consider that fifteen hundred miles of railway – at the rate of a mile on each side – would improve the land it passes through to the extent of nearly two million acres. Now at twenty-five years' purchase, this would be the equivalent of twenty-four million pounds' worth of improvement in the value of the land. You'd have your railways, in fact, for nothing, and a permanent rise in the general standard of value and living for those who live off the land.'

Rothschild followed Disraeli's arguments with interest.

'With so obvious an advantage,' he said, 'why does nobody take it?'

'There's a lack of domestic capital in Ireland,' said Disraeli. 'It needs the daring of a Rothschild to seize the opportunity.'

Rothschild shook his head.

'For mechanical change,' he said, 'there must be a vital will. Is that present in Ireland today? I doubt it.'

Before Disraeli could comment, he changed the subject.

'I hear, Mr Disraeli, that there's some talk of your standing for another constituency.'

'Yes,' said Disraeli gloomily. 'It's my purpose to obtain a Parliamentary seat. I am distressed, sir, that you with your attainments and authority are for the time being denied that possibility.'

'It will be a struggle,' said Rothschild. 'I don't imagine that it will always be so. The Bill to relieve Jews of their disabilities is too much of an annual event for it never to succeed. The English public will eventually acquiesce – if only out of boredom.'

They both laughed, and Rothschild rose and gave Disraeli his hand.

'Meanwhile,' he said, 'you must get into Parliament soon. Your talents, Mr Disraeli, are not to be wasted.'

Disraeli flushed, and bowed.

'When you have a constituency and you hold a subscription, we will be honoured to contribute.'

Disraeli bowed again.

'I'm obliged,' he said, and added, 'I trust your father will soon be well again.'

'Thank you,' said Rothschild, leading him to the door. 'And if you are free to dine at Piccadilly next Thursday, we should be delighted to see you.'

The chatter in the City streets was like a scherzo, the Bank an Acropolis lit with a sublime radiance by the autumn sun, the phaetons planetary chariots. From its pedestrian beginnings, Disraeli's meeting with Rothschild had taken wings. The modest, watchful, legendary young man had promised him support, and reinforced it, after a careful examination, by his invitation. Lyndhurst, now in Paris, would be interested and pleased, even though for the time being he was preoccupied with Miss Georgina Goldsmith. Was it love? Disraeli had seen her portrait, and she was certainly a handsome woman, a wealthy woman, the daughter of a banker who only needed a baronetcy and two thousand acres to be absorbed with time into the aristocracy; she would be an admirable consort for the Chief Baron. She'd be a perfect prop for Lyndhurst who, lacking inherited wealth to keep up his magnificent establishment at George Street, was always short of money to supplement his emoluments. There had, indeed, been a rumour that just before a great dinner for a Minister at Lyndhurst's home the bailiffs had arrived, and Lyndhurst had dealt with the embarrassment by dressing them up in his footmen's livery.

Yes, Miss Goldsmith would be useful. But did he love her? Disraeli had no doubt Lyndhurst would always be the willing vassal of any woman possessed of a dimple and large breasts. When he had first met Lyndhurst with his tall, erect figure, his Roman head, his logical and encyclopædic mind, and his effortless style, he had thought him a Jupiter. It took a little time for him to realize that Lyndhurst had a voluptuary's mouth and a weak chin, and that his brilliant and unique memory was a compensation and a cover for his intellectual inertia. But not in his personal life. Disraeli had never met anyone, not even D'Orsay, who applied himself with such dedication to his personal pleasures, whether at a *guingette* or some splendid and private soirée in the Faubourg St Honoré.

And yet, there were few men who could evoke such affection. In the past two years Disraeli had become in fact Lyndhurst's secretary, the repository of his confidences. Lyndhurst repeated to him the Duke of Wellington's intimacies, and together they discussed and analysed them. When Lyndhurst spoke in the House of Lords, Disraeli was always there with his notes and supplementary information, patient through the most tedious debate, though he had little relish for the Augustan manner, much preferring the vehement contradictions of the Commons. Lyndhurst had shown him many kindnesses, but the time of apprenticeship must soon be over. It wasn't his destiny to be a permanent and nameless mouthpiece; and he was beginning to tire of the polemical Letters of Runnymede in *The Times*, in which Lyndhurst had encouraged him to abuse the Whigs in extravagant terms reprobated even by Barnes, the editor, himself a trenchant controversialist. The truth was that Lyndhurst, while fighting his battles at second hand, wanted to be esteemed by friends and adversaries alike.

As Disraeli turned into the Strand, he thought that he would never yield to so feeble a self-indulgence. To love – to be loved – yes. But to defer to an enemy for the sake of a smile – that would never be his part.

He wondered how Henrietta would accommodate herself to Miss Goldsmith – or Miss Goldsmith to Henrietta. A birdcatcher went by whistling, and Disraeli glanced at the sad linnets in their cages. The catcher, not the birds, was singing. That's how it always had been and would be. How long could his own relationship with Henrietta last? The Lyndhurst connection, whatever it had been long ago, was virtually extinct, he was sure, surviving vestigially as a tradition of friendship towards which he himself had developed a habit of indulgence. But nothing was static; everything had to change.

Sykes would be back in the spring. And then? Disraeli's mood darkened, and the elation of his meeting with Rothschild began to fade. Sykes had maintained a bizarre correspondence with Disraeli, some of it written in German, some in Italian and some in English. *Mein lieber Disraeli; mio caro Disraeli.* Sometimes Disraeli thought his correspondent mad – the transitions of language, the restlessness of his itinerary, the waverings of intention, his hypochondriac introspection, the fact that he wrote to him at all, his wife's protector, in this insistent and mocking way.

Disraeli had written to Sykes's doctor, and the reply had come from Lucca that, 'Sir Francis is tolerably well, but his impatience is such that he will not complete his cure but hurries from one spa to another.' That might be; but he would certainly come back at some time. And then? Would he still be complaisant? What form might his objections take? His complaisance would be as intolerable as his objections, because Disraeli would then be irrevocably committed to a nexus more binding and less rewarding than marriage, one which he could scarcely break without dishonour, while constantly embarrassing his friends and acquaintances by its ambiguity.

Marriage, he had no doubt, would be fashionable again. The old king was ill, and couldn't survive for long. A young queen would usher in a new age. And he, on the threshold of the Parliamentary career that would surely open up for him, might be left enveloped in the cerements of a dead liaison.

Disraeli shook his head as he walked, startled by a heresy he was reluctant to admit even to himself. Good God, how could he have such a thought about Henrietta, Henrietta whom he loved and who loved him with an intensity that he had never felt with any other human being? He remembered the King's Theatre, the Grange and the sea beneath his room, and the river parties and their first embrace in Upper Grosvenor Street when disaster had turned to triumph, and all the hundreds of happy hours that had followed and his pride in Henrietta. One day, no doubt – one unhappy day when the world pressed too hard on them, they would have to part. He had noticed in the last few months how Henrietta had changed, how he had found her staring into space, how often lately he had seen her in unexplained tears, how she had reassured him and covered his face with kisses, affirming her love, her unalterable love, 'Come what may.' Come what may! They were like people who live under the shadow of a great and crumbling mountain.

The maidservant, Emmeline, greeted him with a curtsy, and announced that Lady Sykes was out, having learnt that Mr Disraeli had already left for Bradenham.

'No,' said Disraeli, 'I've decided to stay in London a few days more.'

The girl was looking at him with awe as he handed her his hat, his stick, his gloves and his cape.

'When did Lady Sykes say that she'd return?'

The maidservant curtsied again, and said, 'I dunno, sir. Her ladyship left in a real hurry. Her ladyship's going out to dinner, sir, so she must be back by six, sir.'

She spoke with a Norfolk accent, and Disraeli said,

'Do you miss the country, Emmeline?'

He was still excited by his visit to Rothschild, and wanted to talk to somebody, anybody, and Emmeline with her fresh cheeks was better than nothing.

'No, sir,' said Emmeline. 'There's nothing there but fields. In London – it's people. And at night, when the gas lamps are on – '

'What then?'

'It's nice.'

'Yes,' said Disraeli. 'This great metropolis is – nice. I'm going to write a few letters, Emmeline. Where's Carter?'

'Lady Sykes sent him out with a message.'

'I see. Let me know when he's back. I must tell my family in Bradenham that I won't be there next week.'

Emmeline, who had been backing away as he spoke, dodged around the marble head of a bacchante on a podium, and disappeared downstairs.

Disraeli smiled. He was feeling benevolent, and the apprehensions and doubts of half an hour before disappeared.

Henrietta had furnished and decorated the new house with the intention that he should be happy to display it to their friends, and today everything pleased him, the red striped silk of the chairs, the gilt mirrors, the foliate arms of the chandeliers. But his favourite part of the house was the alcove in the dressing-room where Henrietta was accustomed to write her letters and, indeed, where he had written several chapters of his new novel *Venetia*, a study of Byron and Shelley. High above Park Lane so that the sounds of its traffic only reached him faintly, he could see his map of London – the Park, the Row, a glimpse of Piccadilly, Apsley House, and beyond it Westminster. To conquer those few square miles was to conquer a world.

Henrietta's table in the alcove was littered with invitation cards, the strewn contents of a work-basket, programmes, writing paper, Heath's *Books of Beauty*, which Lady Blessington had been editing and to which Disraeli had contributed a poem. Emmeline and the other servants had strict orders never to disturb, or worse still, tidy any papers or manuscripts on that mahogany surface. Disraeli, who liked neatness, carefully assembled the books and laid them on one side. The chaotic state of the table made him feel tender rather than displeased. When Henrietta had an enthusiasm, order had no part in its display, and lately, like many other women in society, she had decided to write a novel. When Disraeli questioned her about it, she said she would show him the manuscript if she ever thought it worthy of his attention. But for hours during the afternoons when she wasn't sitting for her portrait or visiting Lady Cork, she would lock herself in her room, and when Disraeli passed it he could hear the scratching of her quill, as relentless as his own when he was writing.

He wanted to send a letter to Sarah, telling her about Rothschild's invitation to dinner and explaining why he had to postpone his return to Bradenham, and he began to clear the table methodically. First, the work-basket with its scissors and ribbons and reels; it reminded him of the hours Henrietta had spent sewing election favours. Then he took up one of the *Books of Beauty* with a leather book-mark. It opened at a poem by Lady Blessington facing an engraving of Henrietta by A. E. Chalon, and Disraeli looked back at Henrietta, who had been portrayed holding Tou-Tou in her arms and smiling. The original drawing dated from the year before they had met, and Disraeli thought to himself that in those three years Henrietta had changed. She had become thinner, her eyes more anxious, her manner more defiant – and at the same time she had become more beautiful. In the portrait, she had the air of a woman secure in her husband, her children and her household. In recent months she had seemed to Disraeli to have isolated herself as if she lived another life, remote from himself or anyone else. Even when they were in bed, her former posture had changed. Sometimes he would awake to find that she had withdrawn herself, lying with her eyes wide open in the darkness and unmoving, as if by contact she might betray to him a secret.

Disraeli shrugged his shoulders. No man knew the hour of his natural death; nor for that matter could he know the moment when love itself might come to an end. He loved Henrietta. Of that he was sure. Their partings were both an agony and a refreshment, a pain and an aphrodisiac, and each time they met after parting, with their feelings sharpened by the jealousies and uncertainties of their separation, they would be reunited with an urgent passion as if they had only become lovers the day before.

Disraeli finished tidying the table, and took up a sheet from Henrietta's writing-box, half-hidden under a programme of *The Duenna* which they had recently seen at Covent Garden. He was short-sighted, and he peered at her spiky writing. He thought the page might be part of Henrietta's novel, and he hesitated. Then he saw that it was a letter addressed to himself, and he began to read it.

My dearest, my beloved,
    You have scarcely gone, but already I feel the loneliness of being a widow. Yes, to be away from you is to know the darkness . . .

Overwritten! thought Disraeli, and he was about to put the letter down. Henrietta liked writing, and she had indeed written to him a hundred times, devoted and desperate letters in which love was always an extravagant superlative, though with a circumscribed vocabulary. He liked her letters, but they had a refrain which he knew by heart. Out of habit, he read on.

Lately, I confess to you, my angel – *that was new* – I have become frightened. Our happiness is always at risk from the malice of those whose greatest joy is to destroy a reputation.

My poor, unhappy father! He has suffered very much, and is lying ill in Norfolk after a heart attack.

He knew that already.

I have no wish to deepen his sorrow. Some new shock would easily kill him. For him to die unreconciled with me would be an unbearable sorrow. I lie awake and think of it.

And yet, my dearest one, there are great and powerful forces in women as well as men that it is impossible to deny. I did not seek what has happened to us.

'No,' Disraeli said to himself. 'It was an accident, but a reality none the less.'

Sometimes (the letter continued) I wonder how it all can end. The world is very unfair. For a man like you, my dearest one, there is his career, his power of creation. For a woman, there is no creation except through love. But even that is denied to us unless we conform in every particular, whatever the treatment we receive.

We can be spurned and neglected, treated as property, and still we must remain bound to those whom religion and law have handed a power more absolute than any despot's. Francis can come and go as he wishes, and I must remain forever at his disposal. How can it end? I know, my beloved, that you can't answer. All I know is that what I can least endure is neglect. To be abandoned is a form of being spurned. But with your kindness, your gentleness, your magical hands that create imperishable beauty with a crayon – you have made me feel that there is still a miracle I can know – the miracle of reciprocated love.

Disraeli sat down, and his heart-beat began to accelerate with the familiar thud that he could hear in his ears when in the presence of danger. He cast his eyes rapidly over the rest of the page, and saw that the letter was unfinished, as if Henrietta had been interrupted.

I am happy that you will be at Basildon –

And Disraeli wanted the word to be a lapse for Bradenham, and he willed it under his eyes to turn from Basildon to Bradenham.

– and that the children won't disturb you. It is certain he won't be back before the end of January. There are so many political matters to occupy him which weary me and I can never hope to understand.

My dearest one, you have made the autumn days glow like stained glass windows in sunlight. I wish I could be Scheherezade so that I could see you every day and tell my lord an endless story to save me. Did he love her in the end – or did he destroy her? Perhaps one day you will paint for me –

Disraeli put the letter back on the table, and tidied it neatly into position. His hands and his legs were trembling, and he sat looking at the letter as if it were an obscene toad that had been revealed with a flourish from beneath a silver chafing dish.

Henrietta! Henrietta whom he had loved, and for whom he once would have forsworn the world. Around him were the hangings, the curtains, the carpets, the pictures, the odours that were her presence. Because she was there, he had felt invulnerable. A woman who's unfaithful to her husband will be unfaithful to her lover. He remembered the fateful prophecy of Clara Bolton.

A sudden rage took possession of him. The lies, the subterfuges, the ambiguities that she had used to Sykes, she had used to him too. The same language, the same words, just as she now used the same endearments to that clodhopping painter in Fitzroy Square. Maclise. He felt a nausea in shaping the name in his mind. Maclise, the Irishman with his garrulous whimsy and his clumsy silences in company. That was the man she preferred to him, deceived him about, her overt contempt masking her true inclination.

The daylight was fading, but Disraeli read the letter again. My dearest, my beloved. Yet it was impossible. How long had this liaison existed? Only a few days before, they had made love for happy and inventive hours, vigorous and exhausting hours that had left him triumphant and fulfilled. But Maclise must have been in Basildon. There must have been an interval from his attentions for Henrietta's enthusiasm to revive, though afterwards – now he remembered – she had wept, and when he had asked the reason, she said that she was weeping for happiness.

At half past six, Henrietta returned, and, preceded by Emmeline with a candelabrum, made her way to her room. As the light revealed Disraeli she dismissed the maidservant and said,

'Ben!'

He turned slowly, and rose to his feet.

'Dearest,' she said, approaching. 'I had a message that you had left for Bradenham.'

She went to kiss him, but he pushed her arm away.

'What is it?' she asked gently. 'Why is my darling ill-humoured?'

He stood looking at her.

'What is it?' she repeated.

He handed her the letter.

'You must finish your letter,' he said.

She let the pages fall to the ground, and looked back at him steadfastly.

'Do you think it gentlemanly to read another person's correspondence?'

She barred his way as he made for the door. He paused, and she said, raising her voice,

'Is it gentlemanly to read my letters?'

'I have read many,' he said frigidly. 'I know the style.'

His hands were trembling again, and he felt as if a fever had suddenly gripped him. He couldn't continue to look her in the face, but in the mirror he could see that his face was as white as Henrietta's.

She sat down and looked up at him with her eyes large and despairing.

'I love you, Ben,' she said. 'You must know that.'

He picked up her letter, and didn't answer.

'What will you do?' she asked in a whisper.

He sat beside her, and took her hands.

'Nothing,' he said. 'Nothing at all.'

She laid her head against his shoulder, and a current of air, striking the curtains, blew out one of the candles. Disraeli's fingers were on her wet cheek, and they sat in silence for minutes.

From outside came the faint cries of coachmen, the rolling of carriages, distant voices, and in Disraeli's memory the calendar of their relationship recurred – the opera, their first promenade in her carriage, the shore at Southend, *mio caro Disraeli*, the rowers on the Thames and the music, the birds flying startled at his pistol shot, and her hair trailing over his face after their love-making. But that was the hair that had trailed over Maclise's face too, and he felt his arm tighten as he touched her cheeks.

'Don't leave me, Ben,' she said. 'I don't want you to leave me.'

'Tell me about it,' he said.

'There's nothing to tell. There was nothing that touched me. It was – it was – '

'What?'

'Your neglect. You left me. You had other things to do. I was too much alone.'

Now she began to sob, and Disraeli tightened his arm around her shoulder.

'You must tell me everything,' he said quietly. 'Everything. How long did it – has it lasted?'

She hid her face in his chest, and didn't answer.

'How long?' he repeated.

'The third time I went there – we were alone. You sent the carriage.'

'And now?'

'Oh, Ben – I don't know. I love you, Ben. What will happen now?'

'It's all over,' he said in the same voice.

'All over!' she whispered as he drew her to her feet. Her voice was hopeful as if his words contained an ambiguity. He took her in his arms and laid his face against hers, looking at the crimson, unfocused pattern of the wallpaper.

'It's all over, Henrietta.'

Chapter Twenty-One

'The noble Lord from his pedestal of power wielding in one hand the keys of St Peter and waving in the other the cap of liberty – how d'you like that, Baum?' In front of the tall looking-glass, Disraeli was standing in his underclothes, rehearsing the speech he intended to deliver in the House later that day.

'Very good indeed,' said Baum. 'Your stays, sir?'

Disraeli hesitated.

'I think so,' he said. The glum December day needed a contrast and he had already decided that his Maiden Speech on Smith O'Brien's Motion would be brilliant in every respect, in its imagery, its delivery and in his dress. O'Brien was moving that a Commission be set up to investigate what he called 'Sir Francis Burdett's plot' to collect money in England for petitions to upset the results in Irish Elections where Catholics had been victorious. On the sofa, the brocade waistcoat, the braided trousers, the cravat with its cameo-head tie-pin, the black velvet coat lined with scarlet and the three gold chains, expressed the care of his composition. Studying himself as Baum tightened the stays, Disraeli felt calm. A year after the catastrophe with Henrietta, he was liberated at last from an ecstasy that had become a suffocating miasma, though for months after it had lifted he had still longed for Henrietta like an Orpheus in hell seeking his lost Eurydice.

It had been a death, ultimate and irreversible. Nothing could undo it.

*In a drear nighted December
Too happy, happy tree
Thy branches ne'er remember
Their green felicity.*

The lines of Keats came into his mind.

*Was there ever any writhed not at passed joy?
To know the pain and feel it
When there is none to heal it.*

After his last meeting with Henrietta, the news of their parting had quickly spread, and his friends had called and written to him with discreet condolences – D'Orsay, Lady Blessington, the hypocritical Lady Cork, Bulwer, even Lyndhurst from Paris. Sarah had heard in Bradenham. 'I too, darling Ben, have known what loss and rejection mean.' And Disraeli had welcomed the sympathy. Rather a victim than an executioner! He had comforted himself as a man who has suffered a bereavement too deep to discuss and nobly endured.

But the pain, the true pain, had followed when Henrietta wrote him a gentle letter full of admiration for *Henrietta Temple*. It was a postscript for ever to their connection. But she didn't want to leave Disraeli in doubt about Lyndhurst. Between them, since she and Disraeli had first met, there had only been friendship, she swore. Sir Francis Sykes had returned from the Continent and was 'tolerably kind to her'. And she had ended her letter by saying that she would send Disraeli his Turkish daggers to Bradenham.

There had been an interval in January when he had been the guest of D'Orsay in Kensington in the elegant villa that he had taken next to Gore House. But he had been uneasy there. D'Orsay dined out every other night. Lady Blessington was beautiful but fractious, busy with her own writings at which she spent ten hours a day to obtain the means of supporting her lavish household and a spendthrift father.

Then Disraeli had returned to Bradenham, but even there he had felt restless. The sheriff's officers were dogging him in his own county. And with all this, he was eager to play his part in an election at Aylesbury. There, after collapsing outside the George Inn, he had fallen ill with a fever that had lasted many weeks, while Sarah, always present, always reliable, had nursed him, happy, he knew, that he was at last released from an involvement potentially more destructive than his debtors, whom, with Pyne's help, he had managed so far to ward off.

Then in June when the old King died and the young Queen Victoria came to the throne, it was as if a new life had begun for him too. 'The clouds have at last dispersed,' he wrote to Sarah on his return to London. From Derby, Chichester, Dartmouth, Marylebone and Taunton came invitations to stand at the General Election, each of them a compliment to his status as a politician and a controversialist. He had toyed with the idea of being a candidate for Taunton where he had many friends. But at the last moment, on the suggestion of Wyndham Lewis, the MP for Maidstone, a deputation had come from that two-member constituency to the Carlton, asking Disraeli if he would stand jointly with Lewis at the forthcoming election. He had accepted and his election address was the shortest he had ever delivered. He solicited the suffrage of the electors in the interest of the 'ancient Constitution, the Established Church and as one resident in an agricultural county and deeply interested in the land, who would on all occasions watch over the fortunes of the British farmer with vigilant solicitude, because his welfare is the surest and most permanent basis of general prosperity'.

Yes, those were the principles from which he would never deviate, and he reinforced them with a speech at Maidstone against the new Poor Law.

'It is a Bill,' he said, 'that bears fearful tidings for the poor. Its primary object is founded not only on a political blunder, but on a moral error – it's based on the principle that relief to the poor is a *charity*. I maintain that it is a *right*.'

He had spoken the words defiantly in face of farmers not unwilling for the Poor Law to subsidize wages. But his declaration had been greeted with a storm of applause.

And then on July 27th, 1837, it was all over. He had taken the first step. In a terse note to his sister from Maidstone – written at eleven o'clock at night – he said,

Dearest,

Lewis   707

Disraeli   616

Colonel Thompson   412

The constituency exhausted.

In haste,

Dizzy.

When he was dressed, he said to Baum,

'How do I look?'

'You look, sir,' said Baum proudly, 'like a Member of Parliament.'

'I fear, Baum,' he said, 'you don't know what a Member of Parliament looks like.'

But neither of them cared greatly. Both were pleased with Disraeli's appearance and once again he addressed the mirror with the opening of his speech.

'Mr Speaker, sir (a short bow), I shall not trouble the House at any length. I do not affect to be insensible to the difficulties of my position, and I shall be very glad . . .'

'Hear, hear,' said a voice, and Disraeli turned to see Bulwer, looking on with a friendly smile.

'Now,' said Bulwer, 'all you need is to deliver your speech. Will your father be present?'

'No,' said Disraeli. 'It's enough for one Disraeli to suffer this ordeal. D'you know, Bulwer, I'm beginning to feel apprehensive.'

'Everyone does,' said Bulwer calmly.

'It's worse than a duel,' said Disraeli.

'Much worse,' said Bulwer comfortingly. 'You have three hundred adversaries.'

'I shall not trouble the House at any length,' Disraeli began rehearsing again.

'You should forget it now,' Bulwer advised him. 'Words, too often repeated, lose their meaning. Just imagine you're addressing an Association dinner. Remember how you carried them away at Taunton. You told me so.'

'Yes,' said Disraeli more cheerfully. 'That is exactly what I must do – perhaps with a little more reserve.'

'Not too much,' said Bulwer. 'Your style is to be an eagle not a goose. You must be sincere – be yourself – astonish them! That's what I'd do myself, if I had your oratory.'

Disraeli straightened his coat and said,

'Let's leave it to fate. Baum, get us a cab.'

When Baum had gone, Bulwer said,

'Do you miss her?'

'Yes,' said Disraeli. 'Every day of my life. But there's no going back.'

'What will happen to her?'

Disraeli tidied his cravat.

'I don't know. People must fulfil their nature. Accidents may divert them. But in the end, they are what they're destined to be. Henrietta's destiny is to give and receive love. She will compromise for a while with Sykes and he with her. I don't believe, though, he'll tolerate Maclise.'

'Why not?'

'Because for Sykes an artist is next door to a tradesman.'

'A nice discrimination.'

Bulwer didn't smile.

'And Rosina?' Disraeli asked.

Bulwer dismissed the subject.

'Let's take mutton at Bellamy's.'

Late in the afternoon, Disraeli decided that he had a fever, and that he wouldn't be able to speak. He had entered the Chamber several times to follow the progress of the debate, and in the stale atmosphere, his forehead felt clammy, his feet were chilled and his heart had a strange irregular beat. In the Lobby, he had met the elderly Sir Francis Burdett, the Member for Westminster, against whom Smith O'Brien's Motion was directed, and Burdett had taken his arm and walked with him through the corridors. Burdett, dressed in a blue coat, a light-coloured waistcoat, knee breeches and top boots, was the very image of an English country gentleman of a quarter of a century earlier, and Disraeli savoured his company and their contrast in style. Colonel Evans, Burdett's fellow member in Westminster, dark and sallow-faced, raised his hat to Disraeli, and Burdett said, 'There goes a brave and honourable soldier –

wounded in the late war. Whatever you do in this House, Disraeli, remember that you will only be noticed if you charge!'

'I hear, sir,' said Disraeli, 'that O'Connell will be speaking.'

'Very likely,' said Burdett. 'Trounce him in debate as you did with your challenge – ! Good day, Mr Disraeli.'

In the library, Disraeli looked around at the Members dozing in armchairs – Mr Baines, Mr Finch, Colonel Perceval, the same as had prophesied the wrath of God if no reference were made to the Deity in the Reform Bill, Mr Sheriff Humphrey, Lord Dudley Stuart, Serjeant Wilde, and Lord Stanley who had been in Earl Grey's Ministry and then left the Whigs. Stanley was a young man, little older than Disraeli, with red hair and a reputation for being a fluent orator and penetrating debater. He was due to speak on O'Brien's Motion.

Disraeli adjusted his cravat and approached him.

'I hope, sir,' he said, 'to make my début in this debate.'

'Ah, yes,' said Stanley, looking up casually. From an old, though mistaken, conviction that Disraeli had introduced a relative into a disreputable gambling set, he disliked him.

'I should be especially pleased if you would permit me to intervene immediately O'Connell has spoken.'

Stanley's expression changed.

'I had hoped to do so myself.'

'The matter,' said Disraeli, 'is of some importance that goes beyond the immediate debate.'

Stanley rose, and said,

'It's a privilege of a Maiden Speaker to choose his moment. By all means follow O'Connell if you wish.'

He bowed curtly, and walked away.

Disraeli sat in an armchair, and shut his eyes. He still felt as if he had a fever, but now he was committed. The gangplank had been removed. 'I trust the House will extend me that gracious indulgence which is usually allowed to one who solicits its attention for the first time . . .' What next? He had forgotten. What was O'Brien's constituency? – Cork, Limerick? He wasn't sure. He intended to speak for an hour but it seemed to him that he didn't have enough for five minutes. No matter! The occasion would inspire him. He had heard of Maiden

Speakers who had risen, opened their mouths, found themselves incapable of articulation and sat down again. Of one thing he was sure. That would never happen to him, though he had taken the precaution, an insurance against disaster, of asking his sister as well as his father not to attend the sitting.

'I confess,' he had written to Sarah, 'that no one – Lord John Russell, Spring Rice, Thomson, even Palmerston and Peel – holds any terror for me. But in the presence of Father, I feel humble. If I ask you to absent yourself, it's only so that I can bring you myself the news of victory.'

How often, after passion had ebbed and Henrietta lay with her naked arm flung across his chest, had he spoken to her of this occasion, as he idled with dreams of political triumph. But all that was long ago. He wondered where she was – whether she remembered – whether she was at that very moment with Maclise using the words, the endearments, that they had taught each other. My angel, my dearest love. Behind his eyelids, the pain was now contained. Your faithful Henrietta. There was, after all, only one betrayal, the first discovery. Everything else was a number in a calendar, an epilogue. In wounding him once, Henrietta had lost her capacity to wound him again.

Yet the pain remained, the private pain.

> To know the pain and feel it
> When there is none to heal it
> Nor numbed sense to steal it
> Was never said in rhyme.

He would never speak of it, never complain of it, never tell the prurient and the curious how the love that had been the background of his every thought had been poisoned.

'Mr O'Connell on his legs!' an usher called in the corridor, and Disraeli joined the other Members hurrying into the Chamber to hear the Irish leader.

With many excuses, Disraeli picked his way over the seated Members in the crowded bench behind Peel, and good-humouredly they made a space for him to squeeze into. The Speaker had already been told by Stanley of Disraeli's wish to follow O'Connell, and from the other side of the House he was observed with the curiosity and respect appropriate to a Virgin dedicated as a sacrificial offering by some ancient tribe. A Maiden Speech, as he had often observed, was a rite. The novice rises mumbling. The hierophants chant an incantation of 'Hear! Hear!' And then after the litany, a general Hallelujah is sung.

He had deliberately delayed his return to the Chamber after the opening speeches. He wanted to show that he wasn't going to be intimidated even by O'Connell's ready-made reputation. Yet when he entered the Chamber, and heard O'Connell already speaking, at ease and in command of the House, fresh-faced and benevolent, able to rouse even his opponents to laughter, his wig slightly tipped back and surrounded by the Irish Members, among them Morgan and his other two sons, Maurice and John, he felt a quiver of doubt. He wished that he had been present at the beginning of the speech.

O'Connell was arguing that to put the Irish victors to the expense of resisting a petition for the annulment of their election was an abuse of justice, since the unlimited resources available to their English and Protestant adversaries as a result of an open subscription would deny the poor the chance of defending themselves against the rich. What is more, many of the Protestant subscribers might themselves sit in judgment on the petition. He spoke in a relaxed and humorous style, twitted a young opponent that while he, O'Connell, had never been touched by England's criminal law, the other had the advantage of him in that respect, 'though no doubt he would grow out of it', and ended by saying that 'the people of Ireland knew that the funds raised for petitions would be used against them, adding insult to injury'. The procedure was unfair. It should be rejected. He spoke with restraint, not allowing himself to rouse the Irish Members to anything more than hurt and dignified cheers.

As O'Connell's speech came to an end after nearly an hour, Disraeli pulled down his waistcoat, tightened his grip of the notes he held in his left hand, and fixed his eyes on the Speaker. . . . 'Those funds,' O'Connell ended, 'will be instrumental in making one Party triumphant, and they, the Irish people, will yet again be the victims.' O'Connell sat down, and the 'Hear, hears!' went on and on.

Disraeli rose with several other Members, and he heard his name called by various voices in several parts of the Chamber. 'Mr Disraeli!' said the Speaker, and Disraeli stood while the cheers for O'Connell gradually subsided. For the first time in his experience, his audience was behind him as well as in front of him, and as he stood, so the benches seemed to fall away and he felt the blood draining from his head. The notes in his hand were quivering, and he transferred them to his right hand which he then held behind his back. This wasn't like the hustings or the Association dinner. In those first few seconds, the scene was constantly changing. Members were coming in from Bellamy's, and talking at the Bar. Others were changing places, some leaving, some arriving, in a distracting movement. At political dinners, the claret gave gusto to the toasts. Everyone was on the same side and there was a following breeze for every sally. Here in the Chamber, the flushed faces were ready for sport. The country gentlemen were looking for a quarry, and MPs who never spoke in the Chamber except to interrupt were sitting with their legs spread in a disengaged after-dinner attitude. But even in this mood, the tradition of courtesy was present, and the House fell silent as the Speaker said, 'Order!'

'Mr Speaker, sir,' said Disraeli. 'I trust that the House will extend to me that gracious indulgence which is usually allowed to one who solicits its attention for the first time.' He could hear his own voice speaking the well-rehearsed words, and it seemed wonderful to him that it was he, Benjamin Disraeli, delivering them in the Chamber of the House of Commons in the presence of Peel who sat in front of him and Palmerston and Spring Rice and John Cam Hobhouse and Mahon and Robert Inglis. Yes, he was speaking and they were listening, and this was his hour, long fought for, long suffered for, when he would establish his genius for England to recognize.

'I have,' he went on, 'sufficient experience of the critical spirit which pervades the House to know how much I need that indulgence of which I will prove not unworthy by promising not to abuse it.'

His voice had become stronger, the dark blurs in the crowded Chamber had turned into recognizable figures, and the tremor had begun to fade as he paused, encouraged by friendly cheers that rewarded his modesty.

He looked around him, and then turned his gaze on O'Connell who was observing him with a curious though detached expression, as he sat with his arm affectionately linked in the arm of his son Maurice, and his posture drew Disraeli's attention as he prepared to launch himself into the next passage of his speech. It had never occurred to him that O'Connell might share the same kind of family intimacy as he had with his own father, whose image, half approving, half disapproving, yet always staunch in his support, came to Disraeli's mind in a counterpoint to his theme.

'The honourable and learned Member for Dublin . . .' he said, but as O'Connell raised his broad-brimmed hat in acknowledgement of the reference, the tone of the Chamber altered. Hitherto there had been a generalized goodwill: now there was a differentiated reaction that followed the pattern of the factions in the House. The Irish Members stopped their whispered conversations, the Radicals leant forward as if preparing to adjudicate between their allies. Mr Place paused in eating an orange, and the Members on the Treasury Bench and the Opposition Front Bench composed their faces into neutrality.

'The honourable and learned Member for Dublin,' Disraeli said, 'has taunted an honourable Member who has previously spoken with having uttered a long, rambling, wandering and jumbled speech. For my part, I can't help feeling that the honourable and learned Member for Dublin has taken an example from the one he has attacked. Indeed, there is scarcely a single subject connected with Ireland which the honourable and learned Member has not touched on in his rhetorical medley.' He spoke the last words scornfully.

From his own side came a polite laugh, but from the Irish Members below the gangway came a growl, not very loud, more like the growl of an animal that has been disturbed. O'Connell muttered something to his son about Disraeli's chains, and the growl turned into a hostile laugh that ran through the benches. Henry Grattan pointed a taunting finger at Disraeli, who, now that he had established his opponents, tried to engage O'Connell on an issue which had no relevance to the debate. 'The honourable and learned Member favoured the House with an allusion to Poor Laws for Ireland,' said Disraeli. It was an old and notorious dialectical trick, one sometimes used with great effect by Peel, to ascribe to an opponent an argument he had never used. It was one which experienced Members of Parliament always watched for and quickly identified.

At that, there was a loud 'No! No! No!', a cry of outrage from Members in all parts of the House, but most particularly from the Irish. It was one thing for a veteran debater to try and invent an opponent's argument. For a new Member to do so was an insolence. Disraeli, surprised at the uproar, apologized.

'I may be wrong,' he said, 'and if the recollection of some Members differs from mine, I regret it. But at any rate there *has* been an allusion to the Irish Corporations Bill. Is that not an irrelevance?'

'We'll choose our own irrelevances,' shouted an Irish Member.

'That I will concede,' said Disraeli, and the laughter began again. He had briefly lost the train of his argument, but he quickly recovered it. For a quarter of an hour, he urged that the fund in favour of petitions was defensive, not offensive. Its purpose was to produce justice for the Protestant constituencies of Ireland. As Disraeli praised the subscribers to the petitions funds 'as men who seldom partook of the excitement created by the conflict of parties', the Irish members fell into a hostile silence. But when he spoke the words, 'I will now have something to say with respect to Her Majesty's Government,' all the resentment suppressed by a conventional forbearance burst out. As Disraeli's confidence had grown, so had the displeasure of the House at the manner in which he had presumed to lecture it. O'Connell's opinions were unpopular; but his person was admired. Even in arguing an acceptable case, Disraeli with his curled hair, his Jewish face, his rings glittering in the candlelight, his sneers, his self-assurance, his elaborate chains, his ostentatious air which went far beyond the *convenances* of a dandy, was personally unacceptable. When he had attacked O'Connell, the squires had mimicked his manner. Now that he was turning his attention to Her Majesty's Government, it was clear to them that their fox had broken cover.

O'Connell had inspired a project to raise funds for the Liberals. 'This,' Disraeli said, 'was a project of majestic mendicancy.' At that, there was a shout of View-Halloo from near the Bar, a roar of laughter from the Rads and an outburst of cock-crowing from the Irish Members. Disraeli couldn't distinguish between the subtleties of the opposing shouts. This wasn't the scene that he had so often imagined in which he was borne forward by the acclamation of his audience. Those flushed, sweating faces in front of him weren't the faces with the admiring eyes that he had visualized as celebrating his triumph. The nods of agreement and 'Hear, hears!' with which Peel and his friends had greeted his opening phrases had changed into a stiff-necked neutrality. In the face of the uproar, Disraeli had already discarded his carefully prepared and logically constructed speech on the subject of petitions. His body felt chilled and he recognized that now his task was not to overwhelm his opponents but to salvage his own dignity, to save himself from a unique Parliamentary humiliation and a social disaster.

He drew himself up, and paused, waiting for the baying country Members to subside.

'Order!' called the Speaker rising to his feet.

Disraeli sat and rose again in the silence that followed. He straightened his cravat and said,

'I have only a little more to add, sir. I only ask another five minutes of the House.'

Again the ironic 'Hear, hears!' broke out, and Disraeli saw that apart from the taunting faces, there were some who sat in an embarrassed silence while others, like Peel himself, were restraining their smiles.

'Is that asking too much?' he said.

There was a shout of 'Yes', and more laughter.

Desperately, Disraeli said, 'I stand here tonight – not formally, it's true, but effectively as the representative of a considerable number of new Members of Parliament.'

'You can't even speak for yourself,' an Irish Member shouted, and again the uproar rose. Each of Disraeli's sentences produced an antiphon of groans and mocking laughter. In his hand, he held the peroration of his speech written with detailed care, the climax of an occasion which was to have ended with prolonged applause. Now that the improvisations were over, he would end with all the eloquence that had enabled him to be victorious over the country dullards. He raised his voice. The sweat was running in rivulets down his face and neck as he referred to the coalition of the Irish Members and the Whigs. 'When the House recalls that in spite of the support of the hon. and learned Member for Dublin and his well-disciplined band of patriots (loud cheers) – when the House recollects the new loves and the old loves in which so much passion and recrimination is mixed up between the noble Tityrus of the Treasury and the learned Daphne of Liskeard – ' the laughter and the cheers grew and someone shouted 'Clever boy!' – 'notwithstanding that the *amantium irae* has resulted as I always suspected in the *amoris integratio* –' 'Latin too!' came a voice, and the cock-crowing grew louder – 'notwithstanding that a political duel has been fought, but in which recourse has been had to the arbitrament of blank cartridges – ' the ironic cheering had now become a steady din, and Disraeli shouted his words to overcome it – 'notwithstanding emancipated Ireland and enslaved England, the noble lord might wave in one hand the keys of St Peter and in the other – '

But now the uproar was total, blanketing the end of his sentence in a clamour of laughter, jeers, groans, conversation and shouts as if the Chamber were a cockpit, a prize-ring.

Disraeli paused for a moment, looking with rage and contempt at the mob that faced him. It had happened to him before when he was a schoolboy, facing a taunting, bullying gang.

'Ah, Mr Speaker,' he said when at last he could be heard. 'See the philosophical prejudices of man!'

He was interrupted by a loud laugh.

'Yes, I would gladly have welcomed a cheer, even from the lips of those opposite.'

As if he had reflected on their manners, the Irish Members again in a single voice began to chant their ironic 'Hear, hears!', while the jeers rose around him and Peel turned his head to give Disraeli a half-pitying frown as if to urge him to end a painful scene.

Disraeli stopped again, and now, he squared his shoulders. It was over. The speech, so carefully prepared, so disastrously delivered, was ended. His début was a failure.

'I am not at all surprised,' he said when he could be heard again, 'at the reception I've experienced. I have begun several things many times, and I've often succeeded at the last – though many had predicted that *I* must fail, as *they* had done before me.'

There were jeering shouts of 'Question! Question!', and now the clamour had taken on a new and angry note, the good humour evaporated. The fox had turned on the hounds.

Suddenly Disraeli shouted high above the din, in a terrible voice that brought a silence in the Chamber, 'I sit down now. But the time will come when you will hear me!'

He sat, and Lord Stanley immediately rose to address the House, which, as if conscious that the baiting of Disraeli had gone too far, now relapsed into its normal good humour. It was customary for the Member who followed a Maiden Speaker to congratulate him, irrespective of the merit of his speech. Lord Stanley ignored the scene that had just taken place. He spoke as if Disraeli's speech had never taken place.

While Stanley was speaking, Disraeli sat with his face flushed. Instead of the acclamation that he had expected, he had ended his speech amid derision, abuse and frigid indifference from those he had most wished to impress. Lord John Russell, the Leader of the House, hadn't stirred his head at the height of the pandemonium. Peel had twisted around with a smile to observe him. On the Ministerial benches, Spring Rice, the Chancellor of the Exchequer, and Sir John Campbell, the Attorney General, had entered into a colloquy as if they were too well bred even to notice the general brawl.

If there was one minute comfort, it was that those he loved

hadn't witnessed his discomfiture – his father, his sister, Lyndhurst. Sara Austen? Well, she might have found satisfaction in the opportunity of consoling him for being as fallible as anyone else. *Amantium irae, amoris integratio.* The anger of lovers, the harmony of love. Henrietta would hear of it. The anger of lovers. The noble Tityrus. The learned Daphne. 'The stain of borough-mongering has assumed a deeper and darker hue.' The baying mouths. A mob as vile as in Finsbury Square. The carefully rehearsed phrases of his speech rattled in his memory. And the notes at his side, thumbed with sweat marks, were the memorial of a shaming episode.

The debate had several hours to go, and he decided that he'd sit through it all to avoid the artificial courtesy of his friendly acquaintances, the sneers of his adversaries, and the backs of those who didn't care to salute him after the fiasco.

What had gone wrong? He was mystified. He had hoped to carry the House or at least the Opposition with his attack. Instead, it had all turned against him. He had spoken fearlessly, but that too was a reproach. He had presented himself to the House as a man of elegance both in dress and language. But the House had preferred the slovens of debate. And so he had failed. He would have to write and tell Sarah. Yet how could he tell her of failure when all her life was concerned with his success.

In his mind, he began to compose a letter to his sister. 'I made my Maiden Speech last night, rising very late after O'Connell, but at the request of my party and with the full sanction of Sir Robert Peel.'

'At the request?' Well, it would hearten Sarah to feel that he had some backing.

'My début was a failure.' That, at least, she would soon know from the newspapers, but he would explain it to her. He *hadn't* been incompetent. He *hadn't* broken down. No, the Rads and the Repealers had organized the uproar. They had been determined to shout him down. But Peel had cheered him.

At the Division, Disraeli walked with his head erect into the Lobby, conscious that acquaintances who would otherwise have greeted him, avoided him. Other Members jostled each other in twos or threes, discussing the debate. As he neared the Tellers, the Marquis of Chandos, nicknamed the Farmers' Friend, came up to him, and said,

'Well done, Disraeli. I congratulate you.'

Disraeli shook his head. 'Failure, I'm afraid,' he muttered.

'Ah no, my dear fellow, Peel doesn't think so. Not a bit. I've just spoken to him. Some think you've come a tumble. He says, "The very reverse. Disraeli will make his way." Congratulations, my dear fellow.'

After Chandos's greeting, a few Members gave him a courteous salute, and the Attorney General, Sir John Campbell, short-sighted, raised his eye-glass to peer at him.

'Ah, Mr Disraeli,' he said in a husky voice with its rolling Scottish overtones, 'that was a splendid battle you were engaged in. And that image – "In one hand the keys of St Peter and in the other" – but how was it completed?'

'In the other the cap of liberty, Sir John.'

'A good picture.'

'I fear your friends wouldn't let me complete it.'

Campbell smiled.

'They will,' he said. 'Have no fear. The mob at the Bar won't always be there.'

Disraeli went on to collect his cloak. Outside the Palace Yard, a group of Members were gathering to walk to St James's. He didn't want to join them, and set off alone. He wanted to draw his cloak around him in the December night as if it were a shroud so that he could blot out in the darkness the record of his humiliation. There were humiliations that could turn to triumphs. But this humiliation had been total. Whitehall with its hissing primroses of light should have been his avenue of victory. Instead, it had turned to a *via dolorosa*. As a novelist he had known humiliation at the hands of the critics. As a lover – and he smiled in the darkness – there had been that moment of disaster in his first rendezvous with Henrietta at Upper Grosvenor Street when the world and its beauty had seemed to collapse in sordid failure, only to achieve a transcendent resurgence. But his débâcle that night in the Chamber was total. He would have wept, were it not that he had always despised tears.

Behind him, he heard steps, and he turned.

'Good heavens, Ben. You've made me run,' Bulwer panted.

'I doubt if I deserve such energetic attention,' said Disraeli.

'Indeed you do,' said Bulwer. 'I want you to dine with me on Saturday. There are one or two excellent people who heard your speech tonight. And one in particular wants to talk to you of its merits.'

An east wind was blowing down Whitehall, and Disraeli flicked the corner of his eye that had begun to water.

'No, no,' said Richard Lalor Sheil, whom Bulwer, to Disraeli's surprise, had invited to meet him. 'You misunderstand O'Connell.' O'Connell's deputy had been a friend of Bulwer for several years, and a contributor to the *New Monthly Magazine* of 'Sketches of the Irish Bar'. But whereas O'Connell was massive and measured, Sheil was diminutive, lively, with a shrill loud voice, speaking exceptionally quickly as if to make sure that not a word should be lost in the time available. Now, after dinner at Bulwer's, stretched out on a sofa with his gouty leg on a foot-stool, he was giving Disraeli some advice while Tennyson D'Eyncourt, the Whig Member for Lambeth, and Bulwer were talking to a Tory Member Mackinnon in the room overlooking Piccadilly.

'You and O'Connell have a common quality, Mr Disraeli.'

'And what is that, sir?'

'Pride. Proud men are natural victims of mischief-makers and gossipers. And then, even when they recognize their error, they're too proud to be reconciled.'

'I fear,' said Disraeli, 'that it will never be possible for me to be reconciled with O'Connell. You saw it two nights ago. He has too deep a prejudice.'

Sheil moved his leg in pain.

'This,' he said, 'is the real Inquisition . . . No, you mustn't misunderstand O'Connell. To the contrary of what you say, he has a predisposition to members of your race. Indeed, next week he will be presenting a petition to end the civil disabilities of Jews.'

Disraeli changed his posture nonchalantly. He had no wish to discuss O'Connell, especially in that context. He could still see the pack yelping at the Bar around the Irish leader.

'No,' said Sheil. 'You were inducted into Parliament with fire. I watched you, and felt your speech was Promethean.'

'Promethean?' said Disraeli, sitting up. He liked the word. It expressed his feeling about himself.

'Yes, Promethean,' said Sheil. 'Just imagine, Disraeli. You might have made a fine, cold speech as I did at my début – the best speech I ever made. And it would have been received as coldly as it was made – with cold compliments and glazed eyes and then be forgotten. But instead, you set the Chamber alight. They howled, they crowed, they groaned, they booed. But they noticed you. Next to undoubted success, my dear Disraeli, the best thing is to make a great noise.'

Disraeli smiled. The small middle-aged Irishman with his eager eyes was beginning to lift the gloom that had enveloped him for three days.

'Forgive me my presumption in advising you,' Sheil went on.

'I am honoured, sir,' said Disraeli attentively. 'You are among our greatest Parliamentarians.'

'Not among the greatest, alas, but among the longest in service. Well, then, Mr Disraeli – here is what Polonius might have said if he'd been myself. To begin with, you've a fine voice.' He chuckled. 'You proved that in the din. You've courage too – a fine grasp of language, good temper, and a gift of repartee.'

Disraeli muttered his thanks.

'Very well,' said Sheil. 'Get rid of all that genius for a session. Speak often – you mustn't let anyone think they've cowed you – but speak briefly. And then again, you must play yourself down. Be very quiet. Try to be dull. Don't be too logical – if you're logical, the English think you're trying to be witty. And then again, you must concentrate on details – figures, dates, calculations.'

'Yes,' said Disraeli dutifully.

'I promise you,' said Sheil, 'that if you do this, the House after a bit will sigh for the eloquence that they all know you have in you. You'll get its ear, and I promise you, you'll become a great favourite.'

'Thank you, sir,' said Disraeli.

'Ah, well,' said Sheil, 'here comes Bulwer with the port. I've never allowed the gout to keep me away from it.'

When Disraeli awoke the next morning feeling in good spirits, Baum was drawing the curtains, and the wintry sun drifted into the room.

'Baum,' he called.

'Sir!'

'Why am I in good spirits?'

Baum reflected. Usually his master's questions were rhetorical at that hour of the morning and didn't invite a reply.

'Perhaps, sir – it's your invitation for Saturday.'

'Yes,' said Disraeli, removing his tasselled cap. 'That may be contributory.' After Bulwer's party, he had found on his return to his rooms an invitation to a dinner-party from Sir Robert Peel.

'What else?' he said, stretching himself.

'Well,' said Baum, 'you're like a fellow who's had his first fight. The second one's never so bad.'

'That's true,' said Disraeli.

'And another thing,' said Baum, laying out Disraeli's clothes, 'the English like fair play.'

'Yes, indeed,' said Disraeli. He didn't want to encourage Baum's further ruminations.

After he had taken his coffee, he set off to walk to the Carlton Club. Suddenly, his long and agonizing ordeal in the Chamber changed its quality. Sheil was right. He had been the centre of everyone's attention. In a single hour he had become a Parliamentarian of note. He had no need of pity. *The Times* had written of his 'eloquence'. The Radicals and the Repealers would turn to other enemies, and he would be remembered as one who in his very first speech had stood up to their rancour and malice. Others, the diffident, the insecure, the mediocre and the humble, might make their speeches, and win a muted applause. But for him there must be another and higher destiny.

The year was almost at its end. December 16th, 1837. Soon he would speak again in the Chamber, and again and again. And he would be heard. No one with a conviction could be silenced.

And he was free. For the time being, the duns didn't dare pursue him while Parliament was in session. Henrietta, darling, beloved Henrietta, was no longer his responsibility. And that too, he had to admit, gave his spirit relief, the chance to breathe and grow.

A coach stopped behind him, and he heard Mrs Wyndham Lewis call his name. She was waving her lavender-gloved hand through the window, and she said in her excited voice,

'Oh, Mr Disraeli. What good fortune!'

He took her hand, and bowed.

'Please accompany me,' she said, 'if you've nothing better to do.'

'I could have nothing better to do,' said Disraeli, entering the coach.

'I was so sorry,' she said, 'that Mr Wyndham Lewis was ill and unable to hear your speech.'

'And how is Wyndham today?'

'He changes very little,' she said.

She was wearing a green pelerine mantle and her face was a pretty oval inside the curved brim of her bonnet with the strings fastened under her chin.

'I am so happy your speech was a success,' she said. 'You know, they call you my Parliamentary protégé.'

'I am greatly honoured,' said Disraeli.

She smiled back at him and said, 'I didn't ask you where you were making for?'

'For the Carlton,' he said. 'And you?'

'For Grosvenor Gate. I'll send you back in my coach.'

'Will you stay in London when the House rises?'

'Yes – and you?'

'I will join my family in Bradenham. It's the place where I am most at peace.'

She looked out of the window at the trees of Hyde Park, and said,

'We'll miss you, Mr Disraeli.'

They had reached Grosvenor Gate, and Disraeli helped Mrs Lewis from the coach.

'How hard it is,' she said, 'to know what is an ending and what is a beginning.'

She looked straight at Disraeli as she spoke, and he looked away to the magnificent house rising in three storeys behind her.

'Our beginnings,' he said, 'are when we decide them.'

She ran up the steps to the door which the footman had already opened.

'If she turns her head,' Disraeli said to himself, standing there, 'it's a beginning.'

She turned her head.